Praise for Steven Harper's
novels of The Silent Empire

Dreamer

"This exceptional first novel in a new series is a satisfying and complete work in itself. A diverse array of memorable characters and worlds makes this a book [to] relate to and enjoy." —*School Library Journal*

"This series opener should appeal to lovers of far-future space opera and sf adventure." —*Library Journal*

"In terms of narrative and world building, this is definitely a well-told tale, and Harper's skill at characterization is significantly above average. Moreover, his extrapolation of aboriginal Austrialian myth freshens the shopworn theme of telepathy. Even the future slums he imagines are memorably vivid." —*Booklist*

"A fresh, original story . . . a clever concept . . . an exciting tale." —BookBrowser

"Harper is a promising writer." —On Spec

Nightmare

"A thoroughly solid sequel, highly recommended to those who enjoyed its predecessor." —*Booklist*

"Steven Harper creates a realistic future based on meditation philosophies in vogue today. Many readers will wish they had a time machine so they could travel into the future and learn how to be part of the Dream. [Kendi's] ablility to overcome the traumas he has endured makes him a hero worth rooting for by the enthralled audience." —BookBrowser

TRICKSTER

A NOVEL OF THE SILENT EMPIRE

STEVEN HARPER

A ROC BOOK

SF

ROC
Published by New American Library, a division of
Penguin Group (USA) Inc., 375 Hudson Street,
New York, New York 10014, U.S.A.
Penguin Books Ltd, 80 Strand,
London WC2R 0RL, England
Penguin Books Australia Ltd, 250 Camberwell Road,
Camberwell, Victoria 3124, Australia
Penguin Books Canada Ltd, 10 Alcorn Avenue,
Toronto, Ontario, Canada M4V 3B2
Penguin Books (N.Z.) Ltd, Cnr Rosedale and Airborne Roads,
Albany, Auckland 1310, New Zealand

Penguin Books Ltd, Registered Offices:
80 Strand, London WC2R 0RL, England

First published by Roc, an imprint of New American Library,
a division of Penguin Group (USA) Inc.

First Printing, November 2003
10 9 8 7 6 5 4 3 2 1

*For my cousin David Drake, fellow SF fan
and lifetime friend*

ACKNOWLEDGMENTS

Thanks, as always, to the Untitled Writers Group (Karen Everson, Anne Harris, Jonathan Jarrard, Lisa Leutheuser, Erica Schippers, Catherine Shaffer, Shannon White, and Sarah Zettel) for an unlimited supply of critiques, hilarity, and support.

Thanks also to Jim Morrow, Adam Hardy, Deirdre Saoirse Moen, and Marcie Tentchoff for critiques of the early chapters.

The quote that Ben half remembers in chapter six is from Robert Heinlein.

CHAPTER ONE

"There is no greater fear than the possibility of losing a child."
      —Renna Dell, First Bellerophon Landing Party

Harenn's chair crashed to the floor. Ben Rymar jumped, spilling most of the water in his glass down his front.

"God!" Harenn said from behind her veil. "We have left slipspace."

"How did—" Ben began, but Harenn had already left the galley. Ben scrambled to his feet to hurry after her, shedding bits of ice and swearing under his breath. His tunic clung cold and wet to his stomach.

"Hold on," he protested, catching up. "How do you know we left slip?"

"The *Poltergeist* is a brand-new ship and it still has minor bugs in the slipdrive," Harenn said without slackening her pace. "A good engineer can feel the difference when it shuts down. I am an *excellent* engineer."

"There's still no big hurry. We have to negotiate landing privileges before we can even enter orbit. Five minutes won't make a difference."

"Perhaps not to you." Harenn tapped her earpiece without breaking stride. "Father Kendi, I see we have left slipspace. Have we arrived at Klimkinnar or has something gone wrong?"

Ben quickly activated his own earpiece and checked the communication display on his ocular implant. A flick of his eye highlighted the proper channel and tuned him in to the conversation.

"—lutely nothing has gone wrong, Harenn," came

Kendi's familiar voice. *"We're about thirty thousand kilometers out from Klimkinnar, right on schedule."*

"Half an hour to get there, then," Harenn said to the empty air.

They reached the lift and hustled inside before the doors snapped shut. Although Ben couldn't see anything of Harenn's face except brown eyes above a blue veil, her entire body radiated impatience. A faint smell of bath powder hung about her. With a grimace, Ben pulled the front of his damp tunic away from his body and flapped it, trying to speed the evaporation as the lift rose.

"Apologies," Harenn murmured.

"It's just water," Ben said. "Don't worry, Harenn. We'll get there and we'll find your son."

Harenn made no reply, but rushed onto the bridge the moment the doors opened, leaving Ben behind. He followed more slowly.

The bridge was an oval, with the captain's chair in the center and a large viewscreen at one of the narrow ends. Individual workstations ringed the bulkheads. Two of them—the pilot board and the sensor board— were occupied. Everything was painted in soft blues and greens, and there were no angles anywhere. Even the doors had rounded corners. The place smelled of fresh paint. As Harenn had pointed out, the *Poltergeist* was new—large and well-appointed.

Seated in the captain's chair, Father Kendi Weaver glanced up as Ben and Harenn entered. Kendi was Ben's age—not quite thirty—but where Ben was short and stocky, Kendi was tall and thin, with dark skin, a broad nose, and tightly curled black hair. Despite his relative youth, stress lines had cropped up around his eyes and on his forehead. A gold medallion glittered from a chain around his neck, and a green jade ring gleamed on his right hand. The former indicated that he was a Child of Irfan, the latter that he had reached the rank of Father. Harenn strode to his chair, though her eyes never left the viewscreen and its display of the planet. Like most human-inhabited worlds, Klimkinnar was blue and green with interesting swirls of clouds drifting through the atmosphere. A trio of moonlets danced their way through orbit, while stars glittered on a velvety backdrop. The whole scene was very pretty.

It was also very big.

"So this is where my son is hidden," Harenn breathed from behind her veil. "Where my son is a slave."

"If Sejal's information was correct," Kendi said.

"I hope we can narrow things down a little," Gretchen Beyer put in from the sensor boards. She was a tall, rawboned woman with blue eyes, blond hair, and bland features that would blend easily into a crowd. The gold medallion around her neck matched Kendi's, though her amber ring gave her rank as Sister.

"What do you mean?" Kendi asked.

"Database says Klimkinnar is thirteen thousand, fifty-five kilometers in diameter—a little bigger than Earth," Gretchen said. "Surface area is seventy-odd percent water, but we're still talking about three hundred and eighty million square kilometers." She sniffed theatrically. "Might take a little time to search. More than eight weeks, that's for sure, and that's all we've got."

"It isn't *that* bad," said Lucia dePaolo from the pilot console. "We can find ways to narrow it down. He's got to be in an inhabited area, for one thing."

"Population one point two billion," Gretchen reported.

"But not all of them will be slaves," Kendi countered.

"Slave population three point three million."

"Shut up, Gretchen," Lucia said.

"We will find him," Harenn said with quiet finality.

The dark eyes above her veil were filled with fierce determination. "And we will set him free."

Ben, meanwhile, slid into his customary seat at the communication board beside Lucia's pilot console. Communications had remained dead while the *Poltergeist* was slipping—only the Silent could communicate with ships in slipspace—but now the board leaped with activity. Ben automatically sifted through channels and frequencies to find out which ones carried what kind of information.

"I've already contacted the transportation authority," Lucia told him. She was halfway between thirty and forty and had olive skin, shoulder-length black hair, and a lush body. Her fingers, however, were long and quick, marked by ragged nails and a fair number of white scars. She pronounced her name with a "ch" sound in the middle.

"Permission to orbit?" Ben asked.

"Granted, no problem," Lucia said. "We'll be there in twenty-four minutes."

Ben glanced up. Klimkinnar continued to float on the viewscreen, attended by its three tiny moons. Ben wondered if the moonlets were colonized and if the group would have to search them for Bedj-ka as well. He hoped not. The *Poltergeist*, like all ships commanded by the Children, was only on loan from the monastery. Kendi had managed to get her for just nine weeks. It had taken four days of that time to reach Klimkinnar.

"All right, troops," Kendi said, "we have to find one nine-year-old slave boy whose name has probably been changed to who-knows-what, and we need to do it in as little time as possible."

"Sure," Gretchen said. "Won't take but a minute. After all, we have Bedj-ka's age and gender, the name of the planet where he lives, and the fact that his father kidnapped him away from his mother when he was a baby"—Harenn stiffened visibly beside Kendi's

chair—"and sold him into slavery. With all that information, how can we help but find him?"

"Gretchen," Kendi warned. "Thin ice. Skating.
You."

"Yeah, all right," Gretchen said, relenting. "Look,
we don't know if he's ever changed owners, or if Klimkinnar's the only place where he's lived, or anything
else about him. Slave sales records are usually privileged information, so tracking him that way is going
to be problematic at best."

"Bedj-ka is Silent," Harenn added firmly. "That will
have an impact on where and when he was sold."

Gretchen's blue eyes glittered and Ben tensed for
an explosion. "Yeah, well, I'm supposed to be Silent,
too," she said. "What's that prove? I haven't touched
the Dream in six months."

"No, wait," Lucia said. "It does have an impact.
After the Despair, a lot of Silent—"

"Most Silent," Gretchen interrupted.

"Most Silent," Lucia amended, "lost their ability to
enter the Dream. If Bedj-ka was being raised and
trained as a Silent slave but then suddenly lost his
Silence, his value would have dropped. At minimum
he wouldn't be able to do his primary job, right?"

"What are you getting at?" Kendi asked, leaning
forward.

"I think there's a good chance Bedj-ka was sold
after the Despair," Lucia finished. "He would still be
a perfectly good slave—sorry, Harenn—he just
wouldn't be Silent anymore. We should probably start
with recent sales records, check for nine-year-old
males. It's a good . . . I mean, it might be a good
place to start, Father."

Kendi nodded and turned his attention toward Ben.
"You're the computer genius, Ben. What do you
think? Is the information hackable?"

"We can probably get some data through social engineering," Ben said. "Tricking people into telling us

what we need to know, peering over shoulders to get passwords, that sort of thing. I can hack the networks directly too, but I won't know how long that'll take until I actually start working on it and find out how tight their security is."

"Ballpark," Kendi said. "We're under a time limit, here."

"Uh, a week to figure out who to hack?" Ben hazarded. "Probably another week to sneak in without getting caught and another two or three to search. That's assuming Bedj-ka isn't too hard to find in the first place."

"All life," Kendi muttered. "That's three weeks, maybe four. We have to narrow it down. Otherwise we may not have enough time to find—" He cut himself off.

Harenn touched his shoulder. "Father Kendi," she said hesitantly, "if finding Bedj-ka will cost you the chance to find your own family, perhaps we should—"

"No," Kendi said. "Our mission is to find Bedj-ka."

~Ben? Kendi?~

Ben stiffened at the voice in his head. Kendi's eyes glazed over. The voice sounded familiar, but Ben, still new to the concept of Silent communication, didn't immediately recognize it.

~We need to talk, guys,~ the voice said. *~In the Dream.~*

"What's up?" Gretchen demanded.

"It's Sejal." Kendi rose from his chair. "We'll be in the Dream for a while, troops. Ben?"

Recognition clicked. The speaker was Sejal. A tang of anticipation burst into Ben as if he had bitten an unexpected orange. He bounced to his feet and followed Kendi from the bridge. Sejal was a Silent street kid Kendi had rescued and brought to Bellerophon just before the Despair ripped the Dream to pieces. Sejal had not only survived the Despair with his Silence intact, he had also sensed the general location of Harenn's son Bedj-ka and of two members of Kendi's missing family. If he needed to talk with Ben and Kendi, it was probably because he had narrowed something down. That could shorten their mission considerably.

"Are you sure we couldn't get the ship for more time?" Ben asked, quickening his pace. The rounded blue corridor was wide enough for Ben and Kendi to walk side by side. Walls curved down gently to meet the carpeted floor.

"I'm sure." The strain lines on Kendi's face tightened. "I've tried twice since we left to get an extension, but the Council won't budge."

"It's not like we don't deserve it," Ben growled. "They wanted to give us a parade, remember? Heroes of the Despair, that's us. I think they didn't go through with it only because everyone was so damned busy."

"That's why we don't have more time," Kendi pointed out. "With all the ships drafted into courier work—"

"Yeah, yeah. I know. We were lucky to get the *Poltergeist* for as long as we did."

~*Where do we meet, guys?*~ Sejal's mental voice interjected. ~*Whose turf?*~

"Mine," Ben said as he and Kendi entered the lift. It hummed as they dropped smoothly downward. "I'm still not very good at finding people in the Dream, and it'll be easier if you two come to me."

"You should practice more," Kendi chided, though his dark eyes carried no hint of rebuke. "And you should also comb your hair. It looks like a red haystack."

"Who are you, my mo—my keeper?" Ben said.

"It's definitely a zoo around here," Kendi said. "Between the Council, Gretchen's griping, the pressure Harenn's been laying on me, and you turning into a loose cannon, it's pretty—"

"Hey!" Ben protested. "I've never been a loose anything!"

Kendi looked Ben's body up and down with an appreciative grin. "Yeah. You do look pretty tight." Ben flushed but managed to grin back. Kendi could still do that to him, make him feel embarrassed and empowered at the same time. Ben still liked it. When Kendi took command of the *Poltergeist*, Ben had wondered if it would feel strange receiving orders from him, but so far it had worked out fine. After all, Ben had once been under his own mother's command. Maybe he was just used to taking orders from people he loved.

Now there's a scary thought for the morning, he mused.

~Are you two coming into the Dream or are you just going to muck around being cute?~

"We're coming, we're coming," Kendi said. He and Ben exited the lift and hurried down to their shared quarters.

As captain of the *Poltergeist*, Kendi—and therefore Ben—rated the largest set of quarters on board. Ben luxuriated in them like a cat caught in a sunbeam. The *Post-Script*, their previous ship, had been a cramped, tiny tub, with grimy beige deck plating and barely enough room to turn around in. Their quarters on this ship boasted separate living and sleeping rooms, a private bathroom, a kitchenette, and a small office area cluttered with Ben's computer equipment. An adjustable-gravity workout machine occupied one corner, and built-in shelves contained a scattering of bookdisks. The furniture was plain but comfortable. Klimkinnar and her moonlets created a spectacular view from the window. Precisely half the living room was a complete mess—clothes, disks, more computer parts, and something that looked like an Erector set on steroids cluttered floor and furniture. The tidy half was spartan by comparison, with a short, rubber-tipped red spear hanging on the wall as the only decoration. The setup was the compromise Ben and Kendi had created so they wouldn't kill each other. Ben could trash one half of the living room and all of the office while Kendi kept the other half of the living room and the entire bedroom pristine. The kitchenette wasn't an issue, since Ben, an aggressive non-cook, never set foot in the place.

Kendi took down the spear and pulled a dermospray cylinder from his pocket. Ben pursed his lips and rummaged through the stuff on the floor near the Erector set. Kendi sighed and stripped off his clothes, leaving only a loincloth. Then he bent his left knee, slipped the spear under it as if it had become a peg leg, and pressed the business end of the dermospray to his inner elbow. There was a hissing *thump* as the drug drove home. Kendi cupped his hands over his groin in the classic meditation pose of Kendi's people, the Australian Aborigines. Kendi called them the Real People, and Ben sometimes wondered if that made Kendi a Real Person. He had never asked because he suspected the answer would involve a thwack to someplace tender.

"I'll meet you in the Dream," Kendi said. "And maybe now we should pause to mention how you could save yourself a lot of time by—"

"Found it!" Ben said, triumphantly brandishing his own dermospray. "I'll see you in there."

Kendi shook his head and closed his eyes. Ben started for the bedroom, then paused to look at Kendi. As if sensing Ben's proximity, Kendi opened his eyes again.

"What?" he said.

Ben reached out and ran the back of one finger down Kendi's cheek. "You. You're so different these days. Sometimes I don't even know you."

"What do you mean?" Kendi's pupils were dilated from the effect of the drugs, but his voice sounded tense again.

"It's not a bad thing," Ben said hastily. "I just mean

that you've become Mr. Responsibility lately, all 'we need some options' and 'we'll be in the Dream, troops'. It's so different from . . . before."

"Before the Despair, you mean," Kendi said in a slightly strained voice. "Everyone has to grow up sometime. I guess it was just my turn." He flashed a smile that went straight through Ben. "I'll do something irresponsible after lunch just to keep you on your toes. How's that?"

"Deal." Ben laughed, heading for the bedroom again. Kendi closed his eyes, and Ben paused one more time to look at him. Although Kendi kept his voice and his words upbeat, Ben sensed his tension. If they didn't get the *Poltergeist* back to the monastery in time, Kendi's career would go straight down the recycling tube, hero or not, and Kendi would never command another mission. Ben swore to himself that he'd find a way to shorten the search and give Kendi enough time to find his own family after they located Harenn's son.

Ben stretched out on the bed and turned the dermospray over and over in his hand. Such a weird situation. For Ben's entire life, he'd been the only non-Silent in his family, the only one who couldn't enter the Dream. His aunt, uncle, and cousins had made his life living hell, and although his mother had never said anything, Ben knew she had been disappointed. Then came the Despair and a quirk of fate that had not only gotten Ben into the Dream, but had torn his family out of it, leaving Ben the only true Silent among them.

He set the flat end of the dermospray to his inner elbow and pressed the button. The dermospray thumped and Ben closed his eyes to concentrate on making his breathing deep and even. His heartbeat slowed, and colors swirled across the darkness inside his eyelids. The small noises of the *Poltergeist* faded away. He was floating, drifting, bodiless amid whirling colors. Gradually he became aware of having hands and feet again. The colors faded and cleared, leaving Ben standing on a hard white floor in the center of a giant computer network. Organic data-processing units reached up like fingers, their DNA matrices glowing green and blue. Magnetic fields pulsed, lights flashed, metal gleamed. Transmission lines and data portals opened in all directions around him, ready to transmit or receive.

It was Ben's part of the Dream.

Despite a thousand years of study, no one knew exactly what the Dream was, though the prevailing theory held that it was a plane of mental existence created from the collective subconscious of every sentient mind in the universe. The Silent—people like Ben and Kendi—could actually enter the Dream, usually with a boost from a drug cocktail tailored to their specific metabolisms.

In the Dream distance meant nothing. Two Silent who entered the Dream could meet and talk, no matter where in the galaxy their bodies might be. The Silent could also shape the Dream landscape, form it into whatever environment they desired. Some Silent—Sejal, for one—could reach out of the Dream and talk to Silent who were in the solid world. And a few could actually possess the bodies of Silent in the solid world. Ben hadn't learned to do any of this yet—shaping the landscape was as far as he could go—but he suspected it would come in time.

A few quiet voices whispered on the still air around the network. Kendi said the Dream used to be filled with thousands, even millions, of voices, but Ben had never experienced that. Ben had been in the Dream only once before the Despair, and then he hadn't been paying much attention to details.

Ben automatically searched the network—his turf—for flaws. Looked solid. He concentrated a moment. The Dream swirled, and a computer terminal coalesced into being, one with a crisp and sharp holographic screen. Ben flipped through a series of images, checking security cameras and antivirus programs. Everything was in order, and Ben sighed with satisfaction. This was a good place. A bit unorthodox, but a good place. Every Silent had his or her own turf, full of comfortable or soothing images among which to work. Many Silent created idyllic landscapes or fantastic castles for themselves, but Ben found comfort in his network, a locale where everything fell into place and made perfect sense, where any and every anomaly could be tracked down and explained.

A transmission line glowed blue and disgorged a koala bear. It landed not far from Ben's feet, bounced twice, and skidded to a halt. After recovering its balance, it glanced around the network room with a small whuff of disapproval.

"Tough." Ben grinned. "This is my turf, not yours."

The koala grunted, then turned enormous brown eyes on Ben and held up its arms like a child demanding to be picked up. Ben laughed and felt some of his earlier tension ease. "I am not going to carry you," he said. "What are you, a little kid?"

In answer, the koala bear leaped straight into the air. Even as its hind claws left the ground, its form shifted like quicksilver and a blue-and-brown falcon flapped across the intervening space to land on Ben's shoulder. The falcon's talons gently pricked Ben's skin through the thin material of his shirt, and Ben had to force himself not to flinch. The little raptor leaned over and nibbled Ben's ear in what turned out to be a surprisingly suggestive manner.

"Knock it off, Kendi," Ben spluttered, pushing the beak away. "That tickles."

"But you taste so good."

Ben rolled his eyes. "Is this your attempt to be more impulsive?"

"Maybe."

A presence brushed Ben's mind, requesting permission enter his turf. At the same moment, a message flickered across the holographic screen: MAY I APPROACH?

"Hey, Sejal," Ben said. "Come on in. Kendi didn't even bother to ask."

Another conduit glowed blue and Sejal Dasa slid into the room. He was a dark-skinned teenager, thin, with startling blue eyes and thick black hair that had a tendency to curl. He looked around the network and gave a low whistle.

"Pretty good," he said. "I hadn't seen your turf before."

"Thanks." Ben's reply was self-conscious. "I'm still kind of new to all this."

"Hey, you're one of the elite," Sejal pointed out. "Numbers are still coming in, but it looks like the early estimates were right—only about one Silent in ten can still enter the Dream these days."

Kendi shuddered once on Ben's shoulder. "I guess I should count myself lucky that I can get in at all."

"Any luck changing back into a human yet?" Sejal asked.

"No."

"So how are you guys doing?" Sejal said.

"Tired," Kendi replied. "When I'm not in the Dream, I'm in slipspace. The Order have kept us kind of busy in the last six months trying to track down other Children who were caught out in the field during the Despair."

Ben resisted the impulse to stroke Kendi's back. "How's the new government doing back home? Is my grandma still shaking things up?"

"Yeah." Sejal gave a wry smile. "She's fucking scary, you know that? She was three votes short in the election for party head, and none of the senators who were voting against her would budge. So she talks to three of them. Private, right? And next thing you know, Senator Reza is party head. Just like that."

"Wow," Kendi said.

Ben nodded wryly. "That's Grandma. Heaven help anyone who gets in her way."

"Anyway," Sejal continued, "the new Bellerophon Senate is up and running, and the Independence Confederation of Planets is pretty much gone. I hear tell Empress Kalii just vanished—ran away or something."

"She was pretty popular," Ben said, surprised. "What happened?"

Sejal shrugged. "Got me. It's just a rumor I heard. I do know that the Children are raising their communication rates through the roof—so is everyone else who can still reach the Dream—and since almost nobody can talk between planets these days, everything's starting to come apart. The Empire of Human Unity's falling to pieces." This last came out with a certain amount of glee. "There's talk of recession all over the place. The galactic corps were really hard hit. Their Silent network for orders and money transfers and business communication"—he snapped his fingers— "gone in one shot."

"Any official numbers on how many Silent died during the Despair?" Kendi asked quietly.

Sejal shrugged again. " 'Lots' is the best I can tell you. If you go out there"—he waved a hand vaguely toward Ben's computer network—"the big thing going is trying to find out who survived and who didn't. It's depressing. I'm glad I didn't know anyone very well."

Anyone like Mom, Ben thought, with the twinge of sorrow and loss that thoughts of his mother usually brought. He wondered if time would ever blunt the pain of finding her ruined, broken body on the forest floor, just one of many Silent driven mad with grief when Padric Sufur's insane progeny had cut them off from the Dream. A slow anger began to burn within the sorrow.

Kendi seemed to sense Ben's mood and nibbled lightly on his cheek in sympathy. Ara Rymar had been Kendi's surrogate mother as well as his teacher, and her death had hit him equally hard.

"Sorry," Sejal said, belatedly noticing the effect of his words. "Didn't mean to be a dragdown."

"We're not exactly bundles of sunshine," Kendi said. He adopted a more brisk tone. "So what's going on besides gossip, Sejal? Any good news?"

"Actually there is," Sejal replied. "That's why I wanted to talk to you."

"You've got more information about Bedj-ka?" Ben said. "We've just arrived at Klimkinnar, but a planet's a big place to search. We could use some more info."

"I've been trying. I mean, using the Dream to find people in the solid world is flipping hard these days," Sejal said. "I can reach out of the Dream and touch your minds pretty easy because I know you, but Bedj-ka's more difficult."

"I know," Kendi said. "I'm supposed to be one of the best Silent-finders ever, but these days I'm lucky to find Ben."

"Yeah. Anyway, when the Despair started up, I touched *every* Silent in the universe for a moment, including Bedj-ka. Talk about a major mind fuck." Sejal hawked and spat. "I told you about how I got a flash of the kid being on Klimkinnar, but I know that's not much to go on, so the last couple days I've been working on finding them again. If I listen really hard in the Dream, I can sometimes hear people who used to be Silent and track them a little bit."

"And?" Kendi asked tautly.

"I think Bedj-ka is in a country named Tiq. Does that help?"

Disappointment settled in Ben's stomach. He had been hoping for more than that. Still, searching a country would be a lot easier than searching an entire planet. They might be able to shave off a week, maybe even ten days if they were lucky.

"Tiq," Ben said. "Got it. Anything more?"

"He has a different name," Sejal told him. "That kind of goes without saying, I guess. Most slavers change the names of their slaves."

"In Tiq and not named Bedj-ka," Kendi said. "Great. Any more?"

Sejal shrugged. "I'll keep looking."

"Then I guess we'll see you around," Kendi said, his own disappointment clear from his tone. "Let us know if you find out more."

"Okay." Sejal turned to go, then paused. "Oh, yeah—something else. Bedj-ka's first name was changed to something like Terry or Jerry or maybe Kerry. And his last name is Markovi."

Ben's mouth fell open. Kendi froze, then puffed up his feathers in mock outrage.

"You little shit," he said. "Enjoy the remainder of your life on Bellerophon, kid, because you're dead when I get back."

Sejal laughed mischievously and vanished from the Dream. The network rippled for a moment and Ben felt an inrush of energy fill the spot Sejal had occupied.

"Little bastard," Kendi said happily.

Ben laughed. "Now you know how Mo—how the rest of us felt whenever you played a—"

"Don't," Kendi warned, "finish that sentence." His talons pricked Ben's skin menacingly.

"Wouldn't dream of it," Ben said, wide-eyed.

"Right. I'd better go tell Harenn." Kendi flapped to the ground and changed back into the koala.

"Do you need me on the bridge right away?" Ben asked. "There are a couple things I want to do in here while Lucia lands the ship."

"Should be okay for a few minutes," Kendi said. "We've already got fake trader credentials, so we won't need a hacker at the ready to forge them for us. See you in a few."

Koala Kendi vanished, leaving ripples in the Dream. Ben watched him go, then turned back to his computer network. The matrices glowed, lights flashed, and a soft, empty hum pervaded the air. An empty hum for an empty Dream, thanks to Padric Sufur. Ben's slow anger neared the boiling point. He made a curt gesture and the entire scene vanished, leaving behind the flat, empty plain that was the default environment of the Dream. Another gesture, and the ground shifted. A stone statue rumbled up out of the ground. It was crudely formed—Ben wasn't much of an artist—but it was recognizably the life-size figure of a gangly older man with hawklike features. The man's stony eyes stared at nothing. Ben contemplated the statue, then held up his hands. The Dream shifted and he was holding a sledgehammer. Ben's fury flared into brilliance. With a sudden yell, he swung the hammer with the full power of every muscle in both arm and shoulder. Metal smashed into stone, and the statue's arm flew off in a shower of rock chips. Hatred filled Ben as he swung again and again, relishing the shock and crack of every hit. The statue's head went flying, then its other arm. Tiny bits of stone scored Ben's arms and one fragment slashed his cheek. The torso cracked into three pieces. Ben smashed the hammer into the statue's groin and the legs split away and fell apart. He yelled, screamed, shouted until his throat was raw. Ben's hammer fell again and again until nothing remained but fist-size bits of rubble. At last Ben halted, barely winded from the exertion. He glared at the ruins, then set the hammer down and raised his hands. The rubble quivered, shivered, and reassembled itself into the statue again. Cracks fused themselves back together, leaving smooth stone. When the statue's last flaw had vanished, Ben picked up the hammer and swung.

Father Kendi Weaver shifted in the captain's chair on the *Poltergeist*'s bridge. It felt right to be sitting there, somehow, and that surprised him. He had been under someone else's command—usually Ara's—for so long, he had assumed it would feel odd to be giving the orders himself. But that wasn't at all the case. Rather, it seemed as if everything he had gone through, including the Despair, had been preparing him for this very position.

"We've got permission to land, Father," Lucia said, looking down at her boards. "Tiq has a spaceport, and we'll be landing in about an hour, Irfan willing."

"Where's Harenn?" Kendi asked.

"She went down to engineering," Gretchen told him. "We're in tip-top, but she said it would be easier if she kept herself busy, even if it was make-work."

Kendi nodded. Like Harenn, no doubt, he felt the urge to get out behind the ship and push.

"Restless, Father?" Gretchen asked archly.

Kendi glanced down and realized he was tapping his feet against the deck plates. He forced himself to stop. "Just anxious to get started."

"Sooner started, sooner done, sooner outside having fun," Gretchen singsonged.

"Enough, *Sister* Gretchen," Kendi said, emphasizing her title with a hint of steel. "Since we're in radio range, I want you to start gathering data on the current state of Klimkinnar's government. I know it was one of the Five Green Worlds, but that was pre-Despair, and no one among the Children has heard anything about the FGW since then."

"Yes, Father," Gretchen said with patently false meekness. -

Kendi suppressed a sigh. *Now you know how it feels,* said the memory of Ara's voice, and he could almost hear her laughing at him, wherever she was. In that moment, Kendi would have given up everything—his promotion, this mission, even his limited ability to enter the Dream—to have her back in the captain's chair again while he flew the ship.

The view on the screen brightened as Lucia guided the *Poltergeist* into Klimkinnar's atmosphere. Lucia's entry was smooth, with minimal turbulence, but Kendi still had to bite back words of advice. He remembered how much he had hated unsolicited suggestions when *he* was at the pilot's board.

As they touched down on their allotted section of the landing field, the door slid open and Ben entered the bridge. Kendi blinked. A red line scored Ben's cheek and several small cuts marked his hands. Ben took the communication station and, without a word, began tapping keys.

"Are you okay, Ben?" Kendi asked.

"I'm fine, Father," Ben said. "Give me a minute and I'll access Klimkinnar's network. I should have—"

"What happened to your hands?" Gretchen asked bluntly.

Ben's face reddened. "I had . . . an accident in the Dream. The cuts are just psychosomatic carryover. I'll be fine. They aren't even bleeding. Did you tell Harenn what Sejal found out?"

"She knows," Kendi said, wondering if he should press the point about Ben's hands or just let it drop. Let it drop, he decided. For now.

Ben's console chimed. "It's customs," he said, a little too briskly. "They said they'll inspect the ship in about an hour. No one can enter or leave until blah blah blah."

"Get the bribe money ready," Gretchen said. "Klimkinnar's on the unstable side right now. That means government officials don't know when—or if—their next paycheck will be coming, and they'll be looking for ways to supplement their income."

"What else did you learn?" Kendi asked.

"Klimkinnar's almost completely cut off from the Five Green Worlds," Gretchen said, glancing down at her display. "Their local FGW ruler is called the planetary governor, and she's been trying to hold things together, but it's hard going. Some sectors—countries, if you like—are trying to assert their own sovereignty, and the governor's working overtime to keep them in line. Klimkinnar also does a lot of farming and not much manufacturing, and their economy is dependent on selling food to the rest of the FGW. This means that a lot of imported manufactured goods—read, *most* of them—are going to get expensive until the shipping corps figure out how to operate without Silent communication. The local big corps are also taking advantage of the situation to consolidate some of their own power—surprise, surprise. It all adds up to recession, recession, recession."

"Jerry," Ben said.

"What?" Gretchen said blankly.

"Bedj-ka's name is Jerry," Ben explained as text crawled across his boards. "Names of slaves and their owners aren't privileged information on Klimkinnar after all. I found a slave boy, nine years old, named Jerry Markovi who's registered as belonging to a farm run by one Douglas Markovi. Jerry was a recent purchase, so the records were new and easy to find. Markovi's farm is about forty klicks away from the spaceport. Take us about half an hour to get there if we rent a groundcar."

"Praise be to Irfan," Lucia said. "Good job."

Ben shrugged. "A kid could've done it."

"Don't say it, Sister," Kendi said. Gretchen snapped her mouth shut. "It's still good work, Ben. If we play this right, Harenn'll have her son back after lunch and we'll be popping into slipspace before dinner."

"You want me to tell her?" Ben asked, reaching for his console.

"No," Kendi said quickly, and Ben halted. "Not one word. We still have an hour before customs arrive, and who knows how much time for them to inspect. I'll try to speed things along with the magic of bribery, but it'll still be a while. No use making it worse for Harenn by telling her Bedj-ka's within shouting distance. Just say you're on the networks and have some high hopes."

"High hopes for what?" said Harenn, coming onto the bridge.

"For finding your kid," Gretchen said with utter blandness. "Red over there's already tracking leads while we wait for customs."

"I have money," Harenn said, "if you need to bribe them for more speed."

"There's plenty in the kitty," Kendi told her. "But I'll keep that in mind."

Harenn nodded. Her face, still hidden behind her customary blue veil, was unreadable, but her every movement was taut and filled with controlled tension. Kendi marveled at her discipline. If he had been this close to any member of his own family . . .

He banished these thoughts. Right now they had to concentrate on helping Harenn. Then he could pursue his own agenda.

An hour later, the customs inspection team arrived. Because the Children of Irfan were known in some circles as slave stealers and because the crew wasn't here to conduct official—read "aboveboard"—Child business, Kendi removed his medallion and ring, ordered Gretchen to do the same, and presented the inspector with carefully forged documentation that identified him as a simple trader, the most common guise adopted by the Children of Irfan. He explained their lack of cargo by claiming they'd just finished a one-way delivery run to an outlying station. The customs inspector, a small, dark-haired man with a toothbrush mustache, lost interest in Kendi's story once a certain amount of freemarks found their way into his hands. The inspection itself—perfunctory in the extreme—lasted only twenty minutes. Once he was gone, everyone assembled in the galley, a tradition started by Ara. ("What better place for a briefing? Room to sit, and close to the refreshments.")

Lucia, as was her habit, had put together a snack tray comprised of bite-sized vegetables, sweetened *ruda* nuts from Bellerophon, and crackers spread with mounded peaks of spiced cream cheese. A large pot of fruit tea sat among a set of cups. Kendi caught up a cheese cracker and raised it in thanks to Lucia, who smiled quietly at the unspoken praise.

"This is a good-news briefing, troops," Kendi said. "Ben found Bedj-ka, or Jerry Markovi, as he's called now."

Everyone pretended surprise and pleasure as Kendi finished explaining. Harenn narrowed her eyes above her veil.

"You are a fine liar, Father Kendi," she said. "But only to those who do not know you. How long have you had this information?"

"Since about the time we landed," Kendi admitted sheepishly. "I didn't want you to have a freak, so I kept quiet. Sorry."

"If we only have to go to the farm and offer an outrageous sum to get my son back," Harenn hissed, "why are we sitting at this table?"

"Good point." Kendi rose. "I think Harenn and I can do this one alone. Ben, would you call a rental company and arrange a groundcar for us?" Ben nodded and Kendi continued. "The rest of you can stretch your legs or look around the city, but be ready to go the minute the two of us—the *three* of us—get back." He looked at all of them pointedly. "We've got other fish to fry after we catch this one."

"Nice metaphor," Gretchen murmured as Harenn all but yanked Kendi out of the room. He decided to pretend he hadn't heard, and Ara laughed in his memory again.

Tiq's spaceport was middle-sized and fairly well-appointed. The usual announcements blared from hidden speakers, and the smells of low-quality, high-cost food filled the air. People walked, rushed, strolled, or lounged everywhere. The vast majority of the crowd was human, but that was normal, in Kendi's experience. Most people preferred the company of their own kind, and it was rare for colony worlds to mix species.

Harenn strode through the crowds with single-minded determination, and Kendi had to hurry to keep up. He finally caught her by the sleeve.

"Slow down, Harenn," he warned. "I don't want to lose you in this crowd."

Harenn obeyed with obvious reluctance. "We are close, Kendi. I have been searching for nine years and it seems as if I can feel Bedj-ka's presence, even hear his voice. I want to push these idiots out of my way and run. I want to know if my baby is all right."

"He won't be a baby anymore," Kendi said.

"I know that. It is merely the way I think of him. It is not something I can help."

Kendi wet his lips uncertainly. He was afraid Harenn had pinned her hopes on a joyous reunion of mother and son and that she was setting herself up for disappointment—a position Kendi could empathize with. Kendi knew he should say something, but he didn't know what. An added complication was that Harenn was ten or fifteen years older than Kendi, not someone he would normally reproach or advise. Ara would have known how to handle the situation, and he felt an irrational flash of anger that she wasn't here to do so.

In the end, he decided to be direct.

"Harenn, please don't take this the wrong way, but I want you to be careful," he said as they approached the spaceport's main entrance. "We're going to get

Bedj-ka back, I promise you, but don't think he's going to throw himself into your arms and cry 'Mama!' He won't. I hate to say this so bluntly, but Harenn— he won't even recognize you. He may not believe you when you tell him who you are."

"I am not a fool, Kendi," Harenn snapped. Then she closed her dark eyes for a moment. "All the things you have just said are the things I tell myself over and over. For every night since Sejal told me where Bedj-ka is, I have lain awake thinking about what it would be like to find him again. And I have thought long and hard about what I would do to Isaac Todd for taking Bedj-ka away from me."

"Is Isaac Todd your ex-husband?" Kendi said. "I don't think I've ever heard you mention his name."

"Whenever I say it, I want to wash my mouth and my body," Harenn growled.

Outside the port building, the golden sun of Klimkinnar shone with tropical warmth, and the air was heavy with humidity. For a moment, Kendi was transported back to the muggy frog farm where he had spent three years as a slave, and he forced himself to shake off the memories.

The streets were paved, if that was the word for it, with lush emerald grass. Tiny purple flowers and gray mushrooms peeked between the blades. Green shrubs lined the low buildings and gray sidewalks, and Kendi realized with a start that he didn't know the name of the city. Steady streams of people moved up and down the walks, and groundcars buzzed over the grass, not quite touching the tender green blades. No flitcars crossed the sky—Klimkinnar didn't allow much private air traffic.

A series of empty groundcars queued up near the curb, each with a name printed on the side. Kendi moved down the line until he came to one marked WEAVER. He pressed his thumb to the lock of the vehicle and it popped open. The name erased itself.

"Here we go," Kendi said, and climbed into the driver's seat. Harenn, her blue veil fluttering slightly in the breeze, got in on the passenger's side. Directions to the Markovi farm flashed across the car's onboard computer—Kendi made a mental note to thank Ben later—and Kendi maneuvered carefully into the heavy traffic surrounding the spaceport terminal.

After a moment, Harenn said, "I must admit that I do not understand why we are here."

"Turn left at the next intersection," the computer said in a pleasant, friendly voice.

"Huh?" Kendi scooted around a cargo hauler and made the turn. "We're rescuing your son. What have we been talking about for the last—"

"I mean," Harenn said, "I do not understand why we are here instead of looking for *your* family."

"Oh." Kendi concentrated on driving for a moment. They reached the edge of the city, whatever its name was, and the buildings grew sparser, as did the traffic. "I didn't explain that?"

"No, and I was . . . I was afraid to press in case you changed your mind. Even on the bridge before we landed, I was afraid you would change your mind." Harenn tugged at her veil. "For many years when we were part of Mother Ara's team, I watched you jump every time you thought you had something that would lead you to your family. I know that you and they were sold because you were Silent, but—"

"That's not quite right," Kendi interjected. "My family and I were colonists on a ship that was captured by slavers. I was twelve. A woman named Giselle Blanc bought me and my mother, but someone else bought my dad and my sister and brother. I never saw them again. Three years later, Blanc found out that Mom and I were both Silent, and she decided to sell us for a hefty profit. My mom was sold, and I never saw her again, either. Then Ara bought me and set me free. After the Children of Irfan taught me how to use my Silence, I looked for my family everywhere in the Dream, but no luck. Then the Despair hit, and Sejal touched almost every Silent mind in the universe. He told me he felt a man and a woman who are sure to be my relatives—though I don't know which relatives—and that he felt Bedj-ka, too. That's why we're here."

"This is not what I am asking, Kendi. You are a hero of the—"

"Stop saying that," Kendi said. Traffic cleared and he sped up.

"—of the Despair, and it is true whether you deny it or not. Padric Sufur's twisted children failed to destroy the Dream because of you—"

"And because of Ben and because of Sejal and Katsu and Vidya and Prasad and a whole mess of other people," Kendi pointed out.

"But you are the only one who took advantage of your status," Harenn continued, ruthlessly pursuing the point. "Vidya and Prasad and Katsu and Sejal were content to become a family again and settle among the Children of Irfan. Ben seems to be happy following you wherever you go. But you—well, I do have to say that I have never thought of you as a modest person—"

"Thanks."

"—but you went beyond mere immodesty. You bullied the Council of Irfan into giving you an expensive ship—"

"*Loaning* me an expensive ship."

"—something that usually only a Father Adept is granted, and then you staffed it with not one but *two* so very priceless Silent who can still reach the Dream—"

"Yeah, well, Ben threatened to quit his consulting job, and the Council didn't want to lose him, especially since he's Silent now and they're hoping he'll become a Brother one day."

"—and then you took this expensive ship off to find not *your* family, but *mine*. So I am asking: Why are you doing this?"

Kendi drove in silence for several moments. Then he said, "It's because of Ben."

"This you need to explain."

"When I go home at night—or back to my quarters, anyway—Ben is there. I have somebody, and you . . ." He stopped and felt his face turn hot.

"I have no one?"

Kendi cursed himself. There were a hundred other things he could have said, but he had to choose the one that would throw Harenn's broken family into her face.

"It's not just that," he hastened to add. "It's also because Bedj-ka is still a little kid. He isn't even ten years old yet. My brother would be over thirty now, and my sister's in her mid-twenties. They're adults. They don't . . . they don't *need* their family like Bedj-ka does. So I decided we should find him first."

Harenn looked at him. "That sounds like something Mother Ara would have said."

Kendi stiffened and stared straight ahead at the green road unwinding before him. Trees, fields, and scattered houses rushed quietly past the groundcar. Harenn's remark had pierced him like an arrow, and he didn't know how to feel. Pride mixed with sorrow mixed with . . . relief? To Kendi's horror, his eyes teared up. He firmed his jaw. Not in front of Harenn, not while he was in charge of the expedition and she was under his command, however casual that command might be.

Harenn lightly touched his hand. "Whatever the reason, I am glad you made this choice." Then she turned to stare out her own window, leaving Kendi free to rub his eyes without being observed.

They traveled for some time in companionable silence until the computer said, "Your destination is one hundred meters ahead of you on the right." Harenn sat up straight. Kendi turned down a short gravel driveway that ended in front of a tall, barred gate. From this vantage point, Kendi could see that the trees and brush lining the road actually concealed a high concrete wall that presumably ran around the perimeter of the farm. A sign on the gate read,

SUNNYTREE FARM
A DIVISION OF THE L.L. VENUS CORPORATION
DOUGLAS J. MARKOVI, MANAGER

"L. L. Venus," Harenn said. "The chocolate company?"

"We carried a whole bunch of their stuff when we posed as merchants back on Rust," Kendi said, rereading the sign. "All life—they use slaves?"

"So it would seem." Harenn's voice was tight, and her hands were clasped in her lap.

"But they're a candy company," Kendi said almost plaintively. "They buy *children* to work their farms?"

"It does not matter what a corporation produces," Harenn said. "It will always seek the cheapest method of production."

Kendi tried to estimate out how many pounds of L. L. Venus chocolate he had eaten over the years. The best answer he could come up with was "a lot." He felt slightly sick.

The dashboard screen chimed. He tapped it, and a smartly dressed woman appeared.

"Welcome to Sunnytree Farm," she said. Her voice was impossibly low and smooth, and Kendi figured she was computer-generated. "How may I help you?"

"My name is Kendi Weaver. We need to talk to your manager, please," Kendi said politely, just in case the woman was real.

"Do you have an appointment?"

"I'm afraid we don't, but it's very important. It's a

personal matter about one of his—the farm's—slaves.
Is Mr. Markovi available?" Always go straight to the
top, Ara had taught.

The woman paused blankly, probably to let her program access a database. "Please drive through the
gates to our main office. Please do not leave your
vehicle. Please keep your vehicle on the road at all
times. *Thank* you for visiting Sunnytree Farm."

The screen went blank and the gate swung open.
Kendi guided the car through the opening and into
what felt like another world—a dark and gloomy one.
Slowly Kendi's eyes adjusted to the dim light. The
gloom came from the oppressive shade of a forest of
strange trees, each about twice as tall as a human. The
trunks were thin, less than half a meter in diameter,
and covered with star-shaped flowers that ranged from
white to pink to yellow to red. Amid the flowers were
clumps of lumpy seed pods that reminded Kendi of
rugby balls. They were almost as varied in color as
the flowers, appearing in green, orange, and brown.
Large, flat leaves at the tops of the trees rustled in a
faint breeze. Moss hung from everything, and the
ground between the trees was covered in some kind
of mulch. Water dripped from leaves and branches.
Kendi cracked a window and sniffed. The air was thick
and smelled heavily organic.

The screen beeped again. Harenn tapped it and the
computer-generated woman reappeared.

"Welcome to Sunnytree Farms," she said in an
overly friendly voice. "If you would like guided information about our family-owned operation, just touch
the green button on your screen. Otherwise please
proceed with caution to the main office building.
Thank you!"

Harenn reached down to tap the screen's off button,
but Kendi grabbed her wrist.

"Wait," he said. " 'The greater your knowledge, the
lesser your risk,' remember?"

"Irfan Qasad," Harenn muttered. "Very well." She touched the green button. Kendi continued to drive. Among the trees, he could now make out people. They wore simple clothing, with silver bands around their left wrists and ankles. Slave bands. Memories welled again, and Kendi resisted the impulse to rub his own wrist in sympathy.

"The L. L. Venus Corporation was founded on Earth over eleven hundred years ago, when Lawrence Venus opened a single candy kitchen in the city of Milwaukee," burbled the computer lady. "He eventually expanded this small family business into a global operation. When the chance came, his heirs took the Venus Corporation to the stars. The company has spanned two millennia and operates on twenty-eight different planets, creating delicious chocolates and candies for billions of consumers—the delight of children everywhere."

The workers—slaves—were engaged in a variety of tasks, and they scarcely glanced at the passing groundcar. Some of the adults used hooked knives on poles to cut down the brownest pods, which the children gathered and piled on floating gravity sleds. Other slaves spread mulch, trimmed branches, and performed other tasks Kendi didn't recognize. Harenn watched the children with sharp eyes, and Kendi knew she was wondering which of them was her son.

"The cacao trees you see here at Sunnytree Farm are only the very first step in producing the rich, sumptuous chocolate treats you buy at the store," continued the computer. "The trees are difficult to raise—they require a very specific climate, soil type, and daily weather pattern. Attempts to genegineer cacao trees to make them sturdier and easier to grow have invariably degraded the quality of the beans, so we raise them the old-fashioned way, by hand—exactly as was done on Earth for thousands of years."

The groundcar abruptly emerged into bright sunlight. Kendi blinked until the windshield darkened it-self to compensate. Harenn continued to sit rigidly. A line of slaves stood at an outdoor conveyer belt loaded with lumpy brown cacao pods.

"If you look to your left," said the computer cheer-fully, "you will see the L. L. Venus hands processing the ripe seed pods. First the pods are split in two with a machete." As if on cue, several of the slaves chopped the pods neatly down the middle as they passed by on the belt. "Next, our hands scoop out the mucilage and cocoa beans inside and put it into wooden boxes, which are then covered with leaves." The car passed stacks of leaf-covered crates. "Once the beans have fermented, they are removed and spread in the sun to dry. Each pod will produce be-tween forty and fifty cocoa beans, but it takes more than seven hundred beans to make a single kilogram of—"

Kendi tapped the screen's red button. When Harenn raised her eyebrows at him, he said, "I can't stand that syrupy tone anymore."

"What number of slaves do you suppose this farm owns?"

Kendi looked out at a group of slave children who were using long-handled hoes to spread cocoa beans on screen-bottomed drying racks in the hot sun. Sev-eral of them were barely tall enough to see over the racks.

"Lots," he muttered. "Suddenly the idea of having a candy bar makes me sick to my stomach."

The driveway ended at an enormous mansion, com-plete with cupolas and gingerbread trim. Beyond the house lay a series of low, metal-sided buildings. Kendi assumed they were warehouses, equipment storage areas, and slave quarters. He guided the car into a parking lot near the house. The sun hit him like a hammer when he exited the air-conditioned interior of the car. Harenn didn't seem to notice, and instead headed straight for the mansion's front porch. Before they had reached the top step, the door opened and a man in a red tunic and brown trousers emerged. The L. L. Venus logo was embroidered in gold on the shoulder of the tunic. Kendi took Harenn's arm.

"Let me do the talking," he muttered.

Harenn gave a curt nod of acquiescence.

"Welcome to Sunnytree Farm," the man said. "How may I help you?"

Kendi repeated his request to see Douglas Markovi. "It's extremely important, and I'm afraid we really can't talk to anyone but him."

"Mr. Markovi is very busy," the man said doubtfully.

"I realize that, and I apologize for dropping in with no notice, but it's very important."

"What company did you say you were with?"

"I didn't," was Kendi's only reply.

The man wasn't daunted. "What company are you with?"

"A large private concern," Kendi said. "I'm sorry, but I can't be more specific than that except with Mr. Markovi himself."

Kendi could almost feel the waves of controlled impatience radiating off Harenn. He ground his teeth. In the days before the Despair, another Child of Irfan would have entered the Dream to whisper into this man's mind. If the man had any inclination toward granting Kendi and Harenn an audience with his managerial majesty, the whisper would magnify it and make Kendi's job easy. But nowadays very few Silent could even enter the Dream, let alone reach out from it. Even before the Despair, Kendi had never been good at reaching out or at whispering. Ben hadn't yet learned. Kendi would have to rely on his own powers of persuasion.

The man resisted, and Kendi continued to work at

him. His instincts told him offering a bribe wouldn't be effective, so he continued with a nonstop flow of persuasive talk while Harenn looked on. Eventually the man reluctantly led them to a tastefully furnished waiting room with the curt promise that he would check with Mr. Markovi.

They waited over an hour. Harenn sat like a statue the entire time. Kendi knew she was in agony, but he didn't dare speak to her—the waiting area was probably bugged. Finally the man returned.

"Mr. Markovi has agreed to see you," he said with a certain amount of surprise in his voice.

He ushered them into a large, airy office. A blond man with a prominent chin waited behind a castle-size desk against a bank of windows. A potted cacao tree blocked some of the sunshine streaming in through the glass. The man's tunic was edged with silver, and he forced Harenn and Kendi to reach across the huge expanse of his desk to shake hands. His grip was iron-hard. Kendi gave a mental sigh. The negotiations were going to be rough.

"I'm Douglas Markovi," said the blond man. "What's this about? The computer said you were asking about one of my hands."

"Hands," not *"slaves,"* Kendi noted. *As if those people—those* children—*out there were interviewed and hired.* He decided to try the direct approach.

"My name is Kendi Weaver and this is my associate, Harenn Mashib," he said. "We have a problem that I'm hoping you can help us solve."

Douglas Markovi sat in a tall leather chair behind his desk. He did not offer seats to Kendi and Harenn, though there were smaller chairs behind them. Kendi decided to remain standing for the moment. Although it made him look like an inferior, it did give him and Harenn a height advantage.

"What problem would that be?"

"You have a . . . a *hand* on your farm named Jerry," Kendi said. "According to public record, you bought him two weeks ago."

"I may have," Markovi said. "We acquired several hands recently, but I don't know all of them."

Despite the fact that you give all of them your last name, Kendi growled silently. "Unfortunately," he said aloud, "Jerry is not actually a slave."

"He is my son," Harenn blurted out.

Markovi raised a single blond eyebrow, a trick Kendi hated—the few people he knew who could actually do it invariably used it for sarcastic effect.

"Jerry was kidnapped by his father as a baby and sold without Harenn's knowledge or permission," Kendi said. "This is a violation of Independence Confederation slave code and a violation of the slave codes set down by the Five Green Worlds."

"This isn't the Independence Confederation," Markovi said. "And the FGW doesn't seem to exist much anymore."

"You are correct, sir," Kendi said. He hadn't really expected a legal ploy to work. "However, I'm not asking you to hand Jerry over for free. I'm offering to buy him from you."

"I just acquired him," Markovi said. "And spent a fair amount of time having him trained. Why would I want to sell him?"

"Humanitarianism," Kendi said bluntly. "The chance to reunite a torn family. The chance to let a mother hold her own child again. And the chance to profit by it all. I'm willing to pay you twice Jerry's original purchase price, to reimburse you for your time and effort."

"Jerry, Jerry." Markovi tapped his desk and a holographic computer screen popped into being. "Oh, yes—the damaged goods. Our regular slaver bought him from a small communications company. Little

Jerry was just starting to sense the Dream when the Despair hit. None of the company's Silent slaves were able to reach the Dream afterward, and the company wasn't big enough to survive long without Silent revenue. They went bankrupt right quick, had to sell off their livestock. Looks like we got him for a song."

Harenn's hands were clenched so tightly Kendi was afraid her palms would start bleeding. "Triple price, then," he said, "to ensure it's worth your while. Hard currency."

"Well, here's the thing." Markovi leaned back in his chair and laced his fingers behind his head. "The boy's seen a lot of our operation by now, and security around here's pretty tight. We can't sell off hands who might blab secrets to Venus's competitors."

"How much could he have learned in two weeks?"

"The chocolate business is cutthroat. You'd be surprised," Markovi continued as if Kendi hadn't spoken. "For all I know, you two work for Wexford Chocolate and Jerry is your mole. Wexford would love to know exactly how we do things around here."

Harenn said, "I brought his birth certificate and genetic—"

"Yes, yes, I'm sure you did," Markovi interrupted. "But I'm afraid that I couldn't sell the boy even if I wanted to. FGW law says only a slave dealer can sell hands less than a year after purchase. I sell you this Jerry boy now, and I'm in trouble for trafficking in slaves without a license. Sorry, but you understand where I'm coming from. No sale."

Slaves, not hands, Kendi thought.

"You just said the FGW doesn't much exist anymore," he said aloud, trying to keep his temper. "They aren't in a position to uphold—"

"Sorry, Junior. Can't do it."

"Five times the price," Kendi said tightly. "I might even be able to come up with six."

"Wouldn't matter if you handed me a hundred and your associate here gave me a blow job," Markovi drawled. "Joe and Alex here will show you out now."

Kendi turned. He hadn't heard the office door open, nor had he sensed the two heavily muscled goons gliding into the room. Harenn's eyes went wild. She lunged across the desk and grabbed Markovi by the throat.

"You have to sell him to me," she hissed. "He is my *son*, you bastard! *Give me my son!*"

"Harenn!" Kendi shouted. He grabbed her shoulders and tried to pull her away. Markovi's eyes bulged and he made choking sounds. Joe appeared next to Markovi and pried Harenn's fingers away. The moment he broke her grip, Harenn balled up a fist and socked Markovi in the face. He stumbled backward with a yelp.

"Get them the fuck out of here!" he howled, one hand over his nose. Blood trickled between his fingers.

Joe grabbed Harenn's wrists and twisted her hands behind her. Kendi spun to face him. He was the man who had originally shown them in.

"Let her go!" Kendi snapped.

"Not until we're outside," Joe replied through clenched teeth. Harenn fought his grip, cursing and snarling. He pushed her firmly and none too gently toward the door. Alex put a heavy hand on Kendi's shoulder to escort him away as well. Kendi shook it off with a glare and followed Joe and Harenn out the office door.

"Bitch!" Markovi yelled after them. "You'll never see your little brat again; I'll make sure of that!"

Harenn renewed her struggles, and in the end it took both Joe and Alex to get her out to the parking lot. Kendi, not knowing what else to do, followed.

"Get into the car, sir," Joe said. "Our security computer will take control of your vehicle and drive it from the grounds. If you try to come back"—he cracked his knuckles pointedly—"it'll involve broken bones."

Kendi silently climbed in. The moment he closed the door, the groundcar rushed out of the parking lot and zipped up the driveway. The gates swung open just in time to let the vehicle through and they crashed shut behind it.

"*Thank* you for visiting Sunnytree Farms," chirped the computer. Kendi punched the screen with his fist and it shut up. He turned to Harenn.

"I'm sorry," he said.

"I don't know what to do," she whispered. Harenn pressed a hand against her window. "He is in there and he doesn't even know I am here for him. He doesn't even know."

An unfamiliar, gasping sort of sound issued from her veil. It took Kendi a moment to realize that Harenn was crying. It was the first time he had seen her do such a thing. He found it unnerving, as if he were standing on a boulder that had suddenly shifted beneath him.

"We aren't done yet, Harenn," he said grimly, and laid a hand on her shoulder.

"What do you mean?" she asked, her eyes red above her veil.

"I promised you I'd get your son back and I will," Kendi told her. "I already have a plan."

CHAPTER TWO

"If wealth can't buy you freedom, you have to steal it."

—Collette Martin, Bethlehem Colony

"Exactly what's supposed to be wrong with our system?" Markovi said.

The blond woman shifted an impressive wad of gum from one cheek to the other. She wore a blue jumpsuit with matching cap and carried a toolbox. A holographic ID badge floating near her lapel proclaimed her an employee of Compulink, Inc.

"Look, mister—how many times you want this explained?" she said. "Our programmers found a potential glitch in the programs we installed for your irrigation and fertilizer systems. Nothing has gone wrong yet, but something probably will and I'm here to fix it before it does. We're not even charging you, since it's our fault the glitch is there in the first place. What's the big deal?"

"The big deal is that I received no authorization from the home corp to let anyone examine our equipment," Markovi said sharply. "There are a lot of spies in this business, and—"

"Yeah, yeah. You want me to fix this thing or do you want fertilizer spraying every which way at noon on Tuesdays?"

"I'll have to call the home corp first."

"Sure, fine. What do I care? I'm paid by the hour."

Markovi turned and walked into his office. Gretchen Beyer picked up the toolbox of computer equipment and followed. She was surprised at how calm she felt. By all rights her heart should be hammering. There was no doubt in her mind that if Markovi learned who she was, her broken body would turn up in a ditch somewhere. Ben had uncovered a fair amount of information on chocolate companies, and it had turned out that these particular corps were more paranoid and secretive than many fascist police agencies. L. L. Venus had no public information officer, no press agents, and, since it was still a proprietary company, no stock market presence. According to an unauthorized biography of the Venus family and of the Wexford family, both corporations had surveillance and espionage departments dedicated to guarding their own recipes and stealing secrets from their rivals. And their security people had reputations for absolute ruthlessness. By all rights, Gretchen should have been nervous as hell— and she wasn't.

Of course, ever since the Despair, Gretchen hadn't been much in control of her emotional state. One minute she was so depressed she didn't care if the universe ended; the next she was so angry everything seemed tinged with red. Gretchen had been a reasonably skilled and powerful Silent, gifted in the Dream and easily achieving the rank of Sister among the Children of Irfan. Now, however, she was nothing. Sure, she still held her rank, but she couldn't *do* anything with it. The Dream was gone for her. She couldn't reach it, couldn't even feel it. Like every other Silent in her position, she hoped with fevered desperation that this was only temporary, that one morning she'd wake up and sense the familiar Dream around her again.

She hadn't cried at Mother Ara's funeral. In her more despondent moments, Gretchen felt that Ara had it pretty good, had taken the easy way out during the Despair. Jump off a balcony, all the pain stops. Gretchen couldn't blame her for doing it, not when she knew exactly how Ara felt. But Ara had left an unholy mess in her wake, including the impact on Ben. Gretchen liked Ben, had even had a crush on him once, though now she sometimes found herself angry at him for gaining what she had lost. And then there was Kendi. He had once been her equal. Now he was her superior, both in rank and in the fact the he still had the Dream. She respected him, though she'd never say so except under extreme torture, but she was mighty pissed at him, too. That was the problem. Everything was mixed up, and each time Gretchen thought she'd figured out which direction was up, she turned out to be ninety degrees from reality.

Better, then, to concentrate on the job at hand. Slavers and slave owners were a concrete problem Gretchen could handle. Besides, Gretchen had always felt that the best thing to do for a bad mood was to spread it around.

Markovi strode to the office wall that held his main viewscreen. He was reaching out to tap it and call the home corp when the latches on Gretchen's toolbox gave way. Computer tools and parts spilled in a spectacular jumble across the carpet close to the wall.

"Oh, hell," Gretchen grumbled. "Hey, can you give me a hand here? I asked for a new toolbox, but nooooo . . ."

Markovi gave a put-upon sigh and knelt to help her gather up the scattered materials. He didn't notice Gretchen palm a chip half the size of a fingernail and stick it to the wall just beneath the viewscreen.

Once the mess was cleaned up, Gretchen thanked Markovi and he tapped the viewscreen. "HQ," he said. "Extension one three six."

A moment later, a dark-haired man with a mole on his cheek appeared. Gretchen barely recognized

Ben. Harenn, the resident makeup expert, had done a good job.

"Requisitions," Ben said. The computer changed his voice, making it deeper. *"Samson speaking."*

"Doug Markovi at Sunnytree," Markovi said. "I have a computer technician here who says she's supposed to fix a glitch in our sprinkler and irrigation system. But I didn't receive any authorization for it. Can you confirm?"

"One moment." "Samson's" fingers clicked across a keyboard and his eyes tracked as if reading an offscreen display. *"You said Sunnytree, right? It's here. You should have gotten the authorization yesterday."*

"I didn't get it."

"One moment." More key clicks. *"Nope. Computer confirms arrival. Everything's in order from this end."*

Markovi folded his arms. "Well, it's not in order from *my* end."

"Look," Gretchen interrupted, "it's getting close to lunchtime and I don't want to be dicking around here all day. You don't want me to fix the glitch, I won't fix the glitch." She pulled a computer pad from her pocket and tapped at it. "Just thumb here to indicate you refused service. When your fertilizer system goes kaflooey, give Compulink a yell and we'll try to get someone down here, but since you refused the free repair, it'll count as an emergency call and you'll pay full emergency rates."

"Hey!" Ben said from the screen. *"Emergencies run triple."*

"Not my call," Gretchen said. "Thumb here, please." She thrust the computer pad at Markovi.

Markovi hesitated. "Look, I'm only—"

"Just thumb it," Gretchen said. "I've got other calls to make today."

"No, that's all right," Markovi said, putting his hands behind his back. "Fix the glitch."

"You sure?" Gretchen said, waggling the pad. "Because I can be out of here in—"

"Just fix it," Markovi snapped.

Gretchen put the pad back into her pocket with a shrug. "You're the boss. Can you have someone show me where your equipment mainframe is?"

Markovi nodded to her and tapped the viewscreen off without saying good-bye to Ben, who would deactivate the chip remotely from the *Poltergeist*. Then Markovi called a husky-looking man into the office.

"This is Joe," Markovi said. "He'll show you what's where."

Gretchen chewed her gum noisily and followed Joe out to the farm proper. The smell of mulch and damp moss assailed her, and the hot sun burned high overhead. Joe took Gretchen to what looked like a wooden barn. Inside however, were no stables or animals. Instead they entered a series of tiled corridors and equipment bays full of machines Gretchen didn't recognize. She hoped she wouldn't have to comment on any of them. Fans hummed and overhead pipes gurgled. The air was cool, and no slaves were in evidence. Gretchen glanced around as if in idle curiosity but was careful to memorize the route back in case she had to make a hasty exit.

"Mainframe's in here," Joe said, opening a door and gesturing inside. He was a big man who bulged in places where nothing should bulge, and Gretchen wondered how many weapons he was carrying. Still chewing her gum and keeping her face bland, Gretchen peered suspiciously into the room. It wouldn't be impossible that Markovi was on to her and had somehow told Joe to bop her over the head or zap her with something nasty and lock her in some kind of prison cell. But the room beyond was full of computer equipment. A lone technician tapped at a keyboard. He glanced up as Gretchen entered. Joe shut the door behind her, leaving the two of them alone. Loud classical music floated from hidden speakers.

"Hey," Gretchen said. "I'm Denise Fell with Compulink. Gotta fix a glitch before it becomes a problem."

"Vince Mays," he said without turning down the music. "Systems operator. What's the glitch?" Gretchen cracked her gum and explained. Mays said, "There's a terminal over there. Do what you have to."

Gretchen sat at the indicated keyboard. A single tap brought up the holographic screen, and she positioned herself between it and Mays so Mays couldn't read over her shoulder. Then she pressed a finger to her ear. The implant in her ear canal sprang to life.

"Okay, Ben, I'm in," she subvocalized. Mays's music helped cover the sound. "You still have access to my eye implant?"

"I'm with you," came Ben's voice. *"Put your pad on the desk so the IR beam can link up with the mainframe. The program I put in it should hack you root access, just like a real Compulink tech would normally have. Sunnytree's equipment mainframe isn't linked to the outside, so their computer's security probably isn't all that great—they'll be figuring you can't hack what you can't get to."*

Which was why Gretchen had to show up with a wad of gum in her mouth and a toolbox in her hand.

Gretchen set the pad on the desk and pretended to click computer keys while the pad did its work. She was getting nervous. Vince Mays could walk over and check out what she was doing at any moment, and getting her ass off the farm would be problematic if she were discovered. Gretchen shot Mays a covert glance, but he seemed more interested in his own screen than in hers.

"Don't forget the copycat," Ben reminded her.

Swearing softly, Gretchen fished a flat black box from her toolkit. Red lights skittered around the edge when she pressed the activation button. After a moment, a small screen displayed the message, TWO HUNDRED FIFTEEN LOCAL FREQUENCIES DETECTED, along with a list of numbers. PLEASE INDICATE WHICH FREQUENCY YOU WISH TO COPY.

Gretchen ran a stylus down the entire list to select all of them. WORKING, the screen said. Gretchen set the copycat back in her toolbox and turned back to the computer pad. It was still breaking into the mainframe. Her hands were shaking now and she forced them back into steadiness. She peeked at Mays. He was looking directly at her. Gretchen's mouth went dry around the gum.

"What?" she asked.

"Just wondering what you're up to over there," Mays said with a smile. "Will it take long?"

"Shouldn't."

"Maybe I can help." He started to get to his feet. Gretchen's heart leaped into her throat. If he got a look at her screen, he'd see she hadn't even logged in yet and would know something was up.

"Nuh-uh." She held up both hands, partly to indicate negation and partly to block his view of her screen. "Company policy. If I get help from someone who isn't a Compulink employee, the union will have conniptions."

"Funny." Mays frowned. "I've helped Compulink people before."

"New policy." Gretchen rolled her eyes. "You know how bureaucrats and bean counters get."

"Around here everyone's a bean counter," Mays said with a grin. At Gretchen's blank look, he added, "Cocoa beans?"

Gretchen forced a laugh, though she was ready to bolt for the door. "Guess I'm not very quick on the uptake today." She blew a gum bubble to cover the pounding of her heart. What the hell was taking Ben's program so long? "I better see what trouble I can get into on your network, then."

She turned back to her terminal, pretending to work but actually holding her breath. Mays didn't come up behind her. After a moment, she sneaked another peek. His attention was back on his work.

At last—at *last*—the pad flashed. The holographic screen on the terminal flickered and Gretchen had root access.

"Got it," she murmured. "And next time you should be doing this, Benny-boy."

"*I would have,*" Ben said in her ear, "*except I'm the only one who knows how to tap the communication system and reroute Markovi's calls. Okay, here's what you do next.*"

As Ben spoke, printed instructions scrolled across the bottom of Gretchen's eye—her ocular implant at work. She did as instructed, accessing the section of the mainframe that oversaw the farm's automated equipment and uploading a single program. Then she downloaded several files of information and she reached into her toolbox to check the copycat.

FREQUENCIES COPIED, said the screen. Gretchen switched it off, wiped Ben's hacking program from her pad in case she was caught, logged off the mainframe, and closed her toolbox.

"Both jobs are done," she muttered to Ben. "I'm on my way out."

"*Great job,*" he said. "*I'll tell Kendi.*"

"You're all set," Gretchen announced to Mays, and held her pad out to him. "Be a pal and thumb this service acknowledgment, would you? The company doesn't care who thumbs the thing, and I don't want to track down that guy Markovi again."

"Sure thing." Mays pressed his thumb to Gretchen's pad and his hand brushed hers. "It's about lunchtime," he added, looking straight into her eyes. "You want to catch a bite or something?"

Oh, brother, Gretchen thought. *Ah, well. At least he isn't one of the grabby ones.* Gretchen smiled at him with a demure shake of her head. "I have two more calls to make before I can break. Maybe another time."

"Yeah, sure." Mays turned back to his computer with an air of "nothing ventured, nothing gained," and Gretchen let herself out of the room, heart pounding again. A few moments later she was back in her groundcar and winding her way back to the entry gate. Slaves continued their work among the cacao trees, and Gretchen wondered if one of them was Bedj-ka. A grubby boy who was loading a gravity sled with seed pods paused in his labor long enough to wipe the sweat from his face. Gretchen found her appetite for chocolate had disappeared. At last she reached the entry gate.

The dashboard computer chimed and Gretchen jumped, certain she had been discovered.

"*Thank* you," chirped the computer, "for visiting Sunnytree Farms."

Gretchen slapped the screen to shut it off and sped back toward the city. Once she was a safe distance away, however, she pulled onto an empty side road and peeled the Compulink signs off both car doors. She tapped one corner of each sign, and both promptly erased themselves. This procedure she repeated with her Compulink holobadge. It vanished, leaving behind a blank chip. Then Gretchen skinned out of her jumpsuit, revealing an ordinary shirt and trousers, and sprayed the cloth with the contents of a small flask. The jumpsuit disintegrated into dust, which blew away in the slight breeze.

Safely anonymous and sure no one was following her, Gretchen drove into the city, returned the groundcar to the rental company, and took a bus back to the spaceport. But only when she was safely aboard the *Poltergeist* did she finally breathe a sigh of relief. Gretchen trotted into the galley—she felt she deserved a shot of something that would burn all the way down—and found Lucia working at one of the tables. A set of slave bands, one shackle for the wrist and one for the ankle, lay open on the table in front of her, along with a set of microtools.

"Did you get the frequency?" Lucia asked.

Gretchen set the copycat on the table. "Got a couple hundred of them, along with the tracking files. It's your happy job to figure out which frequency is the right one."

"Not a problem." She reached for the copycat with her scarred hands. "It'll take me a couple hours, but it's just tedious, not hard."

"Better you than me." Gretchen stretched. "When does everything go *foom* at Sunnyass?"

Lucia switched on the copycat. "Two days. Then the real fun begins."

"Your technician said this bug was fixed!" Markovi roared. "What the hell's wrong with your piece-of-shit company?"

Gretchen kept her head down and her cap pulled low as she and Lucia opened the back doors of the van. Ben had already exited from the driver's side. Markovi's face was beet red beneath blond hair. Joe stood behind his boss, doing his best to loom threateningly and succeeding nicely.

"Don't worry, sir," Ben said placatingly as he shut the van door. It had a Compulink logo emblazoned on it, and the trio of "troubleshooters" all wore blue Compulink jumpsuits, caps, and holobadges. Ben's little chip had rerouted Markovi's frantic call, allowing the Children to answer Sunnytree's summons in Compulink's place. "We'll track down the problem and fix it right away."

"You goddammed well better!" Markovi snarled. "I've got six dozen hands who can't work because the goddammed sprinkler system keeps spraying goddammed fertilizer every goddammed ten minutes."

"Are your hands all right?" Ben asked. "Raw fertilizer will cause burns after—"

"Don't you think I know that?" Markovi snapped. "My hands are all sitting goddammed idle in their goddammed quarters, and they'll have to stay there until you fix the goddammed problem which your goddammed company said was goddammed fixed. I'm more worried about those cacao trees. They're goddammed delicate, and too much fertilizer will kill them, you understand me? Goddammed *kill* them. I'll sue Compulink for every goddammed credit you've got!"

Ben nodded, and Gretchen wondered if he was suppressing an urge to punch the man right in the middle of his goddammed face. God only knew Gretchen wanted to do it. Not only did the man enslave children and yell at people, he had permanently ruined her taste for chocolate. The last, in Gretchen's mind, justified capital punishment.

But Ben only made soothing noises at Markovi while Lucia and Gretchen clambered down from the rear of the van and grabbed hold of an enormous crate, also decorated with the Compulink logo. The tool belt around Gretchen's waist made an unfamiliar weight, and a heavy flashlight banged against her thigh. She kept her cap low and face down in case anyone recognized her as the original technician, though if that happened, Gretchen would simply claim that she had done the original job to the best of her ability and was now on the team that would unsnarl the problem. It would be a better bet than trying to explain away a disguise if anyone saw through it. Harenn, of course, had wanted to come along the moment Ben intercepted Markovi's frantic call, had even been willing to remove her veil, but Kendi had vetoed the entire idea.

"You're emotionally too close to the entire affair, Harenn," he had said, "and you might not make good decisions—like trying to throttle Markovi again. It'll have to be Ben, Lucia, and Gretchen." And in the end, Harenn had agreed.

Lucia tapped a pad mounted to her side of the crate and the container floated upward two or three centimeters, allowing her and Gretchen to guide it out of the back of the van. Once clear of the rear doors, the crate drifted toward the ground and hovered just above the gravel driveway.

Ben waited for a pause in Markovi's tirade. "We'll take care of everything, sir," he said. "We have enough parts in that crate to build you an entirely new system if we have to, free of charge."

"Just fix the goddammed glitch," Markovi growled.

"Of course, sir," Ben said meekly.

Markovi stormed toward the office building, leaving his goon behind. Ben turned to him. "So can you show us the equipment we need to look at?"

Gretchen, of course, remembered where everything was, but she didn't want to call undue attention to herself.

Joe folded his arms. He loomed almost a full head taller than Ben. "Computer equipment or sprinkler equipment?" he said in a heavy voice.

"Both," Ben replied. "Once we fix the computer, we'll have to give the sprinkler system a once-over to make sure everything's okay."

Without a word, Joe turned and walked away. Ben shot Gretchen and Lucia a glance before hurrying after him. The two women gave the crate a shove, and it slid easily forward. They guided it into the huge equipment barn Gretchen had visited and

toward one of the equipment bays. Pipes clanked
and gurgled, and pumps chugged steadily.

"All the sprinkler equipment goes through here,"
Joe yelled over the noise. "The equipment mainframe is through that door." He pointed, and
Gretchen recognized the room she had worked in
earlier.

"Got it!" Ben yelled back. "Thanks! We'll get
right to work!"

Joe gave a curt nod and left. Gretchen, who was
bent over the crate, let out a sigh of relief. Ben took
hold of her arm.

"Go!" he shouted. "We'll keep things busy down
here!"

Gretchen gave a smart salute and trotted out of
the equipment bay, tool belt and flashlight dragging
at her hips. Once the equipment noise had faded,
she tapped her earpiece.

"Myra?" she said.

"On-line," said the *Poltergeist*'s computer.

"Track copied frequency 'Bedj-ka one' and upload
tracking information to my ocular implant."

"Working," said the computer. A moment later, a
small red arrow popped into Gretchen's field of vision along with a digital readout that said, 107 ME-
TERS. The arrow pointed to Gretchen's left. Lucia's
copycat had worked as advertised, detecting and copying all the broadcast frequencies used on the farm—
including the one that tracked the movements of the
individual slaves. Like most slave owners, Sunnytree
used slave shackles and a computer to keep its slaves
from escaping. Each set of wrist- and ankle bands
continually broadcast its whereabouts to the main
computer and delivered a debilitating electric shock
if the wearer left the boundaries of the farm. Most
wristbands also monitored conversation, delivering
punishing shocks if the slave spoke words such as

escape or *revolt*. Lucia had isolated Bedj-ka's frequency and uploaded it to the *Poltergeist*'s computer.

Gretchen, figuring that the slaves probably weren't housed in the equipment barn, hurried toward the exit. The arrow slowly turned until it was pointing down and the numbers went up, telling Gretchen that Bedj-ka was a hundred and thirty meters behind her now.

Outside, Gretchen paused a moment to let her eyes adjust to the hard sunlight. The smell of cacao tree mulch and cacao blossoms hung heavily on the air. The edge of the green, leafy cacao tree grove was about fifteen paces ahead of Gretchen, and she caught sight of a bunch of metal pipes rising up from the ground. A moment later, liquid sprayed from the tops of the pipes and Gretchen caught the sharp scent of chemical fertilizer. Markovi's glitch.

No one else was in sight. Markovi had said the hands—slaves—were all in their quarters, and Gretchen guessed the office staff was all inside with the air-conditioning. Sweating beneath the golden sun, she trotted around the perimeter of the equipment barn until the arrow pointed straight ahead and the number ticker informed her that Bedj-ka was only seventy-three meters ahead of her. A concrete pathway led to a series of what appeared to be large white bunkhouses, and Gretchen assumed they were the slave quarters. The arrow steered her to the second bunkhouse. Gretchen shut off the tracker, then rapped on the whitewashed door. It opened on a middle-aged man with a whipcord body and a leathery, burned-in suntan. A silvery band encircled his wrist.

"Yes, mistress?" he said.

Gretchen tried not to grimace at the man's deferential tone and the title he had bestowed on her. "I'm part of the team that's here to fix the sprinkler and fertilizer system," she said. "We need a runner to help us out, and Mr. Markovi told me I could find a kid named Jerry here. He's supposed to come with me."

"Yes, mistress." The man vanished into the bunkhouse. Gretchen tried to peer inside, but the interior was too dim to make out more than shadows and shapes. She did get the sense of a large space filled with what were probably bunk beds. Snores and grunts issued from the room, indicating that many of the slaves were taking advantage of their enforced idleness to catch up on lost sleep. Gretchen, who had grown up in South Africa on Earth, remembered reading about apartheid in history class and times when workers who were slaves in all but name learned to sleep standing up on long bus rides to and from their jobs. You caught sleep when you could.

"Here he is, mistress," the man said, pushing a boy out into the sunlight and closing the door. Gretchen looked down at the kid. He was short, barely coming up to Gretchen's breastbone, with dark eyes and a headful of straight black hair. Thin build, sharp nose, fine-boned face. Gretchen put his age at nine or ten, despite his lack of height. The boy met Gretchen's gaze for the briefest of moments before dropping his eyes to his ground.

"Jerry?" Gretchen asked. She had to be certain this was the right boy.

"Yes, mistress," he said quietly. "Yatt said you need a runner?"

"I do. Jerry, are you new to Sunnytree Farm?"

He glanced up at Gretchen in puzzlement. "Yes, mistress. I haven't even been here a month. If you want someone else as a runner, someone who knows the farm better, I can go get—"

"No, that's all right, Jerry," Gretchen said. "Let me see your hands, please."

Even more puzzled, Jerry held up his hands, palm up. Blisters mixed with calluses, and his nails were broken and dirty. Gretchen took hold of both his wrists for a moment, then let him go. No Silent jolt, but she hadn't been expecting one. The Despair had robbed her of that.

"Walk with me, kid, and quick," she ordered, and headed back toward the equipment barn. The boy hurried to keep up.

"Mistress?" he asked. "Is something wrong?"

"I don't have a lot of time to explain," she said, "so listen hard. I stuck a chip to your shackle when I grabbed your wrists. It broadcasts a silence loop to the farm's computer so it can't monitor what we're saying."

"Mistress?" the boy said hesitantly. "I don't understand."

Gretchen reached into her jumpsuit and fished out her gold medallion. It was a risk to wear it, but experience had taught Gretchen that the medallion often convinced suspicious slaves faster than mere words. "Do you know what this stands for, Jerry?"

The boy halted and stared, forcing Gretchen to stop as well. Awe mixed with excitement on his face. "Everyone knows what that is. You're a Child of Irfan."

"That's right," she said, tucking the medallion away again. "I'm here with a couple other members of our order to get you out of here. You game?"

"But—but I'm not—" He hesitated, clearly afraid of her reaction. "Not Silent. Not anymore. That's why they sold me."

Gretchen's heart twisted in sympathy and she struggled to keep her voice steady. "Your Silence doesn't matter to us, Jerry. *You* do. Are you in or out? I need to know now."

"In," the boy said to Gretchen's relief. She

wouldn't have to bring up his mother to convince him. Kendi had told her to save Harenn for later, if possible. No sense in overwhelming the boy.

"Then let's get moving," Gretchen said, hurrying down the path toward the equipment barn again. "We don't have a whole lot of time."

"How are you going to do it?" the boy asked. "Do you have a plan? Are you going to kill the master?"

"Never mind the details," she said, "and no, we aren't planning to kill anyone."

"Oh." The boy looked disappointed. "Will it take long? Are we going today?"

"No, it won't, and yes, we are. Now come with me and don't ask so many questions. We'll tell you everything you want to know, but later."

They rounded the corner of the barn—and came face-to-face with Joe. Gretchen only barely managed to avoid slamming into him. The boy dodged behind Gretchen with a gasp.

"What are you doing out here?" Joe demanded. "And what's with the kid?"

Gretchen's heart thudded hard, but she managed to keep her face expressionless. "We need a runner, one who knows the farm," she said. "So I co-opted one of your hands. We didn't figure you'd mind."

Joe frowned. "We run a tight ship here, lady. This kind of thing needs to be— Hey! Aren't you the tech that came by to fix the sprinkler glitch in the first place?"

"That's me," Gretchen said. She drew her flashlight from her belt and tapped herself on the chest with it. "Corporate HQ says the fix-it program had some bugs— a glitch within a glitch. What are the odds, hey?"

"I don't like this," Joe growled. "That man and that woman coming here to ask about a hand we just bought, then this glitch pops up and I catch you running around with the same kid those two were asking about. I better call Mr. Markovi."

Adrenaline sang in Gretchen's blood. "You don't have to call him," she said, pointing with her chin to a spot past Joe's shoulder. "Here he comes now."

Joe turned to look and Gretchen slugged him with the flashlight. The man staggered in surprise but didn't fall. Gretchen hit him again, and this time he went down. Gretchen glanced quickly around. The main house was blocked from view by the equipment barn, and no other workers were in sight. A small bit of luck to balance out the big chunk of bad.

"Fuck," Gretchen muttered, looking down at Joe's motionless body. "Now what?"

"There," the boy said, pointing to a clump of ornamental bushes next to the equipment barn. "I'll help you drag him."

"You're quick on the uptake," Gretchen said as she grabbed one of Joe's wrists. The boy took the other. Together they dragged him toward the bushes.

"Faster on it than him," the boy said. "That was a really old trick."

"Still works," Gretchen pointed out, her calm voice belying the tension she felt. Someone could come by at any moment, might even be watching them now.

Once Joe's limp form had been stuffed into its leafy hiding place, Gretchen bent down and extracted his earpiece. Then she took the boy's hand and all but sprinted back toward the barn, only remembering at the last minute to slow down to a brisk walk when they came into sight of the house. Once they were in the equipment barn, however, they ran all the way to the equipment bay, where Ben and Lucia were waiting. Computer parts and sprinkler equipment were scattered over the floor.

"Complication," Gretchen said as loudly as she dared above the noise. "Joe got suspicious. I had to hit him to keep him from calling Markovi, and I don't know how long he'll be out."

"Vik!" Lucia swore. She opened the nearly empty equipment crate. "Get in, Jerry—hurry!"

The boy needed no further urging and jumped into the crate. Ben and Lucia carefully piled equipment on top of him while Gretchen kept a lookout; then they shut the lid and maneuvered the crate out of the bay.

Gretchen felt as if a big sign hung over her head and flashed GUILTY! GUILTY! as they emerged with the crate into the bright sunlight and steered it toward the van. Ben tapped his ear and muttered to empty air while Gretchen and Lucia opened the van doors.

An alarm sounded just as they got the crate inside.

Douglas Markovi sat in his office and fumed. This stupid glitch had so far cost him an entire day's work, and it would show on the weekly statement. No doubt HQ would blame him for the whole thing and it would probably cut into his bonus, all because that goddammed bitch of a technician hadn't done her job right. He'd have to talk to legal about that, see what damages they could recover from Compulink. Meanwhile, maybe they could set up some lights in the cacao groves, get the hands off their lazy asses this evening and get some honest labor out of—

An alarm blasted through the room. Markovi jumped.

"Attention! Attention!" barked the computer. "A hand has left the boundaries of Sunnytree Farm. Attention! Attention! A hand has left—"

Markovi waved a frantic hand over his desk computer and the holographic screen popped up. The alarm continued to blare. "Billy, close down the exits and show me which hand has left the farm. And shut off that goddammed noise!"

The alarm instantly shut off. "All hands are accounted for," the computer said.

"What? But you just said someone had left."

"Please restate request."

Markovi ground his teeth. "Billy, explain the inconsistency in the last two reports."

"No inconsistency found. All hands are accounted for."

The vidscreen chimed and flashed the words INCOMING CALL. Markovi tapped his desk. Alex appeared on the wall looking worried. *"What's going on boss? Did someone go AWOL?"*

"That's what I'm trying to figure out," Markovi snarled. "Get your ass down to the quarters with Joe and do a physical head count. I want everyone—"

He was cut off by another blast of alarm noise. "Attention! Attention! A hand has left the boundaries of Sunnytree Farm. Attention! Attention!"

"Billy, shut the fuck up!" Markovi yelled, and the computer obeyed. "Billy, run a count of all hands."

"All hands are accounted for."

"Billy, did any shackle bombs go off?"

"Negative."

"What the hell?" Alex said.

The vidscreen flashed another incoming call, and a moment later one of the Compulink techs—the wimpy one whom Markovi had yelled at earlier—appeared on it.

"Sir," said the tech, *"we've been tracking the glitch, but it isn't exactly a glitch."*

"What do you mean?" Markovi demanded. "Does this have something to do with the alarm system?"

"I think so, sir," the wimp said. *"Your system doesn't have a glitch—it has a virus. That's why our original fix didn't work. I think it's spreading to other systems in your mainframe, including the alarm system. That's why it keeps going off, just like the sprinkler."*

"How the hell did we get a goddammed virus?" Markovi barked. "Our goddammed system is isolated."

The tech shrugged. *"We can try to track it down for you, sir, since we're here."*

"How much is this going to cost?" Alex asked from his half of the vidscreen.

"It won't be our emergency rates, sir," the tech said. "We're already on the premises, so—"

"Attention! Attention! A hand has left the boundaries of Sunnytree Farm. Attention! Attention!"

"Shut up, Billy!" Markovi screamed. Then to the tech, "Just fucking fix it!"

"We'll have to shut off the alarm system for a while," said the tech.

"No way!" Alex said. *"What if someone runs off for real?"*

"Your hands won't know the system is off-line unless you tell them," the tech said. *"And it'll only be for about ten minutes while we clean and reboot the computer system. How far could they get even if they found out?"*

"Attention! Attention!"

Markovi had had it. "Billy, shut up and take the hand alarm system off-line for ten minutes. No more."

"Acknowledged."

"Now get off your ass and get to work," Markovi ordered. The tech nodded and vanished from the screen.

Ben poked his head into the van. "Go!"

Lucia dePaolo muttered a quick prayer to Irfan and set to work, her white-scarred hands moving with swift, serene efficiency. The boy watched with both interest and trepidation as Lucia forced open the control panel on his wristband with a tiny pick and started on the electronic lock within. He stood inside the crate while Gretchen kept a lookout through the van window. His bands were newer than the ones she was used to picking, and they were going to take longer to work than she had thought.

Serene must you ever remain, she thought. *Serene like Irfan herself.*

"What if you make a mistake?" the boy whispered.

"I won't make a mistake," she told him quietly. "Just hold—" She broke off and stared at the band.

"Hold still?" the boy asked.

"Seven minutes left," Gretchen said.

Lucia's face remained expressionless, belying the pang of fear that temporarily overwhelmed her usual calm. The wristband contained a small detonator—another new feature. These shackles would do more than shock. Any slave who left the boundaries of the farm would probably lose a hand and a foot—easily repairable if he were found quickly enough, and a one-footed slave wasn't likely to be running anywhere. The bombs would doubtless also go off if she didn't get the bands removed before the alarm system came back on-line and detected tampering. Lucia spent several precious seconds debating whether she should first remove the shackles or disarm the bombs.

Remove the shackles, she decided. *Once they're off, the bombs won't matter.*

Lucia took a deep breath and murmured a short mantra to restore her peace of mind. This was a simple puzzle, one she could solve with Irfan's help.

Grandmother Irfan, grant me speed, she thought, and tried to hurry without making any time-wasting errors. The boy was counting on her. Father Kendi was counting on her, too, and Lucia would have been hard-pressed to decide which one put her under more pressure. When Harenn had told her that Father Kendi was looking for a pilot on a new ship, Lucia had jumped at the chance. Father Kendi—touched by Irfan herself and a hero of the Despair. How could she refuse such a chance?

"Five minutes," Gretchen said, then gasped. "Oh, shit—it's that Alex guy. He's coming over to the van."

Wasting no movements, Lucia pushed the boy down into the crate and slid in after him. She fumbled around in the dark for a moment, pulled a flashlight from her belt, switched it on, and put it in her mouth. The boy huddled, scared and unhappy, on the floor of the crate as Lucia grabbed for his wrist again. Dim light, cramped quarters, time running out. Another deep, calming breath. Irfan was with her; everything would be fine.

"You guys seen Joe anywhere?" she heard Alex say.

"Not lately," Ben said. "Why?"

"I can't raise him." Alex paused. "Aren't you supposed to be working on the computer virus?"

"Nancy's already gotten started," Ben said. "She'll have the alarm system cleared up pretty quick, so Denise and I came back here for the program disks we'll use to check the rest of the system." His voice got louder. "You *did* bring them, didn't you, Denise?"

"They're in here somewhere," Gretchen shot back. "Probably won't take more than *three minutes* to find them."

Lucia pressed another section of the lock with her electric stylus and the wristband popped open. Lucia caught it just before it thudded to the floor of the crate. Mouth dry as a raisin, she reached for the boy's ankle band. This one should be easier, since she now knew the lock mechanism better, but she had little time, so little time. The boy was shaking noticeably. He had to know about the shackle bombs. Telling the slaves about such a thing would be a powerful deterrent against escape.

For a moment Lucia considered stage-whispering to Gretchen that she needed more time, that Ben should contact Markovi and tell him to keep the alarm system off-line for a few more minutes. Then she realized that as "Nancy" she was supposed to be working on the computers in the equipment barn and there was no way Gretchen or Ben could know that she needed more minutes. Activating her earpiece and explaining to Ben over the radio, as "Nancy" would have done, would eat up too much time.

"Two minutes," Gretchen murmured.

Mother Irfan, please, Lucia silently begged. She started to change another connection in the ankle band, then froze. Completing the circuit she had been working on would set off the detonator. Another couple of millimeters of movement on her behalf and the bomb would have exploded in Lucia's face, taking the boy's foot and probably killing Lucia in the bargain. A trickle of cold sweat slid around her temple. Quickly she searched for a way to bypass the circuit, isolate it from the detonator. Reroute that piece over this way, cut that bit over there. Clip the red connector first or the green one? Green. Then red. Now a pulse with the stylus—

The ankle band came off.

"Done!" she said hoarsely. "Go!"

"Those disks aren't here," Gretchen said loudly. "We'll have to go back and get them while Nancy finishes up. It'll only take *a minute.*"

"Better go," Ben said, presumably to Alex. "Time is money, after all."

Lucia poked her head cautiously out of the crate in time to see Ben all but leap into the driver's seat. He slammed the door and drove away as quickly as he dared. Just as the van was about to round the first bend in the driveway, Lucia caught sight of a figure through the van's tinted rear windows. It was a man, and he was staggering as if drunk.

"Who's that?" she said, pointing.

Gretchen glanced out the window. "Shit! It's Joe. He can't call for help because I took his earpiece, but once someone sees him—"

Ben floored it. The van careened around the driveway curves beneath the dark shade of the cacao trees. Lucia's heart was in her throat, and no amount of deep breathing slowed its pounding. How long would it take Joe to sound the alarm? And what would—

"Vik!" she cried, and dove back into the crate. Shoving aside the startled boy inside, Lucia scrambled to recover the slave shackles. The van rounded another curve, making the job harder. The boy lost his balance, fell against her. At last Lucia thrust the bands at Gretchen. "Toss these out the window. Quick!"

Gretchen obeyed and the shackles vanished into the mulch surrounding the cacao trees. A moment later, a muffled *boom* rattled several trees. Pipes rose out of the ground and sprayed fertilizer again. The main gate was in sight—and it was shut. Ben aimed a remote control at it, and they began to grind open. Before the van reached them, however, the gates froze, then started to slide shut. Ben swore and tried the remote again. Nothing.

"They've figured out what's going on and changed the codes already," Ben said. "Hold on to something!"

Lucia just managed to grab the crate's rim before Ben slammed his foot down. The van leaped forward. Behind her came a yelp and a thud from the crate as the boy lost his balance. Gretchen was flung backward against the rear doors. They popped open. Gretchen shrieked and barely managed to snag a cargo handle. Her feet dragged the ground behind the speeding van.

"Gretchen!" Lucia launched herself from the crate. The van rushed toward the closing gates, but Lucia didn't dare spare a glance to see if the opening was wide enough for them. She caught Gretchen's wrist and pulled, but Gretchen couldn't get any purchase on the rushing ground to aid in the effort. Lucia braced herself against the floor and, with a bone-cracking heave, yanked as hard as she could. There was a horrendous screech of metal and a shower of sparks as the gates scraped the sides of the van. Then they slammed shut on Gretchen's foot. Gretchen screamed and tumbled into the van on top of Lucia. Lucia disentangled herself, got the doors shut, and turned to look at Gretchen's tight, pale face.

"My foot," Gretchen moaned. "Oh, god, my foot!"

Steeling herself, Lucia looked down, expecting to see crushed bone and spurting blood. Nothing of the sort greeted her. Gretchen's shoe was missing and her trouser cuffs were torn; that was all.

"You still have it," Lucia said. "Blessings to Irfan for that. Let me have a look."

Ben, meanwhile, had turned onto the main road and was once again driving at breakneck speed. Lucia touched Gretchen's foot, and the blond woman howled in pain.

"It's broken," Lucia said. "And you have some abrasions on your legs. We'll have to have Harenn take a look when we get back to the ship. You were lucky, I think."

"It sure as shit doesn't feel lucky," Gretchen growled. "God."

The van slowed, and Lucia glanced out the window in time to see Father Kendi detach himself from a patch of brush near the Sunnytree Farm wall. A thin rope hung over the wall behind his hiding place. The other end, Lucia knew, was tied to the slave shackles that carried a frequency she had taken from the copycat. Father Kendi had been hauling the shackles over the wall with the rope and then tossing them back in order to set off the escaped slave alarm.

Father Kendi hopped into the passenger seat. "What happened to the van?" he asked. "We're going to lose our damage deposit."

"We had to make a break for it. The van almost got caught in the gate," Ben said. "So did Gretchen, for that matter."

"Just drive, computer boy," Gretchen snapped. "My foot isn't getting any less broken back here."

Kendi looked suddenly panicked as the van moved

onto the road and zipped back toward the city. "They know what we did? All life—they'll call the cops."

"Not for a while, they won't," Ben said. "They'll have to find the chip Gretchen installed first. Until then, they're going to find they can't reach anything but one of the downtown porn shops. I give it an hour, and by then we'll be long gone."

Kendi laughed, then turned in his seat to face the boy. "So you're Jerry, huh? I'm Father Kendi of the Children of Irfan. How's it feel to be a free man?"

"I'm really free?" the boy said in wonder. He held out his bare wrist and looked at it.

"Damn straight," Kendi told him. "And not only that, there's someone back on our ship who's dying to meet you."

CHAPTER THREE

"We must protect our children not because they are innocent, but because they are powerless."
—Ched-Balaar Child-Rearing Manual

Harenn Mashib sat stiffly at the pilot's board of the *Poltergeist*. If she moved, even dared to blink, she would start clawing at the walls. Kendi had just called to tell her they had Bedj-ka and that she needed to make sure the ship was ready for takeoff. Harenn wasn't a pilot, couldn't fly even a paper airplane, but she could switch everything on, prime the systems, and get takeoff permission from the spaceport authorities. All this she had done. Now all she had left to do was wait.

Harenn felt like she had been waiting forever. She still remembered with excruciating clarity the day she had come home to find her baby missing and her husband gone. Initially Harenn had assumed Isaac had taken Bedj-ka and gone out, perhaps to the park or for a walk. She had enjoyed an hour of solitude, even taken a nap. But when evening came and Isaac didn't return, she became worried, then frantic. She called everyone she knew, everyone they both knew, but no one had seen them. Finally she called the Guardians, the police and legal force for the Children of Irfan. Late the next day a Guardian inspector named Linus Gray informed her that a man matching Isaac Todd's description had been seen carrying a baby on board a slipship. Inspector Gray also told her that his partner had gotten hold of some contacts on other planets, contacts who were experts in the underground slave trade. They had heard of Isaac Todd.

"It seems your husband has been pulling this game for years," Gray told her. "He marries a woman, gets her pregnant, and then sells the child into slavery before vanishing to another planet and doing it all over again."

"But this is not true," Harenn protested. "Isaac loves me, and he loves Bedj-ka."

"According to my contacts," Gray continued softly, "he has unexpressed Silence—genetically Silent but unable to enter the Dream. His Silent genes, however, always breed true. All his children are Silent, and immensely valuable on the slave market. Ms. Mashib, your husband is a con artist of the worst kind. It's probably not much comfort, but you aren't the first woman he's fooled."

Gray continued to talk about how the Guardians would do everything in their power to find Isaac, but now that he was off-planet the odds were low, and so on and on. Harenn barely heard. She was thinking about how insistent Isaac had been about having children, how fierce he had been about making love, how ecstatic he had been when she told him she was pregnant. Her cheeks burned with shame at her naivete and vulnerability.

After Gray left, Harenn barricaded herself in her tiny home, the one that was now only hers. The thought of going outdoors made her sick. Not only was there the crushing grief at the loss of her child, but also the fact that everyone was surely either laughing at her stupidity or clucking their tongues in sympathy. Which was worse? She couldn't tell, but there was no way she could face either one.

In the end, it was the memory of her mother's funeral that saved her. Harenn found herself sitting on her bed with the veil she had worn to the service, which had taken place six months before Harenn met Isaac Todd. The cloth was soft, flimsy, and opaque, like a secret. Harenn had hazy memories of a place with stone walls, dark-haired men, and veiled women, and she knew Mother had fled this place, but Mother had always refused to talk about it. Sometimes, when she was feeling insecure or unhappy, Mother would wear her veil for a few days, then remove it without comment. Mother's death had been a devastating blow in itself, and Harenn had decided to hide her own grief behind the impenetrable cloth, a shield between her and the rest of the world. Harenn looked down at the veil for a long time. Then, with grim determination, she slipped the hooks behind her ears to hide her shame and went out into the world to find her son.

Harenn was already a certified nurse with the Children of Irfan, but nurses with no other skills didn't go on slave rescue expeditions, so Harenn learned engineering and joined Mother Ara Rymar's crew of seekers. Everywhere she went, she looked for clues to her son, and always she came up empty. In the process, Harenn learned the arts of disguise and makeup, making her even more valuable to Mother Ara's expeditions. And always the veil stayed with her. Nine years later, Harenn helped smuggle a Silent street hustler named Sejal out of the Empire of Human Unity, and like a genie showing gratitude at being released from his bottle, Sejal had told her where to find her little Bedj-ka.

Now she sat in the pilot's chair of the *Poltergeist* and waited for his return, afraid to move for fear she would wake from a strange dream. What did Bedj-ka look like? How would he react when he saw her? How would *she* react? Harenn's imagination continued to portray Bedj-ka as a babe in arms, though she knew better. Kendi had said over the communicator only that Bedj-ka appeared healthy and uninjured and that they would be there in less than half an hour.

Out of the entire nine years she had waited, this half an hour was proving to be the longest. Even the busywork she had tried to create for herself among the engines had failed to occupy her mind. In the end, she merely sat and waited.

"Attention! Attention!" said the computer at long last. "Father Kendi has returned to the ship."

Harenn bolted from the bridge. She flew down the corridor to the air lock hatchway, veil fluttering in the breeze. In the entry bay, she skidded to a halt and covered the returning group in one swift glance. Kendi looked triumphant. Lucia wore her usual serene expression, though she was rubbing the small figure of Irfan she habitually wore around her neck. Ben was carrying Gretchen, whose face was pale with pain. And standing next to them, looking shy and uncertain, was a boy with dark hair and eyes. Harenn's breath caught. The resemblance to Isaac was so strong that if she had seen him at random on the street, she would have instantly recognized him as Isaac's son. Harenn tried to speak, but her throat closed up.

"Hi," the boy said to her.

"Bedj-ka?" she blurted.

"This is Jerry," Kendi said. "He says that's the name he's always had. Markovi only changed his last name."

Harenn found she couldn't move. Nine years she had dreamed of this moment, longed and yearned for it. Now it was here and she didn't know what to do.

"Ben, take Gretchen to medical," Kendi said. "We'll get her fixed up as soon as we can. Lucia, get to the bridge and get us the hell out of here before the cops show up."

The three of them left, leaving Harenn, Kendi, and Bedj-ka—Jerry?—alone. Kendi squatted, bringing his head down to Bedj-ka's level.

"Jerry," he said, "remember how I said there was someone on the ship who wanted to meet you?" At Bedj-ka's mystified nod, he continued, "Jerry, this is Harenn Mashib. She's your mother."

Harenn's throat thickened again. She wanted to sweep Bedj-ka into her arms and hold him close, but she still couldn't move.

"Mother?" Bedj-ka said, and for a moment Harenn thought he was talking to her. Then she realized he was only echoing Kendi. "She can't be my mother. My mother's dead."

Something broke and Harenn found she could speak. "Is that what they told you?" she said hoarsely. "That I was dead?"

"That's why we were slaves—all us kids at the Enclave," Bedj-ka said. "Our parents were dead, and the Enclave bought us and we had to pay them back by growing up and working in the Dream. Then that weird stuff happened and none of us could feel the Dream anymore, so they sold us. They said we were no longer blessed."

"I'm not dead," Harenn said. "You were taken from me and I've been looking for you ever—"

"Why are you wearing a veil?" Bedj-ka interrupted.

Harenn tore the veil from her face and flung it aside. Kendi looked startled—it was the first time she had ever unveiled in his presence. The ship rumbled slightly beneath Harenn's feet as the *Poltergeist* took off. Bedj-ka looked at her face and Harenn felt naked. She could feel the tears standing in her eyes.

"What did you call me? Bed-kee?"

"Bedj-ka," Harenn said. She squatted in front of him. "It was the name I gave you when you were born."

"Where was I born?"

"On a planet called Bellerophon in a place called Treetown. It is a city built among trees that are so tall you cannot see the tops from the ground."

"Why didn't you come and get me before now?"

"I did not know where you were." The questions came rapid-fire, and they made Harenn feel as though she were kneeling in some kind of strange dream. "I looked and I searched, but I couldn't find you. Until now."

"I'll leave you two alone," Kendi put in, rising. "Harenn, as soon as you feel up to it, I need you to go down to medical and look at Gretchen. Her foot was broken getting Jer—Bedj-ka out of Sunnytree." And he left.

"That was rigid!" Bedj-ka said. "The gates slammed shut behind the van and I thought they had chopped Gretchen's foot off but it was only broken and Lucia was great the way she got my shackles off even though she couldn't see because it was dark in the crate, but they didn't tell me the bomb in the shackles was a major problem until after it was all over. Are you really my mom?"

The sudden flood of words put Harenn off balance and it took her a moment to realize Bedj-ka had asked her a question. "Yes," she said.

"I always wondered what my mom was like and so did the other kids, I guess, but none of us thought we'd ever get to find out because they told us our parents were all dead, or at least that's what Matron told us. She was really strict but I think she liked us, though Ned hated her because she always punished him whenever he mouthed off to her or called her names. I could tell she was upset when Patron said that we'd all have to be sold now that we'd lost our Silent blessings and couldn't touch the Dream. Where's my dad?"

"Your father?" Harenn temporized. It was the one question she hadn't been sure how to answer. Harenn's knees were getting tired from squatting in front of Bedj-ka, so she simply sat on the floor of the entry bay. Bedj-ka sat next to her, a stream of chatter pouring from his mouth. Harenn noticed he mostly stared straight ahead at the wall opposite them, though every so often he stole a glance at her face. Harenn wanted to put her veil back on, hide behind it. It had become a part of her after so long, and going without was like appearing in public in her underwear. But she left the veil on the floor where she had dropped it.

"I have a dad, don't I?" Bedj-ka was saying. "Everyone has to have a dad. Is he dead then? Is that why you don't want to say?"

Harenn settled on the truth. He would find out eventually, anyway. "Your father's name is Isaac Todd. He was . . . he was the person who sold you into slavery when you were a baby."

"That's what happened to Ginny. She was the only one of us who knew something about her parents, but they sold her, though she didn't say why and I think she used to cry about it at night a lot. I could hear her because when we were real little they let all of us sleep in one big room but when we got older they put the boys and the girls in separate rooms. I thought it was really stupid but Matron said those were the rules. Was my dad mad at me? Was that why he sold me?"

"Your father was . . . a very sick man, Bedj-ka," Harenn said slowly. "He valued money more than human life. You were a beautiful baby who brought me joy in every moment, and I was devastated when Isaac took you from me. If I had known what he was going to do, I would have destroyed suns and planets to stop him." Every fiber in her ached to snatch this child into her arms, but she didn't know how he would respond, didn't want to frighten him. That was one of her great fears—that he would reject her or show anger at her. Hesitantly, with slow, trembling movements, she put one arm across his shoulders. The boy continued chattering.

"The only place I remember is the Enclave and Matron and Patron and the other kids. I didn't like being a slave, especially when I saw other kids who belonged to free parents who could go wherever they wanted and do whatever they wanted, but Matron told us we were Silent and that meant we were blessed and that we had to be protected so we could learn how to go into the Dream and do stuff in there for the Enclave. Matron told us stories about slaves who were beaten or starved or sold away from their families and she said we were lucky to be in the Enclave, but then they sold us anyway and I ended up at Sunnytree Farm and it was really hard work and I was scared of some of the other slaves there because they would look at me funny when I was getting undressed every night but then that Gretchen lady came and I'd heard stories about the Children of Irfan so I knew it would be okay to go with her and now you're my mom? I've always wanted a mom. Besides Matron, I mean."

A jumble of emotions piled up inside Harenn. Apparently Bedj-ka hadn't been abused, had been with people who had taken good care of him, and the Children had taken him out of slavery before anyone had done anything terrible to him. For this she supposed she should be grateful. Instead she felt cheated. She had missed seeing him walk for the first time, saying his first words, attending his first day of school. The tears that had been building in her eyes suddenly spilled over. Bedj-ka noticed them.

"Why are you sad?" he asked with sudden apprehension. "Did I make you cry? Don't send me back to the farm, I promise I won't make you cry again; I really promise."

This time Harenn gave in to her impulse and, for the first time in nine years, hugged her son tightly to her. "I would never, *ever* send you away, Bedj-ka," she whispered fiercely in his ear. "No matter what."

She held him for a moment longer, then released him and stood up. "Now I should go down to medical and see to Gretchen's foot. Come with me?"

"Are you a doctor?" Bedj-ka asked, getting to his feet. "I always wondered what my mom and dad were like and what they did for a living but I never thought about anyone being a doctor."

"I am not a doctor, but I am an experienced nurse and medical technician, so I can perform many straightforward procedures, including healing fractured bones. I am also the engineer for this ship."

"An engineer? Rigid!"

They were halfway down to the medical bay before Harenn remembered she had left her veil on the floor.

Kendi entered the quarters he shared with Ben and flung himself down on the sofa. The living room was dimly lit. With the *Poltergeist* in slipspace, the windows were darkened to block out the nauseating view of swirling, clashing colors. Ben sat cross-legged on the other end of the couch holding a black, star-shaped piece of computer equipment the size of a basketball.

"All life, what a day," Kendi said. "I'm wiped and wired at the same time. How's Gretchen?"

"Complaining as usual," Ben replied. "I suppose that's a good sign. Harenn cleaned her up, put her foot in a heal-splint, and gave her some painkillers. The heal-splint has an antigrav unit on it so she can walk, but it'll take a week or so for the bone to heal completely."

"How are she and Bedj-ka doing?"

"They seem to be getting along okay, but I'm willing to bet they're both overwhelmed."

"I know the feeling." Kendi rubbed his face.

Ben set the piece of equipment aside to run a hand down Kendi's arm, and Kendi scooted over so he could lean against him. Ben always felt so reassuringly solid, something he could cling to when the rest of the universe seemed to wash up and down like an angry ocean.

How, Kendi thought, *did I ever survive without him?*

"When do we get to Drim?" Ben asked, draping an arm down over Kendi's shoulder and resting his hand on Kendi's stomach. He smelled like soap.

"Lucia says three days and two hours," Kendi said. "We spent three days getting Bedj-ka back, so that'll leave us with seven weeks and one day before we have to return the ship to the Children. Bellerophon is a week away from Drim, though, so we actually have only six weeks and a day to look for my family."

"Lucia's flying the ship right now?"

Kendi nodded. "I asked her if she wanted to drop out of slipspace once we were a safe distance from Klimkinnar and get some rest—she looked kind of tired—but she said she was good to go as long as you can relieve in her in a few hours. I can take over from you, and then we can get back to a more regular pilot schedule until we arrive." He puffed out his cheeks. "Then I should double-check our fake credentials, pop into the Dream long enough to make sure Sunnytree or L. L. Venus hasn't decided to spend the money to set up an interplanetary squawk using what few Silent can still get into the Dream, and—All life, how did Ara handle all this without going over the edge?"

Ben laughed, and the vibrations thrummed pleasantly in Kendi's back and chest. "You wanted this job. Keep saying that to yourself. You're doing pretty good, though. I haven't seen any problems on board."

"Yeah, well, this is an easy group to command."

"Even Gretchen?"

Kendi paused. "Okay, you've got me there."

Another laugh. Then they sat in silence for a while. Kendi drank in Ben's solid presence and decided that he'd be perfectly happy if he never got up from the couch again.

"Seriously, though," Ben said at last, "how are you holding up? About going to Drim, I mean."

"Honestly? I don't know. I made myself concentrate

on getting Bedj-ka back for Harenn so I wouldn't think about my own family or how much time it might take to look for them. Sejal said two of them are on Drim, but I don't know which two. Mom and Dad? Martina and Utang? Dad and Martina? I have no idea, and if I think about it too long I want to run screaming up and down the hallways. Bad for crew morale."

"Aren't you worried it'll be another false lead?"

Kendi shook his head. "Sejal was right about Bedj-ka. I'm sure he's right about this. That's one thing I've never questioned." He sat up and gestured at the piece of equipment Ben had set on the end table. "What is that thing, anyway?"

"You don't recognize it?" Ben picked it up. Green lights winked quietly, and a flat screen said ALL SYS-TEMS OPERATING WITHIN NORMAL PARAMETERS.

"Nope. Looks old, though. Something you're refurbishing?"

"You might say that." Ben fell silent and stared down at his hands. Kendi recognized the signs. Ben had something important he wanted to say, but he was having a hard time forming the words. Kendi knew from experience that pushing was the wrong route to take, so he waited quietly, though he burned with curiosity. What could be so important about a junky old piece of computer equipment? Finally, after a long pause, Ben spoke again.

"We talked about having kids one day, remember?"

"Sure," Kendi said, a little surprised. "Adoption. Or one of us could hook up with a woman who'd be willing to donate eggs. Or we could order a cut-and-splice from a lab, have a kid that was biologically both of ours. But those two options would be pretty expensive, not in the least because we'd have to find a surrogate mother. Artificial wombs are fine for most people, but we're both Silent—"

"And Silent babies die in artificial wombs," Ben said. "I know. There's another way." He held up the black star. "This way."

"What do you mean?"

"You know where I came from, right? Mom's team found a derelict ship that had been cleaned out, probably by pirates. But they missed something."

Realization dawned. "That's the cryo-unit Ara found?"

"Yeah." Ben's voice was low and husky.

"All life, Ben—how did you get it? I thought Ara gave it to Grandfather Melthine once she—Oh."

"Yeah. After Grandfather Melthine died, I helped go through his things and it was still there. I sort of . . . kept it."

"All life," Kendi said again. "Let me see." Ben handed it to him and Kendi turned it over in his hands. The surface was smooth and cool, with tiny controls and switches in the center of the star near the viewscreen.

"The other eleven embryos are still alive," Ben said. "All Silent. There were twelve when Mom found it, and it was right at about the time she was wanting kids in a bad way. She had her doctor thaw one out at random and implant it. If the doctor had grabbed a different embryo, I'd still be in that thing."

"And I'd be a hell of a lonely guy," Kendi added, to which Ben gave a small smile. Kendi reached over and brushed tousled red hair off Ben's forehead. "You want to raise one or two of these as our kids."

"I've known about them all my life," Ben said. "I always kind of thought of them as my brothers and sisters. When I was little I used to pretend they were just asleep. Eventually they'd wake up and I'd have someone to play with besides my stupid cousins." He took the cryo-unit back and held it up. "I want to take them out. All eleven of them."

A pang went through Kendi's stomach and his eyes widened. "*Eleven* kids? All at once?"

"No!" Ben laughed again. "One or maybe two at a time. We'll have to find surrogate mothers, but I'm sure we'll find someone. I was an only child, Kendi. Mom tried to set things up so my cousins would be a brother and sister to me, but they treated me like shit my whole life because I wasn't Silent—or everyone thought I wasn't. I've always thought about how wonderful it would be to have a big family, a whole houseful of people who didn't care if you were Silent or not."

"I loved you before you were Silent," Kendi said, putting an arm around Ben's shoulders. "So did your mom."

Another small smile. "I still want a big family."

"I knew that, but—eleven kids," Kendi said. "All life!"

"What . . . what do you think?" Ben asked.

Kendi took his arm back and chewed on a thumbnail without looking at Ben. He knew that if he looked into those blue eyes he would say "Let's do it," and damn the consequences. A year ago he would have said it anyway. The Despair and Ara's death, however, had made him more cautious. Kendi wanted children; he knew that. But eleven of them! How would they support so many? Would it be fair to the individual kids to have such a large group, spread parental love and resources that far? Ben would make a great father, Kendi was sure, but Kendi had doubts about his own parenting abilities. Was he old enough? Wise enough? Smart enough? Imagine having almost a dozen children all looking to him for help and advice and discipline and love. How would he manage all that, even with Ben there?

"I don't know," he said at last.

Ben drew away. "Okay."

"No, Ben." Kendi reached over, grabbed Ben's hand. "Ben, I love you more than anyone in the universe. I love you so much that sometimes it hurts. I would do anything to make you happy—*anything*—because if you're not happy, I'm not happy. That's why I can't answer you right now. I'm scared that I'd be saying 'let's do it' because you want it and not because we *both* want it. I need time to think. I'm not saying no. I just can't say yes yet."

Ben seemed to consider. "All right," he said at last. "I can accept that. It's a big decision. And these little guys aren't going anywhere."

"Do you know anything about where they came from?"

"Not a clue. I only know that they're all Silent and they're all healthy. And we—all twelve of us—share enough DNA to make us brothers and sisters. Originally there were eighty-seven embryos, but only eleven—twelve, counting me—are still viable. The readout says they were put into this cryo-unit thirty-odd years ago, but that's not necessarily when the embryos themselves were . . . created."

"Shouldn't you get a newer cryo-unit?" Kendi said, suddenly worried.

"Not really. I've checked this one several times and it's perfectly sound."

"Okay." Kendi stretched restlessly. "I should take a nap, especially if I'm going to do a pilot shift later, but I'm still wired. Pulling a con always revs me up. Fooling Markovi like that, yanking Bedj-ka out right from under the bastard's nose. All life, it's almost better than sex."

"Yeah?" Ben set the cryo-unit back on the table and ran light fingers down the back of Kendi's neck. Kendi shivered deliciously at the sensation. Then Ben kissed him.

"I did say *almost* better," Kendi pointed out several moments later.

"Let me show you the exact difference."

Four days later, Father Kendi Weaver leaned against the railing on the roof of the Varsis Building and stared out across the city of Felice. The Varsis was the tallest building in town, and Felice's thin skyscrapers and artificial spires moved out to the horizon in all directions beneath him. Ground traffic oozed over streets so far below that Kendi couldn't hear the sounds. Like Klimkinnar, Drim also put severe restrictions on air traffic, so no aircars buzzed between the buildings. Up here was just the sun and the wind and the quiet voices of the other sightseers who had come up for the view.

Kendi looked down at the dizzying drop. The talltrees on Bellerophon had nothing on the Varsis Building, but height wasn't everything. Bellerophon was a city among the trees, built to merge with the treescape and blend with the beauty. Felice grew from the ground like a glassy cancer.

And somewhere out there were two members of his family.

It seemed to Kendi that he should be able to see them from up here, get their attention if he shouted loud enough. The old longings came back, more powerful than ever. His last memory of his sister, brother, and father had been of them weeping as he and his mother were led away by Giselle Blanc. He could still hear punishing electricity crackle, smell the ozone in the air as Rhys Weaver reached out to touch his wife's hand one more time.

Find us! If we all keep looking, we'll find each other. Don't give up!

They were the last words Kendi had heard his father utter. And three years later when Kendi had been sold away from his mother, he had vowed to obey them. Despite many hours spent with counselors and therapists, consuming fury still snarled inside him like a rabid dingo whenever he thought about what the slavers had done to him and his family. He wept and worried about them, too, sometimes in Ben's arms and sometimes curled up by himself. And still he searched.

How many false leads had he come across over the years? Now, at long last, he had a solid one.

It was a lead he had almost lost, too. During the Despair, the twisted children of Padric Sufur had pushed almost every person in the universe out of the Dream. Without the subconscious connection provided by the Dream, all empathy and caring vanished. Some sentients had fallen into a deep depression. Others had been driven insane. All of them showed a total disregard for the lives and feelings of other sentients. If Ben hadn't freed Kendi from a self-imposed Dream prison, if Kendi hadn't managed to delay the twisted children in their attempt to destroy the Dream, if Vidya and Prasad Vajhur hadn't managed to put the children's solid-world bodies into cryo-chambers—if any of these things hadn't happened, the Dream would have been destroyed forever and all sentient life in the universe would have ended within a single generation. The thought still made Kendi sweat.

After the Despair, Bellerophon had been thrown into turmoil along with the rest of the universe. The Children of Irfan had responded to the crisis by falling back and retrenching. All field teams and operatives were to return to the monastery immediately. Some of the teams returned on their own, but many of them didn't, meaning someone had to go out and find them. Kendi, newly appointed to a command position despite the fact that he had only achieved the rank of Father, had run himself and his team ragged tracking down Child after Child. Some were assigned on planets or on stations. Others were members of teams like Kendi's and had ships of their own. The findings of Kendi's team hadn't always been pretty. Losing touch with the Dream had affected the Silent more strongly than other sentients, and several Silent plunged into homicidal rage or suicidal despair. Twelve Children with long-term off-planet positions had killed themselves, and twice Kendi's team had found empty ships floating in space, the crew's dessicated corpses floating in corridors and quarters. Through it all, however, Kendi couldn't stop thinking about what Sejal had told him just after the Despair. Every word was burned into his mind:

I felt every Silent in the galaxy. It was weird. We were a group, but I could still feel individuals. Two of the minds felt similar to yours, Kendi. I can't describe it better than that. One of them was a man, the other was a woman, and they're both slaves on a planet named Drim.

After six months of scrambling around the galaxy retrieving other Children and relaying emergency messages through the Dream, Kendi had finally had enough of waiting. What if someone sold his family? What if they escaped and vanished into the post-Despair chaos? What if they died? Every day brought a greater chance that this precious lead would dry up. Eventually, Kendi had gone to the Council of Irfan. They had been reluctant to loan him a ship, despite the fact that most of the missing field teams were accounted for and most of the Children, bereft of their Silence, had little or nothing to do.

"Everything is too chaotic," replied Grandmother Adept Pyori. "Governments and economies are collapsing. We need all our people close to home in case something happens."

"That makes this the best time for me to go," Kendi shot back. "It takes a lot of time for galactic governments and megacorporations to collapse. I need to get out there before everything falls apart completely and my family vanishes forever."

The blank faces of the Council, however, said they were still unconvinced, and in the end Kendi fell back on emotional blackmail.

"I saved the lives of every single person in this room," he said. "I saved the lives of your family, your friends, and every living creature in this universe. All

I want in return is a single ship and a crew to go with her. How can that be too much to ask?"

The Council had agreed, but with limitations. When they laid down the time limit, Kendi wondered what he would have had to do to get a ship for longer than two months. Create a new universe from scratch?

"We are not doing this to be difficult, Father Kendi," Grandmother Adept Pyori said, as if reading his mind. "Every Silent who can still reach the Dream is precious beyond measure. Have you considered what will happen to us in the next fifty or sixty years? The danger we are in?"

"I don't understand, Grandmother," Kendi replied.

"No new Silent are entering the Dream," she said solemnly. "And one day the remaining Silent who *can* enter it will die."

A cold chill slid over Kendi's body at her words. He had been so busy over the last six months that this hadn't occurred to him. The Children of Irfan was an organization that existed only because of the Dream and the communication it provided. If no Silent could enter the Dream, the Children would disappear, swallowed by history.

The breeze from the top of the Varsis Building continued to wash over Kendi. He felt bold and alive, filled with optimism despite his problems. He would find his two family members on Drim, and perhaps they would know something about the others. Then together they could keep looking. Kendi was also looking forward to introducing them to Ben and telling them about—

"Father?"

Kendi tapped his earpiece. "I'm here, Lucia. What's going on?"

"Ben's found something on the newsnets that you'll want to see. Can you come down to the suite?"

"Is it something you can upload to my implant?"

Kendi asked, already heading for the elevator doors at the other end of the observation deck.

Pause. *"Not really."*

Kendi's stomach tensed as he entered the lift and told it he wanted the eighteenth floor, one of eight floors that made up a hotel within the Varsis Building. The lift obediently dropped. Was the news good or bad? Had to be bad. Otherwise Lucia would have told him something about it.

The Varsis Hotel hallways were plushly carpeted and thickly wallpapered, hushing every sound. A holographic waterfall rushed over stones at an intersection, filling the air with the sound of gushing water. It even smelled of moss. The hotel was on the expensive side, but Kendi saw no reason not to get comfortable digs. Ara would have told everyone to live on the ship, but Kendi found it annoying to go through the spaceport every time he wanted to do something in the city, and had decided the Children could pay for a hotel. He was glad to have insisted on a huge purse of hard-currency freemarks from the exchequer. Without Silent to handle the transactions in the post-Despair galaxy, very little interplanetary banking was taking place, and the population of a fair number of planets, including Drim, was in the middle of a "don't trust the banks" frame of mind. There was also a very real dread that some currencies would collapse. Many financial institutions had closed their doors, fearing bank runs. As a result, physical money had quickly become the norm again. Kendi liked that. It used to be that the decent hotels and restaurants looked askance at anyone offering hard cash instead of electronic transfer, meaning undercover Children either had to set up electronic accounts under false names—risky—or patronize the sort of places that didn't care how you paid as long as you paid—distasteful. Nowadays, Kendi could pay hard freemarks to the fanciest place in town and be just another cautious socialite.

Kendi passed the waterfall and thumbed open the double door to the suite he had rented. The place was bright and airy, with a large outer sitting room, two well-appointed bathrooms, and four bedrooms. Enormous windows looked out over the cityscape. Although the suite sported its own holographic generator that allowed guests to add artwork or chunks of outdoor scenes, no one had been able to agree on a decoration scheme and Kendi had finally shut the system off entirely. As a result, the place was rather plain, done in simple greens and browns.

Ben had appropriated part of the sitting room as a work area, and he had hooked up his own computer to the hotel's network. The man himself was hunched over the keyboard, clothes rumpled, red hair tousled. In other words, looking perfectly normal. Lucia stood behind Ben's chair, one hand on the Irfan figurine around her neck. The holographic display above the desk showed text and pictures.

"What's going on?" Kendi demanded without preamble.

Ben hesitated. Lucia looked perfectly calm, but Kendi felt his whole insides screw up with tension. Bad news, that was what it was, all right. Otherwise they'd come right out and say it.

"Well?" He strode to the desk. "Just tell me. Or do I have to read it for myself?"

"It's bad," Ben said finally.

"I'll go see what Gretchen is up to," Lucia murmured, and quietly withdrew into the room the two of them shared. Kendi's legs went weak.

"Ben, what is it?" Kendi asked. "I can't handle suspense. Just say it. Did you find them? Are they . . . are they dead?"

"I don't know," Ben replied. He reached up and

took Kendi's hand. "Ken, I found a series of news stories. A firm called DrimCom—the 'Com' is short for Communication—encountered a . . . loss. It used to own twenty-odd Silent slaves, but only two of them came through the Despair with their Silence intact. One's a man; the other's a woman."

"My family?" Kendi asked.

"Yeah. I have their holos. Want to see?"

Kendi leaned forward despite his fear. "You know the answer to that."

Ben tapped a key and the text vanished. The head of a woman in her mid-twenties appeared. She was beautiful, with large brown eyes, skin darker than Kendi's, and sharply defined features that included a firm chin. Kendi touched his own chin when he saw her. "Martina," he breathed.

Another hologram appeared beside the first, one of a man in his thirties. The resemblance to Kendi was unmistakable, except for the striking blue eyes. Sejal had similar eyes, and Kendi had once suspected Sejal—wrongly—of being Utang's son. Kendi's throat thickened. The last time he had seen his brother and sister they had been fifteen and ten, respectively. Now they were adults.

"I managed to break into their medical records, including their DNA scans," Ben said. "I ran a comparison. All three of you have the same mitochondrial DNA, which means you're siblings. It's definitely them."

Kendi's heart was racing and he tightened his grip on Ben's hand. "You said there's bad news."

"Yeah." Ben ran his free hand through his hair. "Ken, they've both disappeared."

For a moment Kendi could only focus on the fact that Ben was calling him Ken, a nickname he didn't allow anyone else to use and one Ben used only rarely. Then he said, "Disappeared?"

"Kidnapped. Someone broke into the slave quarters and snatched them both away. No clues, according to the news reports. They're gone."

Kendi's knees turned to water and the room darkened. Eventually he became aware that he was sitting on the floor with his head between his knees. Ben knelt next to him, an arm around his shoulders. Kendi felt as though he were spinning.

"Just breathe," Ben said. "Slow and steady. You'll be okay."

"What is wrong?" came Harenn's voice. "Is he injured?"

"He almost fainted," Ben told her. "The news was a shock."

Kendi looked up and the room swayed. Harenn's unveiled face—*All life, it still looks strange to see her,* he thought incongruously—was looking down with concern. She was rather pretty, with rounded cheeks and care lines around her mouth. Although she had stopped wearing the veil, she continued to cover her hair with a translucent scarf.

"When?" Kendi asked hoarsely.

"When what?" Ben asked.

"When did it happen? When were they kidnapped?"

"Two days ago. The day before we got to Drim."

Harenn looked abruptly stricken. She backed away, her skin gone pale. "Oh, god."

Kendi closed his eyes.

"What's the matter?" Ben demanded. "Harenn, don't you faint, too. What the hell is wrong?"

"Two days ago," Harenn whispered. "They vanished two days ago. If we had first come to Drim instead of going to Klimkinnar to get Bedj-ka, we might have arrived before . . ." She trailed off.

"Oh," Ben said.

Kendi opened his eyes. "Harenn, don't you feel guilty. I need you to be yourself right now. It was my"—he swallowed—"my decision to go to Klimkin-nar, not yours. It's my fault."

"Hey!" Ben grabbed Kendi's hand again. "It's not your fault, Ken. You had no way of knowing. The people who kidnapped your brother and sister—it's *their* fault. The people who enslaved them in the first place—it's *their* fault. Not yours, not Harenn's. Mom would pitch a fit if she knew you were thinking that way."

Mom. Mother Ara. All life, she would have known what to do. Kendi felt as if he were floundering, drowning in a frothy sea. What was the next step? What should he do? He had no idea. And then for a moment it felt like Ara was standing over him.

Wake up, she snapped. *On your feet. If you want to find them, you have to go look.*

"Yes, Mother," he muttered.

"What?" Ben said.

"Nothing. Help me up. Then get Gretchen and Lucia in here. We have a kidnapping to solve."

"Look, I've gone through this with the police twice already," complained the woman. She was dressed in scarlet from head to foot, with a scarf twisted through night-black hair. The small hologram hovering near her collar gave her name as Linda Tellman and her title as first manager. She had an artificial sort of beauty that told Kendi's practiced eye she had been to a fresh-up at least once.

"I know, ma'am," Kendi said, slipping the fake po-lice ID back into his pocket. "But you know how this sort of thing works. Every time you go over it, you may remember some detail you left out before."

"Well, you cop guys are thorough, I'll give you that," Tellman muttered. She gestured at a chair near her desk. "Have a seat, Detective."

"Actually, I haven't seen the crime scene yet," Kendi said. "Could you go through what happened while we walk down there?"

Tellman sighed. "Somewhere in here I do have work to get done, but it can wait, right?"

Kendi didn't answer. He merely followed her through a series of corridors and down two flights of stairs. The DrimCom building, located on the outskirts of Felice, was low and sprawling, with lots of steel and blue-tinted reflective windows. Many of the offices they passed were empty, indications of DrimCom's recent loss of revenue.

As if reading Kendi's mind, Tellman said, "If we can't get these two back, the company's going to go under. There isn't much of it left as it is. We had twenty-six Silent—"

"All slaves?" Kendi interrupted.

Tellman nodded. "But after the Despair, only two of them were able to enter the Dream. We held on to the others as long as we could, hoping their Silence would come back, but eventually we had to sell them. We raised our communication rates for the two Silent we had left, just like everyone else is doing, but then this happened. Our only source of revenue—gone. DrimCom's dying on the vine now."

"You don't seem overly upset," Kendi observed.

"I've got my savings—unlike a lot of people around here," Tellman said. "And I have prospects. My uncle works for Sufur Enterprises, and he says they have positions open, if you know who to talk to."

They reached an area that reminded Kendi of the Varsis Hotel. Numbered doors faced a quiet hallway lit with yellow lamps. Tellman selected one of the doors and thumbed the lock. It clicked open for her.

"These are our slave quarters," she said, entering ahead of Kendi. "The woman's name was Violet. This was her room."

Kendi stepped into the room. It was plainly furnished but bright, with yellow walls and a beige carpet. A light smell of perfumed body powder hung on the air. Several pictures—pen-and-ink drawings, not holograms—hung on the walls. Kendi almost gasped as he recognized Outback landscapes. Unable to help himself, he moved closer to one. A falcon skimmed high above a rocky cliff. At the base of the cliff wall sat a kangaroo. It was leaning back on its tail and staring up at the sky. In the bottom corner, the name *Martina* had been worked into the roots of a bush. Kendi's throat closed. This indeed belonged to his sister. She had eaten and slept and held on to her name in this very room. Her scent still lingered. With a trembling hand, he reached out to touch the glass of the frame.

"Is there something about her drawings?" Tellman asked behind him. "A clue?"

Kendi pulled his hand back and swallowed hard to get his voice under control. "Maybe. Why don't you tell me what happened and I'll look over the room."

"Like I told the other cop guys, there isn't much to tell. The housekeeper was bringing Violet and Brad—that was the other one's name—their breakfasts and found the rooms empty. The doors were unlocked. The housekeeper tried to check with the security computer, but it had been taken off-line. A virus, we later found out. I was the manager on duty, so the housekeeper called me next. I checked Brad's room, and he was gone, too. The moment they left their rooms, their shackles should have set off the alarms and shocked them unconscious, but that whole program was off-line. What with the recent cutbacks, we only have one tech left, and he only comes in every other day. Security was also reduced, but we didn't think it would be that big a deal. In retrospect, we probably should have been expecting this. Functioning Silent are a hell of a lot more valuable than they used to be."

"Was there a guard on duty that night?" Kendi asked, still unable to take his eyes off the landscapes. He had no idea Martina could draw like that. And they had given Utang the name Brad.

"The guard was found unconscious at his post. Hit

with a brain taser. He doesn't remember anything from the past three days. The doctor said that's normal."

"Was anything taken?"

"Besides the slaves? No. They didn't even take their clothes or any possessions. That's why we're treating it as a theft instead of an escape, even though there were no signs of a struggle. My guess is they—Violet and Brad—were hit with the same brain taser that took out the guard."

Kendi looked through Martina's closet. Judging from her clothes, she was a head shorter than he was, and either she liked the color blue or that was all DrimCom provided for her. As he searched, he kept up a running series of questions to Tellman and gleaned a few more facts. The surveillance cameras had been shorted out just before the guard had been tasered, so there were no video or holographic clues. The security files for the entire night had also been erased. A police search of both rooms had turned up no blood and no evidence of weapons discharge.

"What about Brad's room?" Kendi asked.

"Same thing," Tellman said. "No struggle, nothing missing but him. It must have been really weird for him."

"What do you mean?"

"We bought Brad only one day before the Despair hit. We thought we were lucky to have grabbed him. But he was depressed and despondent after the Despair. I don't think he and Violet even met. He refused to come out of his room. We were just about to start a more aggressive treatment program on him—"

Drugs and shocks, Kendi translated.

"—and then this happened. He arrives here, then leaves again. Weird for him. But he's Silent, so he must have been genengineered, and he'll probably adapt. Comes with not being entirely human."

Kendi wanted to hit her, had even clenched a fist, when another woman poked her head into the room.

"Manager Tellman?" she said. "There's a police detective here who wants to interview you."

"Another one?" Tellman said.

Oops, Kendi thought. "Probably my partner," he said aloud. "What's the detective's name?"

"Lena Halfson," replied the woman.

"That's her. Why don't you go down and get her, Manager Tellman, while I finish up in here?"

Tellman left, grumbling to herself about her position being reduced from manager to errand girl. The other woman followed. The moment they were out of sight, Kendi eased out of the room and sauntered swiftly down the hallway in the opposite direction. Then he paused, dashed back to the room, snatched the Outback landscape from the wall, and rushed back out. A bit of searching turned up a back exit. Kendi hurried out of the building to his rented groundcar, kept his back to the police vehicle parked only four spaces over, and drove quickly away, Martina's landscape on the seat beside him.

"How'd it go?" Ben asked when he arrived back at the hotel. "Any good news?"

"You tell me," Kendi replied, and quickly summarized what he had learned. "It sounds like someone snatched them up because they're functional Silent. The question is, who? And how do we find out?"

"Sounds like we need to do a lot of record-checking," Gretchen said, scratching her foot where the heal-splint had recently come off. She and Lucia were perched on chairs by the window while Harenn sat with her son on the sofa. The boy insisted on being called Bedj-ka and wouldn't answer to Jerry. He seemed to be adjusting well to his new situation. Harenn was the one who looked continually bewildered.

"I agree," said Lucia. "We can find out which ships

have left Drim since then, see if any of them might be worth following up on. With Irfan's guidance, we might turn up something there."

"We can also check with other companies on Drim that employ—or own—Silent," Harenn pointed out. "Perhaps one of them has lost Silent as well. Or unexpectedly gained them."

"I can get into the Dream and see if anyone's heard from them," Ben offered. "Now that we have current names and the name of the firm that owned them."

Kendi sat down on a love seat, the drawing on his lap. "Thanks, guys. We'll keep trying, I guess." No one mentioned the fact that if Martina and Utang had been taken off-planet, the chances of finding them were slim. There was no way to track a slipship's course if the captain and pilot logged a false destination with the authorities. It was an advantage that both the Children and the slavers often used when they needed to make a fast getaway. The irony was not lost on Kendi.

"Who drew that?" Bedj-ka asked, pointing to the sketch.

"My sister." Kendi held it up so everyone could see. "She's pretty good. I didn't . . . I didn't know she could draw. I think it's her hobby."

"It's pretty rigid," Bedj-ka said. "Is there a clue in the picture? That's how it always works in stories and stuff—the artist leaves a clue in a painting or a poem or something that tells the good guys where they were taken, right? That's why you took the drawing, right? All we need to do is find the clue and then we could go in and rescue them and—"

"Real life," Harenn interrupted, "is rarely so easy."

"And I already looked for clues in the picture," Kendi said with small smile. "I figured it was worth a shot. There wasn't anything in it, though. Sorry." He set the picture aside, and suddenly he couldn't stand the idea of being in a roomful of people for another second. Anger flared. He wanted to knock something off the desk and rush from the room, but he didn't. Instead he forced himself to stand up with a calm face. "I need some time alone, guys. I'll be in my room if something turns up."

He knew before he got the bedroom door open that Ben was coming up behind him. He turned, caught Ben's eye, and shook his head. "I'm going into the Dream." Then he firmly shut the door.

Harenn Mashib felt the guilt drag at her like a wet, heavy cloak. The sky above Felice was overcast today, blunting the worst of the usual humid heat but still leaving the busy city uncomfortably warm. Harenn's feet ached, her stomach was empty, and she had a headache, but the guilt kept her moving.

"Your pardon," she said, and held up the holos to the next person on the sidewalk. "Have you seen either of these people?"

The man glanced at the hologram of Kendi's siblings and shook his head. Harenn moved on. This was the third straight day she had been at it. Even Bedjka had abandoned her, preferring to stay in the hotel and swim or read or play on the virtual reality networks. She had only allowed him to stay behind after extracting heavy promises from Ben that someone would always, *always* have an eye on him. And Harenn kept at it, shoving the holograms in the faces of random passersby, hoping for a flicker of recognition.

It was a ploy of desperation. She knew it. Kendi knew it. But in the past week, all other clues had been followed, all other avenues had been exhausted. Martina and Utang had simply vanished. It made Harenn's heart twist inside her whenever she saw Kendi's ashen face. Although he had repeatedly assured her that he didn't hold her responsible, she couldn't help but feel that she was. Every night when she looked down at Bedj-ka's sleeping face, she couldn't help but feel that way.

It filled Harenn with joy beyond imagining to have Bedj-ka back. After their first embrace, she had given him another, and then another, and several more, until at last he began to protest. He was a stranger to her, but she was getting to know him, was growing used to his chatter and how much he lived in his imagination. She had finally set a limit on the number of hours he spent on the game networks, insisting he get fresh air and exercise in the real world. He had become angry and she had almost given in to his demands. What if he ran away from her? What if he stopped speaking to her? What if he hated her for doing this to him? More than anything else, Harenn wanted to live in peace and love with her son. But then she had decided that spoiling him would not, in the end, be best for either of them. The anger and pouting that followed had been difficult, but eventually Bedj-ka's bright nature had returned and he had asked to go swimming. Harenn was beginning to feel like a mother again, even if she barely knew her child.

It was a feeling that had come at great cost to Kendi.

So now Harenn searched the streets. The work was no doubt futile, but it made her feel as if she were doing *something,* and it kept her away from the sight of Kendi's haunted eyes.

Another fruitless hour passed. Harenn's headache intensified along with the hunger, but still she kept moving, asking, looking. After a while, Lucia emerged from the crowd.

"Here you are," she said. "What did you do, switch off your earpiece? I've been worried. You've been gone for so long, and Bedj-ka was wondering what was going on."

Another twinge of guilt. "I have lost track of time."

"Any luck?"

"None."

"Let's go back to the suite. Father Kendi ordered room service. He said he doesn't much feel like going out. I think he's about to give up and leave."

Harenn shook her head as they moved along the sidewalk toward the Varsis Building. "That would be a mistake. We are so very close to them."

A familiar scent wafted by. Spicy grilled sausage sizzled on a cart tended by a man wearing a disposable white cap. Harenn wrinkled her nose. Grilled sausage had been one of Isaac Todd's favorite foods, and every time she smelled the stuff, it brought back harsh memories.

"We don't know if we're close to them or not," Lucia said. "That's the problem. We don't have a single—"

A customer turned away from the cart, raising a sausage in a bun to his mouth. A pang shot through Harenn's stomach. She dropped the holo-unit and grabbed the man by the lapels of his shirt. With a strength that surprised even herself, she shoved him into an alley and up against the hard stone wall. The sausage went flying. The man grunted and his eyes widened with shock and surprise as the tip of the large knife Harenn always carried pricked his throat. Lucia gaped.

"Harenn, what—" she began.

"Do you remember me?" Harenn hissed. *"Do you?"*

"Who the fuck are you, lady?" the man yelped. His eyes were saucer-wide beneath straw-blond hair.

"You don't remember, then." Ignoring Lucia's startled questions, Harenn shoved her face closer to the man's. The big knife blade, sharp and unmoving, pressed against his jugular. "I am unsure if that makes me simply angry or absolutely furious. In either case it does not bode well for you."

"Harenn!" Lucia protested. "What's going on?"

"Tell the woman who you are," Harenn growled.

"Lady, I don't—"

"Tell her!" She pressed the edge of the blade into his skin until a drop of blood oozed down the edge. The man cringed. "Tell her your name!"

"I'm . . . it's Marlin Silver."

Harenn pressed harder. "Liar! Tell the truth, or I will slice you open here and now."

"Todd!" the man howled. "My name is Isaac Todd!"

"Where did you say you found him?" Kendi demanded.

"Not far from the spaceport," Harenn said grimly. "I was showing the holograms of your brother and sister around and I saw him. Lucia and I dragged him back to the ship; then we called you."

"She almost killed him—" Lucia began.

"I still may," Harenn said.

"—but I convinced her that he might be a good source of underworld information."

"Hey, there's no need for violence." Isaac Todd raised both his hands in supplication. A silver slave band, fitted by Lucia, encircled one wrist to ensure he wouldn't attack anyone. The man was attractive enough. Square jaw, blond hair, well-molded physique, blue eyes. Bedj-ka was lucky that way, Kendi decided. The boy had his father's features and his mother's coloring. He was going to break hearts in a dozen solar systems when he got older.

Too bad his father is such a shit, Kendi thought.

"What are you doing here, Isaac?" Harenn demanded. "Does it have anything to do with the slaves who were kidnapped from DrimCom?"

"I don't have to talk to you," Todd replied tightly.

"You fail to understand, my husband," Harenn

purred. She leaned forward, pushing her bare face into his. "You will talk to us and you will tell us everything we need to know. I have in this medical bay a wide variety of drugs that will make you reveal everything that ever happened in your filthy life. Some of those drugs have very interesting side-effects. You *will* talk, Isaac, and then I will check the veracity of your answers with my collection of chemicals. The only question is how miserable I will make you in the process. How miserable do you want to be?"

In the corner, Ben shifted with obvious discomfort. Kendi, however, paid him scant attention. Isaac Todd was an illegal slaver found on the same planet in the same city at the same time his brother and sister had been kidnapped. The coincidence was simply too much to ignore, and every instinct Kendi had said that Todd knew something about Utang and Martina. The only question was how much he knew.

"I have rights," Todd said. "You can't do this to me."

"To whom will you complain, husband?" Harenn asked. "The police? Perhaps we should call them right now and see what they say when I tell them we have a man who is wanted on many planets for kidnapping and illegal slave trafficking."

"Who do you work for?" Kendi asked.

Todd remained silent. After a moment, Harenn reached for an instrument tray and came up with a hypodermic needle long and thick enough to puncture bone. It glittered in the harsh overhead light.

"That's not a dermospray," Todd yelped, pushing himself backward on the bed until his back was against the wall.

"How observant you are," Harenn said. "I do have dermosprays, but I am not inclined to use them."

"Harenn," Kendi warned. "The Children have rules about this kind of thing. We don't torture people."

"I am not a Child," Harenn pointed out.

"But you work for us and you do have to operate by our rules," Kendi said.

"Thank you." Todd sighed. But his eyes never left the needle. His face was pale, and a thin sheen of sweat had broken out on his face. Phobic? Certainly seemed to be.

"However, Mr. Todd," Kendi continued, "Harenn is the only one qualified to administer interrogatives. If, in her considered opinion, the best way to give one to you is by a needle, I can't say I'm qualified to counter what she says."

Harenn touched the hypodermic to Todd's arm and he jumped as if she had touched him with a hot iron. "For subjects who aren't cooperative," she said, "the needle is unfortunately the best method of delivery. It ensures the drug gets into the bloodstream instead of pooling beneath the skin."

"I'll talk!" Todd shouted. "Just get that thing away from me."

"Who do you work for?" Kendi repeated. "Keep in mind that we're going to check what you say, and Harenn won't be happy if you're caught in a lie."

Todd licked his lips. "I work for Silent Acquisitions."

Lucia raised her eyebrows and Kendi clenched a fist. Silent Acquisitions was a megacorporation that dealt in Silence in all its forms—communication, research, genengineering, and slaves. They were known galaxy-wide as being worse than ruthless. Kendi and Ara had between them stolen away more than a dozen slaves from them and their subsidiaries over the years, and he had no doubt that both of them were high on the corp's most wanted list, though Ara was now beyond such considerations.

"What do you do for them?" Kendi said.

"I'm a scout for the Collection."

"And what's the Collection?"

Todd shifted nervously on the bed. "Look, if anyone finds out I'm talking to you, I'm dead meat, all right? I've already told you enough to earn me five years in the corp's waste pits."

"And you have kept silent about enough to earn you five stabs with my knife," Harenn growled.

"You may as well keep on going," Kendi said, taking on the part of good cop to Harenn's bad. "You've gone this far, and we're going to get it out of you either way with the drugs. We won't tell anyone where we got the information. What's the Collection?"

Todd hesitated. "I have your word you'll keep where you found out to yourself?"

"Absolutely," Kendi said, tapping his amulet and raising his right hand. "I swear by Irfan herself."

Still Todd hesitated. Kendi suppressed an urge to wrap his hands around the man's neck and throttle the information out of him. Finally Todd cleared his throat.

"After the Despair," he said, "functioning Silent suddenly became really rare and valuable, right? Everyone at Silent Acquisitions is pretty worried about that. I mean, the few Silent we have left will die eventually, and we won't have anything at all. Silent Acquisitions will eventually disappear."

Like the Children, Kendi thought with a twinge.

"SA has people working on that problem," Todd said, "but until they solve it, the company needs a short-term solution, and that's the Collection. Right now, SA will go pretty far to get its hands on new Silent. We need Dream access and genetic material and all that to stay afloat while we look for a solution."

"Genetic material," Kendi repeated, barely keeping the distaste for this man out of his voice. "Right. So?"

"So the company decided we have to be a little more . . . aggressive."

"Don't be cute," Kendi told him. "Be specific. What

do you mean by aggressive? Kidnapping? Murder? Theft? What?"

"All of the above," Todd said. "Once I find functional Silent, the acquisition team is authorized to use whatever methods necessary to acquire them. The team takes them back to SA station for indoctrination. The goal is to make them into loyal workers for Silent Acquisitions."

"Brainwashing?" Lucia said.

"Hey, I never hurt anyone, I swear. I'm not part of any of the acquisition or indoctrination teams. I just scout out potential personnel."

Harenn made a low, cold sound in her throat and Kendi was seized with sudden fury at Todd. Forgetting his role as good cop, he grabbed the front of Todd's shirt and shook him once. "Did you 'scout out' my brother and sister?"

"I don't know," Todd squeaked. "Who are they?"

"They were both enslaved by DrimCom," Kendi snarled, twisting Todd's collar. "Was it your Collection that took them away?"

"I can't . . . breathe," Todd choked. "I can't . . ."

"Ken," Ben said from the corner. "His lips are turning blue."

Kendi released Todd so fast the man fell backward onto the examination bed. Ben pursed his lips. Todd sucked in great gulps of air and massaged his throat.

"Prep him, Harenn," Kendi said. "I want him coked to the gills and ready to talk fluidly and easily by the time I get back. I'm going for a walk. Maybe in the Dream."

"With great pleasure, Father," Harenn said, raising her hypodermic.

"You said no needles if I talked," Todd cried, trying to push himself away. His back was already against the wall, however, and he had nowhere to go.

"Dermospray, Harenn," Kendi said over his shoulder as he left the medical bay. "But use whatever drug you like."

The doors snapped shut behind him, cutting off Todd's protest. Kendi started to stride away but halted when a familiar voice called out behind him. Ben put a hand on Kendi's shoulder.

"Not right now, Ben," Kendi said tightly. "I'm too pissed off to be rational."

"I was scared you'd let Harenn torture him," Ben admitted. "I'm glad you're better than that."

"Have to set an example, right?" Kendi almost snarled. He turned and abruptly strode up the hallway. "He's filth, Ben. He bred his own kids for slavery and arranged for Utang and Martina to be kidnapped, but I'm supposed to be *nice* to him."

"You're getting what you want," Ben pointed out. "That's all that matters."

"That's what Ara always said."

"Actually I think it's a quote from Irfan's writings," Ben said. "In any case, it's true. We'll find out what he knows and we'll find your brother and sister."

"I know where they are," Kendi growled. "They're being held by one of the most ruthless megacorps in the galaxy in what I imagine is one of the highest-security areas of one of the biggest stations in human space. The trouble won't be finding them. The trouble will be getting them out."

"You're going to take on Silent Acquisitions?" Ben asked.

"I have a choice?"

Ben paused. "I'm not sure whether to talk you out of it or egg you on," he said finally.

"Doesn't matter," Kendi told him. "I'm doing it. I just need some time to come up with a plan."

CHAPTER FOUR

"I can't be a religious icon. I make too many mistakes."

—Irfan Qasad

"The Collection has three department heads and one manager," Todd said dreamily. "The manager's name is Edsard Roon. He answers directly to the board at Silent Acquisitions. Board and room, I think. I wanted a pony in my room when I was little, but—"

"Who are the three department heads for the Collection?" Kendi interrupted.

"Rafille Mallory is chief of security. I've only talked to her once. Once upon a time there lived three—"

"Who else is a department head?"

"Elena Papagos-Faye is chief of information services, which means she does the computer stuff. Do you think she could get me a deal on—"

"Who else?" Kendi asked with a mental sigh. The problem with hypnoral, besides the fact that it was damned expensive, was that it tended to unhook the brain-to-mouth filter. The person didn't so much babble as flit from one subject to another, and it was a challenge to keep Todd on topic. On the other hand, hypnoral had no side-effects and was easy to use.

Todd was currently lying on the medical bay bed, arms at his sides, eyes on the white ceiling. His pupils were wide and dark, and a medical monitor strip clung to his forehead. Harenn stood nearby, one eye on Todd himself and the other on the data pad that tracked his vital signs. Ben sat in a chair at the foot of Todd's bed. The lights overhead were harsh and white.

"Ken Jeung heads up research," Todd said. "He's

the last department head. Jeung's a doctor, and he's doing genetic and medical stuff, but I don't know exactly what. There's a lot I don't know. I don't know how many elephants there are on Earth or how much the slavers sold my children for or—"

"What's the computer security like?" Ben interrupted.

"Solid. You can only access Collection computers on the Collection's private network. The network is isolated from the rest of the station. I have access, but only at a basic level. The higher up you go, the tighter security gets. Only the department heads can access the high-level functions, and those are guarded by prints and keys. Did you ever notice that *prints* and *prince* are pronounced the same even though they're spelled—"

"Quiet, Todd," Kendi ordered, and Todd fell silent. "What's the matter, Ben? You can hack this, right? We need high-level computer access to pull this off."

Ben's head was in his hands. "It's an isolated key-and-print system. We're screwed."

"What is a key-and-print system?" Harenn asked.

"It's a system where you need two things to get access—an authorized thumbprint and a matching key. You scan the thumb and slot the key. If you try to get access with only one of them, the system shuts down and shouts for help. If you have the wrong key or print, the system shuts down and shouts for help. Key-and-print systems are absolutely impossible to hack unless you have world-class hacking programs, the kind of stuff a major government might have. I don't have anything remotely close to that kind of power." This last he said with a kind of horrified awe.

"No system is unbreakable," Kendi said, trying to hold on to optimism. "I think Lucia can make an artificial thumb from a latent print. That won't be hard. What are the keys like?"

"Each one looks like a small cylinder about the size

of your little finger," Ben said. "It contains a chip with rotating, one-use algorithms that are keyed to one person's unique thumbprint. The thumbprint provides the key to the chip's algorithm. Print and key together create the access code for the computer." He ran a hand through his hair. "But it gets worse."

"How?" Kendi asked.

"Todd said the system is isolated. It isn't connected to the SA Station's network, which means that even if we somehow got a synthetic thumb and a key, I wouldn't be able to do anything with them unless I got into the Collection itself and accessed a Collection computer."

Kendi tried to keep his heart from sinking. "Well, we need high-level computer access so we'll have to get our hands on the keys. We'll worry about actual access later." He turned back to Todd. "Tell me about the keys."

"They go everywhere," Todd said. "I screwed Elena Papagos-Faye—or maybe she screwed me—and she told me her key stays with her all the time. The department heads have to report a missing key and that means all four of them have to get new keys and the system is physically shut down until that's taken care of. If they ever take their key off, they have to hide it someplace secure. I know because Elena took hers off before we got into bed and she hid it somewhere but I never saw where. She was a real monster in the sack. She made me kneel between her—"

"Shut up, Todd," Kendi ordered.

"Perhaps we should have him recount his adventure in detail," Harenn said. "It could prove useful as fodder for blackmail."

"Later," Kendi said. "Ben, can the keys be copied?"

Ben thought about that. "Maybe. But it would involve getting our hands on each key long enough to copy it. And if any of the four department heads suspect something, they'll shut the system down and get new keys."

Harenn tapped her data pad. "The hypnoral is wearing off. If you have more questions, you should ask them now before we give him new memories."

"I don't have any at the moment," Kendi said. He leaned closer to Isaac Todd. The harsh smell of hypnoral hung about him. "Todd, when you wake up, you will remember taking a long nap, and nothing more. You will not remember talking to us here and you will not remember answering any questions. Do you understand?"

"Yes," Todd replied languidly.

"You will, however, remember having a terrifying nightmare that froze your very soul," Harenn put in. "The nightmare will involve a hospital bed and many needles. Do you understand?"

"Yes."

Kendi reached down and closed Todd's eyes. Almost immediately, the man began to snore. Ben turned to Harenn. "Was that necessary?" he asked.

"No," was all Harenn said.

The *Poltergeist* popped out of slipspace, and Lucia dePaolo said a small prayer of thanks to Irfan as she always did upon a successful exit. Less than a second later, her flight board was cluttered with long slices of flashing text and urgent messages ordering her to come no closer to SA Station without agreeing to the terms in the attached contract. In the captain's chair, Father Kendi puffed out his cheeks and activated his data pad. Lucia sent over a copy of the contract and the pad beeped in acknowledgment. Father Kendi tapped the tiny computer, ordering it to compare the current contract with the one in the monastery database.

"They haven't substantially altered the stupid thing since the last time I was here," he mused. "I was hoping they'd have dropped the whole issue, what with the Despair and all."

"No such luck," Gretchen said from her own station.

Father Kendi shook his head. "They're still expecting us to hand over fifty percent of everything we earn while on the station and a controlling interest in the ship. And then there's that DNA clause. 'Party of the first part agrees to assign to the party of the second part all rights to the party of the first part's DNA and first work derived therefrom.' They have to be the only corporation around that literally wants you to sign over your firstborn child. Do they honestly think anyone's going to fall for it?"

"Enough people must," Gretchen replied, "since they keep asking."

"Well, at least it means the database's strike list is still valid. You have it, Lucia?"

"Yes, Father."

"Merge the list with the contract and send the whole thing back."

Lucia prepared the new contract—there was no indication anywhere on the original that Silent Acquisitions even considered counteroffers—and sent it. It came back a few moments later with the message, FINAL TERMS ACCEPTED. YOU MAY DOCK AT LOADING BAY XC-14539-MAL. ALL APPROPRIATE CHARGES APPLY.

"We're set, Father."

"Then find the bay and let's dock."

Lucia punched up course information and laid it in. Before her, the viewscreen showed the station itself. The sight was disconcerting, even though Lucia had visited the place twice before. SA Station orbited a star, not a planet, and as a result there was nothing nearby to give the station real scale. Part of the problem lay in its irregular shape. Like many stations, SA Station was a hodgepodge of parts and pieces. Bits had been stuck on as required over time, and Silent

Acquisitions had been in business for a long time indeed. The station's volume easily matched that of a pair of good-size moons, or even a tiny planet. It turned slowly in its orbit, a clunky, uneven lattice designed by a drunken spider. Between the uneven shape and the lack of orbital bodies in the immediate area, Lucia wanted to see the station as toy-size. And then a tiny, tiny grain of sand would skitter across in front of it, and Lucia would realize it was a cargo vessel big enough to transport an entire pod of Bellerophon dinosaurs. It was like watching a picture of a young woman turning into an old hag and back again. The whole thing made her seasick, so she dropped her eyes to the instrument panel and concentrated on following course and flying the ship.

Conversation died away, and a strained silence filled the bridge. Lucia heard a faint tapping—Father Kendi drumming his fingers against the arm of his chair. Eagerness and tension radiated off him, and Lucia suppressed an urge to give him advice about the serenity of Irfan. It wouldn't be her place. Instead, Lucia tried to hurry without compromising ship safety.

Despite long hours spent in meditation and weeks of constant exposure to him, Lucia's awe of Father Kendi Weaver hadn't lessened. Every time she saw him, she couldn't help but remember that he had been instrumental in saving the entire universe. It was he who had held back Padric Sufur's malformed children in the Dream, kept them at bay long enough for Vidya and Prasad Vajhur to put their twisted solid-world bodies into cryo-sleep and end the Despair. True, there were other heroes of the Despair. Ben Rymar had saved Kendi's life and thereby allowed Kendi to save the Dream. Sejal Dasa, son of Vidya and Prasad, had fought Sufur's children to a standstill. But Ben was so unassuming, and Lucia had never met Sejal or Vidya and Prasad. Kendi, however, was something else entirely. He *looked* like a hero—tall and handsome and confident, giving his commands in a firm, clear voice.

Did she have a crush on him?

No. Most definitely not. That wouldn't be her place, either.

A slight thump reverberated through the bridge, and an indicator light on Lucia's board flashed. "Docking complete, Father," she reported.

"Great. I'll get started on the forms—oh, joy—and the rest of you can stretch your legs until we get clearance to disembark. After the customs team leaves, I'll want everyone in the galley for a briefing. Got it?"

"I'll spread the word, Chief," Gretchen said, rising and heading for the door.

Lucia stretched with a popping of joints. Every part in her body felt stiff and achy after hours of piloting. She nodded to Father Kendi, who was already muttering to the forms on his data pad, and left the bridge. Apparently even heroes couldn't escape paperwork.

Lucia's ocular implant flashed the time across her retina. She had five minutes to make it to her quarters before daily ritual. A hurried descent in the lift, a light jog down another corridor, and she was entering her own rooms.

As the newest member of the crew, Lucia rated the smallest quarters on the ship. Living room barely big enough to turn around in, bedroom not much wider than her single bunk, efficiency bathroom, no kitchen. Lucia didn't really mind. The place did have a decent-size window. At the moment, the view was currently of black, star-strewn space. Every so often a point of light crept across the void—a ship or a shuttle. Flat pictures and full holograms covered every inch of wall space. People smiled, waved, made faces, or struck silly poses, and all of them bore similar features. Lucia had six brothers and sisters, a dozen aunts and uncles, nieces and nephews galore, and cousins beyond counting. She smiled fondly at a photo of her parents taken not long after their marriage. They were sitting on a porch swing holding hands. She would have to write them a letter soon, see if Ben would be willing to relay it to Bellerophon through the Dream. There was so much to tell them, though she knew Dad would be a little unnerved when he heard how close she and the others had come to getting caught while rescuing Bedj-ka. She could almost hear his voice, unsettled but touched with pride all the same: *You're just a little kid! My baby girl! You're going to give your poor old dad a heart attack one of these days with these adventures of yours!*

An alarm chimed softly and Lucia shook herself. It was time. Two steps took Lucia to the tiny altar set just below the window. On it stood a small statue of Irfan Qasad carved from smooth white marble. Her features bore a peaceful serenity that calmed Lucia whenever she saw them. In the statue's left hand was a scroll, symbol of communication. The statue's right hand was raised in a gesture of beckoning. Leaves and ivy were etched into her clothing, and a double-helix strand of DNA wound around her upraised arm. At the statue's feet sat a small gold platter and three squat candles. Lucia picked up a striker and lit the first candle.

"Great Lady, let the winds and the oceans, the nights and days, the Dream and the world, be all sweet to us." She lit the second candle. "Wondrous Mother, let us follow the path of your goodness for always, like the stars and planets moving in the sky. " She lit the third candle. "Guide and Goddess, let us know and appreciate the points of view of others. You who are the wise and benevolent lady of speech, shower your blessings on us that we may continue your work."

Lucia took up a stick of incense and lit it from one of the candles. The soft, sweet smoke stole over her, and she felt her muscles relax under the familiar ritual, one she had been performing since childhood. She pressed the base of the statue, and a quiet music filled the room like gentle bells. When the song faded, it seemed to Lucia that a quiet, benign presence filled the room and her heart. Lucia breathed a greeting.

"Welcome, Great Mother, and hear my prayer," she murmured. "Thank you for returning Bedj-ka to Harenn and for granting her the happiness she deserves. Let us find Father Kendi's brother and sister. Let them remain safe and whole until we can bring them to the safety of your bosom. Keep my family safe and well. Let Narmi's pregnancy go well, and touch her child with your blessings. Distract the evil Vik and keep him from tainting our lives with his foul presence."

Lucia paused and took a deep breath, trying to remain calm while saying difficult words. Her throat theatened to close anyway. "And please, Great Lady, do not withdraw the blessing of Silence from your people. Do not allow your servants to scatter like the wind. The Children of Irfan do great good in the universe, and it would be wrong to let them fade away. I beg you, Kind One, to grant my Silent brethren entry into the Dream once again. I give thanks for your blessings and pray for your wisdom. Your will be in all."

She waited a moment, inhaling sweet smoke and murmuring a soft chant. Ifran would not let her children die away. She was good and kind, a force for order and justice. Lucia simply had to have faith everything would work out. There was nothing else she could do. Several long breaths later, Irfan's peace and serenity settled over Lucia like a well-worn blanket. She sighed heavily. Everything would be fine, as long as she kept her faith.

Lucia picked up a small silver snuffer, put out the candles, and doused the incense. A few moments later she was down in the galley rummaging through the cabinets and refrigerator for sandwich fixings. She had already set an enormous pot of coffee on to brew, and the rich smell quickly permeated the room. Lucia's scarred hands laid out new loaves of brioche, thin-sliced ham, hard salami, crunchy watercress, sweet peppers, spicy *benyai* leaves, cheddar cheese, and an assortment of sauces ranging from milky-mild to tongue-blisteringly sharp. The Children of Irfan might be a monastic order, but the monks didn't practice asceticism in food or in living arrangements. The Pathway Church of Irfan didn't require it, either, and for this Lucia was grateful.

Of course, if I had grown up an ascetic, she thought, popping a pungent bit of salami into her mouth, *I probably wouldn't know what I was missing.*

"At it again, I see," came Ben Rymar's gentle voice from the galley door. Lucia turned to face him.

"As Irfan so perfectly put it," she replied with a smile, " 'If I don't, who will?' "

"Definitely not me." Ben leaned casually against the door frame. "Cooking is the anti-Irfan, as far as I'm concerned."

Lucia shook her head. "It's *fun,* you heathen."

"I'm glad someone thinks so," Ben said. "Mom didn't cook, either, and sometimes I think Kendi would be happy eating grubs torn from a rotten log. Ever since you joined the crew, we've been eating high on the hog."

"Thank you, kind sir," Lucia said, pretending to simper. "Just send Harenn the finder's fee for bringing me here."

Ben pulled up a chair and sat facing Lucia over the back. Lucia finished slicing bread, then dealt the round pieces out on the counter like cards and began piling generous portions of sandwich fixings on them. She felt comfortable with Ben in the galley, as if one of her brothers were stopping in for a visit.

"You and Harenn are pretty good friends," Ben observed. "How did you two ever hook up, anyway? I never heard."

Lucia picked up a bowl of sauce and a plastic spreader. "You know that I'm a licensed private investigator, right?" When Ben nodded, she went on. "Harenn hired me to look for Bedj-ka because I'm also a pilot and could more easily check out other planets. I wasn't able to find him, obviously, but Harenn and I got along really well. We'd both been jilted by our husbands, so we already had something in common."

"You used to be married?" Ben said. "I didn't know that."

"I was very young and it didn't last long," Lucia said. "One day Jax up and ran off. No reason, no explanation, nothing. Just divorce papers served from a distance. Later I found out Jax had been sleeping with some *bimbina* even before he and I got engaged." She thwacked an onion in half. "Men are pigs."

"Oink."

Lucia laughed. "Sorry. Sometimes I forget that you're a . . . I mean . . . oh, dear."

"Right."

"Anyway," Lucia hurried on, "Harenn and I became friends. Good thing, too—the PI business was getting a little thin even before the Despair came along. These days my one-woman agency exists only on paper. My contract with the Children is the only thing keeping me from having to move back in with my family. I love them, but they're a big and noisy bunch."

Ben nodded and Lucia thought she saw a hint of . . . envy? . . . in his eyes. Maybe she was wrong. What could she possibly have that Ben might envy?

"So," Lucia said, briskly slathering sauce over selected slices, "how did you and Father Kendi get together, anyway? If it's not too private to ask, I mean."

"It's not." Ben rested his chin on the back of the chair. "But it's a long story. Short version is that we met because Kendi was my mom's student. We were both teenagers."

"Love at first sight?" Lucia said.

Ben snorted. "Not quite. It took me forever to figure out how I felt about him. Even after I did, things weren't easy between us. We were on-again, off-again for years. Mom smacked me upside the head a few times about that, but I didn't really admit to myself how much Kendi meant—means—to me until the Despair hit. Sometimes I think you have to lose something, or almost lose it, to understand how precious it is." He paused, then said abruptly, "Do you ever worry about the Children of Irfan becoming extinct? I know Kendi does."

Lucia's thoughts instantly rushed back to her prayers. "I sometimes worry. But never for long."

"Why not?"

"Irfan would never allow her Children to die out," Lucia said firmly.

At that moment Father Kendi poked his head into the galley. "Lucia, you don't have to do this every time we have a briefing, you know."

Lucia blinked. "Do you want me not to? Isn't the food any good?"

"It's great, Lucia," Father Kendi said. His presence seemed to fill the entire galley. "But it's a lot of extra work for you. I mean, newest crew does the cooking for regular meals, but this goes above and beyond."

"She says she likes doing it," Ben put in, "if you can believe that."

"I do like it," Lucia said. "Besides," she added, greatly daring, "you're all too thin. Eat!"

Ben and Father Kendi laughed and Lucia calmly went back to her pile of sandwiches.

Gretchen and Harenn, chatting amiably, arrived in the galley a moment later and sat down at the round table just off the cooking area. Ben and Father Kendi joined them. Harenn poured herself some coffee. Lucia set the finished sandwiches on a large platter, brought them to the table, and took a seat next to

Harenn. Everyone reached for generous portions and pronounced them excellent. Lucia nodded at the praise, then shot a sidelong glance at Harenn. It still seemed strange to see her without her veil in public. Lucia had, of course, been in Harenn's home any number of times and had seen her unveil there, but never anywhere else. It was a welcome sight, and Lucia was glad beyond measure that Bedj-ka's return had allowed it to happen.

"And how's Bedj-ka?" Lucia asked.

Harenn sipped cream-laden coffee with a faintly distracted smile. "He seems happy, as am I. Bedj-ka thinks it exciting to live on a slipship, and I find that it refreshes my own enthusiasm to watch him see things for the first time. He insists on assisting me with the engines and maintenance, and it is touching the way he tries so hard to help."

"Maybe he'll be an engineer like his mother," Lucia said.

"Perhaps." Her smile grew wistful. "He is certainly intelligent enough. He can already run four basic diagnostic programs and—"

"You sound just like my mother when she boasts about my brothers and sisters and me," Lucia interrupted with a chuckle. "Next you'll be whipping holos out of your pocket to show around."

Harenn's brown cheeks darkened. "I have already made several. Would you like to see them?"

Before Lucia could reply, Father Kendi set his data pad on the table and called for order. Lucia instantly gave him her full attention.

"Todd told us where the Collection is housed," he began, "so let's start there." Father Kendi tapped the pad and a hologram of the station sprang into being above the tabletop. "We got lucky. We're docked here"—one part of the station glowed green—"and the Collection is housed here." Another part of the station glowed red. "It's only one section over, so it's not hard to get to from our dock. The first thing we need is a basic recon. Todd gave me some information, but there was a lot he didn't know." More taps, and the view of the station zoomed in tighter, becoming a cutaway of a section of corridor.

"According to Todd, the Collection is almost completely isolated from the rest of the station," Father Kendi continued. "It's on a block that sticks out from the main structure, and the only way to get to it from the station itself is by this corridor. There are several automated checkpoints along the way, where a computer checks your face, your prints, and your identification holo."

"No retina checks?" Gretchen asked.

"Too easy to fake these days," Ben said. "An amateur can get your retina scan from a distance with nothing but a halfway decent camera. Same goes for infrared heat patterns."

"The Collection," Father Kendi continued, "also has a set of escape pods and two private air locks, but I don't think they'll do us much good—it's damned hard to sneak into an air lock." He paused and took a sip of coffee. "One of the first things we need to learn is what the daily routines are. Ben, I want you and Lucia to set up surveillance on the corridor to do just that. Gretchen, you and Harenn need to find out all you can about the routines of Edsard Roon and the three department heads when they aren't at the Collection. Look at where they live, when they usually arrive at work, any habits they have. We need to figure out how to get our hands on their keys, and any detail, no matter how tiny, might be a help. Lucia, if we lift prints from objects the department heads touch, you can make an artificial thumb that would fool a computer scanner, right?"

"Yes, Father," Lucia said. "The best prints will come from something smooth, like a glass or cup, but I can work with harsher stuff."

Father Kendi nodded. "Good. Ben, what about copying the keys?"

"I've been working on that, and I think I can do it." Ben held up a small silver box the size of a pack of playing cards. "I've been modifying one of the copycats. If I pull this off, all you'll have to do is connect the data port of the key to the data port on this. It'll copy the algorithms and I can make a duplicate key from them."

"How long will the download take?" Father Kendi asked.

"Not long. I'm guessing less than thirty seconds. The trick, like you said, will be getting the keys away from the department heads and then returning each one without anyone noticing."

"That's what I'll be working on," Father Kendi said grimly. "Once we have all the information we can glean, I'll get a plan together. Any questions?"

There were none. As the group rose from the table, Lucia swallowed a final bite of spicy sandwich and Ben put a light hand on her shoulder.

"Let's go play with some toys," he said.

Warmth. Softness. Voices. Whispers. Martina Weaver lay in shifting shadows and semidarkness. Occasional colors flickered around her and she studied them with great interest. From time to time she felt as though she were floating, and then she would be lying on something solid again. It was like trying to enter the Dream but being caught adrift in the moment before it solidified around her.

After what was neither a long nor a short time, the darkness began to brighten. Martina became aware that she was lying on a soft bed with a pillow under her head. The ceiling above her was the color of warm sunshine. A round-cheeked woman with a wide, smiling mouth and a scattering of freckles on her face was looking down at her. She wore a dark green wimple over her hair and forehead. A high, white collar came all the way up to her chin, and her green robe reached all the way to the floor. Her hands were gloved in green. But for the color of her robe and the gloves, Martina would have thought she was a Catholic nun.

"Greet the Dream, Alpha," the woman said cheerfully. "Good to see you awake."

A dermospray made a familiar thump against Martina's arm and the room settled with startling abruptness. She sat up, fully awake and alert, and glanced at her surroundings. Sunlight poured into a window overlooking a tree-studded valley. Green plants hung about the room and stood in pots on the carpeted floor. A desk and chair sat below the window, and a comfortable-looking sofa and chair made a little cluster in one corner. The room also had two sliding doors, both shut, and a wooden wardrobe. Martina shook her head. The last thing she remembered was finishing a series of assignments in the Dream. She had sketched for a while in her room and was thinking about asking if she could have some tea. And then . . . what? The memories were fuzzy. Had she undressed for bed? She looked down and saw she was wearing unfamiliar yellow pajamas. The silvery slave bands which had first been fitted to her fifteen years ago were still on her wrist and ankle.

"What is this place?" Martina demanded. "How did I get here?"

The woman smiled, making dimples in her plump cheeks. "We rescued you, praise the Dream. You and your compatriot."

"Compatriot?" Martina started to swing her legs around to get off the bed, but the woman put a restraining hand on her shoulder. A lifetime of obedience conditioning took over, and Martina stayed where she was.

"The other Alpha," the woman explained. "I think your oppressors called him Brad."

"I never met him," Martina said. "I heard Drim-Com had bought a new Silent, but I didn't—"

"There are no slaves here," the woman interrupted firmly. "No owners, no buying or selling of people. The Silent are chosen, divine, and they can't be bought or sold like simple people."

Martina stared. "Are you saying I'm free?"

"No one owns you," the woman said.

"I can leave?"

The woman smiled her cheerful smile. "Not quite yet. You're just an Alpha, and you aren't strong enough yet."

"What do you mean?" Martina asked. "What's an Alpha? How did I get here? Who are you?"

"Everything in time, dear." The woman patted her arm with a gloved hand. "In the meantime, are you hungry?"

Suddenly Martina was. "Ravenous."

"Then you should eat." The woman tapped a panel on the wall and it slid aside, revealing a legged tray. Delicious smells of meat and gravy filled the room. The woman set the tray across Martina's lap. A generous portion of beef steamed on a plate, surrounded by garden vegetables and a salad accompanied by a small pot of tea. Martina ate quickly—the meat was perfectly done and tender.

"My name is Delta Maura," the woman said. Her voice was low and warm. "I'm your counselor, and I'll help repair the damage that's been done to you."

"Damage?" Martina said with her mouth full.

"The damage done to you while you were a slave." Delta Maura patted Martina's shoulder. "It must have been horrible, dear. No one should have to live through something like that."

Martina set down her fork. "Are you a Child of Irfan? Is this Bellerophon?"

"No, dear. You'll learn more about who we are when it's time. For now, you only need to rest. Enjoy yourself. You have computer access, including games and books. If you need something else, use the computer to send a note to the personal needs adjustor." She patted Martina's hand, and Martina found herself growing annoyed at all the patting. "I have to leave now, but if you want to talk to me, just say so and the computer will let me know."

With that, she left. The door slid shut behind her, and Martina was sure she heard the click of a lock. Martina set the tray aside, got out of bed, and tried to open the door. It had no lock plate, only a slot for a keycard. Martina tried to push the door open. It didn't budge. Martina looked down at her feet. A slave band still encircled her ankle, just as it did her wrist. If she were free, why was she still shackled and kept in a locked room? She felt uneasy, and the meat she had eaten seemed to coagulate in her stomach.

First things first, she decided, and set out to explore the room.

The window turned out to be a holographic display. Tapping it changed the view, and the choices ranged from ocean bottom to forest floor to desert dunes to lunar surface. She set it back on the original valley and opened the wardrobe. The clothes inside—none of them from her room back at DrimCom—consisted of several sets of loose yellow tunics and trousers. Two pairs of yellow slippers were on the floor. A set of yellow gloves hung from a hook. Martina changed out of her pajamas, though she didn't don the gloves. Feeling less vulnerable now that she was dressed, she opened the second door and discovered a well-appointed bathroom complete with toilet, sink, enormous tub, and separate shower. The cabinets contained a variety of toiletries.

Back in the main room, she learned that the furniture was comfortable and that the compartment Delta Maura had taken the food from seemed to be some kind of dumbwaiter. Martina put the food tray back inside it, closed the door, and heard a faint hum. When she opened the little door again, there was nothing on the other side but a blank wall.

The computer did indeed have a variety of games, but all of them were holographic or flat-screen. There were no virtual-reality sims. The library was fairly extensive, but all the books were ones she had never heard of. There was no nonfiction. Nothing she saw contained any clue as to where she was or who owned this place.

It took Martina a moment to realize there was no clock in the room and no clock function on the computer. How long had she been drugged? She had no idea. It could have been a few hours or several days. Even weeks, for all she knew.

Martina perched on the edge of the couch, baffled. Was she a prisoner or a guest? Had she been kidnapped or rescued? She felt off-balance and uncertain. Abruptly she wished for her sketchbook and a pencil. Were her art supplies still at DrimCom? Would she ever see them again?

Martina wasn't worried about being in physical danger. If these people had intended to hurt or kill her, they would have done so already. Plus she was one of the few Silent left in the galaxy who could still reach the Dream, someone far too valuable to harm. If they gave her access to her drugs, she could even get into the Dream and shout for help. Even now she could hear the faint whispers around her, whispers she had begun hearing not long after she had been snatched from the colony ship and sold into slavery.

It was a part of Martina's life that she didn't like to think about, but every so often she had terrible nightmares about that terrible day, about someone snatching her out of cryo-sleep on a colony ship and hauling her, cold and shivering, into a smelly, tiny room aboard a slave ship. Her father and mother had

been there, at least, as had been her older brothers
Evan and Keith. All of them were descended from
Australian Aborigines, but Aboriginal culture in Australia had been almost completely lost by the time the
terrible droughts came and the Outback desert spread
even into the farmlands. In an attempt to rediscover
their roots, a group of Aboriginal descendants had
banded together to form the Real People Reconstruc-
tionists. Martina had only been four or five when her
parents joined the group, and her early memories of
the RPR involved long walks outside, meditation exercises, and eating really strange foods. Keith, her oldest
brother, had gone for the RPR in a big way, even
going so far as to change his name to Utang, which
he claimed was an old Aboriginal word for *strength*.
Evan, her other brother, had hated every aspect of
the RPR, but he had especially loathed the trips to
the Outback when they all went on walkabout.

A few years later, the government had announced
that it was sponsoring a giant colony ship to relieve
Australia's population burden. The journey would
take hundreds of years, but the colonists would spend
the entire journey in cryo-sleep. The Real People Re-
constructionists had petitioned to be included so they
could at last rediscover the ways of the Real People on
a new world, and the government had agreed. Keith—
Utang—had been wildly excited. Evan had been furious. Martina, barely ten years old then, remembered
being uncertain about going but feeling reassured that
her parents and brothers would be there every step of
the way.

Now she had no idea if any of them were still alive,
or even what their names might be. Martina had gone
through three owners, and each one of them had
changed her name. Through it all, she had held on to
that one piece of herself. No matter what her owners
had named her, she still thought of herself as Martina

Weaver. Had her family managed the same thing? She had no way of knowing, and had long ago accepted the fact that she would never find out.

Martina paged through the electronic library again, more for something to do than anything else, and discovered she had overlooked a nonfiction book—*A True History of the Dream* by Dr. Edsard Roon. The title attracted Martina's eye. There were many versions of Irfan Qasad's story, and very few of them agreed on all points. Martina thought it interesting the way different versions conflicted. Her first owner had been a history professor who had bought her as a household servant, and he had allowed Martina to read from his library when she wasn't working. She had read a fair amount, trying to learn what had happened in the centuries her family had been sleeping. Later, when her Silence had surfaced, he had sold her for a tidy profit, but by then she had already acquired a decent background in galactic history.

Martina called up the book, and holographic pages appeared in front of her. The beginning was familiar stuff. Irfan Qasad, captain of a colony ship, arrived at a planet named Bellerophon and became the first human being to meet the alien Ched-Balaar, who had arrived there first. Initially Irfan and her people had been worried that the Ched-Balaar would be hostile, or that they'd tell the humans to turn around and go back to Earth, but the aliens had been happy to share their new world, provided the humans fulfilled one condition.

Martina blinked. She knew this part. The Ched-Balaar had asked their new neighbors to take part in a religious ceremony. There had been drumming in the forests and a gathering of peoples around a great fire. All the humans had drunk a special wine concocted by the Ched-Balaar, a wine that had sent most of them into a stupor. A handful of people had found themselves in the Dream. Irfan Qasad had been one of them, as had her eventual husband Daniel Vik. Here, however, Dr. Roon's version diverged from what she knew.

The Atashi Record indicates very clearly that the Ched-Balaar, otherworldly beings of great power, selected only certain humans to take the holy nectar while the unworthy received nothing but thin beer. The special humans, chosen by the Ched-Balaar, would undergo a transformation. They would become blessed with Silence, and they would come to rule Bellerophon.

But the Atashi Record also reveals that one human, Daniel Vik, used guile and trickery to learn what the Ched-Balaar were planning for their Chosen, and he also learned that he was not to be among them. This made Vik jealous, and he used more guile to ensure that he would receive a portion of the holy nectar.

When the night of the ceremony came, the Ched-Balaar came in procession through the talltree forests of Bellerophon to the central fire where the humans awaited them, the Chosen on the right and the unworthy on the left. Daniel Vik had been seated with the unworthy, but he approached the mighty Irfan Qasad. In her weakness for his fair face and his silver tongue, she allowed him to sit next to her. Irfan took the bowl of holy nectar from the first Ched-Balaar, drank, and passed the sacred bowl to Vik, who drank and passed it to the other Chosen while the Ched-Balaar chanted and beat their otherwordly rhythms.

Irfan, Vik, and the Chosen fell into a stupor brought on by the holy nectar and the mysterious rhythms. They underwent the transfiguration and ascended to Silence in the Dream. But unknown to them, the DNA in Daniel Vik's saliva had tainted the nectar, leaving it corrupt. Although the Atashi Record is very clear on this, further proof is seen in the fact that Daniel Vik was weak in the Dream; he was never intended to go there in the first place. And none of the other Chosen were as powerful in the Dream as Irfan Qasad, who drank untainted nectar.

Martina paused. This was certainly different from everything else she had read—so different as to be laughable. That Daniel Vik had been a filthy bastard who betrayed his own wife and kidnapped one of his children away from her was widely accepted, but the idea that he had sabotaged the Awakening Ceremony was so radical it crossed the line into ridiculous. This Dr. Roon guy must have been laughed out of every academic hall in existence. And what was the "Atashi Record"? She had never heard of it. Shaking her head, Martina continued reading.

Irfan Qasad very quickly grew to power in the Dream, learning even how to reach out of it and contact humans on other planets, people whose genetic structure made them kin to her, and therefore Chosen. She taught them how to reach the Dream themselves. But the other Silent on Bellerophon were weaker in the Dream because of Vik's deceitful taint. Proof of this is seen by how easily Irfan Qasad could reach the Dream; she was eventually able to do so without drugs or even trancing, while all those who drank after Vik could enter the Dream only through heavy use of both.

Later, when Irfan's wisdom uncovered Vik's deceit and she attempted to correct his taint with the use of genetic-engineering techniques, he opposed her at every turn, his silver tongue turning her friends and even some of the mighty Ched-Balaar to his side. This corrupted even Irfan herself, who hid her experiments and produced three Silent children of Vik's issue. All were strong in their Silence, and this angered Vik so much that he became insane. He kidnapped their eldest son and fled her presence.

Still angered beyond reason, Vik next raised an army to try to crush Irfan and the other Chosen. But

Irfan entered the Dream and held him at bay until Vik was cut down by one of his own followers.

Irfan and the other Chosen thought they were rid of Vik's taint at last, but such was not to be. His DNA had tainted the Ched-Balaar's holy gift of Silence. Only Irfan herself was pure; all others tainted. And when people learned to make ships that could travel quickly between the stars, they desired the Silent for use as communication. Pirates in search of Silent and their DNA invaded Bellerophon, kidnapping and plundering and making the Chosen into slaves. Irfan fled into the Dream to seek a solution and remained there for many years. When she returned, she told the Chosen that although their birthright was within their grasp, they would never be free of their shackles until they became as pure as she, and she laid down the Laws of the Atash:

1. The Chosen must separate themselves from impure human society.
2. The Chosen must dedicate themselves to purity of thought and deed.
3. The Chosen must confess their impurities to the Enlightened in order to begin cleansing themselves.
4. The Chosen must give themselves over to obedience of the Enlightened that they may follow them into Light.

Martina shut the book off. Bored or not, there was only so much she could take. Was that thing meant to be a scholarly study or a religious text? For a history, it certainly glossed over or ignored an awful lot. A surviving journal from the time of Irfan Qasad had, Martina remembered, described Daniel Vik as going "insane with fury" when he found out that Irfan had genengineered their children for Silence, but there was plenty of hot debate about whether the reference was literal or metaphorical. It also completely ignored the fact that Silence itself had inadvertently led to the enslavement of so many Silent. If Irfan hadn't done her damnedest to spread Silence throughout the galaxy as a method of intergalactic communication, founding her so-called Silent Empire, then two scientists separated by light-years of space would never have collaborated, never have discovered slipspace, never have learned how to travel faster than light.

And Martina would never have been enslaved.

With the discovery of slipspace, humans and other intelligent life spread quickly through the galaxy, and the poky colony ships vanished from living memory. They coasted slowly onward, their slumbering inhabitants confidently waiting to wake on a new, unspoiled world.

Then the slavers discovered them.

After almost a thousand years, all records of Martina, her family, and the other colonists had been lost or simply wiped. There was no proof that they weren't slaves, no one alive who even remembered they had existed. Dazed by the abrupt exit from cryo-sleep, the colonists had been unable to resist being shackled and herded aboard the slaver's ship. Later, they were hauled onto a space station and auctioned off. Martina had watched Utang being taken away by a slaver, though the slaver hadn't said why or where he was taking him. Then Martina had watched Evan and her mother being taken away by a woman in green. Martina had started to cry. Evan had said something to her, something about staying brave because he would find her one day, but she had barely heard him because she was crying so hard. Then he was gone.

Martina shook her head. It was all in the past—three owners ago, in fact. None of it mattered, and as long as she kept busy, either in the Dream or with her sketching, she didn't have to dwell on it.

Trouble was, she didn't have her sketchbook for drawing or her drugs for entering the Dream. There were the games and books on the computer, but Martina wasn't in the mood to read, and holographic games had never interested her. She rummaged around the computer terminal until she found the stylus, then searched the directory until she came across an art program. It activated at her command. Martina waved the stylus through the air, and it left a bright green trail in three dimensions. She nodded to herself. Three-D art wasn't as fun as drawing, but it had its compensations.

Martina erased the trail and started sketching, just letting her hand go where it would. After a while, she realized she was creating a pair of rough portraits—a twelve-year-old boy with dark skin and eyes and a fifteen-year-old boy with equally dark skin but startlingly blue eyes. Evan and Utang. Annoyed with herself, Martina wiped the air clean and drew a series of animals. A falcon. A kangaroo. A koala bear. And all three reminded her of Evan. The koala had his eyes. The kanga mimicked his posture. The falcon shared his fierce expression. Angrily Martina wiped the holograms again and shut down the program. Then she sat down on the bed and drummed her fingers restlessly against her thighs.

All life, why was she here?

CHAPTER FIVE

"Prostitution is the only job where the least experienced workers earn the most money."
— Inspector Lewa Tan, Guardians of Irfan

Gretchen slid through the crowd, avoiding elbows and insteps. Ken Jeung, head of the Collection's medical department, walked purposefully ahead of her. Jeung always walked purposefully, and somehow people always got out of his way. This made it hell to shadow him through the crowds on SA Station, and Gretchen's nerves were already racked with the effort of doing so without attracting attention—his or Security's. The fact that he was short and dark-haired didn't make trailing him any easier, since he tended to blend in with other humans.

The shimmering lights of FunSec jumped and capered all around Gretchen. Laughter bubbled out of casinos along with the jingling of metal chits. The only illumination was provided by the thousands of moving, glittering lights that flashed the names of the establishments or projected giant holograms toward the faraway ceiling, providing street entertainment and, incidentally, slowing traffic as people stopped to watch. Gretchen suspected the latter effect was a way of making sure people didn't breeze past the casinos, theaters, and restaurants without looking at them. Currently, a three-story tall human salsa dancer in a red dress was doing a highly suggestive routine with a tall green alien, and both were getting a lot of attention from just about everyone except Jeung.

Gretchen stepped around a waist-high creature with long fur and stubby legs, dodged between two humans, and sidestepped something that reminded her of a walking tree. Humans were a majority on SA Station, but only barely, and Gretchen couldn't identify many of the nonhumans. Most of the different species had their own enclaves, but a great deal of mixing went on in FunSec.

The travel corridor was so tall and wide Gretchen found herself thinking of it as a street, complete with sidewalks, doors, windows, and vehicle traffic. Restaurants scented the air with smells of fried food, baked sweets, and other aromas Gretchen couldn't identify. Humans and nonhumans chattered among themselves and with each other while dry computer voices provided translations. Music boomed overhead to accompany the holographic dancers. Vehicles zipped up and down the street, hovering just above the metal flooring. Crowded walkways made zigzags and lattices far above ground level. The only greenery came from the occasional potted tree. The erratic lighting, designed to make FunSec always feel like a nighttime fun spot, left large chunks of shadow, and Gretchen used them to her advantage while following Jeung.

Jeung turned a corner and Gretchen hurried to catch up. By now she was fairly sure of her quarry's destination, but she didn't want to take a chance on being wrong. Her suspicions were confirmed when she reached the next street and saw Jeung mount a short flight of red-carpeted steps that led to a set of gold-rimmed obsidian doors. A uniformed door attendant touched her hat and held the door for him. Gretchen ducked into an alleyway and tapped her earpiece.

"He's at it again," she said.

"Third time this week," came Kendi's voice in her ear. *"And it's only Wednesday. You think you can get in there and get some more info on our friend now that we know he's a regular?"*

"Can't hurt to try. Gimme a few to let him get settled in with his thing of the evening and we'll see."

Gretchen settled back to wait. The door attendant let in three more humans—one man, two women—and let out two more—both men. A huge centipede pittered up the steps and was granted admission. It reemerged a few minutes later. Finally Gretchen judged enough time had passed. She put on a nonchalant air, crossed the street, and sauntered up the steps. The attendant touched her cap and opened the door.

Inside, Gretchen found everything looking like a brothel should. Plush red carpet, scarlet and gold wallpaper, big marble staircase, trays of drinks hovering obsequiously about, and various beings for rent chatting up potential customers. Lighting and music were soft, conversation muted. The furniture setup made nooks and crannies for private conversation, and there was even a small dance floor. Humans and nonhumans mixed freely, most with some sort of beverage at hand.

Or paw, Gretchen noted. *Or tentacle.*

Some of the nonhumans were humanoid, with exotic pelts, antennae, ears, or skin tone. Many, however, weren't even bipedal. Creatures scuttled, slithered, glided, and even oozed around the common room. One looked like a giant turtle with a couch cushion on its back. A human man reclined on the creature, drink in hand. Another nonhuman seemed to be a three-headed snake with amazingly muscular arms. Its tail was twined sensuously around the waist of another human male. Gretchen couldn't decide if she wanted to laugh or barf. And Jeung was nowhere in sight.

"What are you drinking?" said a smooth voice at her elbow.

Gretchen turned. A human woman was looking up at her. Short, boyishly slim figure, curling black hair long enough to sit on. Gretchen couldn't even hazard a guess as to her age.

"Uh, nothing for me, thanks," Gretchen replied.

"Your first time here?" asked the woman.

"Yes."

"I'm Lady Kellyn. This is my place." Kellyn gestured with a bony hand. "If any of the nonhumans catches your fancy, please don't hesitate to ask. If you're looking for human companionship, there's a lovely place three doors down, just past the Security station."

"I'm not sure what I'm looking for," Gretchen replied truthfully.

"Then look around until you see something that intrigues. My souls are all trained in what pleasures humans, but we do have a few rules."

"Such as?" Gretchen asked, curious despite herself.

"We are fully licensed and bonded with SA Station, so all the usual Station laws apply here. In addition, we don't do pain, either giving or receiving, and we don't allow heavy drug use, including alcohol. All of my souls are the genuine article—no genengineering here—but if you get something you didn't expect, we can't issue a refund. None of my souls are slaves, so please don't treat them as such. If you want to try more than one soul at the same time, you must ask me or one of my assistants and not the souls in question, since there are occasional cultural difficulties. We are not responsible for damage to clothing. If you want to be swallowed and regurgitated, we need at least twenty-four hours' notice and you must provide your own breathing apparatus. We take payment in advance but can't accept SA chits. Hard cash is preferable, but cashcards are fine as well."

Gretchen nodded. "Understood. How long have you been in business?"

"Two hundred and thirty-six years," Kellyn said with a touch of pride. "We're the second-oldest pleasure house on SA Station, in fact."

"Impressive." Gretchen hooked a glass of sparkling something from a wandering tray and took a sip.

Champagne. Fine quality, too. "This place is amazing. I'm glad I got a recommendation to visit you."

"Who recommended us?" Kellyn asked, rising to the bait. "I'll send a note."

Here Gretchen colored slightly. "Actually it wasn't as much a recommendation as a piece of accidental eavesdropping. I overheard Ken Jeung raving about your place to a friend at work."

"Ah! You work with Dr. Jeung. He's here tonight, you know."

"He is?" Gretchen darted a frightened glance about the room. The guy on the turtle had been joined by a tiger-striped woman, complete with tail. "Where?"

"He went upstairs with one of my souls a few minutes ago. Is something wrong?"

Gretchen ran her finger around the rim of her champagne glass. "It's kind of embarrassing. I sort of work more *for* him than *with* him and it would be . . . awkward running into my boss. I didn't think he'd come here two nights in a row. Please don't mention you saw me, would you?"

"Of course not," Kellyn soothed. "Though you wouldn't need to be embarrassed."

"Does he come here a lot?"

Kellyn gave a smile full of dazzlingly white teeth. "I'm afraid I can't gossip about the individual habits of my customers."

Gretchen nodded, though she already knew quite a bit about Jeung's habits. Ben, Lucia, and Gretchen had spent a great deal of time reading old news stories, striking up casual conversations with patrons, and once even interviewing a soul who had quit working for Kellyn to open a flower shop. The latter had been extremely talkative, especially about Dr. Ken Jeung.

"Well, *I* can gossip," Gretchen said, still hoping to winkle a bit more information out of Lady Kellyn. "Like I said, I've overheard him talk about this place. He said you're always hiring new people—souls—and he likes to get first crack at them." She sniffed. "I had a boyfriend like that once. Never wanted to do the same thing twice."

"Perhaps you should have brought him here," Kellyn said with a smile of her own.

"Is it true that Dr. Jeung's always first in line for someone new?"

"That would be telling," Kellyn replied. "Do you see anyone you find enticing, my dear?"

A pointed change of subject. Gretchen gave an inward sigh. She had been hoping for confirmation of the information she had already gathered, but it was clear Kellyn wasn't going to give any. "Let me look," Gretchen hedged. "I'm new to all this."

"Of course, no pressure," Kellyn said. "And if you see no one who appeals, we have two new souls who will be starting soon. However, I do have to tell you that drinks and the buffet are included in the price of an hour's pleasure time. If you elect not to share pleasure time with one of my souls, I'm afraid we have to charge you for what you imbibe."

Gretchen nodded acknowledgment. Kellyn pressed her arm briefly and moved away to speak to someone else. After a decent interval, Gretchen wandered up the marble staircase. A tall woman accompanied by a hairy, bearlike creature passed Gretchen on their way down. At the top of the stairs she could go either left or right into a corridor lined with doors. She went left until she was standing directly under the small security camera positioned on the ceiling and she stayed there until the tiny camera mounted on her lapel pin had taken several holos of the empty hallway. Then she did the same thing with the other corridor and headed down the stairs again.

In the main mingling area, Gretchen hung around long enough to make it seem as if she were waffling between a soft creature that reminded her of a baby seal and a thing with a beak and wicked-looking talons, then headed for the front door, where a pudgy human in an honest-to-god tuxedo stood behind a small podium. Some sort of maître d', Gretchen assumed, responsible for collecting money.

"You saw nothing to your liking tonight?" he asked solicitously as he presented Gretchen a bill for the champagne.

Gretchen settled the check, trying to look as if she paid half a day's stipend for a single drink all the time. "Nothing grabbed me. Lady Kellyn says you're getting two new souls soon?"

"Yes, madam. They will have finished their training by the day after tomorrow. I'll be sending out a notice to everyone on our honor roll once they're available."

"Really?" Gretchen put her hand on the pudgy man's podium. When she removed it, a hundred-freemark coin glittered in the soft light beside a small address chip. "I hope I'm on that roll."

The pudgy maître d' swept the chip and the coin into his pocket. "Of course, madam. You will be among the first to hear."

"I'd like to be the *very* first, even if it's only by a few minutes."

"That can certainly be arranged, madam."

Gretchen thanked the man and swept out into the false night.

"A hundred freemarks?" Kendi spluttered. "Gretchen! We have a big budget, but isn't that extravagant for a simple bribe?"

"It didn't even include the champagne," Gretchen added with a winsome smile. "Do you want to hear what I got or not?"

Kendi took a deep breath and closed his eyes to get himself under control. It was only money, and the Children had never stinted when it came to buying, begging, or stealing Silent into freedom. It was just the way Gretchen went about it, so smug and irritating.

They were in Ben and Kendi's quarters, with its half-messy living room. The faint smell of old coffee hung on the air. Behind Kendi on Ben's desk sat holographic displays of the plain corridor leading to the Collection's part of SA station. Ben and Lucia had managed to get close enough to the Collection entrance to release a pair of tiny spider cameras that had crawled up to the ceiling and planted themselves. One of them had wandered too close and shorted out, the victim of some sort of jamming device, but the other had hung back and was transmitting a clear image. At the moment, the display showed nothing but an empty corridor that ended in a door fitted with a hand-level scanner for checking prints. Dozens of people passed through that door every day, presenting an identification holo and submitting to a quick print scan before being admitted. Kendi burned to know what was on the other side of that door, but had to be content with having his team shadow the various department heads to learn more about them.

"All right," he said at last. "What did you learn?"

"The maître d', or whoever he is, takes bribes. I didn't try it with Lady Kellyn. I didn't think it would work."

"Right, right. What else?"

"Jeung has a thing for sex with nonhumans—we knew that from our other research—and he does get bored fast. Whenever they get someone new, Jeung's on her faster than a spacer on . . . well, you know."

Kendi tapped his fingers on the arms of the desk chair, a habit he had picked up from Ara. "Anything else?"

"You betcha. I gave the maître d' guy a mail drop and bribed him to let me be the very first to know when a new soul is ready to start working. He said there'll be two more coming up by the day after to-morrow. I'll bet a year of your stipend—"

Kendi snorted as he usually did when Gretchen made this remark.

"—that Jeung will be there and he'll be heavily oc-cupied for quite some time."

"In other words, we'll have a time and place of his next assignation," Kendi said. "Along with a built-in distraction."

"Astute," Gretchen said. "No wonder you were promoted to Father."

Kendi ignored this comment and thought for a long moment, then rose. "We'll have to put a twenty-four-hour monitor on that mail drop. And be ready to spend the evening with a hooker. I need to go find Ben."

"The message came in, troops," Kendi said. *"Go!"*

Gretchen acknowledged the transmission, left a few SA company chits on the restaurant table, and hurried out the front door. The lights and sounds of FunSec swirled around her in a cacophony she had come to hate over the last day and half. Ignoring all of it as best she could, she picked her way across the street to Lady Kellyn's establishment and let the attendant get the door for her.

Because Silent Acquisitions had been originally started by humans and the station originally built with humans in mind, SA Station kept a twenty-four-hour clock and work schedule. However, Silent Acquisi-tions itself was open twenty-four hours a "day," mean-ing FunSec establishments could expect customers at any time, as people got off work at all hours. Lady Kellyn's was therefore busy, despite the fact that it was barely six-thirty in the evening.

Another fact Gretchen had learned in the last day and a half was that Lady Kellyn did not accept reservations from anyone but preferred—read *regular and wealthy*—customers. On the surface it was an attempt to seem genteel and old-fashioned, but Gretchen suspected that too many people had called for reservations and then broken them, either because the customers chickened out or they didn't bother to inform the brothel of a change in plans. People who had to go through the trouble of making reservations in person, Gretchen imagined, rarely broke them.

Gretchen approached the maître d', still pudgy in his tuxedo. "I just happened to be in the neighborhood when I got the news," she said breathlessly. "You have two new souls?"

"Indeed, madam." The maître d' tapped his podium and brought up a screen. "Would you like to spend time with either of them? They begin seeing customers at seven o'clock."

"Who are they and what are they like?" she asked.

A small hologram of a greenish, cone-shaped creature with a multitude of segmented arms appeared next to an image of something that looked like a giant throw pillow with zebra stripes.

"Tour-rif-na," the maître d' said, indicating the cone creature, "is from the planet Pell-de-ra. Her multiple arms and fingers are especially adept at giving pleasure in many forms and she secretes several specially scented oils for this purpose. Zem"—the maître d' indicated the pillow—"is a very relaxing partner from Rivva. The fur is actually made of mobile cilia which can either massage or excite."

Behind Gretchen, Ben and Lucia came through the door, hand in hand. Lucia wore white gloves to cover her scars. Gretchen ignored them to concentrate on the holograms. She started to point to one of the images, then apparently changed her mind.

"Is . . . has Ken Jeung made a reservation for this evening?" she asked, setting a coin on the podium. "I don't mean to pry, but I work for him and it would be . . . embarrassing for me if I ran into him here. I'd prefer to arrange things so that he doesn't see me."

The coin vanished. "He hasn't called yet, madam, but I'm expecting him to do so any moment. The honor roll notifications went out only two minutes ago. You asked to be first."

"And I do appreciate it," Gretchen said. "He should be out of work any moment now, and I'm sure he'll come straight here, so if I take an hour with Zem"—she pointed to the pillow—"I should be out of sight. Unless . . . oh, wait—are their rooms close together? Where we might run into each other?"

The maître d' began to look a little annoyed, so Gretchen put another coin on the podium. "Their rooms are right across the hall from each other, madam. But don't worry—each room is equipped with a spyhole so you can check the corridor to see if it's empty before you leave."

"Thank you so much," Gretchen said.

"I've logged you in to spend an hour with Zem in the Palace Room beginning at seven o'clock. Go to the top of the stairs, turn right, and go all the way to the end of the corridor. Zem herself will not be spending time down here—she isn't as mobile as our other souls—but she will be ready for you. Meanwhile, you can enjoy the bar and buffet." The maître d's podium chimed for his attention and he tapped it. "Greetings, Lady Kellyn's. Ah, hello, Dr. Jeung. So good to hear from you. Yes, we do have a reservation open."

Gretchen mouthed "thank you" at the maître d', who nodded to her. Then she wandered away. Ben and Lucia were sitting on a couch talking with a hairless, red-spotted humanoid. A bit of searching turned up Tour-rif-na, the green, cone-shaped female Jeung had doubtless made a reservation for. She was massaging the shoulders of a startlingly handsome young man with black hair and liquid brown eyes.

Now why can't the new "souls" look anything like him? she thought wickedly, and tried to remember the last time she had actually had sex. She couldn't. *Great. Gorgeous guy over there who's probably more interested in that multiarmed thing than in me, so I get to spend the evening with a sofa cushion. How the hell did I end up with this kind of life?*

Gretchen tapped her earpiece with a sigh. "Myra, open channel to everyone. Listen up, gang—I think we're set. I've got one of the newbies reserved for seven o'clock, and I'd bet two months of Kendi's stipend—"

"That's Father Kendi to you, if you're going to bet my money," Kendi interjected.

"—that Jeung will reserve the other for the same time. Her name is Tour-rif-na, and her room is across from the Palace Room, though at the moment she's down here socializing. To get to her room, go upstairs, make a right, and go all the way down to the end. Everyone got it?"

A multitude of voices from her earpiece indicated that everyone did.

"Ben, you should get into place as soon as you can," Kendi said. *"If Tour-rif-na is downstairs, it means her room is empty."*

"On it," Ben said.

Across the room, Ben and Lucia both got up and headed for the main marble staircase. A caged lift nearby accommodated patrons and souls who couldn't deal with stairs, but it was empty at the moment. Other customers went up and down the steps fairly regularly, so Ben and Lucia didn't attract any attention. Gretchen snagged a wineglass from a hovering tray and wandered over toward Tour-rif-na, who was still working on the beautiful young man. Tour-rif-na, apparently, couldn't sit down on chairs designed for a human, so she was standing behind him while he perched on the back of a sofa. Her long, long fingers worked gracefully at his shoulders and neck. His eyes were closed in blissful happiness. As Gretchen got closer, she was hit with a powerful scent that reminded her not unpleasantly of earth and grass. The soul had three tiny eyes spaced evenly around the top of her head.

"Are you Tour-rif-na?" Gretchen asked.

"I am," she said. Her voice was almost as deep as a human man's, and Gretchen wondered if that was her normal voice or what the translator in her earpiece had settled on. The young man's eyes popped open and he glared at Gretchen.

"This won't take but a second," Gretchen told him. "I was wondering if Tour-rif-na here could do me a favor."

"A favor," Tour-rif-na said, fingers still working. Two of her other hands stole toward Gretchen's shoulders. Gretchen thought about pushing them away, then decided not to. Tour-rif-na's touch was pleasant, and the gentle pressure of just a moment's massage unknotted several muscles. Gretchen hadn't realized she was that tense. She pressed a coin into one of Tour-rif-na's hands, hoping she came from a culture that understood tips and bribes. It was a pretty good bet that she did—anyone working in a brothel for humans would have to. The young man closed his eyes again.

"I was wondering if you could help me win a bet," Gretchen said in a low voice that the man wouldn't be able to hear.

"What is a bet?"

"A sort of game in which the loser has to pay the winner a forfeit."

"I see," Tour-rif-na said. "And what is this bet?"

"It's very simple," Gretchen said, resisting the temptation to close her own eyes under Tour-rif-na's delicious fingers. "And very small. Let me explain."

A while later, Gretchen sauntered up the marble

staircase toward the Palace Room. At the last moment she looked over her shoulder and saw Ken Jeung hurry in the front door. He spoke briefly with the maître d', and then Lady Kellyn breezed over to greet him as well. She took his hand and led him over to where Tour-rif-na was holding court by massaging three people at once. Good. The tricky part of the evening was over for her.

Gretchen quickly trotted up the stairs and came across Ben and Lucia standing together on the landing. What were they doing out here? She almost paused to ask them, then stopped herself. She wasn't supposed to know them. Instead she made herself sail past them and down the hallway. The last door on the left sported a gold plaque that said PALACE ROOM. Directly across from it was another door with a plaque proclaiming it the Garden Room. Gretchen opened the Palace Room door and saw a large room with pillars that arched up to a high ceiling. Thick carpets lay on the floor, and a fireplace with holographic fire graced one wall. In front of the fireplace was a zebra-striped floor pillow big enough for two humans to lie on. Half wondering if she were the victim of some elaborate prank, Gretchen said, "Hello?"

The pillow sat up. "I can sense your presence," said a musical voice. "My name is Zem. Please enter and be welcome."

Gretchen edged closer to the creature, a little nervous now. The only reason she had made the reservation with Zem was to ensure that Jeung chose Tour-rif-na. What Gretchen actually did with Zem was now immaterial, and she still had one more small job to do.

"Look," she said, "I'm not really here because I want sex."

"I knew that when you entered my room," Zem said. There were no signs of eyes or a mouth, and Gretchen couldn't figure out where the voice was coming from. Zem's fur—cilia—stirred. They were long and silky-looking, with an arresting black-and-white pattern. "You do not smell like someone who is interested in that sort of pleasure. But you do smell lonely. Let me soothe you."

Gretchen almost left, but something held her. Tentatively, like a bird ready to take flight, she sat on the floor next to Zem. Well, why shouldn't she take advantage? Her final task wasn't something she could do until Jeung was done with Tour-rif-na, and that was an hour away.

"Sit on me," Zem said. "Rest on me. That is why I am here."

Again without knowing why but no longer feeling self-conscious, Gretchen crawled over Zem's body until she was in the center. Zem was soft like a gel mattress and she noticed that the individual cilia moved on their own. Zem slowly folded over her until she felt engulfed in a warm body hug. For the first time since the Despair, Gretchen felt as if she had reached a haven, a safe place. The lonely ache left by the Dream's absence receded.

As if reading her mood, Zem said softly, "You are safe with me, safe and warm. Just relax. Just be."

Gretchen closed her eyes and obeyed.

Ben kissed Lucia at the top of the stairs, casting one eye up the hallway as he did so. Gretchen had come by a moment ago, no doubt wondering why they were still here. In fact, they had been here for several minutes waiting for the transceiver to do its job, and that hadn't happened yet. So Ben and Lucia had continued pretending to make out. It felt decidedly strange, as though he were kissing his sister or cousin. Ben had dated women, but not often; he had only rarely felt any attraction. Ultimately he had figured he was just a natural loner. Then Kendi had burst into his life like a fox exploding into a flock of pigeons and he had learned to soar.

"This is weird," Lucia muttered against his lips. "Done yet?"

Ben touched the transceiver in his pocket. "Not yet. Think it's still breaking into the camera system. Shouldn't be much—" The transceiver vibrated once, then lay still. "Got it," Ben said, and they parted. A graceful-looking divan sat nearby, and they sank onto it. Lucia oozed onto Ben's lap and positioned herself so that her legs hid Ben's right hand from the cameras. She was heavy and soft, completely unlike Kendi's whipcord build. Lucia leaned over to pretend she was nibbling on Ben's ear while Ben operated the transceiver in his pocket by touch.

The security system at Lady Kellyn's establishment was far from elaborate. It mostly consisted of a series of cameras hooked to a dedicated computer that sounded the alarm if it saw a violent act or if anyone it didn't recognize went into the wrong place. One person oversaw the entire system and almost never watched the camera monitors directly. There were also anywhere from six to a dozen security personnel on the premises, but they spent most of their time on the first floor. Every soul was also equipped with an alarm button or similar way to call for help if needed. The tightest security revolved around the cashbox. The worst problem Lady Kellyn and her assistants usually had to deal with was a drunken patron, and she didn't hesitate to call SA Security if things got sticky. All this Ben and the others had learned from their previous research. The soul-turned-flower-seller had been the most helpful, especially after Ben had paid enough to cover a month's lease on her shop.

Because Lady Kellyn rarely had problems with security, there were no cameras in the individual pleasure rooms, and the cameras in the hallway were hooked to a wireless system. This made Ben's life much easier, since he could break into the transmission system instead of having to access the camera directly. His transceiver carried in it a photo of an empty hallway taken by Gretchen on her initial visit to the place. All Ben had to do was get it close enough to the camera for his special program to break into the camera's transmitter and upload the image of an empty corridor. The quick vibration indicated that the transceiver had isolated the camera's security frequency. Ben put his hand in his pocket to reactivate the transceiver and upload the picture. His practiced fingers easily found the correct buttons. He was just about to start the upload when a weight settled on the divan and a low, throaty voice said, "Now, what are the two of you doing up here all by yourselves?"

Heart suddenly pounding, Ben leaned around Lucia and saw a woman with leopardlike fur and wide, cat-green eyes. She ran a graceful hand down Ben's back, and he shivered despite himself.

"My name is Carrillen," the woman said. "I've been watching the two of you all evening and you've barely said two words to anyone but each other. Now I find you up here necking. Most humans come here for something more exotic than each other." She licked the back of her hand suggestively with a long tongue.

Lucia slid off Ben's lap. "We were just . . . trying to decide what we wanted to do and got distracted. Mike here is so hot, I just can't keep my hands off him."

"Isn't he just?" Carrillen slid behind both Ben and Lucia on the divan and leaned over them to run her hands down their chests. Her whiskers tickled Ben's cheek. "Maybe I can help you decide what you want to do. We can all three slip into my room and explore the possibilities. How does that sound?"

Her hands moved lower. Ben's mouth was dry and his mind raced. They had to find a way to get rid of Carrillen without arousing her suspicions, and they had to do it before Ken Jeung came up those stairs with Tour-rif-na in ten minutes.

Carrillen licked Lucia's ear once with her tongue, then Ben's. It was a raspy but strangely sensual feeling. Ben quickly took advantage of the gesture. He shuddered hard once, then gently pushed Carrillen away.

"I'm sorry, honey," he said to Lucia. "I know you wanted this, and I'm really trying, but I'm just not sure again."

"You promised," Lucia said, picking up the cue. "Mikey, we talked about it all week and you promised for my birthday we'd try it. And Carrillen here would be perfect." Lucia put out a finger and stroked one of Carrillen's ears. She closed her eyes in feline satisfaction.

"I know, I know." Ben looked miserably down at his hands. "I want to, and then I don't want to. It's Dad all over again."

Lucia made an exasperated sound. "Every time I think we're getting somewhere, you bring him up again. Dad, Dad, Dad. What is it with you? Did we flush all that therapy money down the toilet?"

"Hey," Ben flared, "I'm a lot better than I used to be. We don't sleep with the lights on anymore, right?"

"Why don't I just slip downstairs and get a drink while the two of you work this out?" Carrillen said abruptly. She gave each of their ears one more lick. "Save something for me." And then she was gone.

The moment she was out of earshot, Lucia said, "Dad? I don't even want to know."

"It worked." Ben got up and checked the hallway. Empty. Music and party sounds continued to filter up from the area below. Ben put his hand in his pocket and activated the transceiver. "There. In fifteen seconds that camera will show an empty hallway for five minutes. Let's get out of camera range so we don't seem to just disappear."

They strolled to the staircase as Ben quietly counted off the time. He had just reached fifteen when Lucia grabbed his elbow with a sharp hiss.

"He's coming early," she said.

Sure enough, Ken Jeung was heading for the stairs with Tour-rif-na. Several of her arms were around him.

As one, Ben and Lucia turned and strode quickly down the corridor. The moment they left the line of sight of the party below, they broke into a run. Lucia reached the door across from the Palace Room, a set of picklocks already in hand. Ben resisted the impulse to tell her to hurry. It would take less than a minute for Jeung to reach the top of the stairs and then maybe another ten seconds to reach the end of the hallway. Lucia swore, then yanked off her right glove and went back to work.

"Come on, come on," she muttered. Her tiny computer stylus made a buzzing sound.

Ben thought he caught the sound of a man's laughter from the stairs. He was tensing to do something—anything—when Lucia said, "Got it!"

Without hesitation Ben dove into the room beyond, shut the door, and locked it. Lucia, he knew, would simply stroll down the hallway past Jeung and Tour-rif-na as if she had just left one of the other rooms. He hoped she remembered to grab her glove.

Ben glanced around, looking for a hiding place, and saw that the Garden Room lived up to its name. Potted shrubs, plants, and even trees were everywhere. An enormous whirlpool bath took up one corner, and an ivy-twined bed occupied another. The place was a mélange of spicy smells. One door led to a room with strange plumbing facilities, and Ben assumed that was Tour-rif-na's bathroom. Another door opened into a walk-in closet filled with a variety of outfits, all for humans. There were even half a dozen human space suits. This confused Ben for a moment—did he have the wrong room?—until he remembered that Tour-rif-na didn't seem to wear clothing. These must be costumes for clients who desired them. This made the closet a bad place to hide—Jeung might decide to play spaceman.

Heart still thudding in his chest, Ben checked the bed. Plenty of space underneath. He rolled under it just as the door began to open. Forcing himself to breathe quietly, Ben watched Jeung's and Tour-rif-na's feet—she had three stumpy ones—move into the room. They were talking in low voices.

"But you tremble so," Tour-rif-na said. "I have never had someone so eager. We have an entire hour. We can enjoy ourselves."

Ben grimaced. Thank heavens the floor under the bed was carpeted and free of dust. If he had to spend an hour down here, at least he wouldn't get sore from a wooden floor or have to suppress a sneeze every few seconds. Now he only had to hope the new copycat would work. He didn't feel the same confidence he had shown Kendi. There had been no way to field-test the thing, and it was a rare event for anything electronic to hit the ground running. There were always bugs. Ben had spent hours going over the thing, looking for potential problems, but it was impossible to know for certain if it would work or not until he actually tried it.

Jeung spoke again, his voice too low and husky for Ben to catch the words, and a shirt dropped to the floor. Jeung's feet kicked their shoes off and he stepped out of his trousers. A few moments later, Ben presumed he was naked.

"What is this around your neck, my fine one?" Tour-rif-na said.

"I can't take that off," Jeung said.

"But I am afraid. What metal is the chain?"

"Silver."

Tour-rif-na made a small hissing noise. "The oils I

secrete for pleasure react badly to that metal. Together, oil and silver will permanently discolor your skin and mine. If you cannot remove it, perhaps we should find another soul who—"

"No," Jeung replied quickly. "The door is locked, isn't it?"

"Indeed."

"Then it should be all right." With a slight clink, both silver chain and small, cylindrical key dropped onto the pile of clothing mere centimeters from Ben's right hand. Ben let out a noiseless sigh. Gretchen had done a good job persuading Tour-rif-na to play her part in their "bet." He prayed the copycat would let him do his.

"You wish to use the bath?" Tour-rif-na said.

Ben waited until he heard splashing and quiet moans from the direction of the whirlpool before snaking a hand out and grabbing Jeung's key. He eased the copycat out of his pocket and touched its data port to the key.

Nothing happened.

More splashing, and Jeung let out a harsh gasp. "What did you do?"

"Do you wish that I do it again?"

Ben clamped his lips together and pressed the key to the data port again. Still nothing. A crick started in his neck from holding his head off the floor. God, what had he overlooked? Whatever it was, he had to find a way to fix it under the bed without being noticed by Jeung. Ben set the key down—

—and realized he was trying to download the codes into the transceiver instead of the copycat. In the dim light under the bed he had gotten them mixed up. Cursing himself, he drew the copycat from his pocket. With stopped breath, he tried again.

Red lights flicked on the copycat, then flashed green. Download complete. Ben heaved a noiseless sigh of relief that went all the way down to the soles of his feet. He listened a moment to ensure the splashing in the tub was continuing apace before setting the key back on the pile of Jeung's clothing. Strange smells wafted toward him, and he figured they must be the oils Tour-rif-na secreted. Ben settled back under the bed to wait Jeung out, trying to keep pictures of him and Tour-rif-na out of his head.

A soft chime sounded, and Gretchen woke slowly and languidly. Every muscle in her body felt completely relaxed, as if she had just had a good workout followed by a hot soak and a thorough massage. Zem was still wrapped gently around her in a soft cocoon of safety. Gretchen closed her eyes, supposing she should feel guilty but refusing to do so. After everything she had been through in the last six months, she deserved an hour of sensual delight and relaxation. Then the cocoon abruptly vanished as Zem unfolded.

"Apologies," Zem said, "but your time is nearly over."

Gretchen bolted upright, suddenly remembering she wasn't quite through with the evening. "What time is it?"

"Ten minutes before eight o'clock," Zem replied.

Gretchen scrambled to her feet. "I'm really thirsty. Is there—"

"There is a bar near the door. Help yourself to whatever you like. Did I do something to upset you?"

"No, not at all," Gretchen said. She grabbed a small glass from the bar, wiped it with a napkin, and half-filled the glass with sparkling water, careful to hold the glass at the bottom. "Zem, that was wonderful. Perhaps I'll . . . come back."

"I will be here for the foreseeable future," Zem replied, "and please let Lady Kellyn know you enjoyed yourself."

"I will," Gretchen said, suddenly shy. "I will."

She let herself out of Zem's room. The corridor was empty. Gretchen stood there a moment, as if lost in thought but actually trying to hear sounds from the Garden Room, where Jeung had gone with Tour-rif-na. Nothing. The doors were probably sound-proofed. Gretchen stood there as long as she dared—Ben's fake photo would have long since vanished from the security system, and loitering on camera might arouse suspicion. Finally Gretchen walked slowly away, still holding the glass. She had gone only a few steps across the plush hall carpet when the Garden Room door opened and Ken Jeung emerged with Tour-rif-na. Gretchen ignored them as she continued up the hallway, though she knew they were coming behind her. She could smell Tour-rif-na's earthy scent. When Gretchen reached the landing to the marble staircase, she made a tiny gasp of annoyance and bent awkwardly. Jeung and Tour-rif-na caught up with her.

"Hey, could you hold this a second?" Gretchen said to Jeung, and thrust her glass into his hand. Jeung took it reflexively and Gretchen pretended to adjust her shoe. Then she thanked him and took the glass back, again careful to hold it by the bottom. Jeung nodded, said good-bye to Tour-rif-na, and trotted down the staircase. Out of the corner of her eye, Gretchen saw Ben emerge from the Garden Room. This was actually the riskiest part of the game. It was possible the computer or the person in charge of the security cameras would notice that Jeung had not gone into the Garden Room with a friend. Ben moved quickly but not hurriedly down the hall. Tour-rif-na turned to Gretchen.

"He removed the chain," she said as Ben passed behind her and down the stairs. "I believe that means you will win the bet."

"It does," Gretchen said, "but only if I can trick him into doing two more things. So if you see him again, don't mention the chain to him." Gretchen gave her a fifty-freemark coin.

"I will not," Tour-rif-na said. "But I hope you will let me know the outcome. I am very curious about this part of human culture."

Gretchen laughed. "I'll keep you posted."

Tour-rif-na said she had to ready herself for another client and went back to her room. Gretchen looked down at the party below just in time to see Ben exit with Lucia on his arm. That was everyone. Gretchen wrapped the little glass in the napkin, slipped it into her pocket, and headed for the door. Just before departing, she stopped at the pudgy maître d's podium.

"I had a fine time with Zem," she said. "Worth every freemark and more."

"I will tell Lady Kellyn," he said. "And we hope to see you again, madam."

Gretchen exited the brothel into the swirling noise of FunSec and caught up with Ben and Lucia a few blocks later. She gave Lucia the glass.

"There should be a good thumbprint on it," she said. "The security in that place is a joke. Ben walked right out of Tour-rif-na's room and security never even noticed."

"They aren't expecting major trouble, especially in the pleasure rooms," Ben said with a shrug. "Why spend the money for high-power security when you don't need it?"

"So how'd you like being under Jeung's bed?" Gretchen asked. "Get any jollies?"

Ben flushed. "Hardly. And they spent the whole time in the hot tub."

"How was *your* hour, Gretchen?" Lucia asked sweetly.

"Fine." Gretchen's tone was short.

"Just fine?" Lucia pressed. "No jollies of your own?"

"I said it was fine. Leave it, all right?"

"We should let Kendi know we got the key and the print," Ben interjected diplomatically. "That's where the real jollies are."

"One jolly down," Gretchen agreed, "three jollies to go."

The main door slid open, and Martina leaped to her feet. Delta Maura entered the room, her face wreathed in smiles.

"Greet the Dream, Alpha," she said. Her dark green robe and wimple rustled as she moved, and Martina noticed the white keycard hanging from her belt. "I have fine news for you!"

"What time is it?" Martina asked. A while after she had finished sketching, she had felt tired and had gone to bed. When she woke up, a meal of ham steak, one tiny baked potato, unsweetened tea, and a salad had been waiting for her in the dumbwaiter. How long had she been asleep? A few hours? All night? She couldn't tell. The holographic window was no help—it showed the same sun-drenched valley. There had to be a time display somewhere on the computer, but it had either been disabled or hidden so carefully that Martina, who was no hacker, couldn't find it.

"Measuring time is a human concern, Alpha," Maura said in a slight admonishment. "The Dream is eternal, and your dependence on breaking time down into hours and minutes is one of the impurities that Vik stained us with. The Chosen need to rise above that to become one of the Enlightened, as Irfan Qasad did."

"Are you one of the Enlightened, then?"

A serene smile. "Not yet. I'm only a Delta. But I have enough experience now to begin counseling Alphas like yourself. Enough of that, then—I said I have news for you."

"What would that be?" Martina was a slave, and

knew she was supposed to show proper respect to someone who was either her owner or someone who was higher up in the hierarchy, but Delta Maura had said there were no owners here, and Martina allowed a certain amount of sarcasm to creep into her voice.

"Dreamer Roon has consented to address you and the other Alphas." Delta Maura clasped her gloved hands in excitement. "Isn't that wonderful news?"

"I suppose," Martina replied uncertainly.

"You *suppose*?" Delta Maura said in obvious shock. "Dreamer Roon himself, the first Enlightened one to touch the Dream since Irfan Qasad, and you only *suppose* it's wonderful?"

Martina decided on the spot it would be best to play along. Slaves survived best by blending in, and, Delta Maura's words notwithstanding, Martina still wore shackles.

"Oh, it's wonderful news," she said, putting an awed look on her face. "I was just . . . startled that he would do such a thing. Talk to us Alphas, I mean. He wrote that very interesting book about the history of the Dream, didn't he?"

"You read it, then?"

"Part of it," Martina said. "He certainly has some fascinating theories."

"Fact, not theories," Maura chided gently. "Dreamer Roon doesn't need to postulate. He *knows*."

"Of course. Please forgive me. I'm still learning."

Delta Maura smiled her serene smile. "And we will teach you. Now into the tub. You must cleanse yourself before being admitted to the Dreamer's presence."

After a long bath—Delta Maura stood by to ensure that Martina scrubbed every inch of skin—Delta Maura dressed her in a hooded yellow tunic, loose trousers, gloves, and sandals. Martina's head was spinning with questions. Who had taken her away from DrimCom? If she wasn't supposed to be a slave, why couldn't she walk away free? What was the difference between an Alpha and a Delta? What did *Enlightened* mean in this place? Why did everyone wear gloves? But she kept her mouth shut. A lifetime of enslavement had taught her that, Silent or not, slaves were sometimes given only enough information to do their jobs, and asking too many questions could result in an angry owner who inflicted pain. Best to wait and see what she could learn by keeping eyes and ears open.

Once Martina was dressed, Delta Maura opened the door with her keycard. She hustled Martina out of the room and into a red-carpeted corridor faced with several other doors.

"Put up your hood and keep your eyes on the floor," Delta Maura instructed, "so that you don't meet the Dreamer's gaze by accident. Your impurity would taint his cleanliness."

Martina did as instructed, though it meant keeping a hand on Delta Maura's arm. The unfamiliar gloves still felt strange, muffling. Soft clothing and low voices rustled around her, and Martina became aware that she was part of a procession of people making their way down the corridor. She tried to sneak looks at her surroundings, but the hood allowed only a limited range of vision. All she could see was a circle of floor. The space around her widened enough to echo, then closed in again. The floor alternated between carpet, tile, and metal. Eventually, Delta Maura guided Martina into a kneeling position on a thin floor mat. She knelt, settling her loose clothes around her, and heard more rustlings as Delta Maura and the others apparently did the same. All Martina saw was the yellow fabric of her own trousers. The faint smell of incense hung in the air. Martina listened carefully. The noises around her were subdued, but she got the sense that between forty and fifty people occupied the room. Were they all Alphas paired with a Delta? Martina didn't know, but figured it was a good guess, which meant that there were probably twenty-odd Alphas in the group. All stolen from their owners? Or were any of them here voluntarily? The questions kept piling up.

Martina supposed she should be frightened or frustrated, but she had been sold four times now, and in many ways this was just another change in ownership. Eventually someone would tell her what was going on and she would be given work to do. Delta Maura, despite her strangeness, had so far been unfailingly polite and kind, if uninformative; the food was plentiful, her quarters luxurious. It was proving a pretty good position so far.

After a while, a hush settled over the room and Martina heard footsteps approaching. A voice from somewhere in front of her said, "Welcome, Alphas, and greet the Dream! I am Dreamer Edsard Roon, and I am here to help you find your Enlightenment!"

His voice was rich and powerful. Martina was itching to look up and see what he looked like, but she had been ordered to keep her eyes down.

"You have been rescued from your oppressors, the ones who corrupted and tainted you, the ones who prevent you from achieving true Enlightenment in the Dream. I know you are confused and uncertain, but everything will be explained in time. This is a place of love and trust, and you have nothing to fear here. Irfan has guided you here, and we shall guide you to Enlightenment."

He continued on for quite some time about how special they all were, all Chosen by Irfan Qasad, all above mere humanity. Martina supposed that meant everyone here was human—no aliens. Another scrap of information for the mix.

"We will instruct you in the Laws of Atash," Roon continued. "The first—that the Chosen must remove themselves from impure human society—was fulfilled when we brought you here. The second—that you must dedicate yourselves to purity of thought and deed—you will hear about later today. A demonstration of the third law will occur during this instruction, when you will learn the value of confessing your impurities to the Enlightened. To fulfill the fourth law, you must obey the Enlightened and all those designated as your superiors. They have been there ahead of you and know the way. Trust them. They know what they are doing and will help you join them one day."

He droned on, and Martina found herself only half listening. She needed to go to the bathroom and she felt hungry, despite the fact that she had just eaten. She wanted something starchy and sweet—cookies or perhaps cake. Her knees began to ache from kneeling on the thin mat, but when she started to shift position and sit down, a firm hand landed on her arm in a clear warning to remain still.

"Only Irfan Qasad escaped the foul taint of Daniel Vik," Roon was saying, "but that taint can be erased, and you will learn to enter the Dream freely, without use of drugs or trances, as Irfan did, and as I have learned to do."

That caught Martina's attention. Her ability to enter the Dream was enough to make her valuable, but she wasn't a high-class power. It usually took her an hour or more of self-induced trancing and a heavy dose of her drug cocktail to enter the Dream, and after the Despair there had been days when she couldn't enter it at all. She had heard that there were techniques the Silent could learn that would allow them to enter the Dream without drugs and with minimal trancing, but she had never met anyone who could do it.

Unfortunately, Roon didn't explain further. "You

will come to see that this place is your birthright, that
you belong here among those who love you and will
take care of your every need. Go with the Dream,
Alphas, and good day."

Martina wondered if she should applaud. The
room, however, remained silent, and she didn't
move. Her knees were in active pain now. Footsteps
moved away from the front of the chamber, and after
a moment a collective sigh went through the audience. Martina took that as a sign that she could
move, and she shifted into a sitting position. No one
stopped her. The relief was heavenly, though her
bladder ached.

"You may remove your hood now, Alpha," Delta
Maura said beside her. "Dreamer Roon has left the
room."

Martina pushed her hood back and blinked at the
room. It was a large, rounded chamber set up like a
small stadium, with tiered platforms leading down to
a raised stage, the place where Roon had presumably
been standing. Martina was sitting on the third tier,
which put her at a level with the stage. The tiers were
filled with, as she had surmised, about three dozen
people. Half were dressed in yellow tunics like Martina's—Alphas—and half were dressed in dark green
robes like Maura's—Deltas. The robed women wore
wimples and the men wore hoods. Everyone wore
gloves. Martina didn't see any nonhumans, and low
voices echoed softly as people talked among
themselves.

An Alpha on the tier just above and behind Maura
pushed back his hood and a spasm gripped Martina's
heart. The Alpha had dark skin and tightly curled
black hair and a face etched with depression and sorrow, but his eyes . . . his eyes were a bright, startling
blue. Martina stared. The Alpha stretched, and the
green-robed man next to him murmured something in
his ear.

Martina's heart pounded. It couldn't be. Could it? No one but her brother had eyes like that, and even though she hadn't seen them in fifteen years, Martina recognized them with utter certainty. She was about to call out when a hand grabbed her arm.

"Wasn't that wonderful?" Delta Maura said. "He's such an inspiration."

"Delta Maura, who is that?" Martina asked, pointing at the Alpha. He hadn't looked her way. "May I speak to him?"

Delta Maura shook her head. "Earning a name is part of becoming a Gamma, so you would call him 'Alpha.' The name he came here with is meaningless, as is yours. There is not time to speak just now—you're scheduled for confessional purification. We can't have those N-waves interfering with your personal growth, dear."

Martina considered dashing over to him, Delta Maura or no, but a lifetime of conditioned obedience interfered. An order was to be obeyed. Reluctantly, Martina got to her feet. Then she put a fist to her mouth and coughed loudly. Several people, including the Alpha, looked her way. Martina looked straight at him.

The Alpha's blue eyes widened in disbelief. *Martina?* he mouthed. Martina gave a tiny nod in return as tears filled her own eyes. He *was* her brother. After fifteen years, a part of her family was being returned to her.

"Do you need some water, dear?" Delta Maura asked at her elbow.

"No, thank you," Martina said, barely keeping her tone even.

"Then it's time to go."

As Delta Maura firmly led Martina out of the audience chamber, Martina silently decided that this place was looking better and better. She was sure once she explained what was going on that she would be allowed to speak with him. Dreamer Roon had said this was a place of love, and that meant they *had* to let her see her brother. They *had* to.

Didn't they?

CHAPTER SIX

"You may as well confess—we already know what you did."
—Ormand Clearwater, Bethlehem Colony

A triumphant roar went up from the crowd. Elena Papagos-Faye yelled with the best of them and leaned over the railing to peer down into the shallow gladiator pit, careful not to spill her drink. The person beside her, an auburn-haired man wearing a tight shirt that displayed an impressive build and tailored trousers that showed off some fine assets, pounded a fist on the rail. In the pit below, a six-legged, tanklike creature the size of a small horse finished pulling the arm off its hapless opponent. Black blood splashed over the arena floor and the opponent, a furry, fanged cross between a wolf and a human, howled in pain and fury. It bit and scratched, but claws and teeth got no purchase on the bony armor. The tank pushed the wolf creature toward a section of the floor that sat beneath a heavy metal weight. In the control booth that hovered over the pit, the losing owner shouted frantic instructions at the wolf creature, but blood loss was taking its toll and the creature's movements became jerky and spasmodic. The auburn-haired man shouted encouragement. Elena took another cold sip of her martini. The contest was thrilling, and so was the man.

For the last two days at the Pit, it seemed that no matter where she turned, the man was there—placing bets, shouting at the genegineered battlecreatures, and generally enjoying himself. She also noticed, however, that he didn't actually talk to much of anyone or seem to have any friends—at least, no friends that came to the Pit with him. He was a handsome bastard, too. His clothes and hair were immaculate, styled in the latest fashion. Elena was glad that the current mode favored tight clothes, and her own scarlet dress left little to the imagination. Elena herself was a couple centimeters taller than the man, with long black hair, dark eyes, and a longish nose.

Tonight, she decided. *I'll have him tonight.*

The crowd around the gladiator pit was easily two hundred strong. About half were human. The heavy metallic scent of blood mixed with smells of fried food and spilled alcohol. Bodies pressed around the railing to get a better look at the fight below, but no one seemed to mind the crush. Elena took her eyes off the man long enough to watch the end of the fight. The tank shoved the wolf beneath the weight, triggering a sensor. The weight dropped with a crash, squashing the wolf flat. The crunch sent a thrill through Elena's blood and elicited another roar from the crowd. The man yelled again and leaped back from the railing. His elbow hit Elena's arm, and her martini drenched the front of her outfit in cold gin. She gave a yelp of indignation and brushed frantically at herself.

"Oh, hell," the man said over the noisy crowd. "Geez, I'm sorry, ma'am."

Attraction turned to annoyance. "Idiot," she snapped. "Why don't you watch what you're doing?"

Below, the tank skittered triumphant circles around the pit, clutching the furry arm of its flattened adversary. The weight rose, revealing pulped remains, and a cleanup crew moved purposefully toward them. The crowd noise subsided into conversation, and several people headed back toward the betting area to cash in winnings.

"You should go to the bar and have that taken care of," the man said. "Let me help you. Please?"

Elena's anger abated somewhat at his meek tone. She had, after all, been looking for an excuse to talk to him, and he had literally dropped one on her.

The man solicitously took her elbow. She glared at him to let him know all was not forgiven, but allowed him to lead her through an open archway behind the crowd and into the restaurant-bar. The man got the barkeeper's attention and gestured at the spreading stain on Elena's dress.

"Cleanup, please?" he said. "And then get this lady anything she wants."

"You got it." The bartender, an enormously tall man with biceps big as footballs, caught up a spray bottle, leaned over the bar, and expertly misted the stain. It lightened, then vanished entirely. Elena's dress was perfectly dry. "What are you drinking, ma'am?"

"Oak and Ash," she said pointedly.

The man gave a small, embarrassed laugh. "Thirty-year-old Scotch. I'm that bad, am I? Look, I really am sorry. Can I buy you more than a drink? Something to eat, maybe?" A wide smile spread across his face, one that made him look endearingly boyish. God, he was gorgeous.

"All right," she said in a much nicer tone. "Dinner."

Elena caught up her new drink and swept toward an empty booth without looking to see if he was following her. She was already seated by the time he caught up with her and slid into the opposite seat.

"I'm Devin Reap," he said, extending his hand across the table.

"Elena Papagos-Faye." Her handshake was firm, and she pressed his hand a little longer than was necessary. Devin met her eyes with a meek little smile, then looked shyly away. Well. Gorgeous *and* pliable.

The restaurant kept the lights low. Its tables and booths were of dark, scarred wood. Gritty sawdust mixed with peanut shells underfoot, and a small tin pail of unshelled peanuts sat in the middle of the table. A pair of old-fashioned glass screens displayed the menu where the table met the wall. Another cheer went up from the crowd at the fighting pit beyond the arch, and Elena assumed another contest had begun.

"I really am sorry about the spill, Ms. Papagos-Faye," Devin said.

"It cleaned up just fine, Devin," she said. "Though I think I'm still in the mood for something expensive."

A pained look crossed Devin's face. "Not too expensive, I hope. I've had a run of bad luck with the gladiators lately."

"Oh? The way you were cheering in there, I thought you must have won."

"Not really. I was yelling at the loser because he let himself get squashed. What would you like for dinner?"

They leaned over the menu screen and Elena purposefully brushed her hand against Devin's. He blushed—actually *blushed*—and then casually moved his hand away. Elena burned with desire. She would have this Devin and she would definitely have him tonight.

Elena ordered first—prime rib, the second most expensive item on the menu—and Devin tapped in his own order—simple baked chicken.

"Do you bet much on the gladiators?" he asked.

"Not unless I know it's a sure thing," Elena replied. "And how often does that happen?"

Devin smiled. "Not often enough. So what do you do for a living?"

"I'm a department head for a special project within SA." She made circles with her glass on the table and looked at Devin through her eyelashes. "Very hush-hush. You?"

"Accountant, but I'm an independent contractor."

How boring. "Lucky you."

Devin shrugged. "Pay's lower, but yeah—SA doesn't have its claws in me."

"Does anyone else have their claws in you?" she asked with a small smile of her own.

Devin looked self-consciously down at his hands. "Not right now. You?"

"I prefer to put my claws into other people."

Their food arrived, and the inevitable small talk began. Elena found numerous reasons to touch Devin's hand or forearm during the meal. Twice her foot "accidentally" brushed his under the table. After the second time, Devin stopped pulling back, but the endearing blush that made her want to pull his clothes off him then and there continued to surface.

Around them, patrons of various species came and went. Regular shouts of triumph and groans of despair came from the arena. The table offered a tiny holographic display of the fights, and several times Devin looked longingly at the controls, but Elena deliberately didn't pick up on the hint and he didn't say anything. Good.

Throughout their meal, she let slip a few hints about the Collection. Nothing that would get her into trouble, but enough to impress a little contract accountant whose yearly fee was probably less than what Elena made in ten minutes. She imagined him living in a hole-in-the-wall apartment with three roommates so he could spend his money on clothes and bet on genegineered gladiators.

"So, exactly what's this project about?" Devin asked, leaning forward in fascination. "Sounds like it's big-time stuff."

"Top secret, I'm afraid," she said with a knowing wink. "But it's big. When it finishes, you'll be hearing about it in every corner of the universe. I guarantee it."

He pressed for more details like a puppy looking

for attention. She allowed it until she grew tired of evasive answers and cut off further questions with a sharp retort. He immediately fell into a docile silence and Elena changed the subject. Eventually the meal ended and Devin, once more apologizing about her dress, paid the check.

"Why don't you come back to my place for a drink?" she said, knowing what the answer would be. Already she could imagine what it would be like to have him lying beneath her, to run her hands over that hard frame, to listen to him moan and beg for the release that she would give only when she was ready for him to have it.

"Oh, geez, thanks, but I . . . I can't."

Elena stared. "You can't," she repeated, stupefied.

"I had a great time, though," Devin said, rising quickly from the table and handing her a small datachip. "Here's a com-link code where you can reach me. I hope you'll call. I'd really like to see you again."

And then he was gone.

Elena stared after him in a disbelief laced with a dollop of avarice. *No* one turned her down. Not the men she chose, not Silent Acquisitions, not even Edsard Roon. Not only would Devin Reap beg to come to her bed, he would become enamored of her, fall in love with her. And then, just to show him who was in charge, she would toss him aside.

Elena Papagos-Faye pulled out her data pad, activated the holographic screen, and started a background check on Devin Reap.

"Come on, you can't keep me here forever," Todd lamented.

"You know, Isaac, the beauty of that statement is not only that it is false, but that you so clearly *know* it is false," Harenn replied. "I can do anything to you I like. I can hang you upside down from the ceiling and make a thousand little cuts all over your body that will kill you only after many hours of bleeding. I can give you drugs that will drag every darkness from your head and make each one real for you. I can hire a gang of men to come into this room and beat you and rape you until you wish you had died. All these things I can do, and there is nothing you can do to stop me."

Todd abruptly lunged for Harenn, but the moment he came within a meter of her body, his silvery slave bands snapped and sparked with a blue glow. Todd fell to his knees, moaning in pain. Harenn watched impassively until, gasping, he got to his feet and backed away from her. The *Poltergeist* had no brig, so Kendi had put him in a set of windowless quarters that Ben and Lucia had gone over. There was nothing in the little room that Todd could use to communicate with anyone outside the ship. He had no computer access, and Lucia had installed extra-stubborn locks on the door. Todd's slave bands were programmed to shock him if he crossed the threshold or approached any member of the crew too closely. His only entertainment was a set of bookdisks. Harenn knew she should leave him alone, that solitary confinement was a terrible punishment in and of itself, but Isaac Todd was like a bad tooth. She couldn't help probing it, even though it caused her pain.

"You're a vindictive bitch," he spat.

"You made me into one, Isaac," Harenn said. She was leaning with her back against the door. "You taught me that not even love can be trusted, that anything and everything you have can be taken away at a single stroke. You taught me not to trust my own judgment. You taught me that pain and sorrow can come from any direction, even from someone who loves you. And now you are reaping the benefits of my lessons. Doesn't that make you happy?"

"So you just come in here to torture me?" Todd

plunked down onto the tiny room's only chair. "I wonder if Bedj-ka would like seeing this side of his
mother."

Harenn took a step toward Todd, and he scrambled
out of the chair so he could back away.

"Ever the manipulator," she said. "Still trying to
make me question myself. Still trying to make me
miserable."

"Listen, Harenn," Todd said, holding up his hands
in a gesture of placation, "I never set out to hurt you.
It was just a business thing, nothing personal. Besides,
it's not like you'd had Bedj-ka long enough to form a
real attachment or anything."

Harenn's eyes flashed. "Which do you like better,
Isaac, bread or cheese?"

"Why?" he asked warily.

"Because for the next several days you are going to
have only those two things to eat, and a random one
of them will contain a powerful emetic. Choose wisely
which you consume, my husband. If you choose
wrong, the results will be entertaining."

With that, she turned and left the room. Gretchen
was standing in the corridor outside.

"I overheard part of that," she said, falling into step
beside Harenn. "It's not healthy, you know."

Harenn bristled. "Are you going to tell me how to
run my life?"

"I didn't say you shouldn't do it," Gretchen said
with a wolfish grin. "Everyone needs bad habits. After
seeing the L. L. Venus farm, though, I've lost my
chocolate vice. Maybe I can pick up a new one tortur-
ing prisoners. Need any help?"

Harenn looked at Gretchen, uncertain whether the
other woman was joking or not. "No, thank you," she
said at last.

"So what *are* we going to do with him, anyway?"
Gretchen asked. They were heading toward the galley.

"No matter what you might want, we can't shove him out an air lock, and it'd be a royal pain in the ass to keep him around forever."

"I have given the matter little thought," Harenn said. "I have the impression Kendi has something in mind, but he won't say what."

"Have you told Bedj-ka who he is?"

Harenn shook her head. "And I don't know if I will. What good would it do him?"

"He may find out on his own."

"Not if I can prevent it."

Father Kendi Weaver stared at the holographic display above his data pad without really seeing it. He knew it was pointless to worry about things that were beyond his control, but he couldn't help it. He worried about what was happening to Utang and Martina. He worried about running out of time. He worried about Silent Acquisitions discovering the team's connection with the Children. He worred about the Children of Irfan fading away. And through it all, he had to keep a calm demeanor.

Kendi wasn't used to keeping his emotions under control, except when he was trancing for the Dream or playing a role during a rescue mission. The people around him usually knew when he was angry or happy, frustrated or joyful, and that was fine with Kendi. It was a trait that sometimes exasperated Ara, who often said that while forthrightness was indeed a virtue, tact and subtlety had their places as well. She had held up Irfan Qasad's famed serenity as an example. But Kendi had still preferred to wear his heart on his sleeve.

Now things were different.

Now he was in charge of a crew of people who looked to him for command decisions. He had to come up with plans and strategies, and figure out who would be the best person to implement them. He had to keep a calm expression at all times, since an agitated Father would upset his Children.

At least here in his and Ben's quarters, he didn't have to hide the fact that he was worried. A dozen things could go wrong with the current plan. Elena Papagos-Faye could figure out "Devin Reap" wasn't a real person. She might not be attracted to him, and Kendi would have to come up with a brand-new angle. She might actually entice Ben into bed with her.

Kendi snorted. Absurd. Ben would never do such a thing. Sure, Kendi knew Ben had been involved with women, and he had a suspicion that one such affair had been serious. Kendi had never asked. After all, they'd been on-again, off-again for years and hadn't become a permanent couple until just before the Despair. It wasn't any of Kendi's business what Ben had done during their off-again times. But Ben wouldn't go for a woman now. The very idea was ridiculous.

Even if the woman was beautiful. And wealthy. And sophisticated. And powerful. And—

And just shut up, he told himself.

The door slid open and Kendi looked up. A man with stylishly cut auburn hair and a tight green shirt that exactly matched his eyes entered the living room. Relief flooded Kendi. He wanted to snatch Ben into a ferocious hug, scoop him off the ground, and sweep him into the bedroom. He resisted the urge. For one thing, Ben weighed more than Kendi could safely lift.

"All life, you look incredible," he observed instead. "We should turn Harenn loose on you more often. So how'd it go, Mr. Reap?"

Ben sighed and dropped onto the couch next to Kendi. "Those poor Pit animals. It makes me want to throw up."

"What about Papagos-Faye?"

"She's worse. Every time that woman looks at me, I feel like a side of beef hanging on a hook. When I turned her down, I thought she was going to bop me over the head and drag me home by the hair. God. She makes me go all cold inside." He shuddered.

See? Told you it was a stupid idea.

"Lucia did say Papagos-Faye likes to win," Kendi said aloud. "And that she likes to own things. Between Lucia's shadowing and your computer snooping, we got a pretty good profile on her. You probably surprised the hell out of her by turning her down."

"She's already run a background check on me," Ben said, tapping the side of his head. "My implant warned me that someone checked the files I inserted into SA's consultant records. So now she knows that Devin Reap is single, has no kids, hasn't gotten any consulting work in a while, and is the sort-of survivor of a terrible disaster."

"Good. We still need her key." A wash of emotion crossed Kendi's face and he made no attempt to hide it as he glanced involuntarily toward the window. The module that housed the Collection protruded from the station wall only a few hundred meters away. He had never been so close to his family and yet still so far away. He wondered what they looked like, what their voices sounded like. It had been over fifteen years since the three of them had run through the broken streets of Sydney, but he still remembered with perfect clarity the games they had played together. Decrepit, abandoned houses became pirate ships and smuggler caves. Graffiti became sacred Aboriginal writings. Chunks of broken glass became opals of immeasurable value, treasures that needed to be hidden from the mutant whites who wanted to take them away and enslave the Aboriginal people. As children, they had no idea that Australian history would repeat itself in deep space.

"You're missing them again, aren't you?" Ben asked.

"Yeah." More emotions rose and Kendi set his jaw

against them. "I want them *out*, Ben. And more than that—I want the bastard who brought them there punished. Todd said that the Collection was all Edsard Roon's idea, his program, his everything. I want him to suffer for that. I can't get the slavers that broke my family up, but I can get Roon. I want him to lose everything, just like I lost everything, like Martina and Utang lost everything."

"I don't blame you." Ben put a gentle arm around Kendi. "But you may have to be content with just getting them out. Edsard Roon has all of SA's resources working for him, and we only have the resources of this one ship. If they catch us in any of this, every one of us, including Bedj-ka, will quietly disappear into the recycling vats or into the Collection itself."

"I've been thinking about that," Kendi said, leaning into Ben's embrace. "Maybe we should find a way to send Harenn and Bedj-ka back to Bellerophon, get them out of the way in case something goes wrong."

"Harenn won't go for it. She still feels guilty about saving Bedj-ka first. She wants to see everything through, make sure you find your family."

Kendi sighed. Ben was right—Harenn would hate the idea of being sent back home, but to ensure the safety of her son, he should order her to go. The problem was, he needed Harenn's skills and was afraid he wouldn't be able to rescue Martina and Utang without her.

There was another factor as well. Kendi was adult enough to admit that, despite all his assurances to the contrary, he was damned angry at Harenn. He knew it was irrational, that there was no way for either of them to have known that rescuing Bedj-ka first had been a mistake, that if they *had* known, Harenn would have been the first to insist that they go after Martina and Utang right away. All this his head knew. The trouble was, his emotions weren't listening. Did he really need Harenn's skills that badly, or was he keeping her around out of spite? He wasn't entirely sure.

"I should go change," Ben said, letting Kendi go and starting to get up. Kendi caught his arm and stopped him.

"Why? You look amazing, Ben. Green eyes suit you. So does the darker hair. And the clothes."

Ben's face reddened but he didn't object when Kendi pulled him back onto the couch. Kendi sat on Ben's lap, facing him, and kissed him hard. Kendi felt his own desire rise. He wanted to be close to Ben, feel his body moving against his own. His hands moved behind Ben and pulled the other man closer with an ardor that surprised both of them. A maelstrom whirled around Kendi—love, desire, fear, anger, helplessness, frustration, joy. He had been holding it all for so long, and he focused everything into a single, powerful kiss. When they parted, Ben was panting.

"What's this all about?" he asked.

Kendi wanted to tell him, but it was all such a tangle that he couldn't find the words. He wanted to merge with Ben, become a single person, never be apart from him again. But all he could say was, "I don't want you to start getting ideas about Papagos-Faye."

"No fear of that."

"Let's make absolutely sure."

Elena Papagos-Faye drummed her fingers on the cheap tabletop of the Pit restaurant with ill-disguised impatience. Devin Reap was a mystery, an enigma. His consultant file with SA was annoyingly brief. He had been on the station for only a few months. Before that he had worked books for a passenger ship named the *Merry Widow,* but it had apparently gone into slipspace just before the Despair hit and had never come back. Devin Reap had, by sheer chance, not been aboard because he had been taking a two-week vacation. That was all. Because he was a consultant who didn't work with classified equipment or software, SA didn't keep an extensive background file on him. It didn't even list where he lived—just a com-link code identical to the one he had given her. A high-level check with Domestic hadn't turned up an address, but that wasn't unusual—Reap was likely pirating quarters with someone. It was a common scam. SA partly based its rents on the number of people living in a given place, so two people who officially shared an apartment would one day come home to a rent hike, wiping out the main reason for putting up with cramped living quarters in the first place.

The fact that Elena couldn't learn more about Devin made him even more intriguing. Elena was someone who made her living manipulating information and data, and not having much information on this guy tantalized her. He certainly hadn't volunteered much about himself last night during their second date at the Pit.

Elena smiled, remembering. Their time together yesterday had been filled with entendres that varied from double to quintuple. They had placed some bets and cheered the gladiators together, and Elena had used the latter activity as an excuse to rub up against him in the press of spectators. Devin seemed to be receptive during the entire thing, even flashed her a shy, boyish smile when her hand stole down into a more . . . private area. But when the Pit closed down for the evening, he had thanked her for a fun time, given her a quick peck on the cheek, and vanished.

She checked the time on her ocular implant. He was three minutes late. This was their third date in as many nights—if you counted their first meeting as a date—and Elena had decided that tonight she would get him into bed if she had to put him in chains. And wasn't that a lovely thought? Watching those muscles of his strain against the metal, hearing him cry and

beg as she held back from the one thing that he
wanted. That all men wanted.

"What are you thinking about?" a familiar voice
asked. Devin slid into the seat across from her in what
they had already come to refer to as "their" booth at
the Pit. The fights hadn't yet started, and the place
was quiet.

"You," she replied. "You're late, you know. I'll
make you pay for that."

"I'm sorry," he said contritely. "What can I do to
make it up to you?"

His tone was absolutely serious, with no trace of
innuendo. His wide green eyes suddenly filled with
tension, as if he were afraid she really was angry. God,
he was so wonderfully malleable.

"I'll think of something," she murmured, and slid
her foot up his calf.

He gave that shy smile that made her burn inside.
"Have you ordered yet?"

They called for drinks and Devin asked her how
work had gone that day.

"Well, I can't talk about much," she said. "Just
about everything I do is classified over there. You
know, Devin, I could probably get you a job within
my project. Something on the periphery. You said you
haven't been offered any work in, what, a week?
Two?"

"Yeah. The post-Despair recession. There isn't
much work for us independents, with SA laying off its
regular workers left and right. I have some savings,
but they're going fast."

"Play your cards right with me, and I can get you
something more permanent. And higher paying."
Elena gave him a long look over her glass. "You won't
have to pirate living space with someone else
anymore."

Fear filled his face. "How did you—I mean, I'm not—"

"You don't have to worry, Devin," she said, patting

his hand. So her theory had been correct. "I won't tell anyone your little secret. If you keep me happy, that is."

"I'll do my best," he said, still shy. "I like you a lot, Elena. You're smart and beautiful and . . . and sexy." The last word made him blush furiously.

She leaned across the table and stroked his well-muscled forearm. "Then why don't we go back to my place and discuss . . . new positions?"

"But the fights haven't even started yet," he said. "I mean, that Leeland guy is supposed to have his new gladiator up tonight. Everyone's talking about it. And we haven't eaten yet."

He looked a little scared. Too much too fast? Elena wasn't sure. She decided to back away, get a couple of drinks into him. A little tip to the bartender would make sure his drinks contained more than the usual amount of alcohol, though she didn't want him *too* drunk.

"Of course," she said. "Anticipation only makes it better."

They talked about nothing in particular as the Pit filled up and the first fights began. They watched a few on the in-house holographic display, and Devin pounded the table during the good parts. Elena watched in fascination. He was normally so quiet, but the gladiator fights seemed to bring out the screamer within. She wondered if it was the same for him in the bedroom.

After their dinners arrived, Elena asked, "So tell me about the *Merry Widow*."

Devin paused with his fork halfway to his mouth. "The *Widow*?"

"Your ship," she said. "You were supposed to be on board when it left port but you decided to take a last-minute vacation instead. Lucky for you."

He set the fork down, food untasted. "Yeah. Lucky."

"Tell me about it," she commanded.

"What's there to tell?" His eyes stared across the room at nothing. "I worked on the books, kept the payroll people happy. The *Widow* made a regular shuttle run for passengers and cargo around the Five Green Worlds. I decided I needed a break, so I sat the last one out on Klimkinnar. Then the Despair hit and the *Widow* never came out of slipspace. Someone on the crew probably went . . . you know . . . and that was the end of it."

"You had a lot of friends on board," she said. "And someone special?"

"I—I don't—"

"Tell me," she ordered again.

"Yeah," he whispered, voice barely audible. "I was going to ask her to marry me when she got back. I took the vacation time so I could shop for a ring."

How cute. And trite. Elena sat back in her seat, wondering what would happen if she ordered him to get up and do a cartwheel. "That's why you're not so sure you want to get involved with me, isn't it?"

"Don't get me wrong, Elena," he said quickly. "I like you a lot. I'm just not completely sure of everything yet."

"Perhaps I can firm things up for you."

They finished dinner in time to make their way to the Pit for the new Leeland gladiator. They tried to worm their way to the railing, but the cheering crowd was simply too thick. Snarls and howls rose from the fighting arena.

"Let's forget this and go back to my place," she shouted in Devin's ear. "It's too crowded."

"I want to try again," he yelled back. "Maybe I can muscle a place up front for the two of us."

Elena made an exasperated sound that was completely swallowed up by the noise of the crowd. "I need to go to the ladies' room," she snarled.

"Okay. I'll try to get closer."

Elena headed toward the human rest rooms, furious. What was it going to take? He was emotionally vulnerable, probably horny as hell by now, and thought she was sexy. It was infuriating.

She used one of the toilet stalls and headed for the mirrors to check her face. A few other women were there as well, including two who were obviously friends. Both went in for heavy rouge and eyeliner, and their hairdos ran toward big and tacky. Definitely low on the social scale. Elena was about to brush past them without a second glance when one of them said something that caught her attention.

"It's a male date-rape drug," the first woman was saying. She had improbably blond hair and her dress showed plenty of cleavage. "He'll give you anything you want, and I mean *anything*."

"Really?" The second woman, a redhead, seemed skeptical.

"No joke. Hey, I work for bioengineering, and this is the real stuff. It gives women a slight buzz, but it makes men both horny and pliant. Something about the Y chromosome." She held up a vial of clear liquid with a giggle. "And the stuff keeps him hard as a *rock*. God, honey, he'll do whatever you want, and for *hours*. None of this in-and-out-and-done bullshit. It's the greatest invention for women since the hands-free vibrator. You have to try it on Rick."

"It really works?"

"Oh, yeah. Here, honey. Just try it. What have you got to lose, right?"

The other women in the rest room had drifted out. Intrigued, Elena edged closer to the two friends. "Excuse me," she said. "I couldn't help overhearing. Is that stuff for real?"

The vial vanished into the blond woman's pocket. "Is what for real?"

"I heard you talking about that new drug," Elena said. "Is it for real?"

The woman's nostrils flared. Elena saw dark roots poking through the blond dye job. "Are you with Security or something? Listen, I was just joking around when I said—"

"No, nothing like that," Elena said impatiently. "Look, if that stuff's for real, I'll buy some."

"We should probably get out of here, Marlene," the redhead said.

"Is it for real?" Elena persisted. "I've got cash right here."

"It's for real," Marlene said cautiously. "I'm a secretary over in bio-enj, and one of the researchers owed me a . . . a favor. This stuff is so new, it doesn't even have a name."

Elena licked her lips. It would be perfect. Devin would be hers for the taking. She decided on the spot she had to get her hands on some of the stuff, whatever it was.

"I'll pay you a hundred SA chits for a dose," she said.

"No way," Marlene scoffed. "I only have two doses left. If I give one to Shirley here, that's only one left for me."

"Two hundred chits."

"Honey, you must think I'm crazy. My boyfriend's the best he's ever been when he's on this stuff, and I'm looking forward to some hot action tonight with him. It's not for sale."

"I'll give you fifty freemarks."

Marlene looked startled. "Hard cash?"

"Hard as diamonds." She held up a wad of plastic bills. Marlene eyed it with undisguised greed. SA paid most of its employees in company chits, which were spendable only on SA station, and a fair number of employees discovered that their salaries weren't quite enough to make ends meet after paying SA for rent, food, clothes, and other necessities. SA rarely had problems retaining its workers as a result. Only certain employees were able to specify a salary paid in freemarks, and Elena, of course, was one of them.

"Come on, Marlene," Shirley said, plucking at Marlene's sleeve. "I don't like this. Let's get out of here before Security shows up."

Marlene kept her eyes on the money. "It's all right, Shirl. Listen, hon, maybe I could sell you a dose but . . ." She hesitated and Elena forced herself not to fidget. Then Marlene shook her head. "I don't know. This stuff's hard to get, and who knows when I'll be able to get my hands on some more? Plus, my boyfriend's a real minuteman, if you get my drift. I don't think I can give this up. Sorry."

The chance was slipping away. Recklessly, Elena yanked more bills from her pocket. "I'll give you a hundred freemarks. That has to be, what, a month's rent for you?"

Marlene wavered again. "I—I don't—"

"Marlene, come *on*," Shirley whined. "This is really making me nervous. She's gotta be Security."

"A hundred and twenty," Elena insisted. "That's all I have on me. Come on, help me out, here."

"Well . . ." After an achingly long moment, she finally held out the vial. Elena handed over the money and all but snatched the little bottle from Marlene's carefully manicured hand. A thin smile crossed Elena's face. Devin would learn what it meant to say no to her; he would, indeed.

Now that the deal was done, Marlene seemed to lose her earlier reticence. "Using the stuff's a little tricky, hon," she said. "It has a strong smell, so you can't just slip it in his drink—he'll notice. You have to persuade him to take it on purpose instead. I put some in both our drinks and tell my boyfriend we'll get a little high together. It doesn't affect women much—just gives us a little buzz—but it'll be different for him; you just wait. Best part is, when it wears off, your boyfriend'll think the whole 'do as I say' sex thing was *his* idea."

Elena grinned. "Sounds perfect. Thanks."

"Don't mention it," Marlene said, turning back toward the mirror to examine her lipstick. "And I mean that."

Elena left the rest room, the tight smile still on her lips. She found Devin in the press around the Pit, obviously still unable to find a way closer to their favored spot at the railing. The little vial in her hand gleamed like a diamond. *If no one will give you what you want, sometimes you just have to take it.*

"I can't get closer," he complained over the noise.

She took his arm and pulled him away. "Come on," she yelled. "I have a better idea." He let her lead him away from the Pit and out the door into the street corridor. Vehicles buzzed by and the lights of FunSec glittered and swirled around them. Humans and nonhumans walked, lurched, crawled, and scampered up and down the sidewalk. Overhead, the lattice of walkways swarmed with beings.

"We're going back to my place now," she said in a voice that brooked no argument. "It's time you moved on, Devin. Besides, we have to discuss your new position, remember?"

"Elena, I don't—"

"*Now,* Devin," she snapped.

"All right." His voice was meek again.

With a triumphant smile, Elena flagged down a cab. Men like Devin Reap wanted to be given orders, wanted to obey. She probably could have gotten him faster if she had simply ordered him to come along with her in the first place.

During the cab ride, she gave him gentle, careful caresses. The feel of hard muscle under her questing hands was an incredible turn-on, especially when she

knew that soon he'd do anything she said, anything at
all. For his part, Devin kept his eyes down. Once he
shyly touched her knee but otherwise kept his hands
to himself. When they arrived, Elena paid the driver
and led Devin to her front door, which was set into
an anonymous row of similar doors. She opened two
locks, pressed her thumb against a pressure plate, and
opened the door.

Elena, of course, ranked a great deal of space. She
had five rooms to herself, all of them with extrava-
gantly high ceilings and a wide expanse of floor. The
furnishings were simple and minimal, to further em-
phasize this latter quality. Elena's quarters also had
large windows that looked out into deep space, though
she could change them into holographic scenes of anything she wished. Devin looked around, obviously
awed.

"Clarence," she said, "deactivate interior security
cameras."

"Acknowledged," replied the computer.

"Wow." Devin whistled. "You could put three of
my apartment in just this living room."

"I'm not head of information services at my project
for nothing," she said. "Will you excuse me for just
a moment?"

Without waiting for a response, she went into the
bathroom, which was as spacious as the rest of her
quarters, and removed her access key from the hidden
pocket on the inside of her belt. Elena herself had
written the security protocols that demanded Roon
and the department heads keep their access keys on
their persons at all times, and if anyone *did* remove a
key, it had to be hidden in a secret place. Elena had
no direct control over the other two department
heads, and Roon had explicitly ignored her advice
about not installing a Collection terminal in his home,
but Elena could make damn sure her own key was

safe. She certainly wasn't going to show the key to Devin, or leave it unmonitored in his presence, not even if he was about to be drugged out of his mind.

Elena opened the medicine cabinet above the sink and pressed a hidden switch. A small door in the back of the cabinet slid open, revealing a space just big enough for her key. She set it inside, closed the compartment, flushed the toilet, and went back into the living room. Devin was sitting on the couch, nervously drumming his fingers on his knees. He jumped to his feet when she entered the room.

"I was thinking," he said, "that I should probably be going. You have to work tomorrow, and I shouldn't—"

"Just stay right where you are," she said, heading for the bar and uncorking a bottle of champagne. "You can't leave without having at least one drink." She filled two glasses and dosed them both liberally from the little vial while Devin fidgeted nervously. He was so cute when he did that, so innocent-looking. Could he be a virgin? Wouldn't *that* be a kick!

The lighting was low, and Elena ordered the computer to put on some soft music. Then she brought the champagne flutes over to him. A sharp smell issued from the bubbling liquid.

"What is this?" Devin asked as she handed him one.

"Champagne," she said, "laced with a little something to give us both a hit."

"A drug?" he asked, looking doubtfully at the flute.

"I'm taking it, too," she purred. "It's meant to enhance our pleasure."

"Well . . ." He wavered.

"Drink it!" she ordered.

He gave her a wide-eyed look, then drank. In exultation, Elena emptied her own glass. The champagne had a distinctly acrid taste to it. She set her flute on the coffee table and drew an unresisting Devin down to the sofa. She kissed him, and he kissed back with tentative uncertainty. God, he was handsome. Her hands were shaking with desire. She kissed him harder. In a moment he would be hers, all—

Ben backed away from Elena Papagos-Faye and waved a hand in front of her face. No reaction. He picked up one of her hands and dropped it. It fell limply. Her eyes were blank and staring beneath dark hair as she sat motionless on the couch.

Ben wiped his mouth with a grimace. He could still taste Papagos-Faye's tongue, and it seemed like her cold hands were still roving all over his body. For some reason, a memory from lower school popped into his head—

girls have cooties

—and made him snort. He wanted to contact Kendi, tell him that everything was going fine so far, but Elena Papagos-Faye had set up antibug screens all around her house, and outgoing transmissions were therefore only possible through her own com-link, something Ben didn't want to risk using. Best just to find the key and get this over with.

"Stand up," he said, and Papagos-Faye got obediently to her feet, her eyes still glassy. Steeling himself, Ben searched her carefully. She stood pliantly, not speaking or moving except as he moved her. First he checked for a chain around her neck. Nothing. Then he checked wrists, waist, and ankles. Nothing. The pockets of her dress contained only an SA identification holo and a small makeup kit. Ben did a more thorough search, opening her dress and searching the seams of her clothes and her underwear. He found a secret pocket on her belt, but it was empty. He even ran his hands through her hair in a strange parody of a caress. Nothing.

Ben was getting nervous now. The drug would wear off soon, and he had to find the key *now*. Where would it—

The bathroom. She had gone into the bathroom. What if she had taken it off in there?

Leaving Papagos-Faye standing where she was, he dashed into the bathroom. Swiftly he checked all the drawers and all the cabinets. He checked the toilet and under the sink. With growing apprehension, he checked the time on his ocular implant. The drug would wear off in less than half an hour. Grinding his teeth in frustration, he checked the top of the doorsill, the top of the medicine cabinet, and inside various bottles of medicine. Nothing. The tension in his stomach grew tighter. There were a million places to hide something as small as a computer key, and it could be literally anywhere. He had been counting on her keeping it somewhere on her person, as Jeung had done.

Fifteen minutes. Ben searched through the piles of towels in the linen closet, checked the drains in the sink and tub. Nothing. He started to sweat. It had to be here somewhere if only he could—

Ben smacked himself on the forehead with the palm of his hand and ran back into the living room. Papagos-Faye was standing exactly where he had left her.

"Elena," he said, "where did you put your computer key?"

"In the secret compartment in my medicine cabinet." Her voice was dreamy, just like Isaac Todd's had been when Harenn and Kendi were questioning him. "Or is it called a medicine chest? My grandmother always called it—"

"How do I open the secret compartment?"

She told him. Ben left her talking about the buttons on her dress and rushed back to the bathroom. He found the compartment, opened it, and found the key. A rush of exhilaration filled him. Quickly he pressed it against the copycat he took from his pocket. It flashed green to indicate a successful download. Ben returned the key to the compartment and dashed back to the living room. Nine minutes left. He took a small white card from a plastic envelope in his pocket, pressed Elena's thumb to it, and returned the card to his pocket. Then he led Elena to the bedroom.

Seven minutes. Ben undressed her, messed up her hair, and tossed her clothing all over the room. He did the same to his own hair and clothes. Just for effect, he knocked a lamp off the nightstand and tore a hole in one of the silk sheets. Then he ordered Elena to climb into bed and he lay down naked beside her.

One minute.

"Listen to me, Elena," he whispered in her ear. "This is what you're going to remember when you wake up. . . ."

Sixty seconds later, Papagos-Faye blinked once, stretched languidly, and turned to look at Ben. He put an amazed and startled look on his face.

"That was . . . incredible," he said in a shocked voice.

"Wasn't it just?" Papagos-Faye said. "And now, Devin, dear, I think we need to call it a night."

Five minutes later, Ben was staring at Papagos-Faye's front door as the locks engaged with a click. He shook his head, then touched the copycat in his pocket and walked away, whistling a happy little tune.

"How'd it go?" Kendi demanded. "Did everything work as planned? How do you feel?"

Ben plunked down onto a chair in the medical bay with a heavy sigh. It felt good to be back in the *Poltergeist* where the territory was safe, familiar. Kendi's presence also calmed him. Already the memory of Papagos-Faye's cold, busy hands was beginning to fade.

"Without a hitch, yes, and yuck," he said.

Kendi grinned a wide, white grin of relief and leaned over to clasp Ben in a quick, hard hug. Ben's heart swelled. Suddenly every harsh moment he had spent with Elena Papagos-Faye became worth it. A half-remembered quotation came back to him, about love being a condition in which someone else's happiness becomes essential to one's own. He understood it entirely. Kendi's happiness spread into Ben like warm gold, and in that moment Ben would have braved vacuum without a space suit for him.

"You're welcome," he said, unable to keep his own smile hidden. "All right—I want my own hair and clothes back now."

"Momentarily," Harenn said. She was using an enzyme comb to carefully strip the red dye from Gretchen's hair. At one of the counters, Lucia was meticulously fluffing a blond wig that had black roots.

"You got everything, then?" Kendi asked.

Ben held up the copycat and the little card in its plastic envelope. "Key and thumbprint. The hypnoral worked just fine, and so did the antidote I took when Papagos-Faye wasn't looking. I told her to remember some pretty amazing things about me." His face clouded as something occurred to him. "What am I going to do when Papagos-Faye calls me again? I mean, you can tell people to 'remember' stuff when they come off hypnoral, but it doesn't do posthypnotic suggestions. I couldn't tell her not to—"

Lucia laughed over her wig, a rich, musical sound, and Gretchen snorted from her chair. Harenn gave a small smile as the comb changed the last of Gretchen's "red" hair back to its usual cornsilk blond.

"Benny-boy," Gretchen said, "you have a lot to learn about women."

"I dated my share," he protested.

"Three women is *not* a share," Gretchen said.

"Look," Ben said, flushing, "if you think—"

"Don't get your undies in a bunch. All I'm saying is that you've never dated *this* kind of woman, okay? She isn't going to call you back. In fact, *you* need to call *her*."

Ben shuddered at the thought. "No way."

"She's right, Ben," Lucia said. She set the wig on a stand and put the fluffing pick in a drawer. "Remember, Devin Reap is supposed to be a weak, clingy sort of guy. She'll think it strange if you *don't* call. I guarantee you she's already set her com-link to route your calls to her voice mail. Leave a message asking when you can see her again, and then call two or three more times over the course of a week. Sound a little more desperate each time, and I promise you won't hear a thing from her."

"If you say so," Ben muttered.

Kendi patted Ben's arm. "Hey, I don't understand women, either. Close your mouth, Gretchen."

"Did I say anything? A single word, even?"

A while later, Ben and Kendi were back in their quarters. Ben's hair, though still fashionably cut, was back to its usual bright red, and he had changed out of the embarrassingly tight clothes into his usual relaxed-looking tunic and trousers. It felt wonderful to lounge on a comfortable sofa in a quiet room instead of leaning over a hard railing in a cacophonous gladiator ring, and it felt equally wonderful to have Kendi's hands moving over his shoulders in a warm, gentle massage instead of with a cold, insistent probing.

"Did I tell you how proud I am of you?" Kendi said.

"Once or twice," Ben admitted, closing his eyes in bliss. "But you can tell me again."

"I'm very proud of you. That was great work, and we wouldn't have Papagos-Faye's key without you."

"Two more to go—Rafille Mallory and Edsard Roon." Ben paused. "Any idea how we're actually going to get *in* there once we have the keys?"

"Not really," Kendi admitted. "I need more information about Roon, and I'll probably have to interrogate Todd again, see if there's anything we missed. I just wish we had more time. The *Poltergeist* is due back at Bellerophon in only fourteen days."

"I don't like having Todd on board. What if he escapes? It'd be over for us in less time than it takes to say so."

"We're being careful, Ben. All of us. You know that."

"I guess." Ben closed his eyes, deciding not to let himself tense up during a good shoulder rub. "The paranoid part of me wonders what we've overlooked, is all. He's probably getting pretty bored and restless in there with nothing to do but read."

"I don't feel the least bit sorry for that bastard," Kendi said harshly. His fingers dug deeper into Ben's shoulders and he winced. "As far as I'm concerned, boredom isn't even the beginning of what he deserves. All those women he seduced just to sell their babies." He dug harder. "All life, it makes me vomit just to—"

"Shoulders! Shoulders!" Ben yelped.

"Sorry," Kendi said, contritely lessening the pressure. "Still a touchy subject with me, I guess." He stopped kneading and came around to sit on the sofa beside Ben. Outside, a ship coasted by the window so close that Ben could almost see passengers in the windows before it passed out of view. Ben turned a little and faced Kendi, his own private universe. What in the world had taken him so long to figure out how deep his feelings ran, how miserable he had been whenever Kendi wasn't in his life? Ben rarely talked with his friends about his love life, and most of them, he knew, had quietly assumed it was Kendi's mercurial temperament that made their earlier relationship so stormy. None of them, except perhaps Ben's mother, had suspected that Ben had repeatedly been the one to call things to an end while Kendi's devotion had never flagged. Ben still didn't know exactly why he had avoided commitment for so long. Perhaps it was because he had grown up without a father at home and he hadn't learned how to form solid relationships with men. Whatever the reason, he had gotten over it, and thank god for that. He never wanted to be apart from Kendi again.

"I have something I need to tell you," Kendi said.

"Oh?"

Kendi took Ben's hand and stroked the back of it in a familiar gesture. "I've been thinking a lot lately. I've lost a lot of people I love. My entire birth family. Ara. Pitr. I've been scared a lot lately, scared of losing more people I love. Eventually I'll run out of people, and I'll be alone." He paused. "It occurred to me that I'm going to lose people, no matter what happens. It's an unavoidable fact. I don't ever want to run out of people to love, Ben. I especially don't want to lose you. Those embryos Ara found, your brothers and sisters, are a part of you, and if I have them, I'll always have you, no matter what." He paused. "Ben, I want to have children with you. Eleven of them."

The universe froze. Ben's mind stopped moving, then made a joyous leap, as if he had just seen a rainbow in a stormy sky. He couldn't speak at first, but finally he made himself say, "You mean it?"

"Absolutely. Hey, I have to pass all this Real People wisdom on to *someone* before I— What's wrong?"

Ben didn't understand the question. For once, everything was completely right. Only when he felt something warm running down his face did he realize he was crying. "Sorry," he said in a thick voice. "You caught me off guard."

Kendi gathered him close. "You never have to be *on* guard with me, Ben. And really, there was never any other answer I could give."

"We'll have to find a host mother," Ben said.

"About ten of them, come to that," Kendi said wryly, and Ben had to laugh.

Martina Weaver sat on a hard chair, trying not to stare at her brother. She and the others were arranged in a big circle that alternated yellow-clad Alphas and green-clad Deltas. A male Alpha occupied a chair in the center of the circle. Utang sat almost directly across from Martina, and he was looking at her as well, though his face was blank.

"Begin," ordered one of the Deltas.

"Uh, I'm not . . . not sure," said the center Alpha. He was in his forties and ran toward plump. "That is . . . how do I—"

"The source of all impurity is envy, which creates N-waves in your mind," the Delta said. "Envy of someone else's possessions leads to laziness or greed. Envy of someone else's position leads to ambition and pride. Envy of someone else's food leads to gluttony. Envy of someone else's body leads to lust. What is it you envy, Alpha?"

The Alpha's face grew red and Martina felt embarrassed for him. He clearly wanted to be anywhere but here. Meanwhile, it was all Martina could do to keep her seat. Her brother—her *brother*—was sitting only a few meters away and she couldn't even talk to him. She wanted to jump up and run to him more than she had wanted anything in her life. It crossed her mind that perhaps she should say something, tell one of the Deltas. But before she could do so, something else— a slave's instincts?—had advised caution. She didn't know all the rules in this strange place, and she had the distinct feeling that revealing her relationship to Utang would be a mistake. So she kept silent and held her gloved hands folded neatly in her lap.

"What is it you envy, Alpha?" the Delta repeated, more sharply this time.

"I envy everyone who isn't sitting in this chair," he said with a weak smile. This drew a small ripple of laughter from the Alphas and hard pokes in their sides from the Deltas.

"The Confessional is not a place for levity," the Delta said. "Confess! What do you envy?"

"Nothing. I envy nothing."

"Did you wake up this morning with an erection?"

This question clearly caught the Alpha off guard. "What? I . . . That's none of—"

"Computer records indicate that you awoke with an erection this morning and you masturbated in the shower," the Delta said. "But you have refused to confess your impurity. The N-waves course through your brain even as we speak. Only by confessing what you have done can you rid yourself of them and become one with the Dream. Confess!"

Martina stared at the Delta in disbelief. They spied on the bathrooms? What "impurities" had she committed that had been caught and recorded?

The Alpha looked like he wished the floor would open up and swallow him. "I . . . I . . ."

"Did you wake with an erection?" barked the Delta. "Answer!"

"Yes," the Alpha said in a small voice.

As one, the Deltas pointed at him with green-gloved fingers. "Impure!" they boomed. The word echoed like thunder through the room.

"Did you masturbate in the shower?" snapped the Delta.

"Yes."

"Impure!" roared all the Deltas. Delta Maura elbowed Martina in the side and gestured sharply at the central Alpha. The other Deltas did the same with their own charges. The Alphas, including Martina, all pointed and said, "Impure," though without much force or conviction.

"Did you lust after women while you committed this impurity?"

"Yes."

Another nudge. "Impure!" everyone thundered.

"What other impurities did you commit?" the Delta asked.

Tears were leaking from the Alpha's eyes now. "I . . . I envied other people their freedom."

"Impure!"

"I was hungry and wished for more food," he said.

"Impure!"

"I envied Dreamer Roon's ability to enter the Dream without drugs."

"Impure!" By now, the chorus was strong and solid. Martina said it automatically, as did Utang across from her. The man confessed two more impurities, then broke down and cried, whether from simple humiliation or genuine sorrow at what he had done, Martina couldn't tell. Either way, she didn't blame him for the tears. The Delta got up, knelt next to his chair, and put an arm around him.

"It is finished for now," he said in a kind, fatherly voice. "You've confessed some of your impurities and they will bring you no more N-waves. You are that much closer to Irfan now. Come."

The Delta took the Alpha back to his chair and gave him a small chocolate snack cake. Martina's stomach growled and she found herself staring at the Alpha as he ate the cake. Her earlier craving for sweets awoke. Perhaps her current envy would be a good impurity to confess.

The Delta in charge chose another Alpha, a young woman, for the Confessional. She sat down, nervously gathering her voluminous yellow trousers around her.

"You reek of impurity," the Delta intoned. "The N-waves radiate from your mind and spread your filth to all those around you. You must rid yourself of these things. Confess!"

The Alpha twisted her hands in her lap, refusing to look up.

"What impurities have you committed?" the Delta demanded.

"I guess I . . . I envied Dreamer Roon his ability to enter the Dream so easily."

"Impure!"

"I wanted more food."

"Impure!"

The relentless confessions continued. Most of the Alphas broke down crying, and each got a small snack cake. Martina found herself shouting and pointing with full enthusiasm. At first the fervor had been pretended, an attempt to blend in, but the ritual gesture and shout began to take on a life of its own. The words rang through Martina's body, echoing around the bare room and banging against her very bones. The confessions came more readily. Alphas confessed to anger, greed, pride, unhappiness, and lust. One woman said she envied Martina her beauty. At every turn, the word *impure* thundered through the room.

Finally Utang was chosen. He sat down without looking at Martina. Indeed, he didn't look at anyone. Misery was carved into his very posture. The Delta called out to him to confess.

"I woke with an erection," he said. This was a fairly standard confession among the male Alphas by now, though Martina found herself embarrassed again. The sound of his voice also brought her to the edge of tears. It was a sound from her childhood, and one she had thought she'd never hear again.

"Impure!" boomed the circle.

"I disbelieved Dreamer Roon when he said he could enter the Dream without drugs."

"Impure!"

"I became angry at my Delta."

"Impure!"

"I . . . I . . ." Utang seemed to cast about for something to confess. "I had lustful thoughts about that woman," he said, pointing at one.

A shock cracked through Martina's body. She cried out in pain, as did the other Alphas. Utang stiffened, then went limp with a moan.

"That was a lie," said the Delta. "In the Dream there are no untruths, and every lie you tell sends you farther away from it than any other impurity. For that reason, all your fellow Alphas have suffered. You do not need to fabricate impurities, Alpha. You have plenty enough to confess."

Utang opened his eyes. They were glazed with sorrow. Several of the Alphas were rubbing their shackled wrists and glaring at him with undisguised anger. Martina found her own temper rising, though her ire wasn't directed toward Utang.

He didn't shock us, she thought, *but the others are angry at him? How dare they! It's the Deltas' fault, not his.*

Utang was guided back to his seat. He sat staring down at his hands while the others continued to glare. The Delta didn't give him a snack cake.

"Your turn, dear," Delta Maura said with another elbow nudge. Martina was starting to find the woman annoying.

Martina got up and took the central chair. It felt strange. All eyes were on her, even the ones behind her where she couldn't see. Abruptly, she felt vulnerable and alone.

This is foolish and stupid, she told herself. *I am not impure. I am not filthy or horrible. These people are trying to make us think so, but it isn't true.*

"Confess, Alpha!" barked the Delta. "What impurities have you committed?"

Martina decided to get it over with. "I envied the other Alphas their cake."

"Impure!"

Martina had to force herself not to shrink back into the chair at the shout. It was even louder and more forceful when she was sitting here, alone in the center of the circle. She felt naked despite her voluminous clothing.

"I disbelieved Dreamer Roon's writings," she said.

"Impure!"

"I questioned the wisdom of Delta Maura."

"Impure!"

Martina cast about for more. Except for Utang, the other Alphas hadn't been allowed to leave the Confessional until they had confessed to at least four or five impurities. But Martina couldn't think of anything she had done that was impure. There had to be something. *Think!*

Inspiration struck. "I wanted to keep track of time."

"Impure!"

"I tried to disobey my Delta during Dreamer Roon's speech today."

"Impure!"

"I was proud of the fact that I was keeping my name." Martina blinked. Where had *that* come from?

"Impure!"

The word pounded at her body. To her horror, Martina felt a few tears leaking from her eyes. Then she decided to take advantage of it and pretend to be more upset than she already was. She dropped her face into her hands and let her shoulders shake in false despair. The biosensors in her slave shackles, the ones that had no doubt caught Utang's lie, wouldn't catch a falsehood she didn't vocalize—she hoped. Besides, the tears wetting her gloves were real.

She felt no shock, and after a moment a light touch on her shoulder told her she could rise. Delta Maura seated her in the half circle and gave her a snack cake. Martina tore the wrapping away and wolfed it down. The sugar raced through her, creating a momentary high that mingled with a sense of relief. She felt immeasurably better.

"Confessional has ended," the Delta said. "You may stand and speak to one another."

The Alphas all got up and stretched. Martina almost bolted across the circle to Utang, but forced herself to move casually. He met her halfway.

"Martina?" he asked softly.

"All life," she said, a lump rising in her throat. "It's me, Keith. Or is it Utang?"

He shook his head. "The Real People deserted me. I haven't heard either of those names in years."

"What should I call you, then?" She couldn't believe she was saying something so insipid and mundane.

"Keith." He reached out to touch her, and a shock coursed through Martina, painful, but not as harsh as the earlier one. Keith snatched his hand back. Suddenly Delta Maura was there, her round face stern.

"Physical contact between the sexes is forbidden," she said, firmly pushing them apart. "The gloves are to protect you from it, but they can't shield you from the N-waves such things generate. Hence your punishment."

They both murmured apologies. When she had walked away, Martina turned back to him and couldn't think of a single thing to say. She still wanted to hug him. Suddenly she needed to touch another human being, skin to skin, no gloves, no cloth. Emotion bubbled inside her and tears gathered in her eyes again.

"Don't cry," he said, his own voice strained. "I don't think we should let them know about . . . about who we are. If this is a place of love and trust, I haven't seen it."

"All life, I feel the same way," Martina said, then gave a tiny laugh. "What are the odds? You and me, both still Silent after the Despair and both brought here."

"The first is more a coincidence than the second," Keith said with a wan smile of his own. "These people are gathering us up. Maybe we'll see Mom and Dad. Or Evan. Have you heard from any of them?"

"No. Do you suppose there's any way to—" She stopped herself automatically. Almost all her life, the word *escape* had earned her a punishing shock from her shackles, and she had learned not to say it. Keith, however, seemed to understand.

"I don't know," he said tiredly. "We'll have to keep

our eyes open. Assuming that there's any place to . . . go to in the first place. We could be anywhere—on a planet, a ship, a station, anything. It's hopeless."

"Time to return to your rooms," announced a Delta.

"We'll talk again," Keith said.

As Delta Maura hooded Martina and led her away, she silently swore she would find a way out of this place. There had to be one.

All she needed was a plan.

CHAPTER SEVEN

"When someone tells me he isn't a thief, I count my money."
   —Drew Fleming, Investigative Reporter, Earth

Rafille Mallory was a plump, motherly-looking woman who kept people in cages. Harenn watched her with hard brown eyes and wondered how the woman could sleep at night.

"That's her?" Bedj-ka said.

"It is," Harenn said. "Stay with me, my son. I don't want to lose her—or you."

Bedj-ka wordlessly fell into step beside Harenn as they threaded their way through the crowd of shoppers. This part of SA Station was given over to consumer goods for the wealthy, and the tall, wide tunnel was lined with expensive shops and exclusive stores. Long balconies created two more floors on both sides of the hallway, and occasional escalators and lifts granted access to them. Potted plants and fountains were artistically scattered about. Brightly colored clothing displays and the rich smell of baking cookies tugged at Harenn's attention, but she ignored them in favor of the woman she and Bedj-ka were trailing.

By now it felt natural to have Bedj-ka at her side, though Harenn still woke up and looked in on him in the middle of the night, just to make sure he was still there, that his return hadn't been a dream. For his part, Bedj-ka had fallen easily into the rhythm of Harenn's life. When they returned to Bellerophon, she would have to enroll him in school, but for now he assisted her in engineering, in the medical bay, and, today, with a bit of spying. She liked having him there.

Despite all this, Harenn still felt strong flashes of negative emotion. She had missed all but the first month of Bedj-ka's life. She had missed his first steps, his first words, his first day of school, and more. Other people, strangers, had been there to see them instead, and how could they celebrate these things properly, when to them Bedj-ka had been nothing more than a slave? Harenn felt cheated and angry, angry at Isaac Todd, angry at the slavers who had brokered Bedj-ka's sale, angry at this Matron and Patron who had bought him.

Bedj-ka, for all his chatter, actually talked very little of his time in the Enclave. Harenn had managed to glean here and there that they were a small group who viewed the Silent as blessed people who needed to be sequestered because their gift made them more vulnerable to the normal foibles of humanity. Enslavement assured easier control, so the Enclave bought Silent children, both to "shelter" them and to train them. Once such Silent grew to adulthood and were able to work in the Dream, they kept the Enclave afloat financially by providing communication services. It was similar to the Children of Irfan, in a twisted sort of way.

Rafille Mallory paused to examine a display of perfume in a store window. An animated sign flashed OBSESS WITH PHEROMONES. Harenn hung back to watch. This was growing frustrating. Three days of shadowing had turned up nothing. The woman had no hooks. Jeung and Papagos-Faye had shown vices that had proven easy to exploit, but Mallory had so far shown nothing. Harenn hadn't even been able to determine where on her person she kept her computer key.

Bedj-ka started to speak, then coughed hard.

"Cover your mouth, please," Harenn said, and pretended to stare thoughtfully into a gushing fountain so she could spy on Mallory, who was smiling at a display of stuffed toys.

"Sorry." Bedj-ka coughed again, this time into his fist. Mallory picked up a small bear in motley colors, considered it, and set it back down again. "When do you want me to do it?"

"Soon," Harenn said.

Mallory wandered into the perfume store, her walk almost a waddle. Harenn decided to wait outside for her rather than follow her inside and risk being noticed. She paid an exorbitant price for two giant cookies from a nearby bakery, and mother and son settled down on a bench to keep an eye out for Mallory's exit. The cookies were warm and soft, made with peanut butter. Neither Harenn nor Bedj-ka much cared for chocolate these days.

"I had a weird dream last night," Bedj-ka announced amid a spray of damp crumbs.

"Do not speak when your mouth is full," Harenn said, taking a delicate bite of her own.

Bedj-ka swallowed and said, "I was walking through the dormitory at the Enclave, but all the rooms were empty and everything made these weird echoes around me. It felt like there were other people there with me, but I couldn't find them anywhere. I looked and looked, and then I started to run, but I still couldn't find anybody. Finally I ended up in the dining hall, and it was empty, too, except the tables were all full of food." He held up the remaining half of his cookie. "There were cookies like this one there, which is why I remembered the dream just now. Anyway, I was hungry, so I grabbed some food to eat it, and then I noticed I was breathing hard and I had to wait until I caught my breath before I could eat. The foods were all my favorite ones—fried chicken and creamed corn and sweet-and-sour fish—and I could eat as much as I wanted and it all tasted really good. That was weird because I never remember stuff like breathing or tasting food in dreams. Then I woke up."

Harenn thought about this. Bedj-ka's dream was fairly straightforward. The empty rooms symbolized his feelings of abandonment and betrayal, while the banquet and its plethora of choices symbolized his newfound freedom. But she wasn't sure that Bedj-ka would appreciate all this.

"Your dream is a good omen, my son," she said. "Dreaming of abundant food indicates good luck for the future, or so the Ched-Balaar say."

"What are they like?" he asked, flipping easily into a new subject. "I've never even seen one, but Father Kendi talks about them sometimes."

"They are strange and graceful," Harenn said. "I enjoy their company—most humans do—and they seem to enjoy ours. They have four legs and two arms and a very long neck that ends in a rather flat head. Their language sounds strange because they speak by chattering their teeth together and by making hooting noises. No human can duplicate the sounds, just as they cannot duplicate our language, except in the Dream, of course."

"Have you ever been in the Dream?"

"Only once, and very briefly. Sejal brought me in. He has the power to pull other Silent out of the solid world into the Dream. I am not Silent, but he was able to bring me there for just a moment."

"Did you like it?"

Harenn smiled at him. "I was not there long enough to form an opinion."

"I was supposed to start training to enter the Dream in two more years," Bedj-ka said wistfully. "But now I guess I'll never get there. The Despair ruined it for almost everyone. I really wanted to see the Dream, too. Everyone says it's really rigid."

Harenn put an arm around his shoulders in a brief

•

hug. "Perhaps it is best that you never entered it. From what I hear, it is devastating to lose the Dream. I know Gretchen is greatly disturbed by what she has lost."

"Is that why she's so mean all the time? She yells at me sometimes even when all I'm doing is walking down the corridor."

"She is very unhappy," Harenn said, making a mental note to have a few pointed words with Gretchen. "And unhappiness makes people do things they would not normally do."

"I was unhappy." Bedj-ka took a pensive bite of cookie. "During the Despair, I was so unhappy I wanted to die. It was awful. I felt completely alone, like there was no one in the entire universe who cared about me or even knew I existed. I couldn't even move, it was so bad."

Harenn's throat thickened. Her son had needed her, and she hadn't been there. The Despair had rocked her, filled her with pain, but she had been used to dealing with pain and had continued to function. The universal depression had ended once Kendi, Vidya, and Prasad had forced Sufur's twisted children from the Dream, but wounds still lingered. The scars ran deepest for the Silent, who had stronger connections with the Dream. Bedj-ka hadn't even entered the Dream, and he said he had wanted to die. She ached with guilt at not being there to share his pain. She hugged him again.

"You were very strong and very brave," she said. "And I am proud of you."

Bedj-ka smiled at her, and Harenn's heart swelled. Then he pulled away and munched his cookie again. A moment later, Rafille Mallory exited the shop. Harenn stood and brushed crumbs from her loose-cut blouse.

"I think now is the time," she said. "Do you know what to do?"

Bedj-ka flashed another smile. He was quite handsome, she realized with a touch of maternal pride. "I know," he said.

"Let me get ahead of her, then. Once you see me signal, do what we rehearsed."

Harenn trotted through the light crowd of shoppers until she was well ahead of Mallory. Then she stopped to admire a display of blue roses in a florist's shop window while she activated the camera in her ocular implant. A tap on her earpiece opened a communiations link with the *Poltergeist.*

"Harenn?" came Ben's voice.

"I am recording visual," Harenn said, "but you should watch as well in case I miss something."

"Got it."

Harenn turned and saw Bedj-ka among the people a little way to Mallory's left. Mallory herself was about ten meters away from Harenn, strolling casually in her direction. Harenn scratched her nose and Bedj-ka nodded. Abruptly he dashed up to Mallory and all but slammed into her. She staggered. Bedj-ka tugged at Mallory's jacket, then with a laugh vanished into the crowd before she could react. Harenn watched carefully. Several other shoppers turned to stare as well.

Mallory regained her balance, her expression startled and surprised. Quickly she patted a tiny pouch on her belt; then she spun to see if she could spot Bedj-ka. A man approached and said something to Mallory, but she shook her head, refusing his apparent offer of help. Then she opened her shoulder bag, rummaged through it, and quickly checked her shopping bags and parcels. Apparently satisfied with what she found, she closed the bags again and, with a shake of her head, wandered off through the crowd again. Harenn moved to follow.

"I saw it all," Ben said.

"The belt pouch?" Harenn said.

"Most likely."

Harenn nodded in private agreement. If Mallory

thought her pocket had been picked, she would check for her most important possessions first. Identification and cashcards were all easily deactivated and replaced, but the same could not be said of her computer key, and Mallory's instincts had made her check for it right away.

Mallory continued on her way, and Harenn continued to follow. Bedj-ka, she knew, would head back to the ship. It would be too risky to keep him at the shopping center in case Mallory spotted him and grew suspicious.

In quick succession, Mallory visited a toy store, two clothing stores, and a candy shop. She emerged from each, sometimes with more bags, sometimes not. The woman clearly liked to shop. Harenn was trying to figure out how this bit of information could work to her advantage when Mallory ducked into a department store. Harenn followed, able to remain inconspicuous in the larger store.

Mallory browsed aimlessly among various clothing displays. Harenn grew bored. The whole thing seemed pointless, and the longer Harenn continued to shadow the woman, the more likely it became that someone would notice. But then the continual guilt she felt about rescuing Bedj-ka first overtook her again, tightening her stomach and forcing her to keep at it.

The store smelled like fresh cloth, and the customers were all human. Mallory paused to try on a series of straw hats, none of which suited her coloring or clothing style, then ambled onward to look at a display of key rings. She held up one shaped like a little silver cat, then put it back.

Or seemed to.

Harenn blinked. Had she seen correctly? To the casual observer, it would appear that Mallory had put the key ring back on the display rack, but Harenn had been watching carefully and was sure she had seen Mallory palm the key ring. Her suspicions were confirmed a moment later when Mallory strolled away and casually dropped a hand into her pocket. Harenn hurried to catch up, but paused long enough to check the key chain display. She saw no silver cats.

All traces of Harenn's boredom vanished. This was quite the fascinating development. Had it been a unique event? Or had Mallory been shoplifting all day? Harenn suddenly wished she had risked following Mallory into some of the other shops.

Harenn's ocular implant flashed a message across her retina. MEMORY FULL, it said. TO CONTINUE RE- CORDING, PLEASE EMPTY MEMORY CACHE. Harenn had forgotten to turn off her implant's record function. Harenn did so and turned her attention back to Mallory.

Mallory headed back to the main mall area. Harenn held her breath as she left the store. Would security pounce on her? Most stores were outfitted with AI cameras that watched customers unceasingly and un- tiringly, looking for exactly this sort of behavior. One of them should have noticed Mallory's move and noti- fied security. But Mallory calmly crossed the threshold into the mall. No alarms sounded, no security guards appeared on the scene. Harenn narrowed her eyes. How had she fooled them?

Harenn remained behind Mallory, hoping against hope that Mallory wasn't done for the day and plan- ning to head back home. With a heavy sigh audible even at Harenn's distance, however, Mallory shifted her parcels around and entered a food court. She bought a plate of noodles and sat down to eat at one of the empty tables in the middle of the court, where food smells from a dozen different worlds and cultures clashed into a mélange of scents both spicy and sweet. More humans strolled by. Aliens were few and far between in this sector, as the stores were geared pri- marily toward products humans used. Harenn waited patiently until Mallory finished eating. She rose, gathered her parcels, and continued on her way, Harenn trailing unobtrusively behind her.

Eventually, Mallory entered another clothing store, this one specializing in leather goods. The fine smell of suede wafted over Harenn, who pretended interest in a pair of boots while never once taking her eyes off Mallory.

Mallory looked at a leather coat, several belts, and a red leather corset before slipping a pair of gloves into one of her bags and striding nonchalantly toward the door. Again, no one raised a fuss as she exited. Harenn stayed right behind her, and a few minutes later got to see Mallory lift a small case of makeup in another department store.

Harenn's mind raced, examining possibilities and discarding them one by one until she settled on something she thought might work. She tapped her earpiece and called Ben.

"What's up?" he asked.

"I know how to get Mallory's key," she reported. "But you must move quickly. Listen . . ."

Rafille Mallory emerged from the bookstore barely restraining a smug smile. Two bookdisks, recently liberated from their shelves, nestled in her jacket pocket. A touch of excitement thrilled through her. All day she had been lifting various objects from different stores and not once had she been caught. She had even paused in one store to chat with a security guard who remained completely unaware that Rafille was carrying several hundred chits' worth of liberated goods. The idiot.

The sense of excitement continued, and Rafille allowed herself to grin for a moment. She *needed* this. Her job was deadly dull—overseeing security for a bunch of captured slaves was no big deal, occupying only a small part of her attention every day. There was no challenge there, not when Roon's indoctrination program was operating fully on schedule. Eventually the Silent drones wouldn't *want* to leave, would believe that their true place in the universe was in Roon's little enclave. She didn't know if the Alphas believed Roon's claim about being able to enter the Dream without drugs. She didn't much care, actually. People were so gullible, so willing to believe in miracles, it had apparently never occurred to any of them to question what he said. Roon wasn't even Silent, and how would they react to *that*?

Rafille checked her pocket. The jammer was still there. Now *that* had been a challenge, coming up with a device that would temporarily disrupt from a distance the AI programs that watched the stores. A part of her felt as if she were cheating, but she still had to avoid the store security guards, both the ones in uniform and the ones in plainclothes. And it was almost impossible to beat the AI programs. Rafille wanted a challenge, but she wasn't stupid about it.

She checked her ocular implant. Time to go home. Her feet were tired, and the packages were growing heavy. She was just turning away from the bookstore when heavy hands landed on her shoulders from behind.

"Excuse us, ma'am," said an unfamiliar male voice. "I'm afraid we need to talk."

Rafille's heart wrenched inside her chest. She wrenched her head around and stared at a man and a woman, both dressed in simple suits. The man was tall and thin, with dark skin. His companion was only slightly shorter, with blond hair and bland features. Each of them had a hand on her shoulders.

"What's this all about?" she gasped, though she was dreadfully certain she already knew.

The man flashed an identification holo. "Security, ma'am. You'll have to come with us now."

"But I didn't do anything," Rafille spluttered. Her heart was now beating fair to shake her blouse, and the bookdisks felt very heavy and conspicuous in her pocket.

"I don't think we should discuss that here, ma'am," the woman said. "If you'll please come with us?"

They had her dead to rights. A hundred different scenarios flashed through her head. She could make a break for it. She could throw the packages into their faces and *then* make a break for it. She could pretend to faint. She could hit the man with her fist and punch the woman in the stomach. Rafille discarded all of these possibilities. Both man and woman were clearly far more athletic than she was, and Rafille doubted she'd get ten meters before they caught up with her. As if reading her thoughts, the man tightened his grip on her shoulder enough to make her wince, a subtle indicator of his strength. Rafille's mouth went dry. She was in deep, deep trouble. If Roon found out she had been arrested, Rafille would land in the job pool so fast, she might well have traveled there through slipspace. She would lose her luxury apartment and almost everything she owned. Her daughter would have to drop out of college.

This isn't fair! she thought wildly. *Why should my daughter have to suffer because of this? There has to be a way out of it. Think, woman. Think!*

The security people steered Rafille toward an empty store. The front windows were obscured by blank beige screens and a sign read, COMING SOON: ANOTHER FINE STORE! The blond woman pushed open the door and the man guided Rafille firmly into the space beyond.

Inside was a great, empty space. The floor was simple gray tile. A few empty clothing racks made a tangled metal jumble, and a sales counter sat off to one side. A line of closed doors marched along the back wall, and Rafille assumed they were fitting rooms. The place smelled of stale air and dust.

"What's going on?" Rafille demanded, deciding to

play the role of indignant innocent. Perhaps she could brazen it out. "What is this place?"

"It's where we take shoplifters for . . . debriefing," the man said, and held up a small computer disk. "We caught you on camera. Would you like to see it?"

"But that's . . . I mean, there's no way you could have . . . How did . . ."

Without a word, the man produced a datapad from his pocket and slotted in the disk. A holographic display popped up. Rafille watched herself in miniature as she palmed the silver cat key ring. Her heart plummeted into her shoes and her hands began to shake.

"Pretty conclusive," the man said. "Would you like to see the rest?"

"No," Rafille whispered. "Oh, god."

The man pulled a large card from his jacket pocket. "Please give me your hands, ma'am. I need your prints."

They were treating her like a criminal? A common thief? Rafille couldn't believe it, even when the man rolled her fingers carefully across the card. They left black prints in their wake, though her hands remained clean.

"Detective Dell here is going to search you now," the man said next. "Hold your arms out to your sides, please."

Rafille numbly obeyed. Detective Dell's search was quick and thorough. It produced the silver key ring, the bookdisks, the leather gloves, two bottles of perfume, a scarf, and the AI disruptor. Dell laid the objects out on the counter in an accusatory row. Rafille didn't respond until she felt Dell's fingers open the little pouch on her belt, the one that contained her computer key. Rafille's hand shot down and grabbed Dell's wrist.

"There's nothing of importance in there," she snapped.

"I'm sorry, ma'am, but I have to look," Dell said neutrally.

"Please remove your hand from my partner's wrist, ma'am," the man said, "or I will remove it for you."

"The key in that pouch is classified property of Silent Acquisitions," Rafille said, obeying with reluctance. "If you tamper with it—"

"I'll set it on the counter, ma'am," Dell said, and did so. "No one will touch it."

"Look at me, ma'am," the man said, and Rafille did so. "My name is Detective Melthine. Who are you, please?"

"Rafille Mallory," she whispered.

"Ms. Mallory, do you have receipts for any of these items?"

Rafille didn't answer.

"I'll take that as a no." Melthine passed a hand wearily over his face. His eyes were a liquid brown. "I'm going to go through the rest of your packages, Ms. Mallory. What will I find there?"

"I think I should call my corporate representative," she said.

"You certainly may, ma'am," Melthine told her, "though you aren't under arrest. Yet."

"Please," she said. "Please, I have the money to pay for all this. I can pay."

"That's as may be; you still broke corporate law, Ms. Mallory."

Dell, meanwhile, went through Rafille's packages, separating objects that had receipts from those that didn't. Something rustled behind the counter, and Rafille shot a glance in its direction. Her possessions, including the key, were still there.

"What was that noise?" she demanded. "Is there something back there?"

"Ms. Mallory, you have a lot more to worry about than a couple of hungry mice," Melthine said. "I'm just eyeballing here, but it looks like you've stolen over a thousand chits' worth of merchandise. That's a serious crime on SA Station, Ms. Mallory."

"You'll never make it stick," she said.

He held up the data pad. "We've got several hours of images here. Hard to discount evidence like that."

How had they gotten around her jammer? There must be something wrong with it. Or maybe there were technological developments in security that she wasn't aware of. No, that couldn't possibly be the case. It had to be a flaw in the disruptor. *Dammit!* What did these detectives want from her? She had already agreed to pay for the stuff, but they didn't seem to—

And then it struck her. She was offering to pay for the wrong thing.

"Listen," she purred, "I'm sure we can come to an agreement here. You have the stuff back. What do you need me for? All it'll mean is a lot of paperwork for you to fill out. I can make it worth your while."

"Ms. Mallory, are you offering to bribe me?" Melthine asked.

"It's a simple exchange," she said. "I'm sure you can use the money, and I have plenty."

"Listen to her," Dell said. "Miss Moneybags here thinks she can buy her way out of trouble. Just like a rich bitch."

"I'll give you each a hundred chits."

"Ma'am, attempting to bribe a detective is a crime under—"

"But you aren't corp cops," she pointed out. "You're store security. Look, I have a daughter in college. If I get arrested, I'll lose my job and she'll have to drop out of school. Is it fair to punish her for what I did? I'll give you two hundred chits each."

"No deal," Melthine growled. "If I got caught, I'd lose *my* job."

Aha! So the only thing holding him back was the threat of getting caught. Rafille sensed a potential advantage and rushed to press it. "Who's to know?" she countered. "*I* won't say anything; that's for sure. Two fifty."

"How am I going to explain company chits getting into my account from yours?" Melthine said, and Rafille knew in that moment she had him. It was merely a matter of the amount.

"I'll pay you in freemarks, then," she said. "A hundred each."

A gleam entered Melthine's eye. "One fifty."

"Done!"

"Hey, I never agreed to anything," Dell protested. "My job's on the line, too."

Melthine put a hand on her shoulder and turned to Rafille. "Will you excuse my partner and me for a moment?" he asked.

The two of them walked to the other end of the store and conversed in low tones. Melthine made a great many wild gestures, but Dell folded her arms and looked stubborn. Rafille strained to overhear, but she couldn't make out any words. Her heart pounded. Melthine was on her side, but could he persuade his partner? Her entire career rested in the hands of this man, this stranger. Rafille had never felt so helpless in her entire life.

At last, Melthine said something that made Dell bite her lip. Her posture relaxed and she gave a single stiff nod. Melthine trotted back over to Rafille.

"She won't give in for less than two hundred freemarks," he said. "Hard."

Rafille let out a long, heavy sigh of utter, pure relief. "You got it."

Melthine and Dell took the money, counted it, and stuffed it into their pockets. "Take the stuff you paid for," Melthine said, "and get the hell out of here. I think it goes without saying that I'd better not see your face around this mall ever again."

"Not hide nor hair," Rafille promised fervently. She snatched her computer key from the counter, returned it to her belt pouch, gathered up her parcels, and all but bolted for the door. Once outside, she took a deep breath and felt her knees go slightly weak. Definitely time to head home for a drink.

As she strode swiftly toward the mall exit to find a taxi, it occurred to her that she should technically turn in her computer key and get fitted for a new one. After all, it had been out of her sight for quite a while. Then she shook her head. No, the paperwork would be immense, and she certainly didn't feel like explaining why she needed a new key. Besides, what would a couple of low-grade rent-a-cops have done with her key for the few moments it had lain on the counter?

After Rafille had left, Harenn emerged from a fitting room and strode into the main part of the empty store. Lucia popped up from behind the counter like a jack-in-the-box. Harenn smiled.

"Did you get it?" Kendi asked.

Lucia held up the copycat in one scarred hand. The lights were flashing green. "I got it. But I have to say that my heart about stopped when she asked what was behind the counter."

"You and me both," Gretchen muttered.

"Did everything go well?" Harenn asked. "I could not hear everything."

"It all went perfectly." Father Kendi grinned. "Good work, Harenn. Great plan on short notice."

"Do you think she suspected anything when you took her into an empty store instead of a security office?" Harenn asked.

"Are you kidding?" Gretchen scoffed. "She almost wet her pants when we grabbed her out there."

"Best of all, we keep getting paid." Kendi held up the wad of cash. "Between her and Elena Papagos-Faye, we won't need to dip into the kitty for a month."

Harenn nodded in satisfaction. "They are paying for their own demise."

"All right," Lucia said, "we have keys and prints for security, research, and information services. Just one left to go."

"Edsard Roon himself," Kendi said.

Ben Rymar howled like a wild thing. Storm clouds swirled in the sky above him and a few drops of rain spattered the dust at his feet. In front of him, the crude statue of Padric Sufur stared impassively at nothing. Thunder rumbled in the distance. Ben howled again and raised a fist. Lightning cracked down from the clouds and smashed into the statue. It exploded, sending stone fragments whizzing in all directions. The thunderclap smashed Ben's very bones. He flung himself flat on the ground, arms wrapped around his head. Shards rained down all around him and a few stung the backs of his hands. After a moment the rain of stone stopped. Ben uncurled himself and sat up. Where the statue had been stood a charred, blackened hole. Ben sighed and ran a hand through his hair.

Okay, he thought. *That may have been a mistake.* Still, it had felt good. And he had grown better at manipulating the Dream around him. It was easier than he thought it would be. From the descriptions he had heard from Mom's students over the years, he had assumed that shaping the Dream would be difficult, but that didn't seem to be the case. The Dream responded well to his touch, almost as if he had been born to it.

"Still pissed at him, huh?"

Ben, still seated, twisted around. Sejal was standing behind him, his strangely blue eyes looking both amused and concerned.

"I didn't even feel you coming," Ben said, surprised.

"You were busy, and you're still new at this," Sejal said. "Besides, I didn't want to interrupt, so I kept quiet."

"You saw what I was doing?"

Sejal spread his hands. "I'm no fan of Padric Sufur, either. Looks like your interest in him is more personal, though."

"I hate him," Ben growled. "Mom died because of him."

Sejal nodded. "Lots of people's moms—and dads—died because of him. I don't know how he can live with himself."

Ben worked his jaw for a moment in an attempt to keep fresh grief from running down his face. It still hurt, no matter how many statues he destroyed. Mom was dead, gone forever. It had happened over six months ago, and it still hurt as if it had been last week. He remembered finding her body, shattered and broken, at the base of the talltree. He could still feel her ribs grate and shift beneath his hands as he attempted CPR, even though she was already growing cold. And it was all because of Padric Sufur. Whenever he thought too much about it, the rage overtook him, burned with terrible intensity, and Ben knew that if he ever met Padric Sufur face-to-face, he would kill the man without a moment's hesitation. But Ben kept most of it to himself. Some things were too raw to share, even with Kendi. Kendi probably had some idea that Ben's grief was far from abated—Kendi's own pain was still an ongoing concern—but Ben doubted he knew just how deep it still ran.

Kendi. The con job. And Sejal was here. An idea popped into Ben's head.

"Sejal," he asked urgently, "where exactly are you these days?"

Sejal shrugged. "Around. Why?"

"We could really use your help. You can still reach through the Dream and possess non-Silent in the solid world, right?"

"Not as easily as I used to, but yeah." Sejal's tone

was wary. "And before you ask, no, I can't pull people who've lost their Silence into the Dream. I've already tried."

"That's not what I was getting at," Ben said. "I meant that you could help *us*. God, with you on the team, we could get Kendi's brother and sister out of the Collection in ten minutes. All you'd have to do is possess the people on the project, and Martina and Utang could walk right out. How fast can you get to SA Station? Should we come and get you?"

Sejal shifted uncomfortably. "I'm not exactly able to go anywhere right now, Ben."

"What? Why not?"

"I'm sort of busy. I just popped into the Dream to take care of some stuff and I noticed you were in the neighborhood, so I thought I'd just say hello. I can't really go anywhere right now."

"But—"

"I'm sorry, Ben. Look, I have to go. I'll see you around, all right?" And Sejal vanished so abruptly it created a wash of Dream energy that almost bowled Ben over. Slowly he got to his feet. The anger, initially directed at Sufur, shifted toward Sejal. What was Sejal doing that was so important? He wasn't a Child of Irfan, took orders from no one except his parents as far as Ben knew. Kendi had saved Sejal's *life*, for god's sake.

Ben took a deep breath and tried to calm down. Sejal wasn't usually mean or thoughtless. Maybe he had a good reason for refusing to help. What it might be, Ben had no idea. In any case, it was obvious that getting assistance from Sejal would not be an option, and there was no point in expending energy getting angrier about it. He needed something else to think about. Ben waved a hand, banishing the charred hole in the ground and replacing it with the featureless, blank plain that was the default condition of the Dream. Faint voices whispered on the air, just barely audible. Ben closed his eyes and concentrated on what he wanted to see. Around him, the Dream shifted and shimmered, bending to his will. Ben opened his eyes and smiled.

He was standing in a large nursery. Eleven cribs lined the walls, each one different. Shelves stood filled with toys, and happy animals capered across the brightly colored walls and ceiling. Gauzy curtains floated in balmy spring air that breezed through open windows. Ben admired it for several moments, trying to imagine what it would look like filled with babies and children. He snorted, knowing the answer. Toys would be scattered all over the room, some of them broken, while shrieks and cries bounced off the walls. Someone would be laughing, someone else would be crying, and yet another someone would be howling in indignation over some slight. Far from idyllic.

With eleven children, Ben knew, there would be days when he would wonder why he had ever thought having even one was a good idea. But he was equally sure there would also be days when he would wonder how he had lived without them. He was eager to experience both.

Then he sighed. It would be a while. First they had to free Kendi's brother and sister, and after that they'd have to find host mothers. Still, it was fun to dream and plan, especially when he knew that eventually it would all come true.

Assuming they didn't get caught stealing slaves from Silent Acquisitions. Assuming they *could* find host mothers. Assuming they could afford eleven children. Assuming the Children of Irfan didn't simply disappear.

Ben bit his lip. It was hard to imagine the Children of Irfan fading away. The monastery had always been there, a comfortable constant in his life. He knew every building, every walkway, every tree and balcony. He couldn't imagine them empty and lifeless, bereft of the people who had lived and worked there for almost a thousand years. As well imagine the sun going out. But when the current generation of Silent died, the Children would indeed die with them.

Ben gave himself a shake. *Boy, you're in a mood,* he thought. *Go check on Kendi, see how he's doing.*

And he let go of the Dream.

"You want a favor," Harenn said. "I can tell."

Kendi blinked innocently at her from the medical bay door. "How could you possibly know?"

"It is a psychic power found among all mothers. That, and you are holding something behind your back."

With an unrepentant grin, Kendi produced a star-shaped piece of equipment and set it on the counter. Harenn instantly recognized the object as a small cryo-unit, though very old.

"What does it contain?" she asked.

"Silent embryos. Ben's brothers and sisters, to be specific."

"Ah." Harenn picked up the cryo-unit and examined it with interest. "I have heard the story. I was unaware that Ben had . . . inherited the other embryos."

"We want to take them out and raise them as our kids," Kendi said, leaning one hip against the counter. "One or two at a time."

Harenn blinked at him. "You wish to become parents? Congratulations! I think Ben would make a fine father."

"Thanks," Kendi said. "We want to— Hold it."

"And what is it you wish me to do?" Harenn continued with a perfectly straight face. "Be a host mother?"

"Nothing like that." Kendi laughed. "Though we'll have to address that issue eventually. What I'd like is a detailed gene scan. All we know about these embryos is that they're all healthy and they're all Silent. Ben says he and Ara never ran any other tests on them, but you could perform a few, couldn't you?"

"What sort of tests do you have in mind?"

"See if there are any matches in the databases that might tell us who the parents are or where they came from. Or even how old they are. Whatever you can come up with."

"Genetic scans will not tell me their relative ages, unless the gene patterns are from an extinct group. Still, this is an interesting mystery. I will see what I can do."

Kendi thanked her and turned to go, then turned back. "Harenn, do you think I'm ready to be a father?"

"No," Harenn said.

"What? Why not?"

"No one is ever truly ready to become a parent," Harenn said with a small smile. "Even those who think they are. Parenthood is too powerful, too unique to each individual. So I do not think you are ready. But I think you will learn quickly and I think you will learn well."

"Oh. Thanks. I think."

"I will run your tests as soon as I have a chance," Harenn told him.

"Thanks for that, too." With a wave, he left. Harenn looked thoughtfully at the empty doorway for a moment, then stared for a long time at the cryo-unit.

A small snip, and a tiny hole opened in the fabric covering Martina's index finger. Martina held her breath, waiting for some kind of shock or even an alarm. Nothing. Martina set the scissors down with an internal sigh of relief and shot Keith a brief glance.

Martina was worried about her brother. It was hard not to stare at him over the pile of robes, even though staring at a member of the opposite sex created more

N-waves and would earn her a warning shock. Keith was bent industriously over his work, the needle dipping swiftly in and out of the fabric. His depression seemed to have vanished entirely, which was why Martina was worried.

The other Alphas sat in a circle on the hard floor, their legs swathed in piles of yellow fabric. There was no conversation, just the rustle of cloth, the snip of scissors, and the occasional low murmur from a Delta pointing out flaws. The Alphas wore special gloves, thinned for the extra sensitivity required for sewing.

How long had she and Keith been here? Martina had no idea. Whenever she tried to keep track of the time, something happened to make her reckoning slip away. Sleep cycles were irregular. Sometimes Martina and the other Alphas were kept awake for so long, they were collectively ready to pass out on the floor. Some began to hallucinate. Other times Martina knew they couldn't possibly have been awake for more than a few hours before being sent to bed. Sleep time, when it came, was always too short. Martina had no way of knowing for sure, but judging from her level of fatigue, she and the others weren't getting more than five or six hours of sleep at a time.

Food was another problem. At first it had been fairly plentiful, if heavy on the protein. Lately there had been less, and mealtimes were also irregular. Martina was almost never full. Every so often, the Deltas handed out sweet snack cakes, and the unaccustomed sugar sent Martina soaring—until she crashed back to earth a few minutes later. She craved starchy foods almost constantly. Bread slathered with butter, mashed potatoes swimming in gravy, pasta peeking out from heavy tomato sauce, and even plain boiled rice danced in her dreams and made her stomach rumble.

Days—if they could be called that—were spent in a variety of ways. The Alphas spent a great deal of time in mind-numbing labor such as hand-stitching robes or scrubbing floors with stiff brushes or washing clothes in great tubs. Other times the Alphas sat through meditation exercises, though these came easily to Martina and the other experienced Silent. A certain amount of time was set aside for study, mostly of Dreamer Roon's book. The more Martina read of his work, however, the more convinced she became that the man had no idea what he was talking about. His stories about Irfan Qasad and Daniel Vik were ludicrous. True, no one questioned the fact that Vik was one of the greatest fiends in all history. After all, the man had been a blatant racist who had kidnapped his own child away from his wife, collaborated with terrorists, and done his best to wipe all Silent from the face of Bellerophon. But Martina seriously doubted that the taint of his genetic material coursed through the bodies of all Silent, causing their impure N-waves. For one thing, Martina herself had been born before the founding of the Bellerophon colony and couldn't possibly be touched by the "taint" of Daniel Vik. The same applied to Keith, for that matter.

And then there was the Confessional. Martina hated it. Every moment she sat in the chair listening to Alphas and Deltas shout "Impure" at her was pure torture. She told herself over and over that there was nothing wrong with her, that she was not impure, that the peccadilloes they wrung from her were nothing more than normal human behavior. Lately, however, she left the Confessional feeling wrung out, exhausted, and filthy. If the circle was supposed to cleanse her, it was failing miserably. Martina had considered mentioning this to Delta Maura, but had almost as quickly decided against it. Something told her that confessing any such thing in this place would be a fatal error.

But Keith appeared to be loving it.

Through the little snatches of conversation she had

managed to steal with him, Martina had gathered that Keith wasn't completely well on a mental level. His previous owners had apparently been hard on him, and there were . . . other factors.

Martina stole a glance across the sewing circle at Keith. His forehead was wrinkled with concentration as he worked. His Delta leaned down and put a gloved hand on his shoulder. Keith stiffened and a momentary touch of fear crossed his face. The expression was familiar, and a long-buried memory stirred within Martina. All at once she was back on the slave ship, still shivering with cold leftover from cryo-sleep. A slaver named Feder was herding her family down a long corridor that smelled of cold metal. The Weavers—Dad, Mom, Evan, Keith, and Martina—were the last ones to leave the colony ship, and Feder stayed right behind them. The new slave shackles were heavy on Martina's wrist and ankle.

Feder, a dark-haired man with a long nose and thin lips, put his hand around Keith's shoulder as they walked. Keith tried to shrug him off, but Feder only tightened his grip. The smile that crossed his face made Martina feel cold and scared inside. She wondered how Keith felt.

"What's the matter, kid?" Feder asked. "You don't like friendly people?"

Before Keith could respond, Dad's hand shot out and grabbed Feder's wrist. "Don't touch my son," he said in a low, deadly voice.

Feder's free hand darted to his waist. Dad collapsed to the floor, screaming in pain. His bands glowed blue. Mom dropped beside him, wanting to help but not knowing what to do. Martina stared with wide eyes, scared and uncertain. She had never heard her father scream like that. Evan began to cry, and Keith looked dazed. Dad's screaming continued for a long time, then abruptly stopped. The blue glow on his bands faded.

"Touch me again, you bastard," Feder told Dad in

a voice that carried up and down the passenger bay, "and I won't shock just you, hey? I'll shock your wife—or your kids. Now get up. No talking."

Mom and Dad slowly got to their feet. Martina's throat was thick and she stifled sobs. Around them, other slavers herded the other members of the Real People toward the large double doors at the other end of the passenger bay. Her family was at the very end of the line. Bare feet shuffled and padded on the cool metal deck. Feder walked in front of Martina and her family with his arm draped around Keith's shoulders, as if the two were old friends. The look of helpless outrage on Dad's face mirrored the way Martina felt. Evan was obviously trying not to cry again, and Rebecca took his hand.

"I read some of your files before we woke you up," Feder said to Keith in a bright, friendly tone. "The whole ship is from Australia back on Earth, but you bunch call yourselves the Real People, hey?"

Keith didn't respond. The muscles on Feder's arm tightened. "Hey?" he repeated.

"Yeah," Keith said, barely audible.

"A great idea," Feder said. "Starting fresh on another planet, reestablishing tribal ways. Too bad it's not going to work out."

Silence. The arm tightened again. "I guess," Keith mumbled.

"What's your name, kid?"

Pause. "Utang," Keith said, giving the Real People name he had chosen for himself only a few months before. Martina rarely thought of Keith as Utang, even though Keith—Utang—used it regularly.

"Your ship's behind the times, kid," Feder said. "Now that we got slipships, these old slower-than-light heaps are just about junk. Barely worth salvaging. But people—now, that's different. People never devalue, hey?"

"I guess."

"You wouldn't have wanted Pelagosa anyway," Feder continued. "It was colonized by the KLO Syndicate and the Freebanders four, five hundred years ago. They're not taking immigrants. But don't you worry— we'll find a good home for you. Might even buy you myself, hey? Boss gives us our pick at cost-and-a-quarter. Been saving up for a new cabin boy. What do you think?"

"I . . . I . . ." Keith stammered.

Martina's stomach churned. There had to be some way to help her brother, but she couldn't think of anything.

"You don't have to answer, kid," Feder said kindly. "Know why?" He clamped his arm around Keith's neck. Martina heard him gasp and choke. Dad looked ready to leap, bands or no bands, but Rebecca put a hand on his arm and gestured sharply at Martina. Martina felt a stab of guilt. Dad wasn't going to help Keith because he was afraid Feder would shock her. It was her fault Dad couldn't do anything.

"You don't have to answer because you don't have a choice," Feder said. He abruptly spun Keith around to face his family and grabbed Keith's cheeks from behind with one big hand. With a nasty grin, he gave Keith's ear a long, wet lick. Martina wondered why he would do such a thing. Then Feder gave Keith a shove that sent him sprawling.

"Now move your lazy ass!" Feder barked.

Keith waved off Dad's help and got up on his own, ankle bands and wristbands shining in the ship's harsh lighting. His face was hard, but Martina caught tears at the corners of his eyes.

Feder herded them through the double doors into the corridor and from there into a tiny cell with two other families. The cell contained nothing but a few sleeping pallets on the floor and a single sink and toilet in the corner. It all stank of urine and fearful sweat. The coverings on the pallets had clearly not been washed in years. Two round portholes looked out into black, star-strewn space. Feder slammed the door shut, and it locked.

Martina looked out one of the portholes and by craning her neck was barely able to make out the colony ship. A stiff umbilical cord chained it to the slaver ship. The colony ship was a giant cylinder, gray and impact-pocked, and looked slow and clunky compared to what Martina could see of the slaver vessel, which was sleek and flat. The colony ship was spinning to provide gravity, and the slaver vessel had matched the spin, though from Martina's perspective, the stars were rotating around the two ships instead of the other way around.

"Do you realize," said Dad behind her, "that the mutants have enslaved us again? As they did our ancestors?"

Gary, the father of one of the other two families in the cell, shrugged. "They enslaved the other groups, too. And the crew."

"How can they get away with this?" his wife Anna cried. She held twin boys not even a year old on her lap. "We're not slaves. We never were. What about our records? Citizenship and all that?"

Mom shook her head. "We left Earth over nine hundred years ago. Even if any of those records survived, how would we access them? Telephone? Fax? I overheard some of the slavers talking, and it sounds like they do this all the time. The slavers find a colony vessel like this one, hit the crew with a surprise attack, and enslave the whole lot. Who's to prove we *aren't* slaves?"

"We need to pool our knowledge," Dad said. "Compare notes about what we've all seen or overheard so we can form a plan of escape or rebellion or—" His bands glowed blue and he cried out in pain. Startled, Martina spun from the window in time to see her father writhing on the floor. Mom crouched near him, looking as helpless as Martina felt. After a long moment, Dad stopped squirming. His bands were no longer glowing. Martina bit her lip.

Once they had determined that Dad had suffered no permanent damage, Gary gestured at the walls. *Listening devices?* he mouthed.

"Probably," grunted Liza, the mother of the third family. She was a large woman, with heavy breasts and thighs. "Either they're eavesdropping or the computer is programmed to listen for certain words. They shock us if we talk about . . . anything important."

"We should still pool information," Dad said stubbornly. "Just don't use those words."

The adults did so, gesturing for Martina and the others to remain silent. Two shocks later, they knew that sometime in the nine hundred years since the Real People had left Earth, someone had invented slipships, which allowed for faster-than-light travel. The slower ships and their claims on habitable planets had either been forgotten or purposely ignored. These slavers were from a government called the Five Green Worlds, though the colony ship had been found in unclaimed space.

The cell grew close and stuffy. Martina did a quick count. Six adults, three teenagers, four preteens (counting herself and Evan), and two babies for one sink and toilet and maybe eight sleeping pallets. How would they—

The porthole exploded into multicolored light. The quiet talk instantly died. Martina stared. The stars and darkness had vanished, replaced by psychedelic swirls of color. Martina's eyes felt as if something were twisting them, and nausea turned her stomach. She looked away from the porthole and felt a little better.

"I think we've entered slipspace," Gary said. He scrambled to the toilet and threw up.

They spent several days in slipspace, though the only way to mark passing time was by how often the slavers came by. Three times a "day" the door opened and someone handed in diapers for the babies and bowls of food, usually some kind of mush. No silver-ware—they had to eat with their fingers or slurp directly from the bowl.

There was nothing to do but talk, and even that was limited. Anyone who said a wrong word received a shock. They learned not to say *revolt, escape, run, kill, attack, hurt, organize,* and a good dozen other words. The families also learned to sit with their backs to the portholes, since a single glance at the colors outside brought on violent headaches or nausea. Most of the time, everyone sat and stared at the walls, sunk into a dull apathy. Martina's skin itched and she wanted a shower. The cell smelled of unwashed people and babies that needed changing.

The adults took turns comforting each other and the children. Everyone went through at least one session of weeping despair. One time Martina wondered what had happened to the shell collection she had put into her suitcase, and the realization that it was probably now the property of one of the slavers choked her throat and made tears run down her face.

"It's just a stupid shell collection," she sobbed when Rebecca put her arms around her on the pallet. "Just some stupid shells." But she couldn't stop crying for a long time.

That night—which was night in name only, since the lights never dimmed—Martina lay on the crowded pallet with Evan squashing her on one side and Keith pressing her on the other and found herself wishing they would get wherever it was they were going, get it over with.

The next day was the worst. The door slid open not long after breakfast, and Feder stood framed in the entrance. The Weaver family gasped as one. Feder didn't say a word. Instead he crooked a finger at Keith. Keith flinched and Martina's heart pounded hard. Dad got slowly to his feet and stood between his son and Feder.

"No," was all he said.

Feder's hand went to his belt and pain tore through Martina's body. She screamed. Mom pulled Martina's writhing body to her, but there was nothing she could do to stop the pain. The pain went on and on, ripping at her muscles and tearing at her head like hot knives. Dad flung himself at Feder, but before he could touch the man, his own bands glowed. Dad dropped to floor, face pale with agony. Martina continued to scream. The others stared uncertainly and the twins began to cry. Martina screamed and screamed. She couldn't stop herself, or even think. She wished she were dead.

"Stop it!" Mom cried. "Leave her alone!"

And then Keith stepped over Dad and stood in front of Feder, eyes downcast. Feder removed his hand from his belt. Dad's and Martina's bands faded to silver and their cries stopped. The hot pain ended, but Martina's whole body still hurt. She whimpered in Mom's arms, glad to feel them around her. Feder took Keith by the shoulder and the two of them left. The door slid shut.

Martina sat in her mother's embrace, trying to stop crying. She had never felt so helpless. His brother was at this moment being . . . what? Beaten? Killed? Raped? Martina was only ten years old, but she had heard the older kids on the streets of Sydney talk about that kind of thing. Some of them took money for it. Martina didn't know for sure if that was what Feder had in mind for her brother, but she couldn't think of anything else he would want.

Everyone in the cell sat and waited like the family of a hospital patient expecting bad news. Mom and Dad looked like statues. Martina's soft cries were the only sounds. She felt bad, guilty. Something awful was happening to Keith, and it was her fault. If she had been able to stop screaming, stand up to the pain, maybe Feder would have left Keith alone.

A long time later, the door slid open. Everyone came quietly alert as Keith entered the cell. Martina caught a glimpse of Feder's smirk before the door shut. Keith made his way to a corner of the cell and sat down, his face a blank mask. Mom approached him, but he turned his back on her. He continued to shun all forms of contact for the rest of the day, and in the middle of that night's sleep cycle, Martina awoke to hear him crying softly. She didn't know what to do, so she did nothing. Eventually the crying stopped and Martina fell back into restless sleep.

Martina forced herself to look down at the seam she was stitching so she would avoid looking at Keith. Feder had come for Keith several times before they reached the station where Martina and her family had been auctioned off. She had thought she'd forgotten that, buried safely in the bottom of her mind, but now it felt as if it had happened only a few days ago. Had Feder carried through on his threat to buy Keith as a cabin boy? Martina didn't know, though she also remembered a slaver—not Feder—coming for Keith at the end of the auction and taking him away. It could easily have been for Feder. Fury rose in Martina's chest and the yellow seam blurred before her. How long had Keith been abused by that man? And then, to top everything off, Keith had turned out Silent. Feder, or whoever had initially bought him, had probably sold him off at a healthy profit, just as Martina's first owner had done. He had doubtless been trained by his new master, learned how to enter the Dream—and then been wrenched away from it during the Despair. Martina herself had almost jumped off a building, and she hadn't ever encountered anyone like Feder. No wonder Keith was unbalanced.

Keith's Delta said something to him, and he smiled.
Martina wondered what it was. A warning tingle from
her shackles reminded her not to stare and she quickly
turned her attention back to her sewing. How long
were they going to do this? Dreamer Roon said in
one of his lectures that hard labor drove away N-
waves, bringing them closer to Irfan and making them
readier to enter the Dream without drugs. Martina
had her doubts. She suspected it was make-work, but
to what end? And why the weird sleeping and eating
patterns? A way of reinforcing Roon's power over
them? Martina had been a slave for most of her life
and was used to obeying orders from her owner, so
why did Roon need to establish dominance? It was a
puzzle, something to think about during the intermina-
ble labors of the day.

A soft chime sounded. "Time," called Delta Maura.
Martina tensed. She was taking a risk today, a small
one, but a risk nonetheless. With a false sigh of relief,
Martina set aside the half-finished robe, then surreptitiously pulled at her left glove, tightening it over her
fingers and exposing the little patch of skin. The
Alphas rose and stretched the kinks out of arms and
legs. Keith neatly folded his work first. When Martina
got to her feet, she swayed, as if dizzy. Immediately,
Delta Maura was at Martina's side.

"Are you all right, dear?" Delta Maura asked.

With her left hand, Martina grasped Delta Maura's
wrist just above her green glove and pretended to
steady herself. The tiny patch of Martina's bare skin
came into direct contact with Delta Maura's. Martina
braced herself.

Nothing.

"Alpha?" Delta Maura said. "Is something wrong?"

"I'm fine," Martina managed. "I sometimes get a
little head rush when I stand up too fast."

This was no lie and therefore didn't earn her a
shock. Delta Maura nodded and stepped away, folding

her hands in front of her. Martina's heart was pounding. She had felt nothing. It had been drilled into her from childhood that when two Silent touched skin to skin for the first time, they both experienced a physical jolt. The jolt was the physical manifestation of a newly established psychic link that would allow the two Silent to find each other in the Dream faster and more easily than two Silent who had never touched. It was also a highly reliable test for Silence.

Delta Maura was not Silent.

Martina's head swam beneath this staggering concept. All the Deltas were supposed to be Silent, trained by Roon himself. But Delta Maura clearly wasn't. Was this true of all the Deltas?

That's the reason for the gloves and the rules against touching each other, Martina realized. *So we won't find out the Deltas aren't Silent.*

It made a terrible sort of sense. Working Silent were rare these days. How had these people—she still didn't know what the group was called—found so many of them and retrained them in the few months since the Despair? It was something Martina hadn't considered until now, but she had been dealing with strange food, sleep deprivation, and mind-numbing labor. Was this the reason for all that? So no one would ask too many questions?

One of the Deltas—Keith's Delta—cleared his throat pointedly and the Alphas fell silent.

"I need to announce," the Delta said, gesturing at Keith, "that this Alpha has been doing exemplary work of late and is deserving of high praise. Very soon he will be promoted to Beta. All praise the Dream!"

"All praise the Dream!" everyone repeated automatically. Keith smiled, glowing at the kind words. Martina felt an unexpected wash of jealousy. Ridiculous. She quashed the feeling and filed it away as something to trot out during the Confessional.

"You may now return to your quarters for a few moments of free time," the Delta finished.

As the Alphas filed out of the sewing room, Martina managed to get next to Keith. "Congratulations," she said wryly without looking directly at him. He gave her a glance that was almost shy.

"Thanks," he said.

Now Martina *did* look at him. She had heard no trace of irony in his voice. Deciding on the direct approach, she said, "You like it here, don't you?"

"Of course," he said. "I don't have to worry about anything here. There are fewer N-waves in my brain, and I feel freer than ever. Didn't you hear? Pretty soon I'll be a Beta!"

Martina worked her jaw. How could he be buying into this place? Sure, she might be a slave, but she was *Silent,* and used to better treatment than this.

"I didn't like it at first, either," said another Alpha, the plumpish man who had been the first to sit in the Confessional. "But now I'm thinking it isn't so bad. Out there"—he made a vague gesture toward the corridor walls—"we're slaves to the Dream. In here, we're free. No one can hurt us or look at us like we're freaks because we're Silent. Dreamer Roon *cares* about us. He's trying to help us get into the Dream without all those drugs. If putting up with some weird stuff now and then is part of the price, I'm willing to pay it."

Martina couldn't believe her ears. True, she had thought at first that the deal was pretty good—nice quarters, nice clothes, not having to put in long hours in the Dream—but they didn't outweigh the other factors. Not even close. And now she had learned that at least one part of the whole place was a lie.

Martina threw a glance over her shoulder. The Deltas were following, doubtless listening in on the conversation. Best to play along. "I'm starting to think so, too," she said. "I do miss the Dream, though. Do you think they'll give us our drugs back and let us back in?"

"That will come when you are a Gamma," Delta Maura said from behind. "For now, you must concentrate on Dreamer Roon's teaching, dear."

"I'll try, Delta," Martina said with pretend disappointment.

"Do you hear the Dream whisper to you?" Delta Maura asked.

"At ni—just before I go to sleep," Martina replied, remembering at the last moment not to make references to time. "I used to hear it all the time, but ever since the Despair, I've only heard it a little bit."

"The Despair was a time of cleansing," Delta Maura said seriously. "It was a time when the unworthy were weeded out of the Dream. Those who were cast out had too much of Vik's evil taint about them, and they deserved their fate. You are all chosen by Irfan herself, and her blessings run strong within you."

Pride in herself welled up. Martina fiercely shoved it aside. The words were false praise from a fake Silent. No one knew why some Silent could still touch the Dream and others couldn't. The idea that it had anything to do with Irfan Qasad or Daniel Vik was ludicrous. But the words still made her feel special, part of an "in" crowd, maybe even a member of a secret society or a cult.

Martina stopped dead in the corridor, causing the Alpha coming up behind to bump into her. She apologized and made herself keep moving, though her mind was whirling again. She entered her quarters and sat down on her bed, trying to fit her mind around another new idea.

The place was a cult.

Martina should have recognized it sooner. She had read about cults in her first owner's library, had heard about Silent who were members of such groups. Everything that had happened in this place, she realized, was part of an indoctrination process. The separation from society, the enforcement of strict rules, the sleep deprivation and low-carbohydrate diet—all designed to break down psychological barriers and force the "recruits" to embrace the cult itself. Martina was amazed that she hadn't seen it all earlier.

The question was, why go through all the trouble? Martina got up to pace the floor between her bed and the computer desk. She desperately wished she could go outside, get some fresh air and sunshine to clear her mind, but the closest thing to any of that was a stupid hologram on the wall.

Martina continued to pace. She was a slave, had been one for most of her life. She had been stolen away from her owners at DrimCom, but she didn't feel like a kidnap victim. From her perspective, one owner was pretty much like another, as long as she wasn't beaten or otherwise mistreated. None of her work in the Dream enriched her personally, so why did she care who paid for her services? Martina had no children, no husband, and no really close friends, so it wasn't as if she would be a prime candidate for running away after being bought—or stolen—by someone else. Why, then, go through the trouble of all this indoctrination?

The answer, when it came, seemed obvious. Loyalty. Martina—and, presumably, the others—felt no loyalty toward any owner, present or past, and would happily run to freedom, given the chance. But fully indoctrinated members of a cult were something else. Their loyalty to the cult and its leader ran strong and fierce. They invariably resisted anyone who tried to remove them from the cult's enclave. Roon's program was designed to create a group of absolutely loyal Silent who wouldn't dream of running away and who would do their best to return if kidnapped. In a universe where Silent were rarer than free-floating plutonium, such followers were worth a hundred times more than ordinary Silent slaves. A thousand times more.

And it was starting to work. Keith, already emotionally vulnerable, was clearly ready to buy into Roon's fictional world. So was that other male Alpha. Martina herself had begun to weaken, despite the fact that she had been suspicious of late and doing her best to resist.

A feeling of hopelessness washed over her. She had to get out of this place, and fast. She also had to somehow persuade Keith to come with her. But how? Her every move was watched, even when she was alone, and she was still shackled.

No. There was no such thing as a perfect security system. Security systems were designed and used by people, and people made mistakes. Martina sat down on her bed to think. How had her kidnappers managed to deactivate her shackles at DrimCom? They must have done so—otherwise they would have shocked her the moment she crossed the building's threshold. If they could do it, she could do it. And the cameras in her quarters could be foiled. An "accident" could cover them up or knock them off-line entirely. All she had to do was find them.

Martina nodded. It was a place to start and gave her something to think about, concentrate on during the mind-numbing labor. And in the meantime, she would have to play the role of good little Alpha, persuade the Deltas she was glad to be here. If they thought she was a willing participant, they would be less likely to watch her closely.

But how would she stop them from indoctrinating Keith?

CHAPTER EIGHT

"The best way to get a child to do something is to forbid him to do it. The same goes for an adult."
—Renna Dell, First Bellerophon Landing Party

Kendi looked up from the display holo as Ben entered their quarters and flopped down onto the couch with a heavy sigh. It was shift change at the Collection. The holographic screen showed the door scanning a steady stream of people—IDs and prints—in a ritual Kendi had seen dozens of times over the last few weeks. In about half an hour, another stream of people would emerge from the same door. Kendi assumed the people coming off shift had to brief the people coming on. Kendi wondered why the Collection needed all these employees, and he desperately wished they could hack the computer system to find out. The Collection's system, however, was still physically isolated from the rest of the station, and the only way to get access was from within. It was frustrating in the extreme, knowing the Collection and his family were so close, yet so untouchable.

It was also difficult because Kendi had only a vague sketch of a plan. He hadn't told anyone, not even Ben, that he had almost no idea what he was doing. Every instinct he had, however, told him that the department head keys were crucial to freeing his brother and sister. Kendi hated keeping secrets from Ben, but he didn't think Ben would react well if he knew Kendi was insisting on stealing the keys before he knew what to do with them.

And then there was the time limit. The *Poltergeist* had to be back on Bellerophon in eight days, no excuses or exceptions. If it came down to it, Kendi would happily end his career with the Children if it meant liberty for his brother and sister, but he didn't want to do that. For one thing, his parents were still out there somewhere, and they were next on his list.

"I take it you got nothing," Kendi said to Ben.

Ben shook his head. His red hair was dark with sweat. "If I didn't know better, I'd swear Roon was a saint. He doesn't drink, he doesn't touch recreational drugs, he doesn't visit hookers, and he doesn't gamble. He doesn't even seem to have a favorite restaurant. I thought today I might actually get something on him because he deviated from his routine and made an extra stop on his way home from work, but no dice." He ran a hand over his face and grimaced. "God, I need a shower. I'll give you the details when I'm done."

He got up and headed for the bedroom, shedding clothes as he went. Kendi watched the muscles of Ben's back bunch and move beneath smooth skin as he pulled off his shirt and dropped it on the floor. Trousers, underwear, and socks followed. Kendi continued to watch Ben's naked form until it disappeared into the bedroom and, presumably, headed toward the bathroom. A few moments later, he heard the hiss of running water. Kendi drummed his fingers on the desk. He should watch the displays. He should look for an anomaly among the workers that he could exploit. He should look for subtle clues about what was really going on inside the Collection. He should—

"The hell with this," he muttered.

Less than a minute later, he drew aside the back corner of the shower screen and stepped into the shower behind Ben, whose face was upturned under a luxurious spray. Water had drenched and darkened his hair and ran in rivulets down his back. Kendi felt an aching, heavy need to be close to Ben, become so close that their bodies would melt and run together like drops of water. He put both his hands on Ben's shoulders. Ben jumped and turned partway around.

"Need someone to wash your back?" Kendi asked, moving his hands lower.

"That's not my back," Ben pointed out with a grin, and turned back to the shower.

"How about this?"

"Nope." Ben closed his eyes with a sigh. "You'll have to keep trying."

What started in the shower finished in the bedroom. Ben, still slightly damp, sprawled on his stomach next to Kendi, who was lying on his back but still pressed close to Ben. Kendi's skin was warm on Ben's. The soft light and lack of angles in the room were soothing and restful. The window showed gleaming stars against an utterly black background, and Ben could pretend there was no Collection, no SA Station—just a universe that was completely empty except for him and Kendi.

Ben shifted and winced at a slight twinge. Kendi's lovemaking had been intense, even a little rough, and Ben was sure he'd have a few bruises in the morning. He didn't care. Everything about Kendi had lately been more intense—and just plain tense—and Ben was glad to offer him some relief. Ben was just drifting off to sleep when Kendi spoke.

"So what happened today? You said Roon deviated from his routine."

"Hm?" Ben roused himself. "Deviated. Yeah, he did. It wasn't anything big. He gets off work every day at the same time—not during the shift change for the rest of the workers—and then he goes home. He takes the same route every single day, and once he gets home, he stays there. Except today."

"What did he do today?"

"He went to an art gallery."

"Art gallery?" Kendi rolled over and propped his head up on one hand. "Did you follow him inside?"

Ben shrugged. "Of course. I swear he looked at *everything*. Paintings, sculptures, holograms, sensories—you name it. There was a special exhibit on. He wandered around for more than two hours. Finally he bought a painting. He ordered it delivered and walked out. I followed him home, but nothing else happened."

"What was the painting about?" Kendi asked intently.

"Does it matter?" Ben said, surprised.

"It might. No detail is too small; you know that."

Ben closed his eyes and cast his mind back. Kendi, he knew, had the flawless short-term memory required for Dream communication work, and could faultlessly remember pages and pages of text for short periods of time. All Children were trained this way so that written communication could be transmitted word for word to other Silent through the Dream. But Ben hadn't gone through the mnemonic training, and he hadn't paid too much attention to the specifics of Roon's purchase. He hadn't thought it would matter, though now he realized his mistake. He closed his eyes and thought.

"It was an exhibit of circus art," he said after a while. "And Roon bought a painting of a circus animal. An elephant? Yeah, an elephant."

Ben felt the bed move and heard the rustle of sheets. He opened his eyes. Kendi had gotten up and was yanking open the closet door.

"What's up?" Ben asked.

"I have to go talk to him." Kendi pulled out an outfit he rarely wore because it was so dressy—an electric-blue silk tunic with matching trousers that set off his dark skin and eyes.

"Talk to who?"

"The art gallery owner." He pulled a long length

of red cloth from the closet and expertly wound it into a turban. A purple amethyst lapel pin completed the ensemble. Ben gnawed his lower lip, feeling as if he had let Kendi down. If he had done a proper job shadowing Roon, Kendi wouldn't have to go back to the gallery. Ben felt had somehow blown it, but he didn't know what he had done wrong. Kendi didn't seem upset, but still.

"How do I look?" Kendi asked.

"What look are you going for?" Ben countered, sitting up.

"Wealthy collector."

"Works for me. Um . . . do you want me to go with you? Back you up?"

"No, I'll be better off alone. Send out the troops if you don't hear from me in two hours."

And then he was gone, leaving Ben alone on the bed.

Bedj-ka ghosted along the walkway, staying close to the shadows. Insects chirped among the talltree leaves, and his feet made only a tiny whisper of sound on the wooden path. The forest was almost completely dark beneath the talltree canopy, though enough silvery moonlight filtered through the leaves to let him see where he was going. The house, built into the branches of the talltree, lay about ten meters ahead of him. Like most Bellerophon treehouses, it sported a wide balcony that went all the way around it. Golden light shone from the house windows, and a pair of enormous, shaggy humans guarded the front door. Bedj-ka halted where he was. He knew from experience that if he got much closer, the two men would spot him, no matter how many points he put into his stealth skill. This time, however, he had a different idea.

Just before reaching the discovery point, Bedj-ka oozed carefully over the rail of the walkway. The forest floor was shrouded in shadow, and Bedj-ka was grateful for that—he didn't have to look at the hundred-meter drop. Beneath the walkway was a fine polymer netting made to catch objects or people that slipped over the edge. Bedj-ka dropped fearlessly onto the netting and scuttled along the stretchy strands like a spider until he had made his way to the rear of the house, opposite the side with the guards. The men didn't stir. Bedj-ka reached up, got a hand on the walkway, and hoisted himself back onto it. This brought him almost directly under a rear window of the house—and got him past the guards unnoticed.

Rigid, he thought. *It worked.*

Voices filtered out of the open window.

"Where would she run to?" demanded a husky male voice. "Where's she hiding?"

"I don't know," replied a woman in shaky tones. "How would I know?"

The sound of a slap, a grunt of pain. Bedj-ka's throat tickled. He swallowed hard to suppress a cough and slowly raised himself up until he could peer through the window. A big, shaggy man in black was glowering down at a woman who was holding her cheek and trying to look defiant. Three other men in the room held energy pistols on a small crowd of scared-looking humans of varying ages. Some were younger than Bedj-ka.

"Maybe I should kill one of the others," the shaggy man snarled. "Maybe then you'll be more forthcoming." He gestured at one of his men, who leveled a pistol at a boy Bedj-ka's age. "Tell me where Irfan Qasad is hiding, or the boy dies."

"I can't tell you what I don't know," the woman cried. "Please, Mr. Clearwater. I really don't know where she is. None of us do."

"Max," Clearwater said. Max tightened his finger around the pistol. Bedj-ka made an odd gesture, and the scene instantly froze. He stared through the window, trying to think. Bedj-ka had already died seven times, and he didn't want to make a mistake that handed him death number eight.

Okay. The shaggy man was Ormand Clearwater, leader of the pirates. That he already knew. Irfan Qasad was hiding in the woods less than a kilometer away from Treetown, but she had no idea what the pirates were doing or why they had invaded Treetown. All she and the other escapees knew was that the pirates had slipships and a lot of weapons. Bedj-ka had volunteered to go spy on them to learn more, and Irfan had flashed him a grateful look before nodding and sending him off. She hadn't actually said whether or not he should rescue anyone, and the only weapon Bedj-ka had was a knife.

A sudden cough exploded from Bedj-ka's throat. He put a fist to his mouth and coughed several more times, then swallowed. Was he getting sick? He hoped not. Good thing he had paused the game.

Bedj-ka stared at the frozen scene for a long moment. Maybe Clearwater was bluffing, or maybe the woman did know something and would reveal it now. Regardless, Bedj-ka was sure that if he charged through the window, he would die.

Or would he just be captured?

Bedj-ka suddenly wished he had read more about Bellerophon's history. The sim was supposed to be historically accurate, and he had the feeling he was playing the part of a real person. If he knew what that person had done, Bedj-ka might know what to do now.

Clearwater continued to train his pistol on the cowering woman. Bedj-ka did know that Clearwater was actually a minor player in all this. The *real* villain was Daniel Vik, who was even now amassing an army to attack Treetown and the new Silent who lived there. Irfan—and Bedj-ka—had to find a way to stop Clearwater and rid Treetown of the pirates before Vik got wind of their presence. If he knew how vulnerable Treetown currently was, he would almost certainly invade in force and the Silent would be wiped from the face of the planet.

Bedj-ka drew an "S" in midair. The letter glowed briefly, then flashed and vanished, indicating the game had been saved. If he blew it, he could just restart from this point and try again. Bedj-ka drew his knife and made the gesture that would restart the scene.

"Hold it!" he shouted, and dove through the window. Everyone turned in surprise. Clearwater's face shifted into a mask of rage—

—and then froze again.

"Time expired," said a dry computer voice. "Do you wish to save the game before exiting?"

Bedj-ka sighed. "No." The scene vanished, replaced by the blank inside of sim goggles. Bedj-ka pulled them off, removed gloves, boots, and earpieces, and stepped off the little trampoline that could become rigid or soft, depending on what sort of surface the sim called for. He considered calling Mom to ask for more sim time, but ultimately decided against it. She always said no, and he didn't feel like arguing with her right now.

A coughing fit seized him, followed by a hefty sneeze. Definitely a cold. He grimaced. Getting sick meant you had sinned and were being punished. It also meant being confined to bed, having to drink horrible-tasting medicine several times a day, and having the other children pray over you. He didn't want to go through that here.

What had he done? Bedj-ka tried to think. He hadn't disobeyed Mom that he remembered, though maybe he hadn't obeyed her as fast as he could have. He didn't like Sister Gretchen very much. Did that count? He didn't know.

Bedj-ka put the sim equipment on the shelf in the living room of the quarters he and Mom shared. They were nice, a lot nicer than the Enclave had ever been. Everything was done in soft blue, and several windows looked out into space. There was a big living room, a bathroom with both a shower and a tub, and two bedrooms. The rooms were also *quiet*, with no gongs to mark meditation time and no bells to mark learning time, eating time, and play time, no shouts and yells of other kids. The only sound was the soft rush of the ventilation system. Bedj-ka liked that. He could be alone whenever he wanted.

In this place, Bedj-ka had his own room. It was small, but it had a door he could close and a bed that stood by itself instead of in a long row of other beds. It also had a window. Bedj-ka had his own closet with seven whole outfits Mom had bought for him on Drim and on SA Station. He had unlimited access to the galley and could get something to eat whenever he liked, as long as it wasn't too close to mealtime. He had bookdisks and sim games and other toys, all things Mom had bought for him. She limited the amount of time he could play sim games, but he could read all he wanted. Bedj-ka liked reading. The Enclave had taught him how, but Matron and Patron had made it clear a lot of stuff was forbidden to the Silent. Silent were weaker than other humans, more prone to corruption, and they had to be sheltered. When Bedj-ka had brought this fact up with Mom, however, her face had gotten all tight. The next day, he had found a small library of bookdisks in his room, ones filled with histories and fairy tales and stories of adventure the Enclave had forbidden. Bedj-ka had devoured most of them. At first he had felt guilty and wondered whether he would get corrupted, but nothing had happened, and then Mom had asked him about some of the books at supper. That had been a suprise. He hadn't known she'd read them too. Mom wasn't corrupt. She had gotten him away from the chocolate farm.

Except now he was getting sick. Was reading the

books a sin after all? How could it be, if Mom did it? Matron always said Silent children sinned more than the non-Silent. Maybe it was a sin for him but not for Mom.

He coughed again, hard. After the spasm passed, he got a glass of water from the bathroom. At this rate, the whole ship would know he was getting sick. He groaned inwardly at the thought. Then it occurred to him that if Mom was nice about the books, maybe she would be nice about him getting sick, whether he had sinned or not. Maybe he should tell her. She was a nurse, after all.

Bedj-ka checked the computer. It said Mom was working down among the engines. He hesitated for a moment, then told the intercom system to page her.

"Yes, Bedj-ka?" came her voice.

"I'm off the sims," he said.

"Did you do your lessons?"

"Course I did. The computer won't let me play until I'm done." He paused, suddenly uncertain again. The cough came back, and he suppressed it.

"Is something wrong? I'm nearly done down here and will be up soon."

"No," Bedj-ka said. "Nothing's wrong. I just wanted to see what you were doing."

"I am resetting the gravity generators. If you get bored, you may come down here and help me, if you like," she said.

He didn't like, though he only said, "Okay. Myra, close channel."

Bedj-ka coughed again, then wandered aimlessly around the quarters for a while, not quite sure what he wanted to do. He didn't really *feel* sick—he was just coughing—and he wasn't tired enough to lie down. If Mom treated him like Matron and Patron had done at the Enclave, he'd be stuck in bed soon enough, so he decided to wander around and enjoy a little freedom.

The ship's corridors seemed to be empty. Where was everyone? Probably out scouting the Collection again or something. Bedj-ka only had a hazy idea of what Father Kendi, Mom, and the others were up to. Mom had told him he didn't need to worry about it, and eventually he had given up pestering her for information.

Bedj-ka continued to wander, stopping to look out the occasional window at the ships coming and going from SA Station. A few minutes later he found himself outside the Forbidden Door. He passed it without stopping, then, when no one appeared in the corridor, reversed direction and passed it again. Stopping outside the door was disobedient, but no one had forbidden him to just walk past it.

Curiosity burned. Someone was in there; that he knew. Ms. Lucia made food for whoever it was, and Sister Gretchen delivered it. Twice Bedj-ka had arranged to be in the vicinity when Sister Gretchen opened the door, and both times she had noticed him lurking and ordered him away. When he had asked Mom about it, she had gone quiet and her mouth tightened in an expression that meant he'd get no answer.

Mom. Bedj-ka put his arms out on either side of him and pretended to tightrope-walk along a carpet seam. It still felt strange knowing he had a real mom. And not only was she a real mom, she was a totally *rigid* mom who traveled on a spaceship and played sneaky tricks on bad people and rescued slaves. Slaves like him.

Bedj-ka wobbled a bit, then coughed and had to windmill his arms to keep his balance. The Forbidden Door remained stubbornly shut. Mom thought he didn't know she checked on him every night. Bedj-ka, however, was a light sleeper, and she always woke him up when she looked in. It made him feel secure, knowing she always checked. At first he had been afraid that she might take him back to the cacao farm, or sell him to someone else. And then he had been afraid it would all turn out to be a hallucination, or maybe that he had gotten into the Dream after all and was making it all up for himself. As a result, he had been afraid to let Mom out of his sight. By the time the *Poltergeist* got to Drim, however, Bedj-ka had begun to feel secure enough to let someone else watch him, and on the ship he didn't need much direct supervision. Bedj-ka liked Ms. Lucia best. She told him stories about Irfan Qasad and her adventures back in the days before slipspace. It was because of her that Bedj-ka had tracked down the historical sim games.

But now he was lurking outside the Forbidden Door again. Bedj-ka glanced up and down the blue hallway. No one was around. He dashed up to the door and pressed an ear against the cool surface. Nothing but the faint hum of ship machinery. He concentrated, trying to tune out the noises of the ship and catch even a tiny sound from within.

"Hey, shortie," came a gruff voice. "Move it!"

Bedj-ka jumped away from the door. Sister Gretchen had moved up behind him, carrying a covered food tray. Bedj-ka blushed and tried to think of something to say. Sister Gretchen saved him the trouble.

"I told you to stay away from this door," she snapped. "You've got no business in this part of the ship. You want me to tell your mom what you're doing?"

"No," Bedj-ka said with a touch of belligerence. Sister Gretchen wasn't his mother and she couldn't tell him what to do. Besides, she was a real bitch, no matter what Mom said about her.

Sister Gretchen shifted the tray to one hip. "Listen, kid, I'm only going to tell you this one more time. There is a very dangerous man behind this door. He's a real son of bitch, and he'd happily slit your little throat if it gave him a chance to get away." She took a step toward him and he backed away. "You ever feel a knife slice through you, kid? Ever watch your own blood pour through your hands and make a puddle on the ground?"

Bedj-ka didn't answer, though his hand stole unconsciously to his neck.

"I didn't think so," Sister Gretchen said. "That's what'll happen if you ever open this door. And if I ever, *ever* catch you lurking around here again, I'm going to have Lucia fit you up with a pair of slave shackles that'll shock the living piss out of you if you come within ten meters of this door. You got that?"

"You can't put shackles on me," Bedj-ka said, anger rising again. "I'm free now."

"You'll be dead if you come near this door again," Sister Gretchen shot back. "Now get the hell out of here."

Bedj-ka turned and marched away with all the dignity he could muster, though his heart was pounding hard enough to make his neck muscles pulse. Yet another coughing fit struck him, and he was starting to feel warm now. He thought about telling Mom about what Sister Gretchen had said, then realized that would involve telling her why she had said it. Best to keep his mouth shut and hope Sister Gretchen did the same.

And then, sin or not, he'd have to find a way to talk to the person behind that door.

"Are you looking for something in particular, good gentle?"

Kendi turned. A tall, willowy being with red skin and enormous yellow eyes had approached him from behind. He—the voice was deep enough to make Kendi think of the creature as male—had long, graceful limbs and topped Kendi by almost a meter.

"I'm always looking for something unique to add to my collection," Kendi said with a small smile. "This one isn't quite to my taste"—he gestured at a messy blob of colors titled *Circus Day*—"but I'm sure you have better." He sniffed. "You certainly couldn't have worse."

"What sort of work is to your taste?"

"Realistic paintings and sculptures, especially of circus animals."

"Then you should follow me, fine gentle, and I will guide your steps to something more to your liking. I am Pnebran, and this is my gallery."

Pnebran turned and walked away, swaying like a sapling in the wind. Kendi followed, trying not to bounce in the lighter gravity of the gallery. The place was built on a spiral. A large open space opened all the way up to the ceiling, and a single wide balcony wound its way around the wall, corkscrewing a path to the top. Occasional staircases and lift platforms provided shortcuts. Floors, walls, and ceilings were white so as not to detract from the artwork displays that lined the walls. Statues, paintings, holograms both static and mobile, living sculptures, and sound symphonies each had a niche. Creatures of many shapes and species moved slowly among the pieces. Every work had a price discreetly displayed somewhere on it, reminding the viewer that this was not a museum.

"You have arrived at an appropriate time," Pnebran continued. "I am displaying my annual exhibit of circus pieces."

"I know," Kendi said. "That's why I'm here."

Pnebran made a languid gesture, and Kendi wondered if his bones would break under the full gravity of the rest of the station. Was Pnebran a prisoner in his own gallery? If so, why did he stay on SA Station?

"The first three tiers are all circus artwork," Pnebran said. "Here we have a lovely display of Pallingram's early work. The colors are carefully muted and almost hypnotic. You're familiar, I'm sure, with the fact that his work always has a dark edge to it."

Kendi looked with pretended interest at the four paintings. They did indeed hold a dark quality to them. The clowns creating a living pyramid in the first painting looked ready to leap onto the audience and devour them. A tiger in the second was clearly about to slip its leash and attack the red-clad ringleader.

"Fine examples," Kendi said. "What else do you have? I'm especially interested in the rarer works."

"Would you like to touch my Koochi?"

Kendi bit back a reply that would probably have gotten him ejected from the gallery and simply nodded instead. Pnebran led him to a blank section of white wall. "There," Pnebran said with another gesture. Kendi laid his palm on the wall. Crowd noise crashed over him and he smelled roasted peanuts.

"Preeeeesenting the Amazing Gambolini Brothers!" boomed a voice. More cheering thundered through the air and an elephant trumpeted. Smells of cotton candy and caramel apples wafted by. Then sounds and smells abruptly vanished. Kendi took his hand from the wall in amazement.

"Olfactory and auditory neural interface," Pnebran said proudly. "I have heard rumors of a Koochi that combines three senses but have been unable to find such."

"Breathtaking," Kendi said, meaning it. "What is the price?"

"Eight hundred thousand freemarks," Pnebran replied.

"A steal," Kendi said, barely managing not to choke. "What else do you have?"

Pnebran showed Kendi several other pieces, and Kendi pretended polite interest in each. Other guides of Pnebran's species shepherded other customers through the gallery around them.

"Have you sold many pieces during this exhibition?" Kendi asked casually.

"We just opened it yesterday, gentle, so not yet. It is a popular exhibition, however. The idea of a traveling group of performers appears in so many cultures that it is nearly universal, as is the artwork that springs from the concept, so we have people of many species who wish to visit."

Kendi nodded. "I'm especially interested in pieces with elephants in them. I had heard there were a few here."

"We sold one such just today," Pnebran said. "*Gray Elephants on Parade* by Wimpale."

Kendi seemed to grow excited. "Do you have more Wimpale?"

"I am afraid I do not."

"Dammit! Who bought the piece? No, let me guess—Edsard Roon."

"You know him," Pnebran observed.

"I know who he is," Kendi replied ruefully. "Does he often buy from you?"

"He is one of our favored customers. He has, in fact, one of the finest collections of circus art I have ever seen. And his memorabilia collection goes beyond the status of mere treasure."

"I've never seen his collection," Kendi said absently. Something stirred in his head.

Pnebran, meanwhile, led Kendi to another painting. A group of human circus folk were gathered around a downed elephant. "Yemark's work is not so much dark as delightfully depressing. This is one of his earlier ones. The elephant is diseased and soon to be put out of its misery."

Diseased. The word froze Kendi's world. He stared at the painting for a long moment. Ideas and possibilities rushed through his mind. Abruptly one idea crystallized, and excitement surged through him. It took him a moment to realize Pnebran was speaking to him.

". . . you well, gentle?" Pnebran asked. "Do you like the painting? The price is—"

"I'm fine," Kendi interrupted, wishing the curator would shut up. "I just . . . I'm receiving a call. Excuse me?" He turned away and pressed a hand to the side of his head, as if listening to someone on his earpiece, and he used the time to examine his idea from several sides. Disease. A ship. Roon's key. Elephants. It would work. He was sure of it. Excitement jumped around Kendi's head and made him want to leap up and slap the ceiling. In this gravity, he might be able to pull it off.

Instead, he turned back to Pnebran. "I have to leave, sir. How long will your exhibit be open? There are some pieces I want to look at more closely."

Pnebran made a graceful gesture Kendi took for a slight bow. "We close in twelve more days."

Kendi thanked him and rushed away.

Ben glared down at the pile of rubble beneath his feet, then lifted his Plexiglas face mask and swiped at his sweaty face with one sleeve. The little sledgehammer pulled with substantial weight at his other arm. It wasn't working anymore. Smashing Padric Sufur flat with a hammer used to give him a certain amount of satisfaction, but lately it hadn't done much for him. Maybe he needed to try something else. But what?

He wished he could create the real thing, a Dream simulacrum that would move and talk. And bleed. But Mom had always said that no one could create people in the Dream.

A feathery touch on Ben's mind warned him that someone was nearby.

~Hey, you,~ came Kendi's voice. ~What are you up to?~

Ben quickly banished the sledgehammer, face shield, and remains of Sufur's statue. "Come on in," he said aloud.

A falcon swooped in from the plain gray sky. It changed into a kangaroo in mid-drop and landed lightly in front of Ben. The kangaroo had a pouch. Before the Despair, Kendi's fragment animals had always been female, a trait that seemed to have carried over into Kendi's current state. The one time Ben had tried to rib Kendi about this had resulted in such an explosion of temper that Ben had never again remarked on it. Nowadays Ben always thought of Dream Kendi as "he," regardless of the gender of his animal form.

"Where's the computer system?" the kangaroo asked.

Ben shrugged. "I'm playing around with other stuff. How did things go at the gallery?"

"Pretty good. That's why I'm in here, in fact." Kendi gave Ben a capsule description of his conversation with Pnebran. He kept bobbing up and down in obvious excitement. "I've got it, Ben. I know how to do it."

"Do what?"

"Get them out."

"You mean you didn't before?"

"Not completely," Kendi admitted. "But then it hit me in the middle of the art gallery, every detail. I think it'll work. And it won't take that long."

Ben called up an armchair and plunked down into it, bringing himself down to Kendi's eye level. "So what's the plan?"

Kendi looked away. "I'm not . . . I don't think I should tell you all of it."

"Why not?"

"In case."

"Kendi, who am I going to tell?" Ben asked, nettled.

"No one—unless Silent Acquisitions gets wind of what's going on and captures one of us. Anyone will talk under drugs or torture. You know that."

"How am I supposed to help if I don't know what the hell is going on?" Ben demanded.

The kangaroo took a hop forward and abruptly changed into a koala bear, which looked up at Ben with enormous brown eyes. "Please don't be angry, Ben. I need your support in this. I don't want anything to go wrong."

"You're only doing that because you know koalas are cute," Ben growled.

"Is it working?" Kendi asked, reaching up to place a warm, clawed paw on Ben's leg.

Ben sighed. "All right. What do I need to do?"

"Help me find Valeta's messenger. I need to cash in a favor."

"A favor?" Ben echoed. "From the Emporium?"

"And then I need to talk to Vidya and Prasad. You said Sejal can't—or won't—help us, but I'll bet those two will."

~Relay, please: Hey, Val. What's up lately?~

~Relayed out of Dream to solid-world messenger. Awaiting response. Relaying response: Kendi! I haven't heard from you since before the Despair. How're the Children holding out? I hear you guys are expensive these days.~

~Relay: Got that right. Listen, remember that time back on Nipon? The stalker who came after you?~

~Relaying response: I'll never forget it. Why? What's—Oh, no. Aw, Kendi. Not now. This isn't a good time.~

~Relay: "Whatever you need, whenever you need it. I don't care if I have to move a planet." Those were your exact words, Val, and I need you.~

~Relaying response: Just me or the whole Emporium?~

~Relay: The whole enchilada, Val. Probably won't take more than a week.~

~Editorial comment: She is wailing. Relaying re-

*sponse: I'll have to reschedule an entire engagement,
Kendi. Can't this wait six months?~*

*~Relay: Sorry, Val, no can do. I'm under a time limit
here, and I'm afraid I have to lean hard. I need this,
and you owe me.~*

~Relaying response: Kendi, I can't just——~

*~Interrupt: "I wouldn't have an Emporium if it
weren't for you, Kendi. Thank god you were here. I
owe you everything."~*

*~Editorial comment: She is sighing. Relaying re-
sponse: You made that one up. I'd never say something
like that.~*

*~Relay: I can probably come up with a recording.
Look, Val, this is the most important job I've ever
pulled, and I can't do it without you and your people.
You know—the ones who still have a job because of
me?~*

*~Relaying response: I hate you. Editorial comment:
That remark was sarcastic in nature. Relaying response:
I can leave in two days, no sooner. If you're at SA
Station, it'll take me two more days to get there, give
or take.~*

*~Relay: Actually, I need you to stop at Bellerophon
first and pick up a couple of passengers.~*

*~Relaying response: Bellerophon? That'll add an-
other day.~*

~Relay: No worries there.~

*~Editorial comment: She is anticipating more infor-
mation. Relaying response: So are you going to tell me
what this is all about?~*

*~Relay: Only when you get here, love. See you then.
End transmission.~*

"Rent a slip shuttle? From SA? Father, that'll cost
a small fortune."

"I know, Lucia, but I don't want to take the *Poltergeist* out."

"And where you do want me to go?"

"There's a . . . semilegal shipyard orbiting one of the moons around Artemis. Do you know it?"

"I know it. It's just outside the boundaries of the Five Green Worlds. One of the owners is actually a distant cousin of mine."

"Does he owe you any favors?"

"One or two. Why?"

"Cash them in, Lucia, and *I'll* owe you a favor. A big one. See if you can get him to give you a discount—a one hundred percent discount, if you can manage it."

"On what?"

"An old, clunky ship. It doesn't need to have slip, gravity, or even life support. As long as the hull is intact, it'll work. The less it costs, the better—rent for the shuttle will eat up most of the cash we have left."

"All right. What am I supposed to do with this ship?"

"Haul it to a point a few parsecs away from SA and set it to drift relative to the station. Then leave it and come straight back here."

"Yes, Father."

"Aren't you going to ask what it's for?"

"I'm assuming you have your reasons."

"A refreshing change from everyone else. Leave as soon as you can get the shuttle, Lucia. And thanks."

"Irfan blesses you, Father."

"Let's hope she blesses all of us."

"I need everything you can get your hands on about circuses, Ben. History, current shows, clowns, animals, the works. In great and excruciating detail."

"Text? Holovid? Pics?"

"The works. I need to become a three-day expert. I learned a fair amount from that time with Valeta, but I need a refresher if I'm going to pull this off."

"Sure. I'll even throw in a subroutine to weed out repeat info."

"Great. But you'll have to hack it out of SA's library databases. I don't want there to be a record of what I'm reading just in case someone starts sniffing around. It'll also be cheaper, and I'm starting to worry about money."

"Shouldn't be hard. It's not like the library computers guard station secrets or anything, and they won't be that well guarded."

"Thanks, Ben. I owe you."

"What? I don't keep track. You know that."

"Sorry. Sometimes I get into favor-cashing mode and don't get out. But I'll still pay you back. There are lots of . . . favors I'd love to owe you. Think creatively about what I could do."

"Not if you want me to hack the SA library without getting caught."

Edsard Roon logged off the computer terminal, pulled his key from the receptor, and dropped the chain around his neck as the screen vanished. Enough work for now. These days he too often found himself arriving home after a fourteen-hour workday only to spend another hour at his home terminal. Time for a break.

He kicked off his shoes, took a deep, cold pull from the frosted glass that hovered at his elbow, and sank into a supremely comfortable easy chair with a sigh. Caffeine, his one weakness. Edsard didn't allow himself alcohol or any other recreational drug. The mind had to stay clear, be precise, firm. Even caffeine had an impact on the thought processes, but, he supposed, everyone needed at least one bad habit. Bad habits, in moderation, relieved stress.

Relieved N-waves.

Edsard snorted. He was a dark-haired man, tall and rangy, with a long, sad face. Work, it seemed, was never far from his mind. He supposed it was his own fault. After overriding Elena Papagos-Faye and order-

ing a dedicated terminal installed in his den at home,
he found himself spending more and more of his mi-
nuscule free time at the computer doing Collection
business. Papagos-Faye had protested the practice, but
Edsard had known there would be times when he
would need the access at home. Besides, no one except Elena even knew the terminal existed—or what
it was for. There was no danger it would be hacked.

After another long drink, Edsard set the glass down
in midair beside him. The house computer caught the
movement and adjusted local gravity generators. Edsard's glass hovered in place at hand level. Edsard wig-
gled tired toes and sank deeper into the chair. Did
enjoying comfortable furniture count as a bad habit?
Perhaps it did, and he had two bad habits.

The study was enormous, large enough to house
three families in some sectors of SA Station. Persian
rugs imported all the way from Earth covered the pol-
ished wood floors. Glass-topped tables with wooden
borders vied for floor space with several couches and
overstuffed chairs. The ceiling was two stories away,
and the walls were all but hidden by display cases.
Each case was crammed with pieces from Edsard's
collection, as if someone had torn pieces from a thousand different circuses and trapped them under glass.
Tom Thumb's skeleton. P. T. Barnum's hat. A set of
tights worn by Ernie Clarke, the first human trapeze
artist to perform the triple somersault. A lock of
Mario Santelli's hair. Tommy Zane's chess set. A scale
reproduction of the railway accident that had killed
Jumbo the elephant. The third eye of Vrilkari no Sen-
cmok, ringleader of the very first interplanetary circus.

Seeded among them all were the elephants. Statues
of elephants, paintings of elephants, holograms of elephants. Toys, blankets, tapestries, signs, hides, and
tusks. Everywhere one looked, an elephant looked
back. Edsard's newest acquisition, a Wimpale painting
called *Gray Elephants on Parade,* hung in a place of

honor lit by a special spotlight. He looked at it con-
tentedly. There were only eight surviving Wimpales
left, though rumor spoke of a ninth in the vaults
owned by Padric Sufur. Edsard possessed three Wimpales. *Parade* now made four. The work had cost over
three million freemarks, and it was worth every single one.

Edsard took back his glass and raised it at the Wimpale in silent toast. A salute to his collection. And,
as always, his mind wandered back toward work—his
other Collection.

The Collection. His best idea ever, despite its sim-
plicity. Use the same indoctrination methods that
human cults had perfected over centuries of practice
to create an army of working Silent who were slavishly
devoted to him—and to Silent Acquisitions. With
working Silent still terrifyingly rare, a stable of Silent
that wouldn't run away even if they could was essential to SA's financial future. And SA *had* to survive.
The collapse of Silent Acquisitions would be equiva-
lent to the collapse of a multisystem government, with
millions of people thrown out of work and thousands
of slaves left without owners. Also, no fewer than five
major economies were tied in with SA's future, and if
SA sank, it would doubtless drag those governments
down with it. No, SA had to continue, and gaining
monopolistic control over the remaining Silent in the
galaxy was the best way to guarantee that. Carinna
Mogarr, the company's CEO, had been slaveringly appreciative when Edsard brought her the idea, though
now she was pressuring him to put some of the Collection to work and find out if similar methods would
work on nonhuman species.

It was all stopgap, of course. When the current crop
of Silent died, Silent Acquisitions would follow them.
But that was still several decades away, and someone,
Roon was sure, would find a solution.

Meanwhile, between overseeing the Collection's

day-to-day operations and playing the part of Dreamer Roon, he was finding precious little time to admire his circus collection. The outing to the circus exhibit had been his first major treat in months. Ah, well. Eventually the Collection would run itself, and Edsard would have more spare time. Several of the Alphas had already been promoted to Beta, and when they reached Delta status, they would take over the training of new Alphas, replacing the current Deltas, who were played by actors. This absolutely loyal base of workers would "recruit" and train more workers, who would, in turn, indoctrinate yet another generation. It was perfect. It was brilliant. And it had been all his idea.

Edsard grinned. Once the Alphas were all nicely pliable Betas, he would start the next phase of the operation. He toyed with the computer key on its chain around his neck as his mind filled with pleasant plans.

"Mr. Roon?"

Edsard glanced up. His wife Annalies Roon, a soft, pale woman with white-blond hair and gray eyes, was standing in the door. He gave her a quizzical look.

"There's someone here to see you. A Mr. Evan Qiwele. He was insistent but not rude."

"What does he want to see me about, Mrs. Roon?"

She gestured at the displays. "He says he a circus enthusiast and he's hoping to see your collection, especially your Wimpales."

Edsard's first instinct was to tell Mrs. Roon to send him away. It had been a long day, and he was looking forward to some time alone. Mrs. Roon would keep the children, and he could spend a quiet hour or two.

On the other hand, it was no fun having a collection if you didn't get to show it off. Edsard's few friends didn't share his enthusiasm, and it would be nice to have a new audience, even one who arrived unexpectedly.

"Show him in, Mrs. Roon," he ordered.

She nodded and vanished. A few moments later, a tall, dark-skinned man wearing blue silk, white gloves, and a red turban entered the room. A smile wide as a crescent moon split the man's face in half.

"Mr. Roon?" He extended a hand and Edsard shook it. "I'm Evan Qiwele. Sorry to drop in on you unannounced, but I was down at a certain gallery today and learned that you beat me to a Wimpale. I had to see if you would allow me to view it."

"Mr. Qiwele," Edsard said politely. "Can I offer you something to drink?"

"Thank you. Scotch and soda?"

Mrs. Roon had already taken up her position behind the bar. Ice clinked and soda hissed. Roon reached for his floating tea glass and gestured for Qiwele to sit on one of the sofas. He accepted the drink when Mrs. Roon brought it, sipped, and looked at the glass appreciatively.

"The Scotch is twenty years old," Edsard said. "I keep it especially for guests."

Qiwele nodded and set the glass down in the air beside him with a restless air. The computer caught the glass and set it to hover.

"I apologize again if I seem rude," Qiwele said, hands tapping on his knees, "but I couldn't help myself. I've been looking for a Wimpale for ages, and just when I think I've gotten a solid lead on one, I learn that someone has whisked it out from under my nose. I congratulate you, Mr. Roon, though I have to say I'm not above trying to convince you to sell it to me. Or perhaps we could arrange a trade? Something in my collection for something in yours?"

Edsard shook his head with a smile. "I doubt that very much. The Wimpales are the jewel of my collection. Have you been a circus enthusiast for long?"

"All my life." Qiwele continued tapping his hands on his knees. "My wife thinks I'm insane. I literally sneaked through a war zone for the chance to examine a Debsi sculpture once. Turned out to be a forgery, I'm sorry to say."

"Debsi isn't really my thing," Edsard said with a smile. "Shall I show you my collection, then?"

"That would be a delight, sir," Qiwele cried with palpable enthusiasm. "Do you still have Lupino's makeup case? I would give a great deal to see that."

"I have it," Edsard told him, surprised and pleased. "How did you—"

"Please." Qiwele held up a hand. "I've heard a great deal about your collection, Mr. Roon, and I've been eager to get a look at it for a long, long time."

Feeling flattered, Edsard got to his feet. Mrs. Roon stayed behind the bar as he led Qiwele to the first display case. They chatted circus as Qiwele examined with happy exclamations each piece Edsard showed him. Qiwele clearly knew what he was talking about, and Edsard found himself glowing with pride as he saw his prizes anew through the eyes of his visitor. A fine man, this Mr. Qiwele.

Despite the growing lateness of the hour, Edsard saved the Wimpales for last, and when Qiwele finally reached them, he let out a long sigh of contentment.

"Let me simply feast my eyes," he said. "No one captures the spirit of the circus elephant like Wimpale."

"Agreed," Edsard said. "His work takes me back to my childhood. I wanted to be a circus performer for the longest time."

"I wanted to be a lion tamer," Qiwele confessed with a wry grin. "I even made a whip. The first time I used it, I broke an antique lamp and my mother banished me to the garden."

"I wanted to be a clown," Edsard said. "Whenever there was a costume party, you would find me dressed in floppy shoes and white makeup."

Qiwele looked him up and down. "That's hard to picture," he said.

"Truth." Edsard held up his right hand, though his eyes took on a faraway look. He remembered the smell of real greasepaint, the ridiculous flapping of overlarge shoes, making silly faces, eliciting bright laughter from other partygoers. The only thing missing was the ring and the roar of an audience. He came to himself a moment later and realized Qiwele was staring at him.

"What?" he asked, suddenly uncomfortable.

Qiwele made his wide, white smile again. "Just trying to imagine you as a clown. It still doesn't fit." He gave an abrupt yawn that nearly split his head in two, and Roon, finding the gesture contagious, followed suit. "Heavens, it's late. I've intruded on you long enough, sir. Your lovely wife abandoned us ages ago."

He leaned against Edsard's desk, the one with the Collection terminal on it. Edsard quickly gestured him over to a pair of armchairs and they sat, despite Qiwele's observation of the hour.

"I trust I'll see you at the Emporium next week," Qiwele said.

"The Emporium?" Edsard echoed, confused.

"The Kalopolis Intergalactic Traveling Emporium of Wonders."

"I know what it is. What do you mean by mentioning it?"

Qiwele scratched his ear. "You hadn't heard?"

"Heard what?" Roon asked with a hint of impatience.

"The Emporium is coming here next week for a short engagement. Three performances only."

Edsard sat bolt upright. "The Emporium is coming *here*? To SA Station? Why didn't I hear about it?"

"Tickets are already sold out, my good man. You really hadn't heard?"

Anxiety mixed with disappointment. The Emporium was the greatest circus in all history. No other even came close. Roon had seen the Emporium's show only twice in his life, and both times he had come away burning to see more. He would happily travel slipspace for a month to catch it, but his schedule was so insane these days, such things were out of the question. Now the Emporium was coming here, right into his own neighborhood, and tickets were already gone. Well, he would see about that. What was the point of having money and power if you didn't use them?

"You must come," Qiwele was saying. He lowered his voice, though they were patently alone. "I'm good friends with the ringleader, and—"

It was Edsard's turn to be impressed. "You know Valeta Kalopolis?"

"I didn't mention that? Our families have been friends for a long time. I'm sure I can arrange tickets for you and your family at the opening performance. They'll be waiting at the box office for you. I insist!"

Relief and excitement flooded over Edsard. The Emporium! "That would be marvelous, Mr. Qiwele. I'm in your debt."

"It would be my pleasure, Mr. Roon. In fact . . ." Qiwele's voice trailed off for a moment, and Edsard leaned forward, eager to hear what might come next. "You know the Emporium uses bleachers? With no reserved seats?"

"Yes," Edsard said. "Part of the charm."

"You've been so kind," Qiwele murmured. "And for a fellow enthusiast of your caliber, I might be able to arrange . . . well, perhaps I shouldn't say, in case it can't be done."

Edsard tried not to squirm. "What? You can't leave me hanging like that. Tell me!"

"No, no. I shouldn't get your hopes up."

It was on the tip of Edsard's tongue to shout, to order Qiwele to tell. This was the *Emporium,* for god's sake. Who did Qiwele think he was, jerking him, Edsard Roon, around like this? But he bit the inside of his cheek. Shouting orders at a guest was not only rude, it probably wouldn't work. He forced himself to keep his voice calm.

"Tell," he said. "After all, I showed you my Wimpale."

Qiwele paused for an agonizingly long time. "I just don't want to make you think this is a guarantee when I can only promise to do my best."

"What? What?" Edsard demanded.

"I'm thinking," Qiwele said slowly, "that I could have a word with Valeta. Arrange something special." Qiwele rubbed his nose. "Tell you what. As I said, I will arrange for tickets to be left at the box office. When you and your family arrive, be sure you sit in seat A-seven. Your wife and children may sit where they like, but *you,* my friend, must sit in seat A-seven. I will try to ensure it remains vacant, but I can't control everything, so you'll want to arrive in plenty of time."

"What exactly are you arranging, Mr. Qiwele?"

Qiwele gave a maddening smile. "A surprise, Mr. Roon. And nothing in the world will make me spoil it for you. The opening performance is in three days, and seating starts at seven o'clock. Seat A-seven. It'll be a dream come true, Mr. Roon. An absolute dream."

After a hearty handshake and a polite good-bye, Qiwele left. Roon stared after him feeling like a child who had been handed an enormous present and told he couldn't open it for three days.

Then his com-link chimed.

One, two, three, four, five, six, and turn. One, two, three, four, five, six, and turn. Isaac Todd paced and paced and paced again. There was frigging nothing to *do*. He was tired of reading, bored with the mini-sim games, and sick, sick, sick of being in these tiny quarters with no frigging *windows*. He had nothing but a bed, a chair, a tiny bathroom, and a combination bookdisk reader and mini-sim player. That was it. He didn't even have a change of clothes, had to stand around naked while he washed out his stuff in the sink and hung it up to dry. Who the hell did Harenn think she was, anyway? She had no right, no *right* to keep him here, let alone stick him with needles.

Todd shuddered and paused in his pacing. The needles. Just thinking about them made him sweat. And then there were the nightmares. He could never remember exactly what they were, or even actually having them, for that matter. All he knew was that three times in four when he woke up in the morning, he was shaking with the memory of fear, the sheets soaked and cold. Harenn was doing it to him somehow; he was sure of it.

At least the vomiting thing had stopped.

Harenn. Damned bitch. He hadn't done anything illegal to her. The kids he had made were his, his to keep or to sell. Besides, Harenn and the other women should have been *glad* for what he did. The kids were all genetic freaks. He had disposed of each one of them, ensuring their mothers didn't have to raise them and earning a tidy profit for himself. In the meantime, the freaks were put to good use. Everybody won. Especially Isaac, who got a steady stream of new sex partners, a good income from the results, and the thrill of outsmarting a bunch of women stupid enough to fall for him.

But now he sat in an inhumanly tiny cell with nothing to do, and that burned him. Inactivity chafed like sand in his clothes. He wanted to act, get out there and *do* something. Anything.

Well, not quite anything. He had been putting off the one thing he *could* do, setting it aside until he could work out some details. Said details had come together yesterday afternoon, but still Todd had avoided acting. So much would depend on how fast he could talk.

With a deep breath, Isaac Todd twisted his left ring finger. It came off. From the base of the finger he pulled a short antenna. Then he pressed the nail. A tiny holographic display popped up. Todd swallowed, then whispered a command to it. A few moments later, the display morphed into a head-and-shoulders view of a man.

"Isaac Todd," he said, mouth almost completely dry. "Reporting in, Mr. Roon."

"It's been over two weeks, Mr. Todd. Where are you? I was just about to go to bed."

"I've been captured by the Children of Irfan."

Mr. Roon's expression didn't change, but Todd noticed his neck muscles stiffen. *"The Children? Are you on Belleroph—No, you can't be. What is your location?"*

"I'm on a ship docked at SA Station. I don't know the name of it—they haven't mentioned it within my hearing."

"Start from the beginning, Mr. Todd," Mr. Roon said tensely, *"and tell me everything."*

Todd explained and Mr. Roon listened.

"So you allowed yourself to be captured, is that it?" Mr. Roon said when he was done. *"And then you let them drug you and make you blab everything you know."*

"We can turn this into an advantage, sir," Todd said. He thrust the hand that wasn't holding the communicator into his pocket so it wouldn't shake. "The Father in charge—I haven't caught his name, either—said he wants to steal away his family. Mr. Roon, he's still Silent."

Roon didn't answer right away, so Todd plunged on. "He once said something about going into the Dream. I also get the idea that at least one other person on this ship is also still Silent. There may be more, sir."

"And?" Mr. Roon said at last. *"I have the feeling that this is going somewhere."*

"If we play this right," Todd replied, "we could grab all of them."

"Of course we can grab all of them. Your signal has already told me where you are. I can simply flood the ship with security troops. We'd get the Silent—and you."

Todd didn't miss the implied threat. "I think that would be a mistake, sir."

"Oh?"

"It would be hard to keep something like that a secret," he explained. "The moment security forces show up, the Children will shout for help and probably dump everything they know about the Collection into public-access networks—and into the Dream. *I* would, under those circumstances."

"To what end?" Mr. Roon countered.

"Partly to tick you off and partly because it would put every Silent in the galaxy on their guard, making the Collection harder to expand. The Children themselves would also come looking to rescue their people, and the groups we . . . liberated our Silent from would want their property back, so you can be sure they'd kick up a fuss. SA Station would be inundated with people trying to destroy the Collection, and someone might even declare war against SA itself. If the Collection's existence became public knowledge at this stage, the whole thing would be ruined."

"You have a point," Mr. Roon conceded grudgingly. *"So what do you propose we do?"*

"Nothing. That's the beauty of it. If they want to get the Father's relatives, they'll have to come to *us*. All you have to do is wait for them. I can feed you information from the inside, let you know when they're planning to move. The moment they try something"—Todd snapped his fingers—"you'll have them. All of them."

Mr. Roon thought for a long moment. Todd held his breath. If Mr. Roon decided to dump Todd's plan and instead take the ship by force, Todd would be in the position of "agent who needed rescue." If Mr. Roon accepted Todd's plan, Todd would be in the position of "agent who came up with a brilliant idea." The latter meant gratitude and a bonus. The former meant the recycling vats or worse.

"All right," Mr. Roon said at last. *"We'll try it your way. Check in with me every two days at this time, sooner if something's going to break. Meanwhile, I'll step up security around the Collection."*

"That would also be a mistake, sir," Todd said with an internal sigh of relief. "If anything, you should ease up a little."

Mr. Roon considered this. *"Because it will make it easier for the Children to get inside where we want them. I see your point."* He eyed Todd skeptically. *"You're adept at turning your position around, Mr. Todd. I'll be watching you carefully."*

And with that, he broke the connection. The hologram vanished. Todd let out a long, heavy breath. Then, whistling a little tune, he replaced his finger.

CHAPTER NINE

*"Call an elephant a rabbit only if it makes you feel
better to say you got trampled by a rabbit."*
              —Daniel Vik, Othertown Governor

The parade was enormous, with elephants. Kendi
leaped and capered and skipped, sometimes tripping
over his enormous purple shoes and landing flat on
his face, to the great merriment of the assembled
crowd. At the very front of the parade marched Valeta
Kalopolis, her long dreadlocks piled under a tall red
hat. She wore the traditional scarlet tuxedo of the
ringleader, and she often twirled her gold-topped cane
like a baton. Behind her came a pair of elephants.
Old-fashioned flat signs on their sides spelled out KA-
LOPOLIS INTERGALACTIC TRAVELING EMPORIUM OF
WONDERS in large, important letters. Then came
Kendi, mixed in with a group of a dozen other joeys
that included Ben and Gretchen. Ben was made up as
a sad-looking hobo while Gretchen sported a fluffy
green wig and a bright blue smile. Kendi wouldn't
have thought that Gretchen would make a very good
clown, but she was making a surprisingly fine job of
it. She skipped and waved and at one point blew up
a long, thin balloon. With a few expert twists, she
transformed it into a dog, handed it to a small child,
and continued on her way.

"I didn't know you could do that," Kendi murmured to her.

Gretchen waved cheerily at the crowd, her face un-
recognizable under white and blue makeup. "There's
a lot you don't know about me."

Kendi grinned and decided to lose himself in his

current role. Hidden beneath the bright, happy makeup, he could pretend that his family wasn't imprisoned, that he didn't have a slaver imprisoned on his ship, even that the Despair had never happened. His only purpose was to make people laugh and forget their troubles as he was forgetting his.

Behind the clowns hovered a broad platform on which acrobats of three different species—none of them human—performed graceful gymnastics. Horse riders came next, leaping on and off steady equine backs in their bright, glittering costumes. A short, squat humanoid who bulged with muscle performed feats of strength while an animal trainer herded a troop of house cats. A real calliope hooted cheerful music. Acts and riders stretched farther back than Kendi could see down the wide street corridor. Even the crowd itself was a riot of color and species that almost rivaled the Emporium itself. Pnebran, the gallery curator, had been correct—the idea of a circus was something almost all species seemed to enjoy. The whole thing was glorious.

And then he caught sight of Edsard Roon. The man was standing, face rapt, in front of the crowd with his wife Annalies and three pale children under the age of ten. Kendi stiffened, then caught himself and waved as if they were any other family in the crowd. The Roon children were quieter than the ones around them, almost subdued, and they didn't dive for the candy Ben tossed their way. Kendi felt a little sorry for them as he passed.

But I feel sorrier for the people their father has kidnapped, he thought.

The Emporium wound its way through the station, passing through wealthy and poor sections alike. The poor sections wrenched Kendi's heart. The wide corridor was grimy, the buildings had few windows, and the air smelled stale. Noisy machinery clanked in the background, and small scavenger animals rustled in alley shadows. Family clusters crowded the walkways, both at ground level and above, all of them determined to get a glimpse of the Emporium. Tickets, Kendi knew, would be too expensive for almost everyone who lived here. Val, bless her heart, slowed the parade down to allow them to get a good, long look. Kendi and the joeys, for their part, worked extra hard to touch the crowd before moving on.

Just over an hour later, right about the time Kendi's feet were getting sore, the Emporium arrived at the entertainment coliseum where the circus would perform. The wide corridor dove straight into a long tunnel that opened directly into a cavernous performance arena. A trio of wooden rings made circles on the floor, and an impressive array of rigging for the flyers and acrobats made a network high above them. Rows of numbered bleachers rose high on all sides, and extra seats had been placed so luckier patrons could sit mere meters from the actual performers. People already crowded the seating areas, and more were streaming in.

The Emporium parade glittered like a dancing rainbow as it cut through the arena to a matching exit tunnel on the other side. Valeta waved, and the gathering crowd cheered. Kendi found a few reserves of energy and turned a cartwheel. Hobo Ben plodded sadly along beside him. Down near the floor in the seat Kendi knew to be A7 sat Edsard Roon, his family beside him. The children were munching candied apples. Mrs. Roon sat with her hands in her lap. Roon himself sat staring at the arena with the same rapt look on his face Kendi had seen earlier at the parade. Kendi smelled fried food and animal manure.

The elephants, followed by the group of joeys, passed out of the arena and into the performer's tunnel. The area under and behind the coliseum was a gray warren of dressing rooms, storage areas, holding pens, offices, and other facilities. The Emporium had taken over the entire thing for a week at tremendous cost. Valeta Kalopolis had groaned that she was going to lose money on this run but hadn't tried to back out of the agreement.

The elephant riders turned the animals down a side tunnel to a holding area where they would await their cue. Kendi dashed ahead of them so he could catch up to Valeta. Her scarlet tuxedo glittered with gold sequins.

"Roon's here, Val," he told her. "You remember what to do?"

Valeta turned and gave him a hard look over the golden head of her cane.

"Sorry. I worry."

"Don't," she said, and linked arms with him. "We're show people from a long line of show people, dearest. Roon won't suspect a thing."

Kendi nodded, feeling suddenly silly in his clown outfit. "I appreciate this, Val. You have no idea what this means to me."

"I'd say it was no trouble," Val replied, "except I'd rather save my lies for Roon. Keep in mind that after this"—she wagged a warning finger at him—"our debt is clearly and carefully paid. Don't even ask for tickets the next time we're in the neighborhood."

"I won't," Kendi promised.

Val squeezed his arm and left. Kendi rejoined Ben, who was waiting in a performer's alcove that gave them a view of the main ring. Gretchen had already gone down to the clowns' dressing room.

"We're all set, Ben," Kendi said. "I guess we have a few minutes to sit back and enjoy the show."

A few moments after the Emporium parade had wound its way through the arena, the coliseum went dark. The murmuring crowd quieted, and Kendi imagined Roon leaning forward with anticipation. A single shaft of light stabbed down to the exact center of the middle ring. There stood Valeta Kalopolis, resplendent with her top hat and cane.

"Ladies and gentlemen!" she cried. "Children of all ages! Welcome to the Kalopolis Intergalactic Traveling Emporium of Wonders!"

The crowd cheered its enthusiasm before the echoes died away. Kendi's mouth, however, was dry and his gaze wandered toward Roon.

"Before we begin our performance," Valeta boomed, "I wish to inform you that everything you see here is absolutely real. The Emporium uses no holograms, no anti-gravity generators, no genetically altered animals or people. The only concession we make to modern times is to use a sound amplification system so that everyone can hear. Ladies and gentlemen, boys and girls, *can you hear me*?"

The crowd cheered again.

"I said, *Can you hear me*?"

Wilder cheers.

"Then let the show begin!"

Performers burst into the arena. A trio of riders leaped lightly on and off the backs of six horses that cantered steadily around the first ring. Two identically dressed clowns stood on opposite sides of a full-size empty mirror frame and duplicated each other's movements. A bare-chested humanoid with scaly orange skin and hulking muscles put a set of strange-looking animals through their paces in the center ring. Kendi, who remembered circuses from his childhood in Australia, found the entire scene a wonderful mix of Earth and . . . other places. Still, he couldn't keep his eyes off Roon.

"He's still there?" asked Ben beside him.

"Free and clear," Kendi said. "The shit who's holding my family—and who knows how many others."

"Any more information on the plan?"

Kendi shook his head. "There will be later, I promise. Did that com signal ever pop up again?"

"Not yet. I'll keep watching for it." Ben leaned against the wall, his sad clown face reflected in his posture. "Ken, I don't like being kept in the dark."

"I know, Ben, and I'm sorry. It won't be for long. Promise."

Ben sighed and Kendi detected a definite note of anger in the sound. Kendi firmed his jaw. He knew exactly what Ben was going through—Ara had done it to him often enough. And Kendi wanted to tell Ben everything, both to include him and to relieve the pressure that was building inside him. But Ara had pounded into Kendi's head that when it came to complex plans, the fewer people who knew what was going on, the better. Although he had chafed under this policy several times, he had also come to realize that she was right. He wondered if Ara had ever felt this way about *him* and wished he could ask her.

"Kendi, is that you?" asked a familiar voice.

Kendi turned. A woman with a pretty, round face was standing behind him. White streaks shot through her long dark hair. Her skin was a little lighter than Kendi's. Beside her stood a man who was close to the woman's age, though his hair was going more silver than white. Vidya Vajhur and her husband Prasad. The two of them had been instrumental in ending the Despair, and Kendi would have lost the battle against Padric Sufur's children without them.

"Vidya!" Kendi gave her a warm embrace while Ben shook hands with the man. "And Prasad! I was wondering where you'd gotten to."

"You and Ben are hard men to find," Prasad said.

"Especially when you hide yourselves under such garish makeup," Vidya added.

"Valeta told me she'd picked you up," Kendi said, "but there was a lot to arrange and I didn't have time to come find you. Is everything all right? How are Sejal and Katsu?"

"As far as I know, they are well," Vidya said, "though I haven't spoken to either of them in some time."

"They are . . . occupied," Prasad added. "The Council of Irfan desperately wants both of them to join the Children, since their Silence was largely untouched by the Despair, but they haven't decided yet. The Council is very worried these days."

"About the Silent dying out," Ben said. "We're nervous, too."

"This is a worry for another day," Vidya said. "Right now we should enjoy the circus."

"Agreed," Kendi said with a smile.

The performances continued. Flyers flipped and twirled among ropes and trapezes. An animal trainer trotted out a pod of small dinosaurs from Bellerophon, and Kendi felt a small stab of homesickness. Up in the stands, food and souvenir merchants hawked their wares. Smells of hot, greasy food spread everywhere. Kendi shifted uneasily. When would it be time for—

"Ready?" Val said behind him. Kendi jumped. He hadn't heard her coming.

"Gretchen's down in the dressing area," Ben said, "so we're set."

Val nodded. "One more act and we'll do it." She trotted away.

"What are you going to do?" Prasad asked. "You said you do not need us to steal Roon's key, but you have not explained why you *do* need us."

Kendi started to scratch his nose, remembered his makeup, and dropped his hand. "I'll tell you later. It's too complicated to go into right here."

The dinosaur trainer ended her act, and Val stepped into the ring to introduce a magician. "Once again I repeat—the Emporium uses no holograms or other special effects. Everything you see is accomplished by skill alone, and the Great Manzini challenges you to figure out how each trick is done."

Ben grabbed Kendi's arm. "He's getting up! Roon is getting up!"

Kendi gasped and wrenched his gaze to Roon's seat. Edsard Roon had indeed risen from his front-row bleacher seat and was heading for the aisle. "All life! He can't get out of his seat now. What the hell is he doing?"

"Who knows? Bathroom break?" Ben hazarded. "What do we do now? Val's going to announce his surprise once the magician finishes up."

Kendi produced a packet of enzyme cloths from one of his capacious clown suit pockets and ripped it open. Roon reached the aisle and headed for one of the smaller exit tunnels used by spectators.

"I've got to get him to sit back down," Kendi said. "Ben, you try to signal Val, see if she can stall one more act's worth."

"I can't," Ben said. "Manzini uses her in his act."

But Kendi had already fled. He shed his clown outfit as he ran, dropping shoes, wig, nose, and baggy suit. Underneath he wore normal clothing. Several swipes of enzyme cloths rid his face of makeup, and he prayed he hadn't missed any. His heart was jerking around in his chest. Roon *had* to get back into his seat or everything would be ruined. Kendi dashed along the hallways, cursing the maze that made it difficult to figure out which way to go. Roon was probably heading for one of the bathrooms, but which set?

Other performers filled the hallways, forcing Kendi to dodge and weave. At one point he snatched a glittering silvery scarf from an assistant animal trainer. "Emergency!" he shouted back over his shoulder. "I'll return it, promise!"

He left the performers' area and entered what he hoped was the main spectator corridor. With shaking hands he twisted the scarf into a turban. Sloppy, but it would have to do. He pelted down the corridor, came around a bend—

—and halted. Roon had emerged from a rest room and was turning to head for a souvenir stand. A light crowd of people kept him from noticing Kendi right away.

"Mr. Roon!" Kendi called, and dashed ahead to catch up to him.

Roon turned, surprised. "Mr. Qiwele. So you *are* here." He shook Kendi's hand in a hard, dry grip. "I want to thank you for this. It's everything I love about the circus. Marvelous!"

"You're welcome," Kendi said. "But why are you out of your seat, sir?"

"Needed a short break. And the collector in me won't let me leave a souvenir stand untouched. It's all part of the experience." He looked at Kendi's throat. "Is that clown makeup?"

Kendi clapped a hand to his neck. *Dammit!* "It is," he admitted. "I shamelessly exploited my connections and arranged to march in the parade with the other joeys. Great fun, that!"

"I thought one of those clowns looked familiar," Roon said. "But you said you always wanted to be a lion tamer."

Kendi forced a laugh. "I can fool a crowd into thinking I'm a clown. I doubt I could fool a lion into thinking I'm a trainer."

"Too true," Roon said with a laugh of his own.

Through the tunnels came the faint sounds of applause. A man's voice boomed, "And now for the grand finale!"

"But you'll miss your surprise," Kendi cried. "Good heavens, man, it's going to be announced any moment. Any moment! You *are* sitting in seat A-seven, aren't you?"

Roon looked at him. "The show's more than half over. I thought perhaps you weren't able to—"

"It's all arranged, sir!" Kendi pushed him with comic severity back to the audience tunnel. "Quickly! You have no idea the trouble I went through. I can't allow you to miss this! Remember—seat A-seven. Hurry!"

Roon turned and said, "Then I thank you again. Really, Mr. Qiwele, this is too much. You must come for dinner sometime. How about tomorrow evening at nine?"

"I would love to come for dinner," Kendi lied, "but I don't remember offhand if I'm free. I shall call you."

Huge applause and cheers burst through the tunnel. Kendi suppressed the urge to drag Roon back to the bleachers and plunk him down on the seat. Roon shook Kendi's hand one more time and finally—*finally*—turned back to the arena. Kendi watched him go, praying that nothing else would go wrong.

"And now," shouted the ringmaster, "we have a special event."

Edsard Roon picked his way up the narrow walkway between the bleachers and sat next to his family with a nod. They didn't respond. Mrs. Roon and the children hadn't spoken much since the performance had begun. Not even Janni, the youngest, kicked his feet or whined. Edsard's little section of bleacher was blue with A7 painted on it. It wasn't that comfortable, but he had refused to bring any kind of cushion or pillow that might interfere with the authenticity of the experience. And a gloriously perfect experience it had been so far.

In fact, it so far had been a gloriously perfect day, exactly what he'd needed to take his mind off the Collection and its assorted problems. The Children of Irfan were involved now, and that made Roon nervous. He didn't like leaving Todd on board their ship and was beginning to regret not ordering security to simply grab the entire vessel. However, he did have to admit that Todd had had a point, self-serving though it was. Todd could prove to be an effective mole, and if Roon played everything right, those busybody monks would walk right into his Collection.

"I hold here a bucket of chips," Valeta Kalopolis was saying. "Each chip has a seat number painted on it. The person whose seat I draw will receive a special treat—the chance to come backstage and be made up as a clown for the final act in the show. Are you ready?"

More cheering. Edsard's mouth fell open and every thought about the Collection fled his mind. This must be Qiwele's surprise. He had arranged for the ring-leader to call out seat A7, no matter what chip she drew. Connections, indeed! Edsard's childhood dream would at last come true. Qiwele was a genius, a prince among men. He would have to give the man a gift of some kind, perhaps even one of the Wimpales. After all, Edsard had five of them and Qiwele had done so much for—

"I do hope they pick me," little Janni said to his sister Mietje. His voice was so low, Edsard was surprised he had heard it. He was also surprised to hear such a thing coming from Janni. The child had shown no interest in the circus before, not the same level of interest Edsard himself showed, at any rate. Indeed, Ruurd, the oldest boy, and Mietje both didn't seem to care one way or the other. But Janni's pale eyes were bright with hope as he perched on his bleacher. Edsard frowned and played idly with the key chain that hung around his neck. Fatherhood wasn't his strength, and Edsard generally stayed out of the children's lives. After all, he had primarily decided to have them in order to complete the family picture, make himself seem more stable to Silent Acquisitions and a likelier candidate for promotion. The children were Mrs. Roon's bailiwick and he left all the decisions regarding their care to her.

But now a bit of paternal interest stirred. He remembered seeing his first circus with his own father and the utter enchantment the performance had wrought. Was Janni going through the same thing?

Perhaps Edsard owed it to his own father to find out.

"And our winner is"—the ringleader stared down at the chip she had drawn and paused for effect—"seat A-seven!"

Another cheer went up. On impulse, Edsard grabbed the startled Janni and hoisted him aloft. "That's my son!" he shouted. "The seat belongs to my son!"

Clown Ben spun around from his position at the dressing room door. "He's coming, he's coming!"

Kendi ducked behind a wall hanging. Originally he'd planned to take part in this stage, but Roon would recognize him even in clown makeup, so he had been forced to leave it in the hands of Ben and Gretchen.

The room was long and narrow. A series of dressing tables with lighted mirrors lined one of the walls and racks of costumes lined the other. Silly props and floppy shoes were scattered everywhere. The whole place smelled of cloth and makeup. Gretchen, still in her clown costume, had already laid out a makeup case at one of the mirrors and stood at the ready. There were no other joeys in the room—Valeta had arranged for privacy. Vidya and Prasad were, Kendi presumed, still watching the show.

"Hold it!" Ben whispered. He was peeking around the door frame again. "He has a boy with him. God— it's his son!"

"His son?" Gretchen echoed. "What the hell?"

Kendi's stomach lurched. Why was Roon bringing his son?

Valeta entered the room, leading Roon and a pale

boy who looked about five or six. Kendi, who had tailed Roon and his family countless times, instantly recognized Janni Roon.

"Moogoo, Bobo, this is Mr. Edsard Roon," Val said gaily, though Kendi could hear the strain in her voice. "And this is Master Janni Roon. Janni is the winner of the clown drawing. Can you make him up, please? I have to get back to the ring."

In a flash Kendi understood what had happened. Roon had decided to hand his prize over to his son. He gritted his teeth. Kendi hadn't counted on Roon being anything but a self-serving bastard. Obviously that wasn't entirely the case. A harsh lesson to learn, Ara would have said. Now what?

Roon was pumping Val's hand. "It was a pleasure to meet you, Ms. Kalopolis. A true pleasure."

Val nodded to him and, with a parting glance at Ben and Gretchen, vanished out the door.

"Well, Janni," Gretchen said slowly, "why don't you have a seat here and we'll get to work. How do you like the idea of being a clown for day?"

Janni didn't answer. He just looked up at Gretchen with shy, pale eyes.

"I think he's too excited to talk," Roon said with a smile. "Should he remove his shirt?"

Ben started to speak, but his voice cracked. He cleared his throat and tried again. "Yes. Here, Janni, we'll hang it up just like this. How do you like the show so far?"

"It's great!" Janni said at last. "Are you a real clown?"

"I sure am," Ben replied. "I started up when I was about your age."

"What do I have to do out there?"

"It'll be really easy. All you'll have to do is ride the elephant and wave."

Janni squirmed with joy. "I get to ride an *elephant*?"

"Sure do. Now, what colors would you like for your makeup?"

He set to work spreading a white base over Janni's face. Gretchen, meanwhile, pulled a data pad out of her pocket and called up a text file on the holographic screen. Kendi stared at Janni's thin chest. It was supposed to be Roon who took off his shirt. But Edsard Roon was standing nearby, shirt still on his body, key firmly out of reach. Kendi bit his lower lip until he tasted blood. The entire plan stood in ruins. He had dragged the Emporium halfway across the galaxy for nothing. There had to be a way to get that key here and now. But even if Kendi could think of a plan, there would be no way for him to implement it. He wanted to punch Roon in the face and take the key by force.

Maybe that was the solution. Maybe once Janni had left, Kendi could knock Roon over the head and hold him prisoner on the *Poltergeist* with Isaac Todd. If Roon couldn't alert the Collection that he had lost his key, the Collection wouldn't know to—

"Mr. Roon," Gretchen said, interrupting Kendi's chain of thought, "I'll need you to sign this waiver of liability. Just a formality, but you know how it goes." She held out the data pad to him.

"Of course, of course," Roon said, not taking his eyes off Janni. "Not a problem." He moved to take the pad.

"Oh! Wait a minute." Gretchen took the pad back before Roon could touch it. "God, what was I thinking? We can't do this. Mr. Roon, your son is a minor. He can't go out into the ring by himself, and he certainly can't ride an elephant."

Janni, whose face was almost completely covered in white base by now, twisted in his chair to face her. "I can't? Why not?"

"What do you mean?" Roon said.

"It's a legal thing on SA Station," Gretchen replied vaguely. "We can't have unaccompanied minors ride animals on the arena floor. Too dangerous."

"You'll be with him, won't you?" Roon said. "And Ms. Kalopolis said I'd be able to watch from the sidelines."

"Ms. Kalopolis doesn't have the legal background I do," Gretchen countered. "And I double as legal counsel for the Emporium. I'm afraid the other performers can't act in loco parentis in these circumstances. Station regulations. I looked them up before we docked."

"But I want to be a clown," Janni said, his eyes filling with tears. "I want to ride the elephant."

"Sorry, kid," Gretchen said. "It's just impossible. You can't go out there alone."

"What if I went with him?" Roon said suddenly.

Kendi held his breath.

"What do you mean?" Gretchen asked.

"What if I went along? You could dress me up as a clown, too, and we'll both ride the elephant. It'll solve the whole problem."

Gretchen paused, then shook her head. "Won't work. Union rules, you know. And we only advertised one clown winner per show. I don't want the Emporium to be brought up on charges of false advertising."

"Aw, come on, Bobo," Ben said. "We can't disappoint this kid. Who's going to know if we don't tell anyone? No one'll even recognize Mr. Roon here, so the union won't say anything. Have a heart."

"Please, Ms. Bobo?" Janni quavered. "Please?"

Gretchen paused, as if thinking it over. Kendi clenched his fists.

"Well . . . all right," she grumbled at last. "But I'm adding a gag order to this waiver. Sign here."

With a grin, Roon scribbled his signature with the stylus and set the pad back in Gretchen's gloved hand. She set it carefully aside and turned to Roon. "Let's get that shirt off, then, Mr. Roon. We'll have to work fast if we want to make the final act."

Still grinning and no doubt gloating that he was about to both have and eat his cake, Roon complied. The key glittered on the chain around his neck. When Gretchen reached for it, however, he snapped a hand over it.

"I can't take this off," he said. "That's nonnegotiable."

"Not a problem," Gretchen soothed. Kendi saw her slip another hand into her pocket. "But I do need you to close your eyes so I can do your lids. Don't open them unless you want a makeup pencil in your cornea. Ready?"

Half an hour later, Ben led the new clowns, one tall and one short, out of the dressing room and down to the elephant bay. Both Roons were chatting excitedly. The moment they were out of earshot, Kendi emerged from behind the wall hanging.

"Gretchen, I could kiss you," he said, and swept her into a hug instead. "You were brilliant."

"All right, all right," she said gruffly, though there was a note of pride in her voice. "Put me down before Ben sees you and gets jealous."

Still laughing, Kendi obeyed. "Where's the copycat? I'll take it and the data pad back to the ship."

"Right here. And don't touch the pad without gloves on or you'll ruin Roon's prints. Put it in this bag."

Kendi obeyed, then looked thoughtfully at the doorway. "You know, we made Roon's fondest dream come true, and he's the biggest bastard in the universe."

"Then we'll do our best," Gretchen replied, "to turn it all into a nightmare."

The coughing fit doubled Bedj-ka over so fast, he almost smacked his forehead on the dinner table. Harenn quickly swallowed a spicy mouthful of minced lamb and set her flat bread down. The galley was empty at the moment. Kendi, Ben, and Gretchen hadn't returned from the circus yet, and Lucia was deep in some kind of meditation in her quarters, leaving Harenn and her son the run of the ship.

"Are you all right, my son?" she asked with concern.

Bedj-ka stopped coughing and reached for his water glass. Before he could get it to his mouth, he sneezed. Water sprayed everywhere.

"Bedj-ka!" Harenn said. "Are you ill?"

"I'm okay," he mumbled.

"That is not what 'okay' sounds like." She slid around to his side of the table and put a hand on his forehead. It was warmer than Harenn would have liked. "Do you feel sick to your stomach? Dizzy? Tired?"

"I'm okay, Mom," he insisted. "I'm not sick."

"I will determine that. Do you want to finish your supper first, or should we visit the medical bay now?"

"I'm not sick," Bedj-ka insisted again, though his argument was weakened by another wet sneeze. "You don't need to put me to bed or pray over me."

Harenn, halfway through the act of rising from the table, halted. "Pray over you?"

"I didn't do anything wrong, did I?" His voice was thick, as if he were about to cry. Confused, Harenn sat down again and put an arm around him.

"Bedj-ka, what is the matter? Tell me what is wrong and we will try to fix it."

"I'm sick . . . because . . . because I sinned." He gulped. "But I don't know what I did. Was it the books? Or that I got mad at Sister Gretchen?"

A slow, angry burn started behind Harenn's eyes. "Bedj-ka, is this what the Enclave taught you? That sickness is punishment for a sin?"

He nodded up at her, his face a picture of misery.

She hugged him hard, wanting to lash out at these people who had done this to her son. How could they teach such a dreadful thing?

"You are sick because you encountered a virus," she said, forcing her voice to remain steady. "No other reason. And here is what will happen. We will go down to the medical bay. I will run tests to determine the structure of your pathogen. I will make you an antiviral. By morning, you will be well again."

"I will?" He sounded startled.

"Indeed. And I will hear no more nonsense about sin making you—"

"Harenn, are you there?" It was Kendi's voice. She tapped her earpiece.

"I am here, but a bit busy. Is this important?"

"Sorry to interrupt, but it is. We got Roon's key with him none the wiser. I need you to have Todd drugged and ready to talk by the time I get back because we need more information about the Collection's security procedures. And then we need to have a . . . conversation." He gave further instructions, and Harenn had to force herself to listen. Bedj-ka waited, his silence puncuated with the occasional cough and sneeze.

"I will have everything ready," Harenn said when Kendi finished. "Though I must also examine Bedj-ka. I think he's come down with a virus."

"Poor kid! Is it bad or can he wait until we're done with Todd?"

"I will have to run a viral analysis for Bedj-ka to determine his treatment, so it would be better if we took care of Todd first."

"Then I'll come down directly."

"Bedj-ka, I want you to wait in our quarters until I call you," Harenn said. "And then we'll have a long talk about stupid people and stupid beliefs."

The hazy fog cleared from Isaac Todd's mind so abruptly it felt as if he had fallen to the medical bay bed. He stared up at the white ceiling above him and felt slightly chilly, as he always did after one of these interrogation sessions. Oddly enough, he didn't feel any fear. Every other time the bitch's dose of hypnoral had worn off, he had come out of it feeling like he had just awoken from a horrible nightmare. This time, however, he felt clearheaded and awake. He was about to say something when he realized people were talking.

". . . do you want something like that?" It was Harenn's voice.

"Because the best way to steal something is to convince the current owner that he doesn't want it anymore. Once you do that, he'll give it to you outright—or sell it to you cheap." The speaker was the leader, the Father whose name Todd hadn't managed to catch. "In this case, we need to convince the Collection that my family are worthless."

Todd froze. Didn't they know he was lying within earshot? Obviously not. Or maybe they didn't care. No. It made no sense for them to discuss plans like this where Todd could hear. So why were they doing it?

The answer, when it came, was obvious. Harenn had screwed up. The dose of hypnoral she had given him hadn't lasted as long as it was supposed to. Maybe he was building up a tolerance for it after all this exposure, or maybe she had accidentally underdosed him. In any case, it was obvious that Harenn and the Father didn't know he was awake and listening. He shut his eyes to keep it that way.

Mr. Roon was going to love this.

"So you're going to make them sick," Harenn said.

"Something like that," the Father said. "If you get your hands on some gelpox virus, can you weaken it so that it won't make them too ill?"

"Easily. I can buy gelpox right here on the station. How do you intend to infect them?"

"Someone will have to get to the kitchen and put it in the food. Once our patients get moved down to their medical facilities, Ken Jeung will test for the virus and find it."

"Gelpox is a minor illness," Harenn pointed out. "The Collection will not try to rid itself of your family for that."

"That's why we need access to Jeung's medical database. We make a few changes to his computer so that when his scanners find gelpox, they'll *say* they found something more serious. Like Selene's disease."

"Not readily contagious, but deadly within two years."

"Right. Why spend resources on someone who's going to be dead soon? Silent Acquisitions policy states that slaves who have outlived their usefulness go into a pool for cheap sale. We just watch for them and make a quick buy. The main problem will be getting inside the Collection to change the computers. We've only got three more days before we have to leave."

"What about the others?"

There was a pause. Todd held his breath and kept his eyes firmly shut.

"Others?" the Father asked.

"The rest of the Collection. All of them were kidnapped, stolen away by force or guile. This plan saves your family but it leaves the others in bondage."

A sigh. "We went through this with Sejal before the Despair, Harenn. The Children can't save everyone. The resources just aren't there."

"That doesn't make it right to leave the others behind." Harenn's voice held a righteous indignation that Todd remembered well from their marriage. He had hated it then and he definitely hated it now. He almost felt sorry for the nameless Father, who was currently on the receiving end of it.

"There isn't anything I can do, Harenn," the Father

said. A pleading tone had entered his voice. "Now that we know about the Collection, maybe the Children can send another task force later to get them out. But we're just one tiny group here, and I'm not a miracle worker."

"Ara would have tried."

"Low blow, Harenn. Besides, you don't know that she—"

"Stop. Isaac will wake any moment now. We'll discuss this later."

"No, Harenn," Father Nameless said tiredly. "We won't."

Todd lay still and tried to breathe normally. He heard Harenn approach his bed and he became acutely aware of the slightly stiff sheets beneath him, of the little current of cool air from the nearby vent, of the smell of cooking oil on Harenn's skin. His heart beat fast. Todd was afraid of Harenn, and he hated himself for it. He fervently wished he could go back in time and stop himself from marrying her, no matter what price he had gotten for . . . what had she named the kid? He couldn't remember. Not that it mattered now anyway.

"Is he awake?" Father Nameless asked. "We need to get him back in his room."

"I judge he has approximately thirty seconds left. Perhaps forty-five."

Isaac silently counted to thirty-eight and stirred. He opened his eyes and saw Harenn looking down at him.

"It is time to return you to your quarters," she said. "Now."

"What did you ask me about this time, Harenn?" he demanded as he always did.

"Nothing of importance to you," she replied. "But I suspect you will . . . enjoy the memory of your dreams."

He didn't speak as she accompanied him back through the maze of blue corridors to his tiny, boring room. The slave band around his wrist prevented him from running, though he desperately wanted to. They had almost reached his quarters when a boy who looked to be eight or nine years old dashed up to them. He had dark hair and eyes that matched Harenn's, but his face . . . Todd blinked. The boy reminded Isaac of holograms of himself taken when he was young.

"I got tired of waiting, Mom, and the computer said you were here," the boy blurted. "Are you ready for me in medical yet?"

"Leave us," Harenn snapped. "Go down to medical. Now!"

"Who's this?" the boy asked, and coughed. "The guy in the room? Rigid!"

Todd took a chance. "I'm your dad."

The boy's eyes bulged and he backed away. "Are you going to cut my throat?"

"What? No. I—" A wrenching shock made him gasp and clutch at the band around his wrist.

"You will be *silent*!" Harenn snarled. "You will not speak to him. You will not *look* at him."

"He's my son, too, Harenn," Todd told her.

"You gave up all rights to him when you sold him into slavery. Bedj-ka, go!"

"But I want to see—"

"Better obey your mother," Todd said. "Or she'll shock you like she does me. She likes shocking people, son."

"Go!" Harenn almost screamed. Bedj-ka flung one last look at Todd, then fled. The moment he was out of sight, another shock sent Todd to his knees. Pain thundered through him and Harenn clapped a hand over his mouth to keep him from screaming.

"The only thing that is stopping my knife, *husband*," she hissed in his ear, "is the possibility that we might still need you. If you speak to him again, you will die, no matter what orders I am given. Is that clear?"

When she took her hand from his mouth, he said, "Perfectly clear." He staggered to his feet—Harenn offered no assistance—and added, "You call me a monster, Harenn. How is what you're doing to me any different?"

"I care nothing about what you say, Isaac." She nudged him forward. "I do not let the words of one who sells children into slavery bring doubt to my mind."

"Maybe you don't," he said without disguising the relish in his voice. "But what about Bedj-ka? I wonder what kind of bedtime story he'll ask for tonight, *wife.*"

She shocked him again, but it was worth it. And when he was back in his tiny room, he made himself wait an entire hour before contacting Edsard Roon.

Kendi could see the trouble on Bedj-ka's face the moment the boy entered the medical bay. Automatically he said, "What's wrong?"

"That guy you've been keeping in that room?" Bedj-ka replied. "I saw him with Mom in the hall. He said he was my father."

Uh-oh. "He said that?"

Bedj-ka nodded. "Is it true? Mom didn't deny it."

A dozen lies rushed through Kendi's head. He could say it wasn't true, that Todd was a prisoner of war, that Todd was a pathological liar. He could simply avoid the question and let Harenn deal with it. After all, he was her son.

But Kendi was captain of the ship, and that made Bedj-ka's relationship with Todd Kendi's responsibility, in a way. Besides, Kendi knew Harenn well enough to predict what she would tell him. Perhaps he could spare her a little pain.

"It's true," Kendi said. "His name is Isaac Todd, and he's your dad."

"Why didn't anyone tell me?" Bedj-ka demanded, then coughed hard.

"We didn't want you to get upset," Kendi replied. "It's still true that he sold you into slavery when you were a baby, and we didn't want you to be afraid he would do it again."

"You should have told me." Bedj-ka's tone was belligerent. Kendi sank down onto a rolling stool so his head was lower than the boy's, and let his arms hang limply at his sides in a nonthreatening gesture calculated to avoid provoking further anger.

"Maybe we should have," Kendi admitted, voice quiet. "Sometimes adults make mistakes. But we figured you'd already been through so much. I mean, I remember how confused I was when Ara freed *me*. We didn't want to make things more complicated for you than they already were."

"He said Mom shocks him a lot. He said Mom likes to shock people for fun."

"That's not true," Kendi said. "I've known your Mom a long time, and she doesn't hurt people for fun." *Only when she has a reason,* added a wry voice in his head. "I think he was trying to make you angry at her by telling lies. Bedj-ka, I know this is hard and it hurts to hear, but Isaac Todd isn't a nice man. He's cruel and mean. That doesn't mean *you're* a mean person. You can be the person you want to be. You don't have to be like him."

"I don't care about him," Bedj-ka said. His voice shook. "He isn't really my father. He didn't raise me."

"That's right. And your mother loves you very much, no matter what anyone might say." Kendi patted Bedj-ka's shoulder. "She'll get that cold fixed right up, too. I'll even bet she won't make you do what *I* had to do when I got sick on the frog farm where I was a slave."

Bedj-ka looked at him, interested despite himself. "You were a slave on a frog farm?"

"Sure was. Anyway, this one species of frog secreted a substance that was refined into an antiviral drug. We slaves couldn't refine anything, of course, so when we got sick, we had only one choice."

"What was that?"

Kendi kept an absolutely straight face. "We licked the frogs."

"Blech! You did not!"

"Absolute truth," Kendi said.

"That's disgusting!" Bedj-ka said just as Ben walked into the medical bay.

"What is?" he asked.

"Kendi was telling me about how he got sick when he was a slave," Bedj-ka said cheerfully.

Ben groaned. "He's not telling that atrocious frog-licking story, is he? It's completely apocryphal, you know."

"Hey!" Kendi said.

"What's 'apocryphal'?" Bedj-ka asked.

"Look it up," Ben said with a smile.

"Before you destroy the rest of my stories," Kendi growled, "do tell me you copied the logarithms into keys."

"Just finished."

"Did you trace the line from Roon's home office?"

"Gretchen did. And we got lucky—there's a hotel right up the street from his house. Gretchen's already got a room."

"Then let's go down there and get to work. Lucia should be back right soon with that clunker ship, and we have a lot to do."

Bejd-ka sneezed hard.

"But first," Kendi said, "we'd better get Harenn down here. Before that . . . *thing* happens."

"What thing?" Bedj-ka said.

"I don't want to worry you," Kendi said seriously.

"Oh, god," Ben muttered.

"Worry me about what?"

"Well . . . back on the farm there was this one slave who sneezed so hard, a big chunk of brain flew straight out of his nose. It landed in a pond and the frogs ate it. I had to cut them open to get it back."

"Disgusting!" Bedj-ka howled happily.

"You're going to do him more damage than the Enclave," Ben said.

Keith bent his head and Dreamer Roon himself dropped the Beta medallion around his neck. Dreamer Roon boomed, "All praise the Dream!"

"All praise the Dream," shouted everyone. Martina mouthed the words but didn't say them. Keith's face beamed with pride, an expression shared by the six other new Betas on the stage. Martina and the other Alphas, along with their Deltas, knelt on the tiered floor, exactly as they had done the first day Dreamer Roon had addressed them.

Roon, Martina reminded herself. *His name is Roon. He made up the title "Dreamer." He made up his stupid book. He made up this whole place. None of it's real.*

She put the thought on her mental list of Confessions—*"I doubted Dreamer Roon's teachings." "Impure!"*—and went back to telling herself it wasn't real. She could get out of here. She *would* get out of here, and she would take Keith with her. A while ago—Martina couldn't measure time in days or hours anymore—she would have thought this impossible, but Martina now had something that might allow her to pull it off.

Martina had a keycard.

She surreptitiously touched the palm of her left glove. The little square of plastic was still there. She had spotted it on the floor on her way to this very ceremony. Most slaves learned a certain amount of sleight of hand in order to pilfer small treats or hide forbidden objects, and Martina was no exception. With a false grunt of annoyance, she had bent over to scoop the object up, then told her questioning Delta that her slipper hadn't been unfastened after all; so sorry for holding up the group. Her yellow robe had no pockets, but she had folded her hands together inside her sleeves and worked the little card into her glove for safekeeping.

Martina was dying to examine the key more closely. Did it work solo? Or did it work in conjunction with a print or retina scan? No, it had to work solo. She had seen the Deltas use keycards to access computer terminals and open doors, and they hadn't used any other scanners. Their prints, after all, were covered with gloves, and retina scans would take too much time for daily tasks like opening doors, especially since the Deltas all wore hoods or wimples that half-hid their eyes and would get in the way of a scanner. A security weakness, but a necessary one—the Deltas couldn't risk one of the Alphas touching them skin to skin by accident and learning they weren't Silent. This was Martina's chance; she knew it. The only problem was figuring out how best to use it.

"You are closer than ever to touching the Dream without the taint of drugs," Roon was saying on the stage. "And let your progress serve as an example to your former compatriots. I know it gets difficult, dear Alphas, but believe me when I tell you that it will one day be worth every moment of discomfort and tribulation. I enter the Dream whenever I wish, with no trancing, no drugs, and no time limits. You can be free, as I am. As these new Betas are close to becoming. As you will be."

Martina tried not to shift. Her knees ached, though not as badly as they had on that first day. Hours spent kneeling had hardened her to that simple discomfort. What she wanted more than anything was to grab Keith's hand and bolt for the door, and the thought filled her with unbearable restlessness. She called upon years of meditation exercises to slow her breathing and bring a measure of calm. At least she didn't have to keep her eyes down anymore. Roon had decided that the Alphas were no longer too impure to gaze upon his face.

"For the immediate future, Betas, you will continue to labor side by side with your former Alpha compatriots," Roon continued. "But your bodies are more pure, so you will receive even better food and more sleep."

The carrot and the stick, Martina thought sourly, and wondered how many people would confess to jealousy N-waves at the next Confessional.

"Soon we will begin the next stage of your training," Roon said. "Some of you will be selected to raise the next generation and see if they are Silent. You will be paired with an appropriate genetic match, though there will be no impure sex. Insemination will be artificial. However, a selected few Alphas, women who are particularly impure, will be partnered with me so that my body can show yours the way."

A small ripple of emotion moved through the kneeling Alphas, quickly silenced by the Deltas. Martina stared, and her stomach wrenched itself into a knot. Was she hearing right? Either she was going to be impregnated with some stranger's child or Roon was going to rape her. Anger and fear fought for ascendency inside her.

Roon continued speaking, haranguing and motivating. The new Betas listened raptly. Martina sneaked looks at remaining Alphas and guessed by their expressions and body language that despite Roon's little bombshell, about two-thirds of them were already willing followers of Roon's project and would strive to become Betas themselves. The remaining third were . . . less than enthusiastic. She made a mental note of these Alphas as potential allies.

After Roon's speech ended, he vanished out a side door. Alphas and Betas stood, stretched, and were allowed to mingle for a time, presumably so the

Alphas could bask in the Betas' presence while the Deltas looked on. A small table to one side held munching food, though it was all finger vegetables and sugarless gelatin salad. Party voices murmured and swirled around the room. Martina managed to worm her way up to Keith and draw him aside.

"Congratulations," she said.

"Thanks." He beamed. "I hope you get here soon. I feel freer of N-waves already. And soon we'll be parents!"

Martina ignored the last comment and lowered her voice. "Remember how we talked about . . . going elsewhere?"

"You mean . . . not here?"

Martina nodded. They both had to choose their words carefully, keep their meaning vague in case the computers in their wristbands interpreted their conversation as seditious.

"Why would I want to do that?" Keith said, clearly puzzled.

Martina tensed. "You like this place, don't you?" It wasn't a question.

"I feel at peace here," he said. "They love me and they're teaching me what I need to know. I have no worries here. Look, if you aren't happy, we can talk to one of the Deltas, and—"

"No," Martina interrupted. Her throat felt thick. "No, don't say anything. Please. I . . . I want to try working it out on my own." She forced a note of sunshine into her voice, though her heart was twisting inside her. "Besides, how could I leave a place that makes my brother so happy? I'm going to work harder. Then I can be a Beta, too."

Keith nodded happily, then winced. A warning tingle shot through Martina's body. She had been talking to Keith—a man—for too long. She smiled a farewell at him and turned away. Abruptly her gorge rose and she had to swallow hard to keep it down.

"Are you all right, dear?" asked Delta Maura, placing a concerned hand on Martina's elbow.

"I'm tired," Martina managed, and wondered how it would look if she threw up on Delta Maura's green slippers. "Is it almost ti—I mean, are we near a sleep cycle yet?"

"Soon," Delta Maura assured her. "Though the ones Dreamer Roon selects for himself won't get much sleep." She said the latter sentence the way she might say she was expecting a com call. Martina swallowed hard again and took a pair of deep breaths.

"Perhaps," Delta Maura said, noticing, "I should take you back to your room a little early. Just this once."

A few minutes later, Martina lay on her bed and stared at the yellow ceiling. The door would open any moment, she was sure of it, and Roon would enter. What would he do? Speak first? Make small talk? Just yank up her robe and shove himself inside her? Martina had been a slave for most of her life, but never once had she been raped. Her Silence—and the value it added to her—had protected her from it. Or maybe she'd just been lucky. Now her luck was coming to an end. She had to get out of here, and she was unfortunately and dreadfully certain that she wouldn't be able to take Keith with her. He had already fallen under Roon's spell.

Martina wanted to cry, wanted to shout and scream and throw something. She did none of it—cameras in the room recorded her every move. So far she had located five of them while tidying her room. It was a strain to act as if nothing were wrong, step naked into the shower every morning with hungry, invisible eyes upon her.

Who else knew about this place? Martina couldn't imagine that her disappearance had gone unnoticed. DrimCom would certainly have called the police. If they had figured out where she was, they would have done something, wouldn't they? Of course, for all she knew, DrimCom had found Roon and he had simply paid them for her. No, that couldn't be. She was far, far too valuable in a post-Despair universe. A place like this had to be a secret, or else it couldn't—

—couldn't function.

Martina sat up. She didn't have to get Keith out. She only had to get herself out. Once she was free, she could tell someone about this place, tell a hundred people, a thousand. The news that Roon had stolen two dozen functioning Silent would crash through the Dream like a thunderclap and bring down the wrath of governments, corporations—perhaps even the Children of Irfan. Roon would be shut down and Keith would be freed.

Now all she had to do was get out herself. She brushed the bit of plastic in her palm and thought long and hard.

CHAPTER TEN

"Hate binds us to our enemies."

—Irfan Qasad

Ben pried up the access panel and, with another glance at the street corridor, dropped into the maintenance tunnel. It was dry and dimly lit, with dozens of pipes and color-coded cables running in various directions.

"How are you doing?" came Lucia's voice in his earpiece.

"In," Ben said, and examined the dozens of wrapped cables. "Let's see. SA datalinks are coded in blue, so it has to be one of these." He brushed his hand across a thick clump of tiny blue cables bound with plastic bands and followed them down the tunnel away from Roon's house. In his other hand he carried a small tool satchel.

"It makes our job so much easier when people act like idiots," Gretchen said.

Ben didn't answer and continued tracing the cables. He came to an intersection, followed the cables to the right, and kept going. The tunnel ceiling was low, and for once Ben was glad he was short. His footsteps were muffled by pipe baffling and the close quarters. A leaky pipe dripped a bright green fluid Ben declined to scrutinize, but otherwise the tunnels were pretty clean. He doubted this would be the case in the poorer sections of the station.

After a few more meters, the cables ended in a junction box with a card access slot. Ben studied the slot for a moment, then opened his tool satchel and extracted a card with a cord dangling from it. He attached the free end of the cord to his data pad, then slotted the card into the access panel. The pad beeped once and displayed a series of codes. Ben removed the reader card and pulled from his satchel what looked like a pack of playing cards. With deft fingers he shuffled through them, found the one he wanted, and slid it into the access slot. The box beeped once and released the lock with a clunk.

"I've got access," Ben said. He opened the box and peered inside at the snarl of cables, hookups, and computer parts. The ceramic on one of the hookups gleamed more brightly than its compatriots, delineating its status as a newcomer. "We have a winner. Let me establish a link; then tell me what you see."

"Waiting," Lucia said.

Ben clipped a shunt the size of a fingernail to the cable just before the hookup. The shunt would intercept signals that passed through the cable, copy them, and transmit them to Lucia's terminal. The shunt had a range of less than a hundred meters, which was why Lucia and Gretchen were currently holed up in a hotel room a little way up the street corridor.

"The computer is asking for a thumbprint and a key," Lucia reported. *"We're in! Praise be to Irfan!"*

"I still don't understand why Roon doesn't use a wireless link," Gretchen said as Ben shut the box and trotted back to the open access panel.

"Security," he said with an ironic snort. "Wireless communication can be intercepted and piggybacked if you know the frequency. Roon probably figured anonymity was on his side. If no one knows about the terminal in his house, no one can look for the cable that hooks it up to the Collection. And even if someone managed to find out about the terminal—Kendi saw it, after all—they'd still wouldn't have his key and print. Or so Roon figured."

"Sometimes even intelligent people can make stupid mistakes," Lucia said.

"And thank god for that," Gretchen added.

Ben climbed the short ladder to the sidewalk, half expecting to be met by a curious Security officer. He had a fake ID and work order in his pocket in case that happened, but no one accosted him. A few electric cars buzzed up the corridor, and foot traffic was limited to a few humans who didn't look twice at a workman climbing out of a maintenance tunnel. The corridor itself was lined with round doors. The owners—or, more likely, their gardeners—had planted trees and flowers and small gardens in pots, and ivy-framed windows looked out onto these little "yards." Far, far overhead, the corridor ceiling was painted sky blue, and an artificial sun shuttled slowly back and forth. Birds sang in the trees, and a group of small children giggled their way through some mysterious game. Despite the homey touches, though, the area felt to Ben more like a shopping mall than a residential zone. He couldn't resist looking up the corridor to Roon's door, a bright red circle beneath a potted elm. The windows were dark.

Ben shut down the projector that created a holographic warning ring around the entrance to the maintenance tunnel, gathered up his satchel, and strolled casually away. When he was sure no one was watching, he ducked into an alley—it was clean and well swept—and removed his coveralls. Beneath them he wore an expensive-looking suit. He sprayed the coveralls with disintegration enzyme, dragged a comb through his hair, and crossed the street, carrying his tool satchel like an overnight bag. A revolving door made of glass and gold spun slowly ahead of him, and a line of cabs stretched up the street waiting for fares. Ben nodded to the blue-clad doorman and entered the hotel. A few minutes later he was knocking on one of the doors. It opened a crack, and a blue eye peered suspiciously at him.

"What's the password?"

"Your mother," Ben said.

Gretchen opened the door with a sigh. "You're no fun," she grumped.

The hotel room was small, sporting a single room, small desk, and two wide beds. Lucia was sitting at the desk, which had a holographic computer display hovering over it. Four rubber thumbs sat nearby, each one a different color. Vidya and Prasad both lounged on one of the beds.

"Ta-da!" Lucia said, gesturing at the display with one scarred hand. It said, PLEASE INSERT KEY AND SCAN PRINT. "I figured you'd want the honors."

Ben nodded. "I'd better get started. Vidya and Prasad, I'll need you two in just a minute. Everyone be ready to run in case something goes wrong. Ready?"

"Get on with it, already," Gretchen said.

Lucia vacated the desk and Ben took her place. His muscles were tense, and he had to force himself to unclench his jaw. Like the situation with the copycat, there was no way to test the print and key system. A mistake here, however, would bring consequences much more serious than being forced to hide under another bed. Taking a deep breath and trying to banish a mental image of Kendi's broken body being fed into a recycling vat, Ben pressed the red rubber thumb to the data pad's scanner and slotted Roon's key. Lucia murmured to herself and clutched the little icon of Irfan around her neck. Ben's tongue felt like sandpaper in his mouth, and he found himself saying a quick prayer of his own.

The pad beeped twice and the display winked out. Ben tensed and Gretchen was already halfway to the door when the display winked back on.

ACCESS APPROVED, it said. GOOD AFTERNOON, MR. ROON.

"No vocal output," Vidya muttered. Her voice was perfectly steady.

"Maybe it annoys him. God." Ben felt limp as a wilted leaf. "Looks like it worked, at any rate. Give me a few minutes."

With Lucia watching over his shoulder, Ben fiddled with the system, quickly familiarizing himself with file locations and downloading whatever caught his eye. Occasionally he paused to read.

"Roon has a private ship," Lucia said, pointing at the display. "It's heavily armed, too. Will that matter, do you think?"

"No idea," Ben replied. "I'll make sure Kendi knows, though."

A moment later, Ben came across a book in the file lists. He copied it to a small disk, which he tossed to Gretchen. "Take a look at this."

Gretchen caught it and slotted it into her own data pad. "*A True History of the Dream,* by Dr. Edsard Roon. What the hell? Roon's a doctor?"

"There," Prasad said. He was standing next to Gretchen. "The fine print says 'Dr.' stands for 'Dreamer.' "

"Roon isn't Silent," Lucia said. "We hacked his medical records first thing."

They continued to talk while Ben worked. First he called up personnel files—all the workers involved with the Collection, he noticed, were human—and found two men and a woman who had been recently laid off. He deleted most of their basic information and substituted information on Vidya and Prasad instead—DNA sequences, ID holograms, and personal communication codes. He did the same for the third person, but uploaded an entirely different set of codes. Then he called over Vidya and Prasad so he could scan their prints and record their voices.

"Cross your fingers," Ben said. "I'm going to log off Roon and log on as Mallory in Security so I can bump up your clearance level."

But the blue thumb and fake key worked perfectly. A few moments later, Ben handed Vidya and Prasad a set of ID holograms.

"These will get you in and out of the Collection," Ben told them. "You were laid off, but in about half an hour you're going to get an automated message recalling you to work for this evening's shift."

"Who is that one for?" Vidya pointed at the third ID holo.

"I'm not supposed to say," Ben said, and slipped the holo into his pocket. "Next up—maps and diagrams from information tech."

The green thumb, which bore Elena Papagos-Faye's print, also worked as advertised, and in a few moments Ben had a complete set of blueprints and diagrams for the entire Collection. Ben logged off the system, shut it down, and ran a relieved hand through his hair.

"We're done," he said.

"All that sweat to get keys and prints, and it only took ten minutes to get what we needed?" Gretchen said. "You didn't even use the yellow thumb."

"We don't need to access research and medical quite yet," Ben said. "Or so Kendi says."

Gretchen leveled a hard look at him. "You don't know the whole plan either, do you?"

"No. But Kendi will tell us what we need to know when we need to know it."

"I'm sensing reluctance." Gretchen smirked. "You're as ticked as I am. Admit it."

"I trust Kendi."

"Of course you do," Gretchen scoffed. "You're both still Silent and Kendi's still your goddammed—"

"Sister Gretchen!" Lucia interrupted, stepping in front of Ben and leveling a hard look of her own. "I think we're done here, don't you?"

Gretchen met her gaze and ran her tongue around the inside of her mouth with small smacking noises. After a long moment, she said, "Yeah. I think we're done. You do what you need to, church girl. I'm going back to the ship."

And she stomped out of the room.

"What was that about?" Prasad asked.

"I can't be angry at her," Lucia said absently. "She's lost too much."

Ben, who was struggling to keep his own temper, took a deep breath and nodded. "Agreed. I just hope she can finish her part in this."

"She will," Lucia said. "I think this sort of thing is all that keeps her going."

Harenn pressed the dermospray to Bedj-ka's arm and activated the release. The drugs thumped home. Bedj-ka rubbed his arm, then rubbed his nose.

"I gave you medication to relieve your cough and fever along with the antiviral," Harenn said. "You will be fine after a good night's sleep."

She turned to the small crate on the counter behind her. The words BIOLOGICAL AGENT: HANDLE WITH CARE marched along the side like red soldiers, and Harenn opened the top as if it might explode.

"Can I talk to my dad?" Bedj-ka asked behind her.

Harenn closed her eyes. It was the question she had been dreading. She pushed the crate aside and laid her palms on the cool countertop without looking around. "Why?"

"I want to see him," Bedj-ka replied. "I want to find out why he did it."

"It is a poor idea, my son." Harenn turned around. Her stomach felt like a ball of heavy ice. "He will only say things that hurt you. Perhaps later you will understand why I cannot let you—"

Bedj-ka's jaw firmed, and in that moment he looked

amazingly like Isaac. "I want to see him. You said I
can make my own choices now that I'm free."

"Within reasonable limits, yes."

"Matron and Patron said the same thing in the
Enclave."

"It is hardly the same thing. You know this very
well."

"All I know is you won't let me see my dad."

Her first crisis as a mother. Harenn had often
watched other parents deal with problems among their
children and felt a stab of envy. Now that it was happening to her, however, she found herself wishing the
situation would go away. The whole thing was a trap.
If she agreed to Bedj-ka's demand, she was setting
him up for a world of hurt. If she refused him, it could
create a serious rift between them at a time when their
relationship was still forming. She couldn't win, no
matter what she did. Hatred for Isaac rolled thick and
black. If he hadn't spoken when he had, none of this
would be happening. If he hadn't stolen Bedj-ka away
in the first place, none of this would be happening.
If . . . if . . . if . . .

"Very well," Harenn said at last. "You may talk to
him during the procedure." That way, at least, Bedj-
ka wouldn't be left alone with him.

"Thanks, Mom." Bedj-ka's eyes were wide and
bright.

"But first I have a few small tasks to attend," she
said. "When I am finished, I will bring him down. You
may sit and wait over there."

Bedj-ka retired to the indicated chair without further comment. Harenn opened the little crate, extracted a plastic vial filled with clear liquid, and slotted
it into the microscope. She examined the virus on the
holographic display with a critical eye. It looked like
a clump of snowflakes. Harenn nodded.

"What's that for?" Bedj-ka asked.

"This I cannot explain to you," she replied. "But it is very important to Father Kendi."

"My ears are burning," Kendi said as he entered the medical bay. "I came down to see how the gene scan is going."

Harenn gestured at the cryo-unit, which sat on a counter across the room. A computer lead was attached to it and the unit's lights were flashing briskly. "The computer is running comparisons. It will take some time."

"How is everything else going?"

"I am examining the biological shipment," Harenn told him. "Would you do me a favor? Go get Isaac and bring him here."

Kendi shot Bedj-ka a look and Harenn braced herself for a barrage of questions. But Kendi merely gave a brief nod and left. Bedj-ka fidgeted on his stool while Harenn put a sample of the virus into a dermospray.

"Mom," he said at last, "what will happen to me once we're done here?"

"You will come home to Bellerophon and live with me, of course. And you will attend school. When you get older, you can decide to apprentice in a trade or business, or you can attend a university. The monastery for the Children of Irfan instructs more than just the Silent, and they have many fine programs. Or you can do something else entirely. When we get back—"

"You mean *if* we get back," Bedj-ka interrupted.

Harenn set down the dermospray. "If?"

"I hear stuff. I don't know everything about what's going on, but I know it's dangerous and if someone makes a mistake, we'll all be dead."

His matter-of-fact tone brought a chill to Harenn's skin. "I suppose you are correct in this. But we will not fail, Bedj-ka. Father Kendi and the others are skilled, intelligent people. We will let nothing harm you."

Bedj-ka didn't look convinced. Before Harenn could respond further, however, Kendi arrived with a sullen Isaac Todd in tow. Bedj-ka got uneasily to his feet. Isaac caught sight of Bedj-ka, opened his mouth, then snapped it shut and looked at Harenn.

"He wishes to speak to you," Harenn said. "You may respond, but remember that I will be listening. It is best that you do not lie, Isaac."

Bedj-ka looked at Isaac without speaking. An uncomfortable silence fell over the medical bay. Kendi leaned against one wall, arms folded, expression neutral.

"What did you want to say?" Isaac finally asked.

"Why did you sell me?" Bedj-ka blurted out.

With a glance at Harenn, Isaac stammered, "I don't . . . look, I . . . ah, hell." He closed his eyes. "Plain and simple, I needed the money. Look, it was nothing personal. It was just that—"

He never finished. Bedj-ka flung himself at his father, both fists flying. "I hate you!" he screamed. "I hate you hate you hate you *hate you*!" One of his blows made a solid connection, and Isaac's breath whooshed out of his lungs. Another fist slammed into Isaac's groin. He paled and doubled over just as Kendi pulled Bedj-ka away. Harenn realized she hadn't been able to move throughout the entire exchange.

"I hate you!" Bedj-ka struggled in Kendi's arms. "You sold me away and I hate you!"

"Harenn!" Kendi barked.

Harenn unfroze. "Take him up to our quarters. I'll deal with Isaac and come right up."

"Hurry." Kendi carried the still-screaming Bedj-ka out of the medical bay, leaving Isaac on the floor. Harenn dragged him to his feet and sat him on one of the examination beds. His face was still pale with pain.

"Now he is hysterical, thanks to you," Harenn said.

"Think of this as your reward." She pressed the dermospray to his arm and thumbed the release.

"What the hell was that?" Isaac gasped, arms crossed over his abdomen from the kick he had received.

"If you are referring to Bedj-ka's attack, I should think that was self-explanatory," Harenn replied. "And I shall definitely have to enroll him in a martial arts class. He has talent. If you are referring to the dermospray—have you ever had gelpox?"

"No."

"Good. I will take you back to your room and there you will stay. By this time tomorrow, if everything goes well, we will be far away from this horrible place."

"What about me?"

"I imagine you will have a long conversation with the Guardians back on Bellerophon, and then you will have more conversations with police forces on other worlds. Enjoy what freedom you have, Isaac. You will have even less of it very soon."

Kendi flopped down onto Harenn's sofa with a sigh. Dealing with hysterical nine-year-old boys wasn't in his job description, unless they had sneaked it in when he wasn't looking. On the other hand, he supposed, it was good practice for becoming a father—small "f." Assuming he and Ben got through this whole thing in one piece, anyway.

The door slid open and Harenn entered. "Where is he?" she asked without preamble.

"In his room. He calmed down and said he wanted to be alone, though I'm sure you'll want to talk to him anyway. I can recommend a good counselor when we get back to Bellerophon."

Harenn lowered her voice. "*If* we get back."

She was echoing his earlier thought, but he forced a smile anyway. "Pessimist."

"Realist," she corrected.

"If you want, Harenn, we can put you and Bedj-ka on the Emporium's ship. You'll both be safe there, and if you injected Todd—"

"I did."

"—then you don't need to stick around for the end. I'll let you know how it works out, I promise."

Harenn opened her mouth, then clamped it shut. Now that she no longer wore her veil, Kendi found it easy to read her expression. He knew she felt it was her duty to stay, to help Kendi free his family the way he had helped Harenn free hers. But now she had to think of Bedj-ka's safety instead of just her own. Kendi had been counting on that.

At last she said, "Very well. I must check on Isaac in an hour to make sure the injection took, and then I will take Bedj-ka over to the Emporium. He will probably enjoy that very much, come to think of it." She stood up. "I should go talk him."

Kendi gave a small sigh of relief that she had agreed so readily and rose as well. "I have a few other things to finish up, too. And then we're going to have a briefing. The last one."

"Only for this mission. There will be others."

"That sounded suspiciously like optimism, Madam Realist."

"Yes." Harenn took Kendi's hand and squeezed it. "Kendi, I hope you know I did not mean what I said about your plan being selfish. I am very grateful to you."

"I know."

"If we do not meet again, I want you to know that I am glad to have served with you—and under you." She looked up at him, brown eyes meeting brown eyes. "You have made history once, Father Kendi Weaver, and I think you are going to make it again."

"By rescuing a handful of Silent from SA? Hardly."

"No. I mean later. Great people rarely touch the

universe only once." She stood on tiptoe, kissed him lightly on the cheek, and hurried into Bedj-ka's room.

"They're going to do it tonight, sir, or perhaps early tomorrow morning."

"How do you know, Mr. Todd?"

"Harenn told me that by this time tomorrow, they would be far away from SA Station."

"Have you learned the Father's name yet? We have extensive files on the Children of Irfan, and it would be easier to keep a lookout if we knew what he looked like."

"I still haven't caught his name, sir. He has dark skin, curly black hair, and dark eyes."

"That describes half the humans who live on this station, Mr. Todd."

"Tall, on the thin side."

"Your powers of description leave much to be desired."

"Sorry, sir. They're still planning to infect the Father's family with gelpox and tamper with the computer diagnostics to make you think they have something more serious and sell them away cheap." He grimaced. "Harenn injected me with gelpox to test the viability of the virus. In a couple days, I won't be feeling very good."

"Gelpox is a child's disease, Mr. Todd—a mere inconvenience. You shouldn't worry yourself."

"Yes, sir."

"If they want to tamper with the diagnostic equipment, they'll have to break into the research and medical labs."

"Yes, sir. If you put extra security in the medical bay, you'll probably get a whole lot more Silent for the Collection."

"You may count on that, Mr. Todd."

"And then you'll come and get me, sir?"

"I won't need to, Mr. Todd. I've already spoken with

Rafille Mallory. She was able to give me a computer virus that will override your shackles and another one that will open your door. I am uploading them into your communicator now. You land on your feet more easily than a cat, Mr. Todd, and I am eager to see you do it again. If you can find your way back to the Collection in time to see everything through, I will reward your resourcefulness. If you can't, you will want to practice your vanishing skills."

"A test, sir?"

"An assignment. Good luck, Mr. Todd."

Martina forced herself not to pace. This was it. She was getting out now. Tonight. Or today, or whatever the hell it was. Pacing, however, might attract the attention of the cameras, and that she didn't want. Yet. First, she needed to run a bath.

In the bathroom, Martina ran hot water into the tub. Moist steam billowed up. Bathing was one luxury the Deltas, with their emphasis on physical purity, did not restrict. Martina was, however, at the beginning of a sleep cycle, and she knew from experience that if she didn't go to bed soon, Delta Maura would come to check on her.

Martina glanced around the tiled room. Several moments' thought and a bit of experimentation had proven to Martina's satisfaction that the bathroom had two cameras in it. One of them observed the shower. Martina had figured this out with a bit of logic. The shower stall had an opaque door on it, but during Confessional, the Deltas always knew what any given Alpha did in the shower. That meant there had to be a camera that spied on just the shower stall from either inside or above.

The bathroom itself was tiled in green squares, and the layout was such that only one place granted a clear view of the entire room—the mirror over the sink. Martina was willing to bet that a second camera lay behind the mirror. Granted, spy devices could be tiny, but mounting—and hiding—such devices on tile was harder than installing them behind a mirror, and why take the hard route when the easy one would work just as well? Further proof of her idea lay in the fact that no matter how steamy the room got, the mirror always stayed clear.

Can't afford to have their spyhole steam up, she thought.

Unfortunately, Martina had no way to test this particular theory until she actually put her plan into motion. Her heart climbed into her throat as she casually undressed down to her underwear and then, as if bored while waiting for the tub to fill, she picked up a bar of soap from the sink and toyed with it. Whimsically, she drew a smiley face on the mirror and made faces at herself. Then, with a light laugh, she scribbled over the mirror with soap until the whole thing was completely blocked out. Just playing around. No harm here. She set the soap down, crossed to the half-full tub, and opened the drain without turning off the water. With a hard swallow, she picked up a can of depilatory cream, propped one foot on the side of the tub, and spread some of it on her leg.

Then she waited.

Her mouth was dry and her hands shook. If this didn't work, if she got caught, she had no idea what would happen to her. Martina doubted it would be pleasant. They wouldn't kill her—she was too valuable for that—but a lot of brainwashing methods were less . . . genial than those that the Deltas currently used. There was also the very real possibility that even if she got out, she would find herself with nowhere to run. As Keith had pointed out, this could be an asteroid or a station or an installation in the middle of a desert. And what about her shackles? They might shock her into insensibility the moment she crossed the threshold. Still, she had to try, had to find out.

A sound reached her ears over the noise of running water. The main door to her quarters had opened.

"Hello?" came Delta Maura's voice. "Alpha?"

"I'm in here," Martina called through dry lips.

Delta Maura entered the bathroom, her green robe and wimple rustling in the thick steam. Her face was serene, as usual, but her eyes went straight to the mirror. Martina suppressed a grim smile. Her theory had proven correct. Delta Maura had been sent in to unblock the camera. If there had been another camera in the room, or if Martina had been wrong about the mirror, the spies, whoever they were, would have simply continued watching.

"Is there a problem, Delta Maura?" Martina asked. The running water was loud, and she had to raise her voice.

"What did you do to your mirror, dear?" Delta Maura said.

Martina laughed. "Just playing around. Didn't you ever draw on the mirror with soap when you were a kid?"

"No."

"It's a pretty design, I think. Look, you can still see the bird."

Delta Maura turned to examine the glass. "Bird? I'm afraid I don't—"

Martina clocked her with the can. Delta Maura collapsed. Martina caught her and lowered her to the floor. Quickly she undressed the woman and shrugged into the voluminous robe and wimple.

Under the robe Delta Maura wore a belt with a small computer box on it. Martina gasped in recognition—a master unit. Master units controlled slave shackles. With trembling fingers, Martina found the tiny key and pulled it away from the unit. A lead wire stretched with it. Martina touched the key to her wristband. It fell open and dropped to the floor. Quickly, Martina touched the key to her ankle band

and released that as well. She stared down at the naked skin left behind. The wristband had been part of her life for over fifteen years, and now it was gone.

Martina shook herself. This wasn't the time for rumination. It was time to leave. At the last minute, Martina remembered to grab the gloves—and she found Delta Maura's keycard. Martina rolled her eyes. She didn't need the one she had found at all. On the other hand, it had given her the idea to escape in the first place. Finally, Martina took Delta Maura's earpiece and slipped it on.

"You can't leave the mirror like that, you know," Martina said as she worked, imitating Delta Maura's voice and praying that the running water would keep a listener from noticing the difference. "We'll have to clean it off."

"I'm almost done over here," she answered in her own voice. "Can you help me?"

Delta Maura's voice: "Well, all right. But let's move it along."

Gritting her teeth to keep herself from grunting, Martina heaved Delta Maura's limp body into the tub. The strain pulled at her back and arms, and she was sweating in the thick, steamy air. Eventually, Delta Maura slid home, with only the top of her head showing above the tub's rim. There was no danger she would drown, since the water was running down the drain as fast as it came in. Martina dropped a towel over her shackles lying open on the floor, then snatched up a washcloth and wiped the soap off the mirror, starting at the top and working downward. She kept her head lowered, pretending to keep her eyes on her work but actually using the wimple to hide her face from the camera. Then she turned back to the tub.

"That's enough water, dear," she said above the noise. "When you finish, go straight to bed."

She reached down, shut off the water, and strode quickly from the room.

"So that's the entire plan," Gretchen said. "Glad you saw fit to enlighten us five whole minutes before we get to work."

"This isn't a good time to argue," Lucia said. "We have our jobs to do, and we need to do them so we can get those people out."

Kendi drummed his fingers on his knees beneath the galley table. Lucia had made her usual delicious spread of snacks, but he didn't feel like eating any of it. Neither, he noticed, did any of the others.

"Just a minute," Ben said. "Kendi, you're planning to break into the research area alone?"

"The fewer to go in," Kendi told him, "the fewer to get caught."

"And killed."

"I'm Silent, Ben, and I can still work in the Dream. Do you honestly think they'd kill me? If I make a mistake, they'll probably just make me part of the Collection."

"That makes me feel so much better."

"And you'll be free to stage another rescue," Kendi finished.

"Sounds like fun," Gretchen drawled.

Kendi firmed his jaw. "I don't know why I'm trying to justify anything. This is the way it's going to happen, troops. You have gripes, take them up with Irfan."

"We'll do as you order, Father," Lucia said quietly. "We're just worried about you. Even Sister Gretchen worries, though she won't admit it."

Gretchen folded her arms. "The only thing I'm worried about is how much my part sucks."

Father Kendi Weaver adjusted his tool belt and shrugged within his blue maintenance uniform. Seemingly without a care in the world, he sauntered up the corridor that led to the Collection.

The corridor, an unassuming gray affair with no doors or windows, was deserted. The files Ben had copied from Roon's directory had indicated that although the Silent prisoners—Alphas, Roon called them—did not have a fixed schedule, most of the workers did. Only a skeleton staff remained on duty for eight of the station's twenty-four hours each "day," giving them some semblance of a diurnal cycle. It seemed most logical to strike when most of the staff were gone.

Interestingly enough, the files also indicated that the vast majority of the workers had no idea what sort of project they were working for. Only Roon, the department heads, another group called the Deltas, and a handful of security folk were in the know. The rest were corporate and blue-collar dupes who would probably lose their jobs when it was all over. But Kendi couldn't let himself feel sorry for them. Not where slavery was involved.

The first checkpoint was a heavy-looking door with a print scanner next to it. Kendi slotted his ID holocard into the key slot, then pressed his thumb to the plate. The plate glowed blue. Kendi held his breath. He knew very well that Ben had used Roon's access to upload a scan of Kendi's prints to the "approved" list, but there was always a moment when you wondered if there had been a mistake.

The lock released with a loud clunk. Kendi pocketed the holocard Ben had forged for him and continued onward. His hands weren't even shaking.

Banish all other thoughts, he told himself. *There is nothing but the objective. No brother, no sister. Just the goal. Irfan said, "Peace and serenity, calm as water."*

The second checkpoint was exactly like the first, and admitted him with no trouble. The third checkpoint consisted of a Plexiglas door through which Kendi could see a pair of human guards watching a series of display terminals. Kendi slotted his card and submitted to the retina scan. Both guards looked up as the lock released and Kendi entered.

"Hey," he said.

The first guard blinked, probably checking the time on his ocular implant. "Late?"

Kendi shrugged. "I called in sick at first, but felt better later, so I decided to come in. You know how it goes—missed hours mean a smaller paycheck."

"I hear you," said the second guard, waving him on.

Kendi hitched his tool belt and moved more quickly, as if he really were worried about missing work time. He turned a corner and found a door labeled LOCK-ERS. Kendi went in.

The place looked like any ordinary place for changing and storing clothes. Gray tiles, benches, rows of black lockers. Deserted. Kendi tapped his earpiece. "I'm in."

"Schematics say the research labs are on the fifth floor," came Ben's voice. *"I'm uploading directions to your implant."*

"Are you logged on to the system as Mallory?"

"Sure am. I'll upload the false hallway displays as soon as you hit the elevator."

Kendi left the locker room, and a transparent red arrow flashed across the bottom of his vision. It led him left, then straight, then left again. He kept his cap low. From time to time he passed other people, all human, and all of whom ignored him. Eventually the arrow took him down another empty hallway to a large lift. The arrow changed into a number 5. Kendi used his card to board the lift and pressed the button for the fifth floor. Once the doors shut, he quickly shucked his coveralls, revealing a skintight black outfit beneath. Kendi replaced the tool belt around his waist and sprayed the coveralls. They disintegrated. Next he pulled a black mask and hood from the tool belt and checked the time on his ocular display. He nodded, satisfied.

It was time to make Roon pay.

CHAPTER ELEVEN

"We are stuck with what we've lived through. The trick is to finish it with a flourish and an outrageous sense of design."

—Valeta Kalopolis, Ringmaster

Delta Maura's keycard opened the door with no trouble. The corridor beyond was empty—sleep cycle. Martina braced herself, then crossed the threshold.

Nothing happened. No shock, no pain, no alarms. She let out a small breath. Her shackles lay on the bathroom floor. There was no reason to believe anything would happen to her when she left her prescribed place, but a lifetime of conditioning could not be overcome in a few seconds of freedom.

Potential freedom, she reminded herself. *Move, girl!*

Martina chose a random direction and went. The problem was, she had no idea where to go. She reasoned there had to be ways in and out of the place, though Martina had never seen them. She should probably avoid places she knew, since they'd be deadends. The kitchen would be a good place to start—food delivery had to come from somewhere. It might provide her an exit, if only she could find the place.

A sudden urge to go find Keith flooded her. She had a master unit. She could release his shackles and they could run together. A firm shake of the head forced the thought from her mind. Keith was lost to her. She would have to get out herself, then find a way to come back for him. And she would.

If she could get out.

Martina opened a door and found a concrete staircase. Up or down?

Down, she decided. Martina had always gotten the

sense that the dumbwaiter in her room came from below, though she had never actually seen it move. In any case, it was something to go on.

She gathered the skirts of her robe in green-gloved hands and headed downward as quickly as she dared. Delta Maura's robe was wide for her and a bit short. Her footsteps echoed off the hard walls. The stairwell was warmer than the corridor, and it smelled like hot metal.

"Did everything go well with your Alpha?"

Martina jumped, but no one was there. The voice had come right into her ear. What had . . .

Delta Maura's earpiece. Swallowing hard, Martina whispered, "Fine. Sorry. I forgot to check in."

"No problem. Where are you headed?"

"I thought I might get something to eat in the kitchen," Martina said, still whispering. The voice of a whisper wasn't recognizable.

"While you're there, would you grab a snack for me and bring it up? You know what I like."

"Of course." Martina tapped the earpiece, ending the conversation. Her heart was beating so fast it made her eyes pulse in time with it. At least she had gotten a valuable clue—the kitchens were on a lower level than the person who had spoken with her.

One level down, the staircase ended. Martina found a door and opened it with her keycard. Voices raised in conversation greeted her. The large room beyond seemed to be an employee dining hall, with rows of long tables and low-backed chairs. Perhaps two dozen people ate from cafeteria trays. Two of them were dressed in green robes identical to Martina's. Martina's first instinct was to flee, but she forced herself to remain in the doorway. None of the diners took the slightest notice of her.

Martina took a deep breath and started across the room. Food smells washed over her and her stomach growled, though she didn't feel at all like eating. The kitchen should be nearby. Martina found herself keeping to the edges of the room. *Stupid.* Anyone who saw a Delta walking as if she belonged there wouldn't think twice. Anyone who saw a Delta trying to sneak about would get suspicious. Martina forced herself to stride openly and firmly. Silverware clattered against plates and people continued to talk. How long before the people spying on her room got suspicious about the bathtub? How long before they sent someone else to check? Martina didn't know.

One of the Deltas looked up, noticed Martina, and waved her over. Martina's veins hummed with adrenaline. She gave a little wave of her own, pretending to misunderstand, and headed for a large set of swinging doors on the other side of the dining room. Before she could hesitate and lose her nerve, she pushed through them.

On the other side lay an industrial-sized kitchen, with rows of gleaming work counters, metal doors, shelves of utensils. White-clad workers chopped and mixed and stirred bubbling pots. The place smelled of cheap meat and tomato sauce.

"Is there something you need, Delta?" asked a voice at her elbow.

Martina stifled a shriek and put a pleasant look on her face. A balding, red-faced man was looking at her inquisitively. An enormous butcher knife gleamed in his hand.

"I'm just looking for the cargo lift where the food shipments come down," she said, trying not to look at the knife. "I don't come back here very often."

"Back there," the man replied, pointing. Then, with a disinterested air, he turned back to his cutting board. The knife made meaty thunks.

Martina breathed an inward sigh at her luck. She hurried to the rear of the kitchen and through another set of swinging doors. Beyond them was a short hallway that ended at another lift, this one big enough to haul freight. It opened to her keycard, so she got in and checked the displays. The kitchen seemed to be in the basement, as she had guessed. There were five floors above her. Which one did she need? Not the first floor—she had just come from there. She thought a moment. Exits were more likely to be on one of the extremes. Fifth floor, then. Martina pressed the button. The lift came to life with a swooping noise that made her jump again.

After a long moment, the doors opened onto another plain corridor faced by several doors. No people in sight. Martina got out and looked for promising signs of an exit. None were in evidence. Martina ground her teeth in frustration. How the hell was she supposed to get out of here? There *had* to be a way.

The doors slid shut and the lift dropped. Martina thought about calling it back again, then decided against it. A stairwell should be nearby—there it was—and she could easily try another floor. Maybe the exit was in the middle, on the third floor? But what if—

The lift made a swooping noise behind her, and the display indicated it was climbing back up. It climbed fast, passing the fourth floor and halting at the fifth.

Gretchen fell backward with a grunt and crashed to the ground. The tray went flying. Food splattered ceiling, deck, and bulkheads as Isaac Todd planted another kick squarely in Gretchen's stomach. The breath whooshed out of her and she lay still. Without hesitating further, Todd sprinted off down the empty corridor, leaving his shackles on the floor behind him. After a long moment, Sister Gretchen Beyer stirred and slowly sat up. Her stomach hurt like hell and every breath burned like fire.

"Well, shit," she said.

*   *   *

Martina Weaver peeped through a crack in the stairwell door as the lift opened. A tall man dressed all in black slipped out and crept down the hall. The lower half of his face was covered with a mask, and he wore a close-fitting hood. A tool belt circled his narrow waist. Martina narrowed her eyes. It didn't take a genius to figure out that this was someone else who didn't belong here. And he probably knew a way out.

The man chose one of the doors, slipped a keycard through the lock, and went inside. Martina stood for a moment, torn by indecision. If she approached the man, he might be willing to let her follow him out in exchange for her silence. Or he might just kill her. All life, was this an opportunity or a trap?

The lift dropped again. After a few more hurried moments of thought, Martina decided to approach the man and take her chances. She was just emerging from the stairwell when alarms blasted up and down the hallway.

Kendi Weaver closed the research lab door behind him and ghosted over to one of the terminals in semi-darkness. The red arrow vanished from his vision. He slotted Jeung's false key into the terminal and pressed the yellow thumb against the plate. A display winked to life, granting him full access, just as Ben's mock IDs and keycards had granted him access to the Collection. It had almost been anticlimactic. Even the cameras in the hallways couldn't detect him—Ben was using Giselle Mallory's security access to upload false images of empty hallways.

The lab itself was pretty impressive, even in dim light. Stone-topped tables were scattered around an enormous room. Cabinets filled with equipment marched along the walls, and silvery cryo-units hummed to themselves, preserving who-knew-what. It smelled faintly of chemicals and singed cloth. The only light came from a table lamp left burning at one of the workstations.

Kendi was still nervous as a hunted lion. Success depended on so many factors beyond his control. Martina and Utang were depending on him—and they didn't even know he was here. Suddenly Kendi was tired of keeping secrets, tired of making plans, tired of the entire business. The idea of settling down on Bellerophon with Ben and a houseful of children became more attractive by the minute.

Kendi shook his head. This wasn't the time to be thinking about that. Forcing himself to concentrate, he produced the yellow thumb and Jeung's key from his tool belt and logged onto one of the terminals. GOOD EVENING, DR. JEUNG.

"I'm on, Ben."

"I can see the display through your implant," Ben told him. *"Access these directories."*

Following Ben's instructions, Kendi searched around until he found the medical database and the files he needed. He was just finishing up when the alarms blared. Kendi jumped, his heart in his mouth.

"Attention! Attention!" shouted the computer over the noise. "Alpha subject has escaped indoctrination area. Lockdown initiated. Attention! Attention! Alpha subject has escaped indoctrination area. Lockdown initiated."

"Shit!" Kendi all but leaped across the room to make for the door. It was locked. With chilly fingers, Kendi produced his false ID card. The door didn't budge. He tried Jeung's fake thumb and his key. Nothing. The alarms honked and blared, pounding his ears into his skull.

"Attention! Attention!"

"Ben!" Kendi shouted.

"I hear it. I've already—"

The door burst open. Kendi jumped back as a small crowd boiled into the room. The lights burst into full illumination, and Kendi shielded his eyes. When they adjusted, he found himself surrounded. Edsard Roon stood red-faced next to Isaac Todd, who looked triumphant. A pair of uniformed security guards, one male and one female, were holding a beautiful young woman in a green robe that was a size too large for her. Kendi stared at her face and the strength drained out of his legs.

Martina . . .

A thousand thoughts and memories poured through him. He wanted to run to her, grab her in a hug. But he remained still. It would be a terrible mistake to let Roon know who she was and what she meant to him.

It was only then that he noticed that Roon and Todd were holding neuro-pistols.

"Alice!" Roon barked. "Silence those damned alarms!"

The alarms went instantly quiet. Kendi's ears rang in the stillness.

"Imagine my surprise," Roon said. "I was on my way up here, acting on certain information that there would be a break-in at the labs, and I happened to stumble onto an escaped Alpha, trapped in the hallway by the lockdown. My luck."

Kendi said nothing. His eyes darted about the room, seeking an exit. Roon noticed the gesture and smiled condescendingly. "Alice, reinitialize lockdown."

The door behind him locked with an audible thump.

"You can't escape, Father," Roon said. "That is your title, isn't it? You're a Father with the Children of Irfan. Except I was led to believe that there would be more of you here. Mr. Todd?"

"I haven't been logged off," Ben murmured in Kendi's ear. *"The hotel terminal is still working. Hang tight."*

Todd's face darkened. "There have to be more of them around here somewhere."

"Alice, page Rafille Mallory and tell her to get her ass down here immediately," Roon barked. The refined, friendly demeanor he had shown Kendi in his home had all but vanished. "Then tell Security to initialize a level-by-level search for unauthorized personnel. Security personnel are hereby granted access through lockdown."

"Working."

"Let me go!" Martina snarled, trying to twist away from her captors. The man expressionlessly twisted her arm until she yelped with pain and stopped struggling. Kendi clenched a fist.

"You, girl," Roon said, reminded of her presence, "are going back to the Alpha pool, though I think we'll have to use stronger methods on you. I think you'll be the first one impregnated by the breeding program, for a start. It's harder for pregnant women to escape, and their children make fine hostages to good behavior."

Martina spat at him. The female guard slapped her.

"Maybe we'll give you twins, then," Roon said, and turned back to Kendi. "I know all about your plan, Father. How you intended to trick us into thinking two of my Alphas were sick with Selene's disease so we'd sell them cheap and you could buy them. Ironic, isn't it? You were trying to rescue this woman, and here she was trying to escape on her own."

"Rescue me?" Martina said. "What are you talking about?"

Kendi still said nothing, though the sound of Martina's voice tore his heart.

"It wouldn't have worked, you know," Roon continued. "We would have sought a second, outside opinion and would have realized the disease was mere gelpox. You Children think you're so smart, so clever. It never occurs to you that other people can be clever, too."

Todd stepped forward and punched Kendi in the stomach. Caught off guard, Kendi doubled over with a groan.

"Don't damage him," Roon snapped. "He's valuable."

"I owed him that," Todd said. "Him and his—"

"Attention! Attention!" interrupted the computer. "Medical emergency level one. Containment of experimental virus XR-476 has been breached. Airborne virus detected. Medical isolation of sector CLCT4 initiated. All personnel are directed to stand by for evacuation. Repeat: all personnel are directed to stand by for evacuation." Alarms, different ones, began to blare as the computer repeated the warning.

"What the hell?" Roon said. "It's got to be another trick. Alice, end medical emergency."

"Unable to comply. Level one medical emergencies must be terminated by direct order of the chief physician of SA Station. Attention! Attention! Biological containment of experimental virus XR-476 has been breached."

"Alice, lower alarm volume in this lab by half," Roon ordered. The alarms and warnings became much quieter.

"That computer's on," Todd said, and dashed over to look as Kendi slowly straightened.

"What's he been accessing?" Roon demanded, neuro-pistol still trained on Kendi.

"Checking," Todd said.

Roon twitched, then pressed a finger to his earpiece. "Edsard Roon," he said. "Yes, Madam Chair. I'm in the research lab right now. No, I have no idea if any of the Silent have been infected. But the alarm is only a—Yes, madam. Yes, I'm familiar with the protocols, but we don't actually have to—No, madam, I would never gainsay you. I know how important the Silent are to the company, but if you would just listen for— No. The entire sector has been sealed off, and there is no company ship big enough to accommodate all personnel in one trip. But that doesn't matter because the alarm is just a—The circus? Madam, I'm afraid I don't understand what that has to do with our current situation. Oh. Yes, I suppose the Emporium's ship would be large enough for everyone, but—"

Roon paused. "Madam Chair, what was the middle name of your second husband?" Pause again. "Just answer the question, Madam Chair. The middle name of your second husband." Yet another pause. Roon looked at Kendi. "She broke the connection. Imagine that. Who was that *really*, Father? It did sound very much like the chair."

Kendi refused to answer. His stomach was so tight, he thought it would burst from his body.

"Take the mask off, Father," Roon ordered. "*Now!*"

Slowly, Kendi obeyed. Martina gasped, but didn't speak. Roon shook his head.

"Mr. Qiwele," he said. "God. I should have known you were too good to be true. Let me guess—you copied my access key when those clowns were making up my face."

"Mr. Roon," Todd said from the computer. "He accessed the medical database and medical safeguards. That, and the records of virus XR-476."

Roon barked a harsh laugh. "So the gelpox was a double-blind. You deserve more credit than I thought, Father. Tell me if I have the right of it. You knew Todd here was communicating with me, didn't you? Do answer. You're going to tell all in a moment anyway. Hypnoral, you know."

"Yes," Kendi said hoarsely. "We detected the signal right off."

"So you arranged for him to overhear certain conversations, knowing he'd relay them to me." Roon kept the neuro-pistol absolutely level. "Then while I was worrying about false reports of gelpox and people breaking into the Collection, this medical 'emergency' would catch me by surprise. Everyone, including the two Alphas you came in here for, would be evacuated to the Emporium's ship, delivered neatly as you please, straight into your hands."

Kendi didn't answer.

"Well, now that I know the medical emergency is no such thing, I'll simply call the *real* Madam Chair and tell her—"

"The release was real," Kendi interrupted.

"What?" Roon said.

"I really did release the virus," Kendi said. "It's going to hit the ventilation system in about ten minutes. Check the logs and the sensors. You have to evacuate, no choice. Your Madam Chair will tell you the exact same thing. Good thing there are only two ways to get out of here—the main entrance and the air locks. They won't let you through the main entrance and into the station proper until you clear quarantine, so that means if you want to avoid little XR-476, you have to escape through the air locks. And the Emporium's ship is the only one close enough with the cargo space to hold everyone. We checked the records. None of the other ships in the area can get here in time."

"I have my private ship."

"Not big enough. We checked that, too."

"Then I won't evacuate," Roon said.

"And let all those Silent die? All those valuable resources? What would Madam Chair say to that, Mr. Roon, especially after all the money Silent Acquisitions sank into this project? Sure, you know the real story, but there isn't anything you can do about it." Kendi gave Roon a crooked grin. "Did you honestly think I'd be stupid enough to walk in here all by myself if there were any way I could fail? You've lost, Roon. Time to admit that."

"Escape pods," Todd said.

Roon looked around at him so fast, he put himself at risk for whiplash. "Explain, Mr. Todd. I'm tired of cryptic phrases."

"The station is equipped with escape pods. Evacuate with those and Security can pick them up, no problem. It'll take longer to gather everyone up, but so what? And you can also destroy the Emporium's ship, while you're at it."

Kendi launched himself at Todd. Roon fired his pistol, and white-hot pain wrenched through Kendi's body. He dropped writhing to the floor. Martina screamed.

"Put shackles on him," Roon told the security guards. "And on the Alpha. Don't forget to remove the Father's earpiece. Then get them both to an escape pod and stay with them until you get picked up."

"We aren't going to your ship?" Kendi asked.

"And risk you finding some way to escape and take over? Hardly. I'm through underestimating you, Mr. Qiwele, or whatever your name is. There's nothing you can do on an escape pod except wait, so off you go. The shackles, guard. Now!"

"Yes, sir," said the male guard, moving to obey.

"No!" Martina screamed, but the female guard clapped a band around her wrist in a single lightning movement.

"Alice," Roon said, "activate sector-wide public address."

"Activated."

"This is Edsard Roon. Due to the medical emergency, we must evacuate immediately." His voice echoed from the loudspeakers as he spoke. "All personnel are hereby directed to move immediately to the escape pods. Repeat: Move immediately to the escape pods. Do not stop for possessions. You will be picked up as quickly as possible. There is no need to

worry—the virus has not yet reached the ventilation
systems. Deltas, remain with your Alphas and Betas.
Alice, deactivate public address."

Kendi tried to fight as the guard clamped shackles
on his wrist and ankle, but his muscles refused to respond. For a moment he was twelve years old again,
torn out of cryo-sleep and shackled in a slave ship.
Then he was being jerked to his feet. Pain marched
through every nerve, and he was only vaguely aware
of Martina beside him.

"Evan," she was saying. "Evan, I'm sorry. I didn't
know you were coming. It's my fault. All life, I'm
sorry. I'm so sorry."

"We'll speak again, Father," Roon said as the
guards hauled them away. "At great and painful
length."

The evacuation was quick and quiet. Only the
Alphas, Betas, and Deltas actually lived in the Collection's sector. Most of the food service, research personnel, clerical workers, and other such employees
were off-shift, meaning only about a hundred people
were present and therefore obliged to evacuate. They
moved swiftly and without panic to a particular corridor on the outer wall of the Collection, where dozens
of small air locks lay open. When three or four people
had filled one of the little rounded capsules, the air
lock cycled shut and a small charge shoved the pod
away from the station. Kendi let himself be half
dragged toward one of the air locks, and he was aware
of people speaking in hushed voices around him as
they boarded their own pods.

"I'm sorry," Martina whispered beside him over and
over. "I'm so sorry."

The guards dragged them, brother and sister, across
the threshold of the air lock. There was barely room
for the four of them, and they crowded against the
pod's rudimentary control panel. A single round port-

hole looked out into empty space. Already several dozen other pods were drifting away from the station. The female guard cycled the lock shut and her male counterpart hit the activator. A heavy thump, and stars began to move slowly past the porthole. Martina slumped to the floor and put her hands over her face.

The male guard put a hand to his ear. "Yes, Mr. Roon, we've evacuated." Pause. "One moment." He tapped the control panel and a small vidscreen winked to life. Edsard Roon's long, serious face appeared.

"I've boarded my ship, Father," he said. *"If you will look out the portal to your left, I'm sure you'll find something worth seeing."*

Kendi couldn't help but obey. An enormous hulk of a vessel was drifting slowly toward a clump of escape pods. The words KALOPOLIS INTERGALACTIC TRAVELING EMPORIUM OF WONDERS was painted in large, fancy letters along one side. A much smaller, sleeker vessel rushed toward it and opened fire. A dozen missile trails streamed forward like hungry fingers. Kendi stared as the big, defenseless ship exploded in a dazzling fireball that dwarfed the sun. Debris pinged off the escape pod's hull. After a long moment, Kendi turned to the male guard and held up his hand. The shackle gleamed, silver and heavy, at his wrist.

"Take this thing off me," he said.

"It would be my pleasure," said Prasad Vajhur.

CHAPTER TWELVE

"If you're ready for it, it isn't a surprise."
—Drew Fleming, Investigative Reporter

"What are you doing?" Roon yelped. *"Don't release him. That's an order!"*

Prasad ignored Roon, and a moment later Kendi's shackles thudded to the floor. Vidya, the female guard, knelt next to Martina and released her shackles as well.

"I apologize for the slaps," Vidya murmured. "There was no other way."

"You're both fired!" Roon bawled. Kendi half expected him to start foaming at the mouth. He edged around the cramped confines of the pod until he could crouch down beside Martina. She looked up at him, clearly confused.

"Evan?" she said. "What's going on?"

"You silly goose." His throat was thick and hoarse. "You were supposed to wait and let us rescue you."

And then, for the first time in fifteen years, he hugged his sister. Kendi's cheek brushed hers beneath the wimple. The Silent jolt rocked him to his heels, but he didn't let go.

"You're Silent," she whispered. "All life. I'd always wondered."

"I told you I'd find you," he said. Warm tears ran down his face. "I told you I would."

"I remember." She pulled back. "What about Mom? She was sold with you. Is she here, too?"

Kendi shook his head. "We were separated. I don't know where she is. I'm sorry."

"How about Keith? He was in that place with me."

"Taken care of." Kendi got up and swiped at the salt water with one sleeve. "We'll talk soon, once I get the rest done. Don't worry."

"I muted the sound for you," Prasad said. His eyes were a little shiny. "I did not think you would want Roon's shouting to disturb you."

"Thanks." Kendi faced Roon on the vidscreen and tapped the mute control.

"—dead!" Roon shouted. *"You won't get two parsecs before—"*

"Shut up!" Kendi snapped. "I've won, and in a minute I'm going to tell you how to salvage your sorry ass, but not if you keep yelping like a dingo with its tail in a twist."

Roon glared at him. *"What do you mean?"*

"First of all, I need to tell you that the rest of the station doesn't even know about this little fiasco. Yet. We used Mallory's access to sever all communication with the station proper, including the distress calls sent out by these pods. Right now 'Ms. Mallory' is contacting SA Station to tell them about the accidental explosion of a derelict ship. No rush to investigate. By the time they figure out what happened, we'll be long gone."

"Derelict ship?"

"We had to provide something for you to waste your missiles on. We'll be picked up by the real Emporium ship in few moments, along with the rest of the pods. The Silent you kidnapped will stay with us, and your non-Silent employees will be set adrift in the escape pods for you to pick up. Everybody wins."

"Except me, you—"

"I said, shut up," Kendi snarled. "I'm getting to your worthless hide. Is Isaac Todd there with you?"

"He is." Roon gestured sharply, and Isaac Todd, expression uncertain, joined his employer on the screen. *"What about him?"*

"Have you ever scanned his genes?"

"No."

"Pity. You had a treasure all along and didn't know it. Don't let him get away—I went through a lot of trouble to ensure you could have him. Think of him as the gift that could save your career."

"What the hell are you talking about?"

"Isaac Todd isn't Silent himself," Kendi said, "but he always fathers Silent children."

All the blood drained from Todd's face as Roon gave him a speculative look. Kendi broke the connection without another word.

At that moment, the pod shuddered. Kendi glanced out the porthole and saw the Emporium's ship—the real one. A gravity beam was gathering the scattered escape pods and bringing them into a wide hold like a mother duck gathering ducklings under her wings. Then the *Poltergeist*, swift and trim, swooped into view.

"We'll take this one, Val," came Ben's voice over Kendi's earpiece—Prasad hadn't taken it as Roon had ordered. "Kendi, is everyone all right?"

"We're fine here," Kendi replied. "And I've got someone for you to meet."

The moment Kendi stepped out of the escape pod and into the cargo bay, a pair of strong arms engulfed him. All the air rushed out of his lungs.

"Oxygen! Oxygen!" Kendi protested with a laugh. "All life, I love you, too."

Ben released him. "Okay, where is she? Val said she has your brother on the Emporium ship, but your sister—"

"Right here." Kendi reached into the pod and helped Martina down. Vidya and Prasad followed, still in their Security uniforms. Kendi turned to his sister and said words he had been rehearsing in his head for months.

"Martina," he said, "this is Ben Rymar. We're part-nered. Ben, this is my sister Martina."

Martina extended a hand and Ben shook it. Both of them gasped.

"Sorry," Kendi said. "I forgot—you're both Silent."

"It's a day for surprises," Martina laughed. "Yester-day I was the prisoner of a weird cult. Today I learn my older brother is a Child of Irfan, he's still Silent even after the Despair, and he's partnered with a Silent . . . man."

"When Kendi is involved," Ben said, "you learn to expect surprises."

"Kendi?" Martina asked, puzzled.

Kendi put one arm around Martina and the other around Ben, then held on tight in case he floated straight up to the ceiling. "There are a lot of long stories to tell, sis. Got a few hours?"

"I have a lifetime," Martina said. "And it's finally *my* lifetime."

Vidya and Prasad went off to change clothes. The Weavers trooped down to the galley, where Harenn was laying out a hastily assembled meal of chicken salad and fruit. Bedj-ka was at the table, sipping a glass of juice.

"So you made it back from the Emporium ship," Kendi said as they sat down. "Where are Gretchen and Lucia?"

"On the bridge," Harenn said. "We have entered slip, and the Emporium is behind us. We will arrive at Bellerophon in two days, exactly in time to return the *Poltergeist* to the Council. Valeta expects that you will aid her in arranging several performances there to help pay for the time she has lost."

"Gladly," Kendi said, and introduced Martina to her and Bedj-ka. "Once we're a safe distance from SA Station, though, I'll want to stop for a bit so we can transfer Utang over here."

Martina's expression clouded. "I have to warn

you—it might not be pleasant. Keith—he prefers that to Utang these days—was buying into Roon's whole Dream cult thing."

"Dream cult?" Kendi asked.

Martina gave a short description of "Dreamer Roon" and his methods of indoctrination. Kendi's mouth fell open and his blood boiled. Ben and Harenn seemed to feel the same way. The food lay on the table, untouched.

"What's a cult?" Bedj-ka wanted to know.

"I will explain later," Harenn said in a flat voice.

"At any rate," Martina finished, "you've shattered the cult for Keith—and a lot of the others. They may not take it kindly."

Kendi's face fell and Ben took his hand under the table. "We'll get into the Dream," Ben said, "and tell the Council we'll need therapists who can deal with this kind of thing. We'll get Keith through it, Kendi; don't worry. You don't have to do everything yourself, you know."

But Kendi couldn't help worrying.

"That's the second time he's called you that," Martina said. "Is that your name now? Kendi? The trickster lizard?"

"I chose it after I became a Child," Kendi told her. "Like I said, it's long story and I'll tell you and Ut— Keith at the same time." *Assuming he'll talk to me.*

"I have to ask you something else," Martina said. "About that man Isaac Todd."

"Bedj-ka," Harenn said, "go up to our quarters. You may play on the sims."

Bedj-ka gave his mother a look, then slid out of his chair and left without arguing.

"Ask away," Kendi said.

"You told Roon he always fathers Silent children," Martina said. "And you arranged for Roon to take Todd prisoner. I don't know what he did—"

"He sold children into slavery," Harenn interjected.

"—but the babies he fathers will be enslaved by Silent Acquisitions. They're innocent, but they'll suffer for what their father did. Is that what you intended?"

Kendi smiled. "Harenn?"

"Isaac Todd will father no more children," Harenn said. "He thought I was injecting him with gelpox to make him a test subject for the plan, but he received another injection entirely."

"What did you give him?" Martina asked.

"A form of the mumps virus genegineered for slave owners who want to castrate their slaves." Harenn gave a rare smile. "It is not contagious, but by tomorrow morning, Isaac's testicles will have swollen to the size of oranges. There is no cure. The disease causes erectile dysfunction and permanent sterility."

"Poetic justice, I'd say," Kendi put in. "Roon's going to be furious."

"And fired," Ben said. "That was mean, raising his hopes like that and then destroying them."

"Yeah," Kendi said happily. "And I'm sure Silent Acquisitions will be pretty mean to Isaac, too. He's failed them twice now, and he blabbed about the Collection."

"We're far enough away from SA Station to leave slipspace for a few minutes," came Lucia's voice over the intercom system. *"We need to drop the SA employees off in the escape pods, and Ms. Kalopolis says a certain person on her ship is demanding transfer to the* Poltergeist."

Kendi tensed again. "We'll meet him in the entry bay."

"Umbilical dock complete," said Gretchen over the intercom. *"Big brother is leaving the Emporium ship and should enter the air lock in a few seconds."*

Kendi felt Ben squeeze his hand and he tried to squeeze back, but he had no strength. Martina stood next to them. She had removed the ridiculous wimple and gloves, but still wore the green robe. It was all the clothing she had. Harenn and Lucia waited a short distance away. Kendi had almost asked the two of them to leave, but then he had realized he drew comfort from their presence, from Harenn's strength of will and from Lucia's calm serenity. So he said nothing.

The entry bay air lock cycled with a rushing sound and slowly slid open. Keith looked exactly like the holo Kendi had seen back on Drim, though he was wearing a yellow robe and was a centimeter or two shorter than Kendi. The latter surprised him. He always remembered Keith as the taller one.

"Evan?" he said. "My god, I'd know you anywhere." Keith ran forward and clasped Kendi in his third hard hug of the day. The Silent jolt snapped through him. Martina joined her brothers. Keith gasped as she touched him—another jolt.

"You aren't angry?" Kendi said after they parted.

"Angry?" Keith said. "Why would I be angry? God, you got me out of that place. And you're a Child of Irfan? You have a lot of explaining to do."

"You believed in Roon," Martina said. "I thought I'd lost you to him."

Keith ran a hand over his face and Kendi noticed he had a few silver hairs. "I figured I'd have a better chance of escaping if they thought I was a believer. It was starting to work—they promoted me to Beta."

"Why didn't you *say* something?" Martina demanded. "I was worried sick."

"I thought *you* had bought into it. All those things you said at Confessional and the way you always worked so hard?"

"That was just a trick so *I* could escape."

Kendi laughed and gave them both another hug. "That's us," he said. "A family of tricksters."

Ben watched Kendi's reunion, feeling happy and, oddly, jealous. It suddenly occurred to him that he would have to share Kendi now. Then he shook his head.

This from the man who wants eleven children, he thought wryly.

After a moment Kendi broke away and brought Ben forward for another introduction. This brought about another handshake and another Silent jolt. Then an uncomfortable silence fell. There was so much to say, but no one knew where to start. Harenn came to the rescue.

"There is still food up in the galley," she said. "Why don't you go up there and talk where it is more comfortable?"

The Weavers agreed to this and headed for the door. Ben started to follow, but Harenn caught his sleeve. "Ben," she said, "Lucia and I wish to talk to you up in the medical bay."

"What about?"

"We'll explain up there," Lucia told him.

Mystified, Ben followed the two women. The soft blue corridors, with their rounded corners and gentle machinery hum, felt calm and homelike after the frenzy of the last several days.

"Don't you have to pilot the ship, Lucia?" Ben asked as they went.

"Gretchen is still overseeing the transfer of the SA employees back into the escape pods," Lucia replied. "She's also launching a signal beacon to make sure SA can find them. It shouldn't take more than two or three hours for them to be rescued. But for now I'm not needed on the bridge."

They reached the medical bay, the place where Isaac Todd had singsonged his way through several interrogations. It seemed as cold and sterile as ever. Ben's little star-shaped cryo-unit sat on one of the counters, lights winking quietly.

"Where did you get that?" Ben demanded.

"Kendi asked me to run some tests," Harenn explained. "He also told me that the two of you want to raise them as your children."

Ben flushed. "He told you that?"

"Why shouldn't he?" Lucia said. "I think you've made a wonderful decision, Ben. That's why we brought you down here."

"I don't understand."

"You will need host mothers," Harenn said. "I would like to volunteer."

Ben stared.

"You and Kendi have reunited me with my child," Harenn said simply. "In the process, Kendi lost his own family and had to risk his freedom to get them back. I can never fully make that up to him—and you—but this thing would be a start."

"I'm volunteering, too," Lucia said. "It would be an honor. Both of you have been touched by Irfan, and I don't mean because you're Silent. Besides, these children need parents, and I want to help."

Ben cast about for something to say and came up empty. At last he only said, "Thank you. Thank you both."

"There is more," Harenn said. "Lucia doesn't know this, but if she bears one of these children, she needs to be informed."

Alarm thrilled through Ben. "Is something wrong with them?"

"Not at all," Harenn said. "Something is merely . . . interesting."

"What do you mean, Harenn?" Lucia said. "Don't be cruel by keeping him—us—in suspense."

Harenn nodded. "Ben, Kendi said you don't know where the embryos come from, that your mother found them on a derelict ship. Do you know how old the embryos are?"

"Only vaguely," Ben said. "The cryo-unit was something over thirty years old when Mom found it, so that would mean the unit is close to sixty years old now, but that doesn't say anything about the embryos. They could be a lot newer."

"Or older." Harenn took a deep breath. "Ben, did you or your mother ever have a comparison done with the monastery's genetic database?"

"No. What would be the point?"

"Curiosity," Harenn said. "I ran such a check with the database carried on this ship. You should sit down, Ben. You too, Lucia."

Nervously, Ben took up a rolling stool. Lucia did as well, a mystified look on her face. Harenn leaned against the counter next to the cryo-unit.

"What's this all about, Harenn?" Ben asked. "What did you find?"

"I ran the check three times," she said. "Every test came back with the same irrefutable result. Those embryos—and you—are the direct issue of Daniel Vik and Irfan Qasad."

Lucia gasped and realization stole over Ben like a cold hand. "What are you saying, Harenn?" he whispered.

"I am saying, Ben, that Daniel Vik was your biological father and Irfan Qasad was your biological mother. In every sense of the word, you are a true child of Irfan."

Read on
for a special preview
of Steven Harper's next novel
of the Silent Empire,

CHILDREN

Coming soon from Roc

Ben Rymar sat on the floor and stared at the holograms on his coffee table. The first showed a pretty woman with pointed features and a long brown braid. She wore a form-fitting jumpsuit with a small captain's insignia at the shoulder. The other hologram portrayed a short, stocky man. His straw-blond hair and enormous blue eyes gave him a boyish look. A handsome guy. Ben puffed out his cheeks and held up a hand mirror so he could compare his reflection with the hologram's. His hair was sunset red, but Ben and the man shared the same long jaw, the same stocky build, the same square features. Their eyes were the same shade of blue.

There was something of the woman in Ben's face as well. Ben made mental comparisons. Same eye shape, same mouth, same nose.

Ben set the mirror down and drew his knees up to his chest. The base of the woman's hologram was inscribed with the words IRFAN QASAD. The base of the man's hologram said DANIEL VIK. They had died almost a thousand years ago, and they were his parents.

He sat on the hardwood floor a long time, trying to wrap his mind around this impossible concept. Irfan Qasad. Captain of the colony ship that had brought humans to the planet Bellerophon. First human to speak to the alien Ched-Balaar. First human to accept the Ched-Balaar's gift of Silence and enter the Dream.

Founder of the Blessed and Most Beautiful Monastery of the Children of Irfan.

Daniel Vik. Yeoman to Captain Qasad and eventually her husband. Second human to enter the Dream. Father of Irfan's children. Genocidal maniac who had tried to murder every Silent on Bellerophon.

Ben got up and went to the kitchen, poured himself a tall, tart glass of juice, and took it out onto the balcony that ringed the house. The early spring sun had finally chased away the heavy winter clouds. Voices, both human and Ched-Balaar, chattered, clattered, and hooted in the distance. Ben tilted the glass and let a few drops of juice fall into the forest below in a customary libation. Beyond the balcony stretched the talltree forest, with its hundred-meter trees above and giant lizards below. Neighboring houses peeked out from the branches one tree over. The original colonists of Bellerophon had taken to the trees to escape the local lizards—inevitably dubbed "dinosaurs"—and their Treetown descendants had never gone back to the ground. Some of the structures, built of iron-hard talltree wood, were reputed to date back to the time of Irfan Qasad herself.

Irfan Qasad. Ben set the juice glass on the balcony rail. It felt unreal, like the news had come to someone else, like—

"You are brooding," said a voice behind him. Ben spun, upset the glass, and caught it just before it fell over the rail. Juice spattered the leaves below.

"Harenn," he yelped. "You scared the life out of me."

"Perhaps I should scare some life *into* you," said Harenn Mashib. She was leaning against the door jamb, her dark eyes half-closed, her arms folded. At her feet lay a star-shaped piece of computer equipment. "I knocked, but no one answered."

"I didn't hear."

"You hear very little lately," she observed. "Kendi has noticed, you know. He asks about you, wants to know if I have any idea what bothers you, and then I have to lie and tell him I know nothing. I dislike lying to him, Ben, especially about something so important."

"Straight to the point." Ben grimaced. "And pulling no punches."

"You have to tell him."

"I will," Ben protested. "I just . . . it hasn't been the right time."

"This begs the question of when the right time will come."

Ben sighed and boosted himself up to sit on the balcony rail. Harenn remained in the doorway. She was a shortish, pretty woman whose choice of clothing ran to voluminous, and she covered her hair with a blue head scarf.

"I don't know," he said finally. "How do you say something like this? 'Hey, love, I just thought you ought to know that Harenn found out who my biological mother is. Can you believe it's Irfan Qasad?' Sure."

Harenn picked up the bit of equipment and brought it over to the balcony. "That information will not change Kendi's feelings for you. And it does not change who you are."

A crisp spring breeze ruffled Ben's hair. He took the cryo-unit from Harenn's hands and stared down at it. The information didn't change who he was. The problem was, he didn't *know* who he was. Or maybe it was that he *did* know.

System lights blinked in a familiar pattern across the readout. Ben knew the cryo-unit itself wasn't a thousand years old, unlike the embryos frozen inside. Those embryos were mere clumps of tiny cells, yet they managed to raise countless questions. Why had

Daniel Vik and Irfan Qasad created them? Who had stolen them away? Why had the thief later abandoned them?

Ben knew part of the story, of course. Ara Rymar, on a mission for the Children of Irfan, had found a derelict ship orbiting a gas giant. A brief examination had proven the ship empty except for the cryo-unit. Back on Bellerophon, Ara decided she wanted a child of her own and had one of the embryos implanted in her womb. Nine months later, Ben came into the world, red hair, blue eyes, and all.

Although a simple scan had revealed that all the embryos were Silent, Ara had never bothered to run a full genetic comparison on Ben or his frozen siblings. No point. The derelict ship had been nowhere near Bellerophon, and it seemed unlikely such a scan would reveal any relatives at the monastery.

After Ara's death, however, Ben had gained custody of the cryo-unit and its contents, and once he and Kendi had decided they wanted children together, it seemed the most natural thing in the world to turn to the cryo-unit and the tiny riches within.

Ben had always wanted to raise his brothers and sisters as his own children, wanted it with an ache so intense it sometimes awoke him late at night when the only sounds were Kendi's deep breathing and the secret cry of unborn infants.

Kendi, however, had been less poetic and more practical. Unknown to Ben, he had asked Harenn to run a full gentic comparison to make absolute sure everything was all right with the embryos. The results had wrenched Ben into a strange and different universe, one where truth hung above him like a hungry sword.

"I am tiring of lying at your request, Ben," Harenn said. "I lied to Kendi when I told him that the database yielded no parental matches. I lied to him when he asked me if I knew what was bothering you. Lucia has joined in these lies, and she finds it a strain because she still holds the famous Father Kendi Weaver in awe, and she fears what will happen when he learns she has concealed the truth from him."

Lucia dePaolo. Ben ran his fingers over the familiar shape of the cryo-unit. Lucia and Harenn had volunteered to be host mothers for the embryos, and Lucia had been present when Harenn had broken the news to Ben.

"You are causing your beloved great pain with this secret," Harenn said, "because he believes you are unhappy about something. You must tell him so his pain will end."

"It's not that easy, Harenn," Ben protested. "If this information gets out, do you know what will happen to me? To them?"

"Tell me what you think will happen."

"Devastation," Ben said bitterly. "God, Harenn— Irfan Qasad is the most famous human being in all history. She changed society across the universe. Without her, humans would never have entered the Dream. People have built religious cults around her. Hell, Harenn—Lucia and her family worship Irfan as a goddess."

"They worship her as a mortal incarnation of divinity," Harenn corrected gently.

"You know what I mean," Ben said. "If this came out, half the universe would show up on the doorstep to have a good gawk, a quarter would probably want to kidnap me and the children for study or worship or whatever, and the last quarter would probably try to . . ." He waved a hand.

"Assassinate you," Harenn finished. "Because Daniel Vik was your father. Or because some people like to target the famous."

"It won't affect just me. It'll affect the kids. They're Irfan's children, too, and they'll get the same attention. And I don't want to be famous. It scares me,

Harenn. Enough people already know who I am and what I did during the Despair. Everyone calls me a hero. They stare in public and they ask questions and I hate it. I don't want this for me, and I don't want it for our kids."

"I still fail to see the problem," Harenn said. "Telling Kendi is not like telling the world. He would not give the secret away if you didn't wish it. Kendi will be the father of these children, Ben. Perhaps not biologically, but certainly in all ways that matter, just as Ara was your mother in all ways that matter. He deserves to know."

"I know," Ben sighed. "Every time I try to say the words, they won't come. And no, I don't want you or Lucia to tell him."

"You have a deadline," Harenn said. She took the cryo-unit from him. "In two weeks, my body will be ready to receive your first child. I will not go through the procedure if Kendi remains ignorant of the baby's nature."

A door slammed inside the house and a voice called, "Ben?"

"Out here, Kendi," Ben called back. Then, to Harenn, "Not now."

"As you say," Harenn replied. "But you have my opinion and my deadline."

Before Ben could say more, Kendi strode out onto the balcony with an excited bounce in his step. Kendi favored the brown tunic and trousers often worn by the Children of Irfan, and the jade ring on his hand indicated he had reached the rank of Father. Like Ben, he was in his late twenties, but the excitement on his face made him look younger. Ben found himself sharing the excitement, even though he didn't know what it was about. Kendi could still do that to him, communicate a mood by his very presence. Ben liked that. He kissed Kendi hello, then backed up a step.

Kendi's eye fell on the cryo-unit in Harenn's hands and his face went tight.

"Is something wrong?" he asked.

"We were discussing parenthood," Harenn said, "and I was using a visual aid. No need for alarm."

"Ah."

"All right, out with it," Ben commanded, changing the subject.

"Out with what?" Kendi said innocently.

"There's something you're dying to tell me," Ben persisted, "so go ahead."

"Sound advice," Harenn murmured. Ben shot her an alarmed look, but Kendi was too excited to notice. "And what is this news, then?"

"You should check your messages, Ben," Kendi said. "Grandma is running for governor."

Second in the *Silent Empire* Series

NIGHTMARE
by
Steven Harper

Kendi Weaver doesn't know he's a Silent.
Hijacked into slavery, he has resigned himself to
a life of servitude. Then the discovery of his
innate gift for dream communication changes
everything. Suddenly Kendi is a very valuable
commodity. He is rescued by the Children of
Irfan, a society dedicated to freeing enslaved
Silents, and taken to their planet, Bellerophon.

But Bellerophon is hardly a safe refuge. A brutal
serial killer is murdering Silents in their
telepathic dreams, and Kendi is soon embroiled
in a world of madness and murder. To catch the
killer, he must enter the victims' dreams.

0-451-45898-2

To order call: 1-800-788-6262

DREAMER

A Novel of the Silent Empire

Steven Harper

0-451-45843-5

THE DREAM...
...is a plateau of mental existence where people are able to communicate by the power of their thoughts alone.

THE SILENT...
These people—known as the Silent—find that the Dream is threatened by a powerful Silent capable of seizing control of other people's bodies against their will...and may be causing tremors within the Dream itself.

THE RISK...
And if the "normals" learn of this, they will do anything to capture the Silent for use as a weapon—and the Dream itself may be shattered forever...

S572

ROC Science Fiction and Fantasy
COMING IN DECEMBER 2003